HE DIED FOR PEACE

HE DIED FOR PEACE

THE ASSASSINATION OF JOHN F. KENNEDY

L. D. SHONO, JR.

Let every nation know,
whether it wishes us well or ill,
that we shall pay any price,
bear any burden,
meet any hardship,
support any friend,
oppose any foe,
to assure the survival
and the success of liberty.

John F. Kennedy

iUniverse, Inc.
Bloomington

HE DIED FOR PEACE
The Assassination of John F. Kennedy

iUniverse books may be ordered through booksellers or by contacting:

iUniverse
1663 Liberty Drive
Bloomington, IN 47403
www.iuniverse.com
1-800-Authors (1-800-288-4677)

ISBN: 978-1-4759-0524-3 (sc)
ISBN: 978-1-4759-0525-0 (ebk)

Printed in the United States of America

iUniverse rev. date: 05/03/2012

DEDICATION

This book is dedicated to the greatest wife a man could ever hope to have. Tracy, you have traveled down this road with me for the last 13 years. I know it was a trip you didn't take willingly at times, but you took it just the same. You have been the driving force behind this book and I am so thankful God has sent you to me. I love you.

FOREWORD

———————————□———————————

Let me say this first and foremost: This is a work of fiction NOT nonfiction. So don't go running to one of your conspiracy theorist buddies and tell them I am revealing the truth. I am NOT. I am just writing a story on what I BELIEVE happened on November 22, 1963.

I will never forget the first time I heard of President John F. Kennedy. I was in the 4th grade at Cherry Ridge Elementary School in Bastrop, Louisiana. My teacher was Mrs. Terry. I don't remember everything she said that day. But I do remember I was instantly intrigued. From that day forth I read everything I could gather on John Kennedy. It didn't matter if it was about his life or his death. I admire what he stood and fought for during his short time as president. He was a man who truly wanted to make a difference and I truly believe he was killed for it. I have read many books on who was responsible for the Kennedy Assassination. From the CIA to the Mafia to Castro to Lyndon B. Johnson to big oil men to he wanted to put an end the Vietnam War. I believe all was involved in one aspect or other. I truly believe his murder was an overthrow of the United States government. I know you are thinking that sound farfetched. I know it sounds like something which doesn't happen in the United States. We want to believe it couldn't happen here in America. But sadly I believe it did happen in 1963. Why do I think it was an overthrow of the United States government? The answer is actually quite simple. It would take more than one entity to pull off something this big. And it would have taken months to plan. It might have even started on the night Kennedy beat Nixon for the White House. Who knows? The question you have to ask yourself is "Who benefit the most with John Kennedy removed from the White House?" Johnson? CIA? Mafia? Oil men? To tell the truth they all benefit greatly.

John F. Kennedy was killed for one reason and one reason only; he wanted peace. It's just that simple. He wanted peace with the Soviet Union and with Fidel Castro. The Central Intelligence Agency threatened this course of plan so President Kennedy threatened to disassemble the CIA. He was able to avoid a full-blown in Cuba, Laos, and Berlin. He wanted to avoid the war in Vietnam. This is where the Central Intelligence Agency drew the line. The end of the United States involvement in Vietnam before the war grew threatened many powerful men's way of life. With the motive out of the way, we need to concentrate on the how. That's the most difficult to discover. I don't know exactly how it was planned or how it was executed. But I have read and researched enough to get a good idea. I don't know all the names of the people who were involved. For that reason this is NOT a work of nonfiction. It is strictly a work of fiction. This is how I chose to tell my version on what happened to President Kennedy on November 22, 1963 in Dallas, Texas. I hope I can carefully lay down the foundation on why President John F. Kennedy was murdered. And I hope I can carefully put that foundation into motion and explain my version on what happened that fateful day.

L. D. Shono, Jr.

PROLOGUE

———————————□———————————

*"**We have been** compelled to create a permanent armaments industry of vast proportions. Added to this, three and a half million men and women are directly engaged in the defense establishment. We annually spend on military security more than the net income of all the United States corporations. This conjunction of an immense military establishment and a large arms industry is new in the American experience. The total influence—economic, political, even spiritual—is felt in every city, every State house, and every office of the Federal government. We recognize the imperative need for this development. Yet we must not fail to comprehend its grave implications. Our toil, resources and livelihood are all involved; so it is the very structure of our society. In the councils of government, we must guard against the acquisition of unwarranted influence, whether sought or unsought, by the military industrial complex. The potential for disastrous rise of misplaced power exists and will persist. We must never let the weight of this combination endanger our liberties or democratic processes. We should take nothing for granted."*

—President Dwight D. Eisenhower January 17, 1961.

CHAPTER 1

———————□———————

"Peace is a daily, a weekly, a monthly process, gradually
changing opinions, slowly eroding old barriers, quietly
building new structures."

John F. Kennedy

On September 16, 1959, Lee Harvey Oswald sat quietly in his room
on the freightliner *Marion Lykes*. He was headed to Le Havre, France.
His final destination was the USSR; Moscow to be specific. He was an
undercover agent for the Central Intelligence Agency; an American spy. It
was a boyhood dream. His mission was to act as a double agent while he
was in Russia. His mission was to try and gather intelligence information
on Russia. Normally there was no guarantee he would even be allowed to
stay in the Soviet Union. But his case wasn't a normal situation. He was a
former United States Marine with classified information he was instructed
to reveal to the Russians. He didn't like betraying his country, but at this
point he had no choice. He stretched out on his bed with his head on his
hands. He thought about his life and the decisions he made which led him
to this day.

On October 18, 1939, Lee Oswald was born in New Orleans,
Louisiana to Marguerite and Robert Lee Oswald, Sr. Two months before
his birth, his father died of a heart attack. She was left alone to care for Lee
and his two older brothers, John Pic (son from a previous marriage) and
Robert, Jr. His mother doted on him to excess, but despite this she was
also characterized as domineering and quarrelsome. She feared she couldn't
care for her young boys adequately so she sent them to an orphanage
and later to boarding school. Lee was rejected at first because he was too

young. But his mother reapplied later and sent him off to the orphanage after he turned four.

At age of 12, Lee and his mother moved to New York City, where they lived with his half-brother John Pic. John had joined the U.S. Coast Guard and was stationed in New York. While Marguerite worked days in a dress shop, Lee spent his time alone at the public library, the museum and endless hours riding the New York City subway system. He was a lonely child. No one was really there for him when he needed someone the most. Although Lee had enrolled in the eighth grade, he didn't set foot in school for almost two months. One day, a truant officer noticed Lee at one of his favorite havens, the Bronx Zoo. As soon as he saw the truant officer, he turned and ran. But it didn't take the truant officer long to catch him. He was taken into court and then sent to a youth detention center for three weeks of psychiatric evaluation. His social worker, Evelyn Siegel, wrote in her report: *"He was a skinny, unprepossessing kid. He was not a mentally disturbed kid. He was just emotionally frozen. He was a kid who had never developed a really trusting relationship with anybody. From what I could garner, he really interacted with no one. He made his own meals. His mother left around 7:00 and came home at 7:00 and he shifted for himself. You got the feeling that this was a kid nobody gave a darn about."* His truancy resulted in visits to psychiatrist Renatus Hartogs, who diagnosed the 14 year old Lee as having a *"personality pattern disturbance with schizoid features and passive-aggressive tendencies."*

One day in New York City Lee came across a leaflet about the impeding execution of Julius and Ethel Rosenberg, who was convicted of spying for Russia. He would later write in his diary: *"I was looking for a key to my environment, and then I discovered socialist literature. I had to dig for my books in the back dusty shelves of libraries."* His behavior in school appeared to improve in his last months in New York. While in New York, he threatened his sister-in-law with a knife and punched his mother in the face. She had been downgrading him and his mother. He had grown tired of it. His mother tried to get the knife from him. He didn't know it was her when he turned and hit her. He would never possibly hurt his mother. He continued to skip school and soon the truant officer came after him once again. Lee and his mother fled New York and moved back to New Orleans, to the edge of the French Quarter. When they left New York there was still an open question before a New York judge if he should be taken from the care of his mother to finish his schooling.

The French Quarter was an area of strip joints and gambling joints where every hustler and pimp in New Orleans plied his trade. But Lee was diverted from the neighborhood's vices by his interest in socialism. He tried to join the Socialist Party's Youth League, but there was no chapter in New Orleans. Before the age of 18 Lee had lived in 22 different residences and attended 12 different schools, mostly around New Orleans and Dallas. His mother was of French and German descent and raised him in the Lutheran faith. He read voraciously and as a result sometimes asserted he was better educated than those around him. Around the age of 15, he became interested in Marxist, solely from reading about the topic. He joined his school's marching band and the Civil Air Patrol, a youth auxiliary of the Air Force.

Although a self-proclaimed Marxist, Lee Oswald wanted to join the United States Marines Corps. He idolized his older brother Robert, Jr., who was himself in the United States Marines. He even wore Robert's U.S. Marine Corps ring. This relationship seemed to have transcended any ideological conflict for him. He tried to enlist into the United States Marines when he was sixteen but was rejected because he was too young. He dropped out of high school and went to work. He failed to receive his high school diploma before he enlisted into the U.S. Marines. Throughout his life he had trouble with spelling and writing coherently. His letters, diary and other writings have led some to suggest he was dyslexic. At the same time some have contended his poor writing and spelling skills were the result of a sporadic education. Just after turning seventeen, he enlisted in the Marines.

CHAPTER 2

—————————◻—————————

"Political sovereignty is but a mockery without the means of
meeting poverty and illiteracy and disease. Self-determination
is but a slogan if the future holds no hope."

John F. Kennedy

Lee Harvey Oswald stood to his feet and walked over to his bag leaning
against a wall. He opened it and pulled out a folder which was marked:
TOP SECRET. He flipped through the pages and photos in the folder.
He couldn't believe that with the contents in the folder he will throw away
everything he ever stood for. He will betray the very thing he swore to
protect when he joined the United States Marine Corps. He was looking
at highly classified information about the CIA U-2 spy plane. He already
knew the information he held in his hand. But his CIA handler gave
him this folder to hand over to the Soviets. He closed the folder and
his returned to his bed. He laid the folder next to him on the bed. He
rested his head in his hands. He leaned forward until his elbows were on
his knees. When he enlisted in the United States Marine Corps, he had
intended to make it a career. But when he met his handler, James Smith,
in Japan, Lee's mind was changed.

On October 26, 1956, shortly after turning seventeen, Lee Harvey
Oswald reported to Marine Corps Basic Training in San Diego, California.
It was the height of the Cold War between the United States and the
Soviet Union. While in San Diego he received extensive training in
marksmanship. He bragged to his mother and brother back home about
his shooting abilities. He claimed he was an expert shoot. But this couldn't
be farther from the truth. Fellow Marines remembered him as a poor

shot. Some of his fellow Marines claimed he couldn't hit the broad side of a barn. One of his Marine buddy who was assigned to the same platoon as Lee remembered him being known as a "shit bird" who couldn't qualify with his rifle. But the sergeant in charge of his training said he was a slightly better than average shot for a Marine, expert by a normal person's standards. He said Lee shot a 212 on the rifle range, earning a "sharpshooter" qualification.

On March 18, 1957, Lee reported to Naval Air Technical Training Center in Jacksonville, Florida. Here he was trained to be a radar operator. This was a job the Marines gave only to men with higher than average intelligence. The course at the training center in Jacksonville was a general introduction to aviation fundamentals. The trainees were shown films of various Navy and Marine aircraft taking off and landing. They also listened to classroom lectures on the flight characteristics of combat aircrafts. He was promoted to private first class and granted a final clearance to handle classified materials specified to be "Confidential." In May of 1957 Lee reported to Keesler Air Force Base in Biloxi, Mississippi. He took the aircraft control and warning operator course at Keesler. He was taught how to use a radar to identify whether incoming planes were friendly or enemies, the techniques for overcoming radar-jamming equipment on Soviet planes and the system for alerting allied planes and if necessary, guiding them to meet an enemy plane.

A couple of months later in July he reported to the Marine Corps Air Station in El Toro, California. After he finished his training, Lee was stationed on the *U.S.S. Bexar* at the Pacific Crossing from August to September. The ship made one stop in Hawaii, where he went ashore. He bought a Hawaiian shirt and took a picture of the statute of Kamehameha the Great. Kamehameha the Great was the 18th century rebel who overthrew the established order and united the Hawaiian Islands under his rule.

James Smith walked into David Atlee Philips' office. David motioned towards a chair. James nodded his head and sat in it. He met David a time or two before now. He was known to be a ruthless agent. He had ran numerous covert operations. James had been involved with just a couple of covert operations himself. He had been looking forward to working with David.

"I hear you have been wanting to get more involved with covert operations ran by the Central Agency Intelligence," said David.

"Yes, sir."

"Good. We have been trying to recruit some new agents. We need new, young, unattached men for the operation we are undertaking," said David.

"And what operation is that, sir?"

"This confrontation with the Soviet Union is really heating up. I think I have heard some people calling it a Cold War. We are training new agents to go over to Russian as so-called defectors. While over there these 'defectors' will attempt to gather information and possibly try to be 'turned' by the Soviets. Would you be interested in acting as a handler for one of these agents?" asked David.

"Yes, sir."

"Good," David said as he stood to his feet. He picked up three files from his desk as he walked over to him. "These are the newest possible recruits. Study them and pick which one you want to work with."

James opened one of the files. After reading for a few minutes, he handed the other two files to David. "I think this one will be perfect. No father figure, no real attachment to family and he is not married. I want to work with this one," he handed the last file to David.

"Ah, Mr. Oswald, nice choice," commented David.

From September to November 1957, Lee Harvey Oswald was shipped out for a posting at an Air Force defense base at Atsugi, Japan. What was unknown to the rest of the world was what kind of Air Force base Atsugi actually was. It was a Central Intelligence Agency base. He was a radar operator at Atsugi Air Force Base. The CIA program which involved the U-2 spy plane mission was based out of Atsugi. The CIA U-2 spy plane mission was a covert operation. Its primary mission was to invade the Russian air space and photograph Soviet strategic sites. The base, which was about thirty-five miles southwest of Tokyo, served as the CIA's main operational base in the Far East. It was one of two bases from which the CIA's top secret U-2 spy plane took off on their flights over the Soviet Union and China. He was a small part in the operation, but he was learning how it worked. From the control room, Lee listened regularly to the U-2's radio communication.

After Atsugi, he was reassigned as a radar operator to the Marine Air Control Squadron No. 9 in Santa Ana California. He continued to have access to secret information which would have been valuable to a Cold

War enemy. It was at this time Lee first met his CIA handler, James Smith. He was approached by his handler while was he was sitting at a booth in a local bar in Japan.

"Your name is Private First Class Lee Harvey Oswald, isn't it?"

"Well, stranger you know my name, but I don't know yours. So I am at an unfair disadvantage," said Lee.

James looked at him for a moment or two. To the normal citizen Lee looked, well, normal. He stood at about five feet nine inches and weighed about a hundred seventy pounds. His dark hair was cut close in the usual military style. His chubby cheeks resembled a chipmunk with a mouth full of nuts. He laughed to himself with that image in his head.

"You can call me James, James Smith," he held out his hand to the young Marine.

"Well, James, it's nice to meet you," Lee shook his hand. "Can I buy you a drink?"

"Sure, what are you drinking?"

"I am drinking a soda. I don't drink alcohol," claimed Lee.

"That's strange. Coming to a bar, but you just drink soda."

"Well, the women in here are nice to look at. And most importantly, I am not like most Marines," he said.

"That's one of things which grabbed our attention about you."

"Excuse me, 'our attention'? Who are you thinking about? Just who are you, Mr. Smith?" asked Lee.

"I work for the Central Intelligence Agency."

"The CIA? You're an agent with the CIA?" this time it was Lee's turned to laugh to himself. "Thought you guys aren't supposed to tell anyone that," suggested Lee.

"Well, I am a different sort of agent. I am what you would call a handler."

"What's a handler?"

"A handler is the one who works as the go-between the Agency and the agent he is working with on a mission. He is the only one who knows how to locate and communicate with that particular agent."

"Nice job, but what does that have to do with me?" asked Lee.

"I am here to try and recruit you. We want you to go to work for the Agency."

"Are you serious? Do you mean like an undercover spy or something like that?"

"Exactly like that. Are you interested?"

"Well, I've got one question; why me?"

"You are the type of man we are looking for."

"And what type of man is that?" asked Lee.

"A man with no real attachments to family, and you're not married. So you would be able to come and go where we need you to go with little trouble."

"What kind of mission are we talking about?" asked Lee.

"Have you been watching the news? Do you know about the confrontation going on between the United States and Soviet Union?"

"Have you already forgotten that I am a United States Marine? Yes, I am aware of the tension between the United States and the Soviet Union."

"We want you to go to the Soviet Union and try to gather information on the Soviets."

"I don't think the Soviets would allow me to enter their country much less stay there. For I am an American after all," said Lee.

"We have taken care of that. You are a radar operator at the U-2 spy plane base, right?"

"Yes, I am."

"When the time comes for you to 'defect' to the Soviet Union we will provide you with some military secrets about the spy plane operation to hand over to the Soviets. This will insure they will allow you to remain in Russia."

"You want me to hand over some highly classified information to the enemy? But by doing that I would be betraying the United States. I don't want to betray my country. That's not why I joined the Marines," said Lee.

"You won't be betraying your country."

"Yes, I will. You want me to go over to the land of our enemy and give them secrets to the U-2 spy plane. The very plane the Soviets have not been able to shoot down, might I add. I think that's considered betrayal, no I would say that's considered treason. And treason is punishable by death," said Lee.

"It's not treason if you work for the United States Government and it concerns National Security."

"National Security? How's that?" asked Lee.

"President Eisenhower and Soviet Premier Khrushchev have a peace talk planned. That peace talk can't happen. If that peace talk was to take place it could end the Cold War between the United States and the Soviet Union."

"Well, wouldn't the end of the Cold War be good for the United States?"

"It would be good, if the Russians could be trusted. But they can't be trusted. The minute the Cold War ends, the Soviets will be making plans on how to betray our trust. That peace talk can't happen."

"So, I turn over the U-2 spy plane secrets and then what?" questioned Lee.

"You hang low; gather a little information, enjoy the sights until it's time for you to come home."

"How do you expect that I would be able to return to the United States after betraying it?"

"Like I said, you won't be betraying America. And just leave your return home to the CIA," replied James.

CHAPTER 3

———————————◻———————————

"Conformity is the jailer of freedom
and the enemy of growth."

John F. Kennedy

On October 18, 1957 as Lee Oswald was celebrating his 18th birthday, his unit received orders to be shipped out to the South China Sea and Philippines. The civil war in Indonesia was heating up. The United States, up to this point, had secretly supported the Moslem generals against President Achmed Sukarno. The United States was now considering an overt intervention which would possibly require a Marine unit landing in Borneo. This presented an unexpected problem for the CIA. The Central Intelligence Agency didn't want their newest recruit out of their sights just yet. They knew very little about him and they didn't trust him just yet. They wanted to have his orders changed so he couldn't leave Japan. But they didn't want it to be obvious to the United States Marine Corps one of their own soldiers was a secret agent. There was no time to go through the normal red tape to get his orders changed. His handler came up with the perfect plan.

On October 27th, as the time for departure drew near, Lee sat on his bunk in his barracks. He held a .22 caliber derringer in his right hand. He was hoping no one knew he had the pistol in his possession. He was not allowed to own a civilian weapon so his handler had given him the pistol. He didn't want to shoot himself, but his handler, James, claimed it was the only way to keep him in Japan. He wasn't finished with his secret CIA training so they needed him to stay. He pointed the barrel at his left arm. He closed his eyes as he pulled the trigger.

As if to highlight the truth of his shooting, Lee almost missed his arm at point blank range. He barely grazed his upper left arm. He screamed out in pain and dropped the weapon onto the barrack floor. He grabbed his arm and fell back on his bed. A Navy corpsman heard the gunshot and he ran into Lee's barracks and saw him lying on the bunk. Blood was seeping slowly through his fingers. The corpsman tore a strip from the sheet began tying a tourniquet on his left arm. Fellow Marine, Sam Jones, walked into the barracks just as the Navy corpsman was tying the tourniquet on Lee's arm.

"What the hell happened here?" asked Sam.

"I don't know. I heard a gunshot and when I came in here I found him lying here on his bunk," answered the Navy corpsman.

"I shot myself," replied Lee.

He was rushed to the United States Navy Hospital in nearby Yokosuka. At the hospital a naval surgeon treated the gunshot wound. As the doctor was stitching up the minor wound, Lee claimed he was shot by a .45 caliber automatic pistol which discharged when he accidently dropped it. He told the doctor this story because he didn't want to reveal he had in his possession a .22 caliber pistol, which would have been a court martial. When the bullet was found and examined it was revealed the pistol was actually a .22 caliber pistol. The doctor reported the incident and Lee faced military discipline. He stayed in the hospital for almost three weeks while recovering from the shooting.

On November 20th, Lee Howard boarded the USS *Terrell County*, bound for the northern end of the Philippine archipelago. The maneuver was code-named *Operation Strongback*. Less than a week after it set up its camp, his unit was ordered to pull up its tents and proceed immediately back to the USS *Terrell County*. The ship headed north toward Japan, and the men assumed they were returning to Atsugi. On the second day at sea, the ship veered around sharply and headed back to Subic Bay in the Philippines. For a week the ship simply sat in the bay. The Marines weren't given a clue to where they were headed.

In early December the *Terrell County* headed out into the South China Sea and met thirty other ships of the Seventh Fleet. For almost forty days, his unit didn't see land. Finally, after a hot and dreary Christmas at sea near the equator, his unit returned to the Subic Bay. The Marines again went ashore and set up a temporary camp on the edges of Cubi Point

Air Base. A few days later the Marines was ordered to take down their temporary camp once again. They were headed, this time, for the island of Corregidor, 40 miles away. Once his unit arrived, they once more set up their radar bubble and arranged sleeping quarters for themselves in the roofless remains of a hospital which was bombed out during World War II. By March 7th the Indonesia crisis had stopped and his unit boarded the USS *Wexford County*. It took another eleven days at sea before the vessel reached their base in Japan.

After returning to Atsugi, Lee was brought up on charges for having an unregistered weapon. He was found guilty on April 11th, and he was sentenced to twenty days at hard labor, forfeiture of fifty dollars in pay and reduction in rank to private. His confinement was suspended for six months, with the provision it would be canceled if he stayed out of future trouble. He was ordered to kitchen duty as punishment. Soon after the court martial, he applied for a hardship discharged. He was hoping he would be discharged in Japan where he had made numerous friends. His request was turned down. He became bitter and began claiming he was being singled out by the Marine Corps.

One night Lee Oswald walked up to Technical Sergeant Miguel Rodriguez at a squadron party at the Enlisted Men's Club. Miguel was the man who Lee believed was responsible for having him reassigned to kitchen duty.

"You've got a lot guts to come in here," he said to Miguel.

Miguel just simply ignored his comment. Miguel figured he was prejudiced against Mexicans. A few nights later Miguel saw him at the Bluebird Café. This was a local hangout for the Marines in his unit. This time Lee spilled his drink on Miguel and tried to start a fight with the technical sergeant. The military police intervened and Miguel signed a complaint against him the next day. In June Lee faced summary court martial. At the hearing he chose to act as his own attorney. During cross examination of Miguel, Lee tried to persuade the court he had spilled the drink accidentally. Miguel insisted Lee had not been drunk and he had purposely spilled his drink. The judge ruled Lee had used "provoking words" and sentenced him to twenty-eight days in the brig and forfeiture of fifty-five dollars. He began serving his sentence on July 27, 1958.

According to his military records, Lee served his sentence from July 27th to August 13th. In truth, he never went to the brig. He was further trained as a CIA agent during that time. When he was "released" from the brig, James Smith instructed him to act as if he was an embittered person. It was time to start planning his "defection" to the Soviet Union. During this time, he subscribed to *The Worker* and strengthened his Russian and began openly espousing the virtues of Marxism to fellow Marines.

CHAPTER 4

—❑—

"A young man who does not have what it takes
to perform military service is not likely to have what it takes
to make a living. Today's military rejects include tomorrow's
hard-core unemployed."

John F. Kennedy

In September 1958, a new international crisis arose as the Chinese
Communists began shelling and blockading the tiny offshore islands of
Quemoy and Matsu. These islands were occupied by anti-Communist
troops loyal to the Nationalist government on Formosa. In anticipation of a
naval intervention in the straits between Formosa and the Communist-held
mainland, Lee Oswald's unit was ordered to set up a forward radar base at
Pingtung on Formosa. Lee and the rest of his unit boarded the USS *Skagit*
which was an attack cargo ship.

One night Lee drew guard duty at the base. About midnight Lieutenant
Charles Rhodes, who was the officer in charge of the guards, heard several
shots coming from the position from which Lee was guarding. The
lieutenant drew his .45 caliber pistol and he ran to the clump of trees
from which he believed the gunfire came. He saw Lee slumped against
a tree and he was holding his M-1 rifle in his lap and he was crying and
shaking.

"What's the matter? What happened?" asked Lt. Rhodes.

"I saw some men in the woods," said Private Oswald. "I challenged
them, but they wouldn't stop. So I started shooting."

"Did you hit any of them?"

"No, sir, I don't think so," replied Lee.

"Who were the men?"

"I don't know. They never said anything," he answered.

"Where did the men go?"

"I . . . I . . . I don't know. Sir, I can't bear being on guard duty anymore," he said almost to himself.

Lt. Rhodes helped him to his feet. He placed Lee's arm around his shoulder and slowly walked him back to his tent. Lieutenant Rhodes reported the incident to his commanding officer. On October 6th, Lee returned to Japan on a military plane. Lt. Rhodes was told Lee was being sent to Atsugi for medical reasons. The truth was he was sent back to the base to finish up his training as a CIA agent.

On November 2, 1958, after his thirteen month tour of duty at Japan ended, Lee Oswald boarded the USS *Barrett* in Yokosuka. Two weeks later, after a quiet voyage, the ship rolled into the San Francisco Harbor. He traveled by bus to Fort Worth, Texas to see his family on a thirty day leave. He stayed at his mother's apartment but spent most of the time with Robert, his brother, hunting squirrels and rabbits with .22 rifles. On December 21st, he boarded another bus and returned to the Marines. Just before Christmas, he reported to his new unit, Marine Air Control Squadron Nine (MACS-9) in Santa Ana, California. It operated out of an old Navy blimp base. The Marine jets and other fixed-wing aircrafts flew mainly out of El Toro Air Base, located across the road from the blimp base. The radar bubble which MACS-9 was assigned to was located on a grassy field near the road separating the two bases. The radar antennas were enclosed by a barbed wire fence. He was assigned to the Bravo team in the bubble.

While most of the men in the unit enjoyed the easy life on the California base, Lee was instructed by James Smith to take a Marine Corps proficiency test on the Russian language. In reading Russian, he received a score of plus four. This meant he got four more answers right than he got wrong. In writing Russian, he scored plus three. In comprehending Russian, he scored a minus five. While his overall score was considered poor when compared to a person who had studied the language, it proved he had actually learned a language which was considered difficult to learn. His CIA training for his mission in the Soviet Union was progressing nicely.

Less than a month later, he took and passed tests which gave him the equivalency of a high school diploma. This made it possible for him to apply for college after his service in the Marines was completed. At the same time he worked to improve his Russian. For hours on end he would seat with a textbook and a Russian-English dictionary, testing himself on words. Once he learned the words he would scribbled them down on in a notebook he kept. By the end of the summer in 1959 Lee had become well known as a Russophile within the unit. One fellow Marine asked him to have dinner with his aunt, Elizabeth Cullen, an extremely attractive airline stewardess from New Orleans. She was studying Russian in preparation for the State Department's foreign language examination. She met him in a cafeteria in Santa Ana. They spoke in Russian for about two hours. She had been studying Russian with a Berlitz tutor for more than a year. She found he had a far more confident command of the difficult language than she did and could string entire sentences together without much hesitation. She asked him how he had learned Russian. He shrugged and replied he had taught himself by listening to Radio Moscow.

That summer Lee also confided in Carlos Delgado, who worked with him for four hour shifts in the radar bubble. Soon they became good friends. Carlos, who was Puerto Rican, was treated by Lee as an equal, not like the other Marines in their unit. He also came to admire the way Lee used his intelligence to knock others, even the officers, down to their "proper size." During their long and uneventful watch in the radar bubble, Carlos decided to teach him Spanish. He found Lee to be a willing and able student. Lee even purchased a Spanish-English dictionary so he could practice on his own. On one occasion he took Lee to Tijuana, Mexico with him for the weekend. After spending a few hours with Carlos in a bar, Lee left him, presumably to meet some friends. He didn't inform Carlos who these friends were. Lee met his CIA handler and an agent who was stationed in Mexico City. They discussed his "defection" to Russia. They informed him the time for his "defection" was nearing. Carlos and Lee's common interest in Fidel Castro is what seemed to strengthen their bond. At the beginning of the year, Fidel had won his guerilla war and assumed power in Cuba. During their many conversations Lee told him he wanted to go to Cuba and help train Castro's troops. At the direction of his CIA handler, he told Carlos his hero was Major William A. Morgan.

Major Morgan was a former sergeant in the United States Army who had joined Castro in Cuba. Morgan had renounced his American citizenship. One of Major Morgan's more impressive achievements was to act as a double agent and lure anti-rebels into a trap in Cuba. At one point,

Lee suggested to Carlos he should accompany him to Cuba, where they both could do the same as Major Morgan. He believed Carlos had some local means of contacting Cubans. Lee continued to press him for someone to contact. One night while on duty in the radar bubble, Carlos scribbled a note telling him to write the Cuban Embassy in Washington, D.C.

When Lee first joined the Marines, he had received few letters, but Carlos now noticed he was getting mail several times a week. Once while he was looking through Lee's locker for a tie to borrow, he noticed several of the letters were from the Cuban consulate. When he started getting letters from the Cuban consulate, Lee started wearing a suit and tie. He would also travel to Los Angeles with Carlos, which was an hour and a half by bus. Lee claimed he was visiting the Cuban consulate. Late one night Carlos was on guard duty with Lee. The Military Police shack called informing them Lee had a visitor at the main gate. Because the visitor was a civilian, they wouldn't let him onto the base. He had to find someone to relieve Lee. An hour later, Carlos passed the main gate and he saw Lee was in a heated discussion with a man in a topcoat. It was a hot California night and it seemed odd to him someone would wear a topcoat on such a hot night. He believed the man was connected to the Cuban consulate in some way. Lee wouldn't confirm his assumption. The man whom Carlos saw talking to Lee was his CIA handler, James Smith.

As Lee's tour of duty drew to an end, Carlos noticed several photographs showing front and profile views of a fighter plane among his belongings. He knew the pictures had been used a visual aid in their classes, but he wondered why Lee had them in his possession. He didn't ask him about the pictures because he knew Lee wouldn't be truthful with him. He feared Lee was a spy but he wasn't sure, so he didn't approach the subject with him. Nearing the end of his duty in California, Lee was instructed his time to "defect" to the Soviet Union had come. Under the direction of his handler, Lee started making careful preparations to go to Russia, applying first to the Albert Schweitzer College in Switzerland. As instructed by his handler, he submitted other fictional applications to foreign universities in order to obtain a student visa. After finishing active duty, Marines were usually required to do reserve duty. James informed him by attending college outside the US he could avoid Marine Corps reserve duty. The CIA didn't want anything to impede his mission in Russia.

In July 1959, Lee Oswald filed papers with the Red Cross to help him get an early discharge from the Marine Corps. He explained to his mother in a special delivery letter, Red Cross representatives would call her to ascertain he was needed at home to support her. Marguerite cooperated with her son by sending her own affidavit and supporting letters from two friends, a doctor and a lawyer. Once this was done, he filed for dependency discharge on August 17, 1959. His request was approved two weeks later, and on September 3rd he was detached from duty. He was transferred to the company headquarters in El Toro across the road to be processed out of the Marines. The next day he filed for a passport in Santa Ana. He noted the primary purpose of his trip was to attend the College of Albert Schweitzer in Switzerland and the University of Turku in Turku, Finland. He cited possible travel to England, France, Switzerland, Germany, Finland, Russia, Cuba and the Dominican Republic. The selection of colleges in Switzerland and Finland provided him cover for his travel to the east. He had his passport within six days.

On September 11th, Lee signed a statement pledging:

> *"I shall not hereafter in any manner reveal or divulge to any person any information affecting the National Defense, Classified, Top-secret, Secret, or Confidential, or which I gained knowledge during my employment . . ."*

This was required of all Marines with access to classified material. He was then officially released from active duty and transferred to the Marine Air Reserve Training Command. On that same day he left Santa Ana and traveled to Fort Worth by bus. He arrived at his mother's home at 2AM on September 14th. The next morning Lee shocked his mother by announcing he planned to board a ship and work in the export-import business. Marguerite was disappointed because she had counted on him to stay home and help support her. After withdrawing $203 from the West Side State Bank, he traveled to Robert's house on Davenport Street in Fort Worth. He spent the entire day with his brother. On September 16th, he showed his mother his passport. She saw a page which was stamped IMPORT-EXPORT. He gave her $100 and then he traveled to New Orleans. The next day in New Orleans he went to the offices of Travel Consultants Inc. He booked a passage on the freighter *Marion Lykes* which was set to leave the next day bound for Le Havre, France. On the application form he described himself as a shipping export agent. He paid $220.75 for the one way ticket. He spent the night in the Liberty Hotel. He wrote his mother:

> "*I have booked passage on a ship to Europe, I would have had to sooner or later and I think it's best I go now. Just remember above all else that my values are different from Robert's or yours. It is difficult to tell you how I feel. Just remember this is what I must do. I did not tell you about my plans because you could hardly be expected to understand.*"

CHAPTER 5

❑

"A nation that is afraid to let its people judge the truth
and falsehood in an open market is a nation
that is afraid of its people."

John F. Kennedy

On October 8th, the freighter, *Marion Lykes*, pulled into the harbor at
Le Havre, France where Lee Harvey Oswald and three other passengers
disembarked. He boarded another freighter and arrived in Southampton
on Friday, October 9th. He informed the customs officials he had $700
with him and intended to spend one week in England before proceeding
to Switzerland to attend college. He left Heathrow Airport in London
that same day on an international flight and landed later that evening in
Helsinki, Finland. There was no direct flight from London to Helsinki
during the time he was in London. So he changed planes at a separate city
in Europe.

At midnight on Friday he checked in at the Torni Hotel in downtown
Helsinki. On Saturday he transferred to the less expensive Klaus Kurki
Hotel. He stayed registered at this hotel for five days. Before leaving,
he traveled to Stockholm to consult with the Soviet Embassy there. He
needed information on the procedure to revoke his American citizenship.

A couple days later, under the guidance of James, Lee visited the Soviet
Consulate in Helsinki. He received visa numbered 403339 which was
valid for a six day trip to the Soviet Union. He also bought $300 worth of
tourist vouchers for the Soviet Union. On the evening of October 15th, he
left Helsinki by train and crossed the Finnish-Soviet border at Vainikkala,
headed to Moscow.

Helsinki was a special type of city. It was the place where a person could travel to get a quick visa into the Soviet Union. This was not routinely known by just anybody. The main people who knew this about Helsinki was people whom worked in the USSR or was involved with Soviet matters. Or in the case of Lee, people who were involved with covert operations with the CIA knew of this information. With the help of his CIA handler, he was able to use this information to gain entry into the Soviet Union.

On October 16th Lee Oswald arrived in Moscow, Russia. He was brimming with enthusiasm about the possibility accomplishing his first mission in the Soviet Union. He was an actual spy for the United States Government. He was living every young boy's dream. On his second day in Moscow, he told his intourist guide, Rima Shirokova, he wanted to defect because he didn't approve of the United States way of life. In his written appeal he said he wanted Soviet citizenship because "*I am communist and a worker and I have lived in a decadent capitalist society where the workers are slaves.*" He was trying to follow his handler's very detailed instructions on defecting to the Soviet Union. His intourist guide introduced him to an older somewhat bald heavy set man in a black suit.

"Why do you want to become a Soviet citizen?" the official asked him in fairly good English.

Lee gave vague answers about the "great Soviet Union."

"The Soviet Union is only great in literature. You need to go back home," the official stated.

Lee Harvey Oswald sat in his chair stunned. This Russian official had rejected his request for citizenship to the Soviet Union. It would appear his first mission would be a failure. He didn't even get the chance to offer up the military secrets James had given him. He practically begged the official to allow him to stay in Russia. The official finally agreed to see what he could do to help him. But he really didn't mean it; he just wanted Lee to leave. Lee, somehow, knew this was what the official was doing. He continued to persist that he be allowed to stay in Russia. The official told him to be patient and go get a hotel room and wait for a reply.

While waiting to hear whether or not he would be allowed to stay in the Soviet Union, Lee's handler set up an interview with Lev Setyayev, a reporter for Radio Moscow. That afternoon a "police official" informed him since his visa was due to expire in two hours, he must immediately leave the country. He was shocked by the Soviets refusal to give him asylum. He quickly contacted his CIA handler. This wasn't how his mission was supposed to go. James made it sound like the Soviets would have no problem letting him stay. Lee met with his handler at a little café-like shop near his apartment.

"What I am going to do? They are going to force me to leave the country?" Lee asked.

"Did you tell them you had Top Secret information to give them?"

"They didn't even give me a chance to tell them anything. I can't let my first mission as a CIA agent be a failure. You don't understand. I have been a failure in everything I have attempted to do. I can't let this be a failure. What am I going to do?" asked Lee.

"First of all stay calm. Second, go back to your hotel room and slit your wrist."

"You want me to kill myself? That's crazy. What will that accomplish? I don't want to be a failure, but I want to live," Lee said.

"You will not die. I make sure your intourist finds you just in time."

"I don't understand. What's the point of me trying to commit suicide?" asked Lee.

"It will show the Soviet you are distraught over being denied the right to stay in the country. And they will then give you just about anything to avoid an international incident."

"Ok, just make sure Rima finds me before I die," Lee turned away and walked out of the café.

About 7:00pm Lee walked into his apartment. He soaked his wrists in cold water, hoping it would numb the pain. He walked into his bathroom and filled his bathtub with hot water. He looked at himself for a moment in the mirror. He shook his head as if to say he didn't really agree with what he was about to do. But James appeared to know what he was talking about. He pulled off his shoe and broke the mirror with it. He picked up a small shard of glass and laid it on the side of the bathtub. He pulled off his clothes and climbed into the bathtub. He picked up the shard of glass and slit his left wrist. He plunged his slit wrist into the steaming hot water. Suddenly everything grew black and he lost consciousness.

Less than an hour later Rima walked into his bathroom. She saw him unconscious in the bathtub filled with hot water. She ran to the tub. She shook him and called his name. She had received a strange call from a man she didn't know. All the man said was she needed to come check on Lee.

She was already worried about him so she didn't hesitate to come to his apartment. It was a good thing she had a key or she might not have found him in time. She felt for his pulse. She could barely feel one in his neck. She ran to the living room and grabbed the phone. She quickly called for help. He was rushed to the hospital where he received five stitches in his wrist. He awakened the next morning to find himself in the insanity ward of Botkin Hospital. After being interview by a doctor the next day, he was transferred to an ordinary ward.

A week later, after being released from the hospital, Lee was taken to the Passport and Registration Office by Rima. While there he was interviewed by four officials. He gave them his discharge papers from the United States Marine Corps. It was at this time he handed over the Top Secret information on the U-2 spy plane he had received from his CIA handler. He was told to wait for their answer. Instead of waiting, Lee was instructed to take a taxi to the American Embassy in Moscow. Although his suicide attempt was no more than an attention-getting ruse, the Soviet government feared an international incident if he attempted something similar again. The intelligence and counterintelligence KGB units considered recruiting him as a spy. But they waited to see what the real reason why he was in the Soviet Union.

On Saturday morning October 31st, Lee Oswald stepped out of the taxi in front of the United States Embassy in Moscow. He walked past the Marine guards into the consulate section. He had almost a smug attitude about him when he glared at the Marine guards. Richard Snyder was the senior consulate officer in Moscow. Richard joined the Central Intelligence Agency in 1949 as an intelligence operative. He served in Tokyo under State Department cover.

Lee walked into Richard's office and slammed down his passport on his desk. Richard noticed he was dressed in a dark suit, white shirt and a tie. He noticed two things the minute Lee walked into his office. It was a cold morning in Moscow, but he wasn't wearing a coat or a hat on his head. He was also wearing thin white gloves. Throughout the meeting, Richard couldn't divert his attention from the white gloves. They just appeared odd to him.

"What can I do for you?" asked Richard.

"I've come to give up my American passport and renounce my citizenship."

Lee laid a piece of paper onto his desk formally renouncing his American citizenship. It said:

> "I, Lee Harvey Oswald, do hereby request that my present citizenship in the United States of America, be revoked.
>
> I have entered the Soviet Union for the express purpose of applying for citizenship in the Soviet Union, through the means of naturalization. My request for citizenship is now pending before the Supreme Soviet of the USSR.
>
> I take these steps for political reasons. My request for the revoking of my American citizenship is made only after the longest and the most serious consideration.
>
> I affirm that my allegiance is to the Union of Soviet Socialist Republics."

Richard could tell he had fully prepared his defection to the Soviet Union. Since it was the State Department's policy to discourage Americans from defecting, he tried to stall him.

"What are your reasons for applying for Soviet citizenship?" asked Richard.

"I am a Marxist," Lee stated with arrogance as crossed his legs and glared at the consul.

"You'll be a lonely man as a Marxist," Richard suggested to him.

Lee didn't show any signs of comprehending his implication the Soviet Union was very far from a Marxist society.

"You know, I was forewarned that you, the Soviet consul, would try to dissuade me out of my decision. So, let me stop you right there. I do not want to hear any lectures from you because I know what I am doing. Don't waste my time and just go ahead give me the forms I need to sign."

Richard realized there was little real possibility of discouraging him from defecting. He tried to elicit as much information as he could from him which would be of operational significance to the State Department or the CIA. He wasn't aware Lee was in fact a spy with the very people he worked for. This wasn't unusual for the Central Intelligence Agency. Very few Agency employees knew who was a spy or wasn't. When Richard asked him when he had first become interested in renouncing his American citizenship, Lee expounded on the American imperialism he had witnessed while serving as a Marine in Japan and other bases in the Far East. Richard pressed him about what he meant by imperialism and Lee replied that his eyes had been opened to the way America oppresses and colonizes foreign people from observing actions in Okinawa.

"Are you prepared to serve the Soviet state?" asked Richard.

"I had been a radar operator with the United States Marine Corps and I have already agreed to furnish the Soviet Union with knowledge I had acquired while in the Marine Corps. I know something which would be of special interest to the Soviet intelligence."

This seemed odd to the American Consul because he didn't ask for this information and Lee had offered it freely. It was as if he knew the Soviets had bugged the Embassy and he was actually offering the information for their ears and not really for the consul's ears. Across the room, John McVickar, another senior consul officer, couldn't believe what Lee had just stated. Richard informed him he couldn't get the forms he needed to sign until Monday. So he stormed out of the embassy. He never returned to sign those forms. If he was really serious about defecting then he would've been back at the embassy first thing on Monday morning. This was what he was instructed to do by James Smith. He needed to leave the door open for his re-entry into the United States.

After Lee Oswald left the Embassy; Richard Snyder reported his intention to Washington. The United States Marine Corps changed their radar codes and began proceedings for an "undesirable discharge" for Lee. He also sent a cable to United Defense Department about his conversation with Lee. He tipped off Robert Korengold, the bureau chief of United Press International, Lee Oswald was about to defect and he was staying in Room 233 at the Metropole Hotel. He suggested to Robert a further interview with him might be an interesting story for his wire service. He rushed over to the Metropole Hotel and knocked on his door. Lee opened the door a few inches.

"Who is it?" asked Lee.

"My name is Robert Korengold. I would like to interview you."

"Why do you want to interview me?" asked Lee.

"I want to interview you because you are an ex-Marine who has defected here from the United States."

"Who told you about me?"

"Richard Snyder at the American Embassy in Moscow told me about you."

"No, I do not want to be interviewed at this time," Lee slammed the door shut before Robert could say anything else.

CHAPTER 6

───────────◻───────────

"As we express our gratitude, we must never forget
that the highest appreciation is not to utter words,
but to live by them."

John F. Kennedy

On November 3rd, going according to the mission before him, Lee Oswald sent the American Embassy a letter strongly protesting the refusal of the consul to accept his renunciation of his American citizenship. He wrote:

> *"My application, requesting that I be considered for citizenship in the Soviet Union is now pending before the Supreme Soviet of the USSR. In the event of acceptance, I will request my government to lodge a formal protest regarding this incident."*

Richard Snyder wrote him in return, inviting him to appear in person to prepare the necessary documents for renunciation of citizenship. Lee didn't reply to the invitation. There was no need for him to reply, because it was never intended by the CIA for him to remain in the Soviet Union. The next day the embassy made a final attempt to contact him. John McVickar personally brought a letter to him from his half-brother John Pic. Lee did not answer his door at the Metropole Hotel. The maid on the floor explained to John that Lee was rarely seen at the hotel. He left the letter at the front desk.

It was determined to make Lee's defection seem more real it had to be reported in the national news. Less than a week later, he granted his first interview to Aline Mosby of UPI. She came to his hotel room with a camera. She saw him in his huge room, furnished with ornate and gilded furniture and overlooking the Bolshoi Theater. She thought he looked even more completely out of place than she had expected. He seemed a bit awkward, but grew more confident as he spoke.

"When did you first turn to Marxism?" asked Aline.

"I lived in New York a short time during my childhood. I turned to Marxism during that time. It was from my observation of the class struggle in New York City. I read about Karl Marx for the first time when I was fifteen years old. When I read it for the first time, it was like a very religious man opening the bible for the first time. My blinded eyes were opened."

"I began to read about Marxist theory when my mother and I moved back to New Orleans. I saw the impoverishment of the masses before my very eyes in my mother. I saw the capitalists everywhere I went in New Orleans. From that moment on, I continued to indoctrinate myself in Marxism for the next five years," he stated.

"Who paid for your way to the Soviet Union?"

"No one paid my way to get here. I saved $1600 while I was on active duty with the United States Marines to finance my defection over here."

When the interview was over, Aline felt as though she had just sat through a two hour lecture instead of an interview. The briefing he received from James Smith proved to be a success. She handed one copy of her story to the Soviet censor and a second copy to the telegraph office, which she knew would send her copy to UPI in New York only after it had been read and approved by the KGB staff in the censor's office. The next day the UPI story appeared in Fort Worth under the headline "FORT WORTH DEFECTOR CONFIRMS RED BELIEFS."

Two days after granting his interview with Aline Mosby, Lee was visited by Priscilla Johnson who was something more than an ordinary journalist. Before coming to Moscow, she worked as an assistant to Senator John F. Kennedy. Then she went on to earn a reputation as a keen analyst of Soviet affairs. She officially worked for the North American Newspaper Alliance syndicate in Moscow as a correspondent. She was also listed in a State Department document of government employees. Her report of her interview with Lee was furnished to the United States Embassy in Moscow on November 17th. It discussed his motives for defecting to the USSR.

"What was the factors contributing to your decisions to defect?" Priscilla asked him.

"My decision was unemotional. I discovered Socialist literature at the age of fifteen. I was looking for something that would give me the key to my environment. My mother had been a worker all her life. And all her life she had to produce profits for capitalists. I am not an idealist completely. I have had a chance to watch American imperialism in action. If you've ever seen the Naval base at Subic Bay in the Philippines you'd know what I mean. Americans look upon all foreign peoples as something to be exploited for profit. For the past two years I have been waiting to do this one thing. For two years I was waiting to leave the Marine Corps and get enough money to come. I spent two years preparing to come here. These preparations consisted mostly of reading. It took me two years to find out how to do it," he answered.

Throughout the four hour interview, he appeared to be well briefed on the Soviets' handling of his case. At one point he sounded like a spokesman for the Soviet government. Despite Priscilla's attempt to elicit information about everybody who had had previous contact with him in the United States, he was just as determined not to name any names.

"To be honest, before I came I had never seen a Communist in my life," he claimed.

Back in the United States, the news of Lee Harvey Oswald's defection to the USSR and his offer to divulge classified information to the Soviets sent shock waves throughout his former radar units in California. Carlos Delgado watched as a group of men dressed in dark suits arriving in November. They had stenographers and literally took over their company headquarters to question Marines about Lee.

On January 4th, Lee was called to the Passport Office and given a residence document instead of citizenship papers. They informed him he was being sent to Minsk and they had arranged for him to receive some money through the Red Cross to pay for his hotel bills and expenses. The next day he received 5,000 rubles from the Red Cross and he was told he would be paid 700 rubles a month in Minsk. He arrived in Minsk on January 7th, and was met by two more Intourist guides. The next day he was greeted by the mayor of Minsk who promised him a rent free apartment. He began working at the Byelorussia radio and television factory as a checker.

CHAPTER 7

———————◻———————

"Do not pray for easy lives. Pray to be stronger men."

John F. Kennedy

World War II ended with just the simple signing of some papers. On September 2, 1945, the representative of the Emperor of Japan signed the surrender papers laid before him by General Douglas MacArthur on the deck of the battleship *Missouri* in Tokyo Bay. The world could breathe a sigh of relief. The bad guys had been defeated and peace could continue to rein throughout the world. At least that was the way it appeared to the everyday normal citizen of the world. What wasn't clear to the normal citizen was a new secret war had already been plotted. September 2nd signaled the start of that secret war.

Also, on September 2nd, in the capital city of Hanoi, in Vietnam, a Declaration of Independence was signed by Ho Chi Minh as president of the new nation, the Democratic Republic of Vietnam (DRV). Before the ink was dry on the documents being signed on the battleship *Missouri*, the first major battlefields of this new Cold War, Korea and Vietnam, had been selected. They were being stocked with military equipment and supplies. All which remained was to create the political climate for the confrontation and to line up the combatants.

During World War II heavy damage was done to mainland Japan by aerial bombardment. Despite this, an invasion of Japan had been considered as the start of a United States victory and an eventual surrender by Japan. When the island of Okinawa became available as the launching site of an invasion of Japan, supplies and equipment was shipped to the island. The shipment was for an invasion force of at least half a million men. But Japan surrendered before the invasion took place. The stockpile of military equipment was no longer needed for an invasion. The smart thing to do would be to return the military equipment to the United States so it wouldn't fall into the wrong hands and be used against the United States. A United States Navy transport vessel soon arrived in Naha Harbor, Okinawa. The vast amount of military equipment was loaded on the ships. But the equipment wasn't headed back to the United States. It had a different destination. Half of the equipment was shipped to Korea and the other half was shipped to Indochina.

The question which begged to be asked was; why wasn't the military equipment sent back to the United States? This took place in 1945 and the Korea War wouldn't start until five years later and the Indochina War, better known as the Vietnam War, wouldn't start until 1965. Did the United States military forces have enough foresight to be able to predict the Korean War and the Vietnam War before they happened?

On September 23, 1945, shortly after the Democratic Republic of Vietnam had issued its Declaration of Independence, a group of former French troops, acting with the consent of the British forces which had arrived in Saigon from their sweep through Burma in the last days of World War II and armed with Japanese weapons stolen from surrender stockpiles, staged a local coup d'état and seized control of the administration of Saigon. All remaining Japanese forces had been rounded up and had surrendered to the British military command in Saigon by November 30, 1945.

By January 1, 1946, the French had assumed all military commitments in Vietnam. Soon fighting broke out between the French and the Vietminh in late November 1946 and by the end of the year guerilla warfare had spread all over Vietnam. All hope for peaceful settlement of this French/ Vietminh dispute evaporated in 1947, and by the end of 1949 the war had become a major international issue.

CHAPTER 8

———————— ❑ ————————

"Communism has never come to power in a country that was
not disrupted by war or corruption, or both."

John F. Kennedy

On October 1, 1945, President Harry Truman disbanded the Office of Strategic Service (OSS). As the legislation for the new defense establishment and the Central Intelligence Agency was being written and debated he issued a directive which created a new department called the Central Intelligence Group (CIG). The CIG was to be jointly staffed and funded by the Departments of State, War, and Navy. The existence of the CIG made it possible to maintain the covert-agent assets of the wartime OSS wherever they existed and to provide organizational cover for former Nazi general Reinhard Gehlen and his intelligence staff, along with their files of former Nazis, anti-Communist agents and spies who were concealed in the undercover networks of Eastern Europe and in the USSR.

During 1947, the Congress worked to establish a new National Security Council (NSC), a new Department of Defense (DOD) with a Joint Chiefs of Staff structure. The creation of the Central Intelligence Agency through the National Security Act of 1947 was created almost as an afterthought. The United States had never possessed, in peacetime, an intelligence agency working on the international level. This was unheard of at this time in the United States. The early creation of the CIA and of the Office of Policy Coordination (OPC) was an inevitable progression after World War II. When it was decided to turn the Soviet Union from a wartime ally to a peacetime adversary, it became necessary to create an organization which could continue the eternal conflict using the networks of agents and spies in Eastern Europe and the Soviet Union became a major characteristic of the Cold War strategy.

After the National Security Act of 1947 was passed, the National Security Council met on December 19, 1947 for the first time. The stipulation in the National Security Act of 1947 stated the Central Intelligence Agency limit itself to the coordination of intelligence. The CIA was originally created to gather information on enemies of the United States. It wasn't meant to be more than an intelligence gathering entity. It didn't take the National Security Council long to break that stipulation. National Security Council Directive # 4 directed the Central Intelligence Director, Admiral Roscoe Hillenkoetter to carry out covert psychological warfare. A special procedures group was set up and it became involved in the covert "buying" of a nationwide election in Italy. The covert operation was successful and in 1948 the National Security Council issued a new directive to cover clandestine paramilitary operations and also political and economic warfare. This new unit was called the Office of Policy Coordination (OPC).

The OPC was brought into the government and created in secrecy. No law existed which authorized such an organization or the wide range of covert functions it was created to perform. When it began, the director of central intelligence, if he was questioned, could have denied he had anything to do with it. This was called plausible denial. The CIA director could not be implicated in any covert operation which was being performed. If the Central Intelligence Agency director was implicated in such operations, then the United States in turn could be implicated. If a covert operation was revealed, then the CIA director had to be able to deny knowledge of the operation. The OPC soon grew from about 300 hundred employees in 1949 to nearly 6,000 contract employees in 1952. A large part of this sudden growth was due to the additional demands for covert action and other special operations which grew out of the Korean War and related activities.

While the CIA administered the operations of this fast-growing organization, with its six thousand employees, it could always rely upon the military for additional personnel, transport, oversea bases, weapons, aircraft, ships, and all the other things the Department of Defense had in abundance. One of the most important items provided regularly by the Department of Defense, was "military cover." OPC and other CIA personnel were concealed in military units and provided with military cover whenever possible. One of the secret methods of the secret war was the special armed forces were used as agitators. These clandestine operations were designed to make war, even though they may have to play both sides at the same time.

The National Security Act of 1947 laid the foundation of a national security state: the National Security Council (NSC), the National Security Resources Board (NSRB), the Munitions Board, the Research and Development Board, the Office of Secretary of Defense, the Joint Chiefs of Staff and the Central Intelligence Agency (CIA). Secretary of State George Marshall warned President Harry Truman that the National Security Act of 1947 would grant a new intelligence agency powers which were be unlimited.

On June 18, 1948, President Truman's National Security Council approved top secret directive NSC 10/2. This directive sanctioned United States intelligence to carry out a broad range of covert operations such as propaganda, economic warfare, preventive direct action including sabotage, anti-sabotage, demolition and evacuation measures; subversion against hostile states including assistance to underground resistance movements, guerrillas, and refugee liberation groups.

This secret directive authorized the violations of international law. It also established official lying as an indispensible cover. All covert operations had to be planned and executed so any United States Government responsibility for them was not evident to unauthorized person, and if uncovered the US government could plausibly deny any responsibility for them. In order to protect the visible authorities of the government from protest and censure, the CIA was authorized not only to violate international law but to do so with as little consultation as possible. In other words the Central Intelligence Agency was held accountable to no one.

In order for the CIA's concept of a Cold War to work, the United States and the Soviet Union had to be enemies by need and definition. Ever since the detonation of the hydrogen bomb, the world's political, economic, and military system has had to be bipolar. The countries without massive weapons and the means to deliver them could not take part effectively in such global warfare. It was politically necessary for each major power to have an enemy. This was necessary even if both super powers knew they no longer had a way to benefit from an all-out war with each other. Neither one could control its own destiny or its own society without the threat of the other. This was exactly what the Central Intelligence Agency wanted to achieve.

CHAPTER 9

---◻---

"Domestic policy can only defeat us;
foreign policy can kill us."

John F. Kennedy

In 1952 it was decided the time had come to replace Elpidio Quirino as president of Philippines. This would not be an easy operation for the United States. He had been a good friend of the United States and a devoted anti-Communist. The reason for the removal was because he had relaxed his businesses with the United States in favor of other countries. The United States maintained the customary diplomatic relations with the Quirino government and they had a strong ambassador in Manila. The ambassador had CIA stations chief George Aurell on his staff. The ambassador urged the Philippines president to hold an election.

Without the knowledge of the ambassador or the station chief, the CIA sent an undercover team into the Philippines. The undercover team was led by Colonel Edward Lansdale and he had access to anti-Quirino Filipinos. He was in the Philippines to train selected Filipino army troops in PsyWar and other paramilitary tactics. His main goal was to overthrow President Quirino and install Ramon Magsaysay as the new president. The men who were selected were trained outside of the Philippines. When their training was complete, they slipped back into the country and into their usual army units. During this time the HUK insurgency was being escalated by secret operations. Throughout the country, news about the growing insurgency was heard; it was everywhere. The rise of this notional Communist influence gave President Quirino what he thought was a strong platform. Then the CIA made their move.

Colonel Lansdale staged mock attacks and mock liberations on countless villages throughout the Philippines. Villages were attacked and destroyed by the HUKs. Captain Ramon Magsaysay and his loyal band charged into town after town. They killed and captured the HUKs and liberated each village. The CIA sent out mass news releases, produced and projected propaganda movies and held rallies to help build the reputation of Captain Magsaysay.

The effort of the CIA was a success and Captain Ramon Magsaysay was made the secretary of defense. When the election campaign began, he ran for president against Elpidio Quirino. President Quirino was shocked when the "HUK killer" hero entered into the campaign for the presidency. The Philippine president had the traditional power to control the ballot boxes and to count the vote. It would appear an honest election in the Philippines would be impossible.

Just before the election, the HUKs stirred themselves and reminded the Filipinos of the brave captain who had liberated their villages. The votes for Captain Magsaysay poured in from all of the islands. He ordered his own loyal troops to guard every voting site. Army men sealed the voting boxes and carried them in trucks to Manila and all of the votes were counted in public. Captain Magsaysay won easily and became the new president of the Philippines.

Elpidio Quirino was stunned by the outcome of the election. The American ambassador and station chief, George Aurell, was also stunned. They realized the CIA had kept them in the dark about the true role of one of its most powerful undercover teams. The CIA pulled off the deal, right under their noses.

Foreign nationals from all over the world were trained in the methods of secret operations, such as, the use of high explosives, sabotage, communications, and so on. They were trained at military bases in the United States under the guidance of the CIA. The CIA concealed its presence on the military bases.

CHAPTER 10

———————☐———————

"Efforts and courage are not enough
without purpose and direction."

John F. Kennedy

By the end of 1953, it became clear Vietnam, Laos, and Cambodia was a region of great wealth. The Indochina region was freeing itself from Japanese occupation and the French control. It appeared to be threatened by Communists, so it was perfect for the CIA to apply its tactics of its invisible war. The Korean War was coming to an end, so the Cold War battleground needed to be moved to a new country. One-half of the stockpiled military equipment needed for a planned invasion of Japan was moved in September 1945 to Haiphong, Vietnam.

Once the equipment and supplies was in Haiphong it came under the direction of Brigadier General Philip Gallagher. He was supporting the OSS and his associate Ho Chi Minh. Once the military equipment arrived in Vietnam it had been moved into hiding until the day it was needed came. In 1954 the time for its use had come.

The Vietnamese Independence League, or the Vietminh, was well armed with new American-made equipment. They were waging a guerilla-typed war against the French. The French were not aware the rebels were so well armed or where the equipment had come from. In 1946, the French thought they could easily have their way so they reneged on giving the Vietnamese their freedom and independence. By 1954 guerilla warfare had grew and the French forces were in deep trouble. They were trapped in a valley at Dien Bien Phu and wanted more direct aid from the United States.

By the middle of January 1954 the beleaguered French had 11,000 troops in fifteen battalions at Dien Bien Phu. The opposing Vietminh had 24,000 well-armed men in nineteen battalions. The National Security Council believed the number of Vietminh could not defeat the French and take Dien Bien Phu. During the National Security Council meeting on January 14, 1954, Secretary of Defense John Foster Dulles suggested the United States prepare to carry on guerilla operations against the Vietminh if the French were defeated, to make as much trouble for them as they had made for the French and for the US. He believed the costs of such operations would be relatively low and such a plan would provide an opportunity for the US in Southeast Asia. The National Security Council agreed. They approved for CIA Director Allen Dulles to develop a plan for certain contingencies in Indochina. The warfare in Vietnam grew from the events of this meeting.

At the end of the meeting, CIA Director Dulles suggested an unconventional-warfare officer, Colonel Edward Lansdale, be added to the group of American liaison officers which General Henri Navarre, the French commander, had agreed to accept in Indochina. The committee authorized the CIA director to put Colonel Lansdale in the Military Assistance Advisory Group (MAAG), Saigon. This marked the beginning of the CIA's intervention into the affairs of the French government in Indochina. It was not long before the reins of government were taken from the French by the Vietminh after their victory at Dien Bien Phu under the leadership of Ho Chi Minh. The Central Intelligence Agency established the Saigon Military Mission in Vietnam. Its mission was to work with the anti-Vietminh Indochinese and not to work with the French. This new CIA unit was not intent on winning the war for the French.

When Ngo Dinh Diem was established as the president of South Vietnam, in 1954, he had no government structure, no armed forces, no police, no tax system, and so on. The United States aided South Vietnam President Diem. The United States armed and fed his troops. The United States provided billions of dollars of aid to the South Vietnam.

President Dwight Eisenhower didn't approve of the United States involvement in South Vietnam. He did not believe in the United States being there. On January 29, 1954, the National Security Council ignored the President and made plans to get on with the business of making war in Indochina. It's not possible for anyone on the NSC to mistaken how opposed President Eisenhower was to placing American troops in Indochina. But they chose to ignore him. Nothing whatsoever would deter them from the essential business of making war.

It was common belief the President was the one who ran the United States. It's believed the Supreme Court assures compliance with the Constitution and all federal laws. It's also believed that the Congress participates effectively in determining the course of the United States' destiny. But the CIA have proven time after time this wasn't true. The CIA was the true leaders of this country.

On April 26, 1954, the Geneva Conference established a demarcation zone near the 17th parallel which divided the former French colonial land into two nearly equal sections. The north would be the Democratic Republic of Vietnam and the south was to become the State of Vietnam and later, on October 26, 1955, the Republic of Vietnam. In the summer of 1954, the CIA's Saigon Military Mission (SMM) had begun its political, psychological and terrorist activities against the native population in the northern regions. It performed many terrorist acts in Hanoi and surrounding Tonkin. SMM agents polluted petroleum supplies, bombed the post offices, wrote and distributed millions of anti-Vietminh leaflets, printed and distributed counterfeit money. These clandestine activities created a rift between the Vietminh and the Tonkinese Catholics. The mission of the clandestine was to carry out unconventional warfare, paramilitary operations, political-psychological warfare, and rumor campaigns and to set up a Combat PsyWar course for the Vietnamese.

Soon the SMM agents transferred more than a million Tonkinese natives from their native homeland to the disorganized, strange, and inhospitable southland of Cochin China. When this mass transfer began in the middle of 1954, the State of Vietnam as a government didn't exist. Yet it was responsible for all of the real estate south of the 17th parallel and of its ancient, settled and peaceful population estimated at about 12 million. The transfer of these total strangers to the already war weary southern population moved them to a boiling point.

At the time the Vietnamese people were considered the most un-Western of all the Asian countries. They had no way to leave their ancestral villages. They could not pack up the family and head down the road for some unknown destination a thousand or fifteen hundred miles away. Indochina was a very ancient country. Vietnam was one of the oldest settlements known to mankind. To those settled village-oriented people, obligations to parents and to the emperor were the cement of the Confucian order. To the Tonkinese, the village was a most important institution.

In the village, the clans were strong, and the basis of the clan was the veneration of ancestors, which ensured strong attachment to the village and to the land. Each village had a dinh, a shrine, which contained protective deity of that village. The cohesive force of the village was a sense of being protected by those spirits of the soil. The village paid a tax to the higher authority and provide young men for military service. In Vietnam, law was not based on authority and will but on the recognition of universal harmony. In Vietnam the traditional demand was not for good laws so much as for good men. Law was deemed less important than virtue. They were the least likely people to ever live to leave their homeland for some unknown and inhospitable alternative.

In 1955, Air Force Headquarters ordered Colonel L. Fletcher Prouty, a career Army and Air Force officer since World War II, to set up a Pentagon office to provide military support for the clandestine operations of the CIA. Colonel Prouty became director of the Pentagon's "Focal Point Office for the CIA. Central Intelligence Agency Director Allen Dulles was its actual creator. In the 1950s, CIA Director Dulles needed military support for his covert campaigns to undermine opposing nations in the Cold War. Moreover, he wanted subterranean secrecy and autonomy for his projects, even from the members of his own government. Colonel Prouty's job was to provide Pentagon support and deep cover for the CIA beneath the different branches of Washington's bureaucracy. In other words, CIA Director Dulles had agents hidden in different areas in the United States Government. CIA Director Dulles ordered him to create a network of subordinate focal point officers in the armed services, then throughout the entire United States government. Each office which he set up was put under a "cleared" CIA employee. That person took orders directly from the CIA but functioned under the cover of his particular office and branch of government.

CHAPTER 11

———————————◻———————————

"Forgive your enemies, but never forget their names."

John F. Kennedy

During the 1940's, Santo Trafficante, Sr. was one of the leading Mob boss in the United States. He was based out Tampa Bay, Florida. His son, Santo, Jr., ran some of the day to day businesses for his father. Trafficante's business interests included several legal casinos in Cuba, a Havana drive-in theater, shares in the Columbia Restaurant, and several other restaurants and bars in Florida. In December 1946, Santo, Jr. was invited to the Havana Conference. During the 1940's, Santo Trafficante, Jr. joined Lucky Luciano, Frank Costello, and Meyer Lansky to set up gambling operations in Cuba. In 1953 his father sent him to Cuba to manage some of the Mafia controlled casinos.

In August 1954, Santo, Jr. took control of these operations when his father died of stomach cancer. During the dictatorship of Cuban leader Fulgencio Batista, Santo, Jr., operated the Sans Souci, and the Casino International gambling establishments in Havana. He had behind-the-scenes interests in other syndicate-owned Cuban gambling casinos which included the Hotel Habana Riviera, the Tropicana Club, the Sevilla-Biltmore, the Capri Hotel Casino, the Commodoro, the Deauville, and the Havana Hilton. Each night, Batista's bagman collected 10% of the profits at Trafficante's casinos.

Santo, Jr. spent time between Cuba and Florida during the late 1950's. In 1956 he was arrested and convicted for gambling offenses. In January 1957, he was released from prison after his conviction was overturned by Florida's Supreme Court. He was arrested in 1957, along with 57 other mobsters at an underworld convention, the Apalachin Meeting in New

York. The charges were later dropped. He returned to Cuba after he was released. His casinos had been shut down after Fidel Castro overthrew Batista in January 1959. He spent time in a Cuban prison before being deported to the United States.

Carlos Marcello was born in Tunis, Tunisia in 1910. He was brought to the United States with his family in 1911. His family settled in a decaying planation house near Metairie, Louisiana. He turned to petty crime in the French Quarters in New Orleans. He was later arrested for masterminding a crew of teenage gangsters who carried out armed robberies in the small towns surrounding New Orleans. The following year he was convicted of assault and robbery. He was sentenced to the Louisiana State Penitentiary for nine years. He was released after serving five years. In 1939 became associated with Frank Costello, the leader of the Genovese crime family in New York. Frank was involved in transporting illegal slot machines from New York to New Orleans. Carlos provided the muscle and arranged for the machines to be placed in local businesses.

By the end of 1947, Carlos had taken control of Louisiana's illegal gambling network. He had joined forces with New York mob associate Meyer Lansky in order to skim money from some of the most important casinos in the New Orleans area. He was also assigned a cut of the money skimmed from Las Vegas casinos, in exchange for providing muscle in Florida real estate deals. By this time, he had been selected as the "Godfather" of the New Orleans Mafia. He continued the family's long-standing tradition of fierce independence from interference by Mafiosi in other areas. He enacted a policy which forbade Mafiosi from other families from visiting Louisiana without his permission.

On March 24, 1959, he appeared before a United States Senate committee investigating organized crime. Serving as Chief Counsel to the committee was Robert Kennedy; his brother Senator John F. Kennedy, was a member of the committee. In response to committee questioning, Carlos invoked the 5th Amendment to the Constitution.

In 1960, he donated $500,000 through Teamsters Union president Jimmy Hoffa, to the Republican campaign of Richard Nixon, challenging the Democrat John F. Kennedy. Before he donated the money, Carlos was visited by Robert Kennedy. He asked for the New Orleans' boss' support in favor of his brother over Lyndon B. Johnson. The New Orleans Mafia boss refused. Robert was angry and swore he would get even with Carlos Marcello.

Sam Giancana was born in Little Italy, Chicago on June 15, 1908. After joining the Forty-Two Gang, Sam developed the reputation for being an excellent getaway driver, a high earner and a vicious killer. In 1926 he was arrested for murder. The charges were dropped when a witness was murdered. In the late 1930's he became a member of the Chicago Outfit. In 1957 he appointed the new boss of the Chicago Outfit. He was arrested along with Santo Trafficante, Jr. and 56 other mobsters in 1957 at the Apalachin Meeting in New York.

In spring of 1954, Mass at a Catholic Church, in Tucson, Arizona, came to an end. A small group of people moved slowly out of the small adobe styled church. Two men from different ends of the law walked in the middle of the crowd. The two men were Joe Kennedy, Sr. and Joe Bonanno. The two men had known each other for almost thirty years. They were different as night and day. One was Irish and privileged and the other was Sicilian and underworld. As different as they were, they knew and understood each other well. Their lives were deeply rooted in the neighborhoods of the American immigrant communities, in which they grew up, among people new to this country, struggling to survive poverty, prejudice, and political powerlessness.

Joe, Sr. was there to see Bonanno because he was looking for money and support for his son, Senator John F. Kennedy. Senator Kennedy had been recently elected to the Senate. The election year, 1956, was coming and Joe, Sr. was hoping for a chance for his son to grab a vice president spot on the ticket. He came to talk to Joe Bonanno because he knew no Democrat got elected without the backing of the Five Families. Bonanno was the Father of one of those Families. Bonanno promised on that day he would do what he could to help him when and if the time came. Bonanno also knew Joe, Sr. well enough to know that if he helped him, then Joe, Sr. would return the favor.

CHAPTER 12

◻

"I look forward to a great future for America—
a future in which our country will match its military strength
with our moral restraint, its wealth with our wisdom,
its power with our purpose."

John F. Kennedy

In 1955, Joe Kennedy, Sr. made a stop in Arizona once again to speak to Joe Bonanno. Once more he was drumming up support for Senator John F. Kennedy. Joe, Sr. and Bonanno spent a couple days together talking about the possibility of fund-raising and political backing. They stayed at the ranch of Gus Battaglia, the Arizona state Democratic Party vice-chairman. Joe, Sr. told him he wanted to get his son, John, on the national ticket; even if it was only to get him prepared for the presidency in 1960. He figured President Eisenhower was unbeatable in 1956. But he figured if his son was positioned correctly, a losing vice-presidential candidate would go to the head of the party in consideration for the presidential nomination in 1960. Bonanno didn't come to aid of Senator Kennedy in 1956, but this would change in the next election year.

In 1959, Joe Kennedy, Sr. sent a Kennedy gofer to contact an intermediary of Joe Bonanno. Senator John F. Kennedy would be on a fund-raising tour through the West, looking to help his upcoming campaign for the Democratic nomination for President. Joe, Sr. wanted the help of the Five Families. Bonanno agreed he would see what he could do to help. He arranged numerous fund-raisers for Senator Kennedy with all the state's top Democrats and leading businessmen attending. Joe Bonanno instructed his son, Bill, to go to New York to see what the other leaders thought about backing Senator Kennedy. He informed Bill it would be a hard sell because the elder Kennedy had enemies. And "Little Bobby" was a bone in the throat, hard to swallow.

Bill Bonanno went to New York and spoke with Joe Profaci, Tommy Lucchese and Carlo Gambino. The support for Senator Kennedy was deeply divided. Profaci didn't trust the Massachusetts Senator. The Mafia leaders in Cleveland and Michigan felt the Families should get behind someone who was more rooted in the unions. Profaci stated Santo Trafficante, Jr. favored Senator Lyndon Johnson because he was known and he was dependable. But at the same time Santo wouldn't really oppose Senator Kennedy because he had taken a strong stand against Fidel Castro. Other leaders, such as Carlos Marcello, strongly opposed him because of Robert Kennedy. Sam Giancana favored Senator Kennedy because he was a playboy like himself. He jokingly told Bill, "Throw him a broad and he'll do whatever you want."

Bill Bonanno reported to his father what the other Mafia leaders' opinion of Senator Kennedy was. There was nothing they could do; they couldn't force the other leaders to support Kennedy. His father decided to just wait to see how the Kennedy campaign was going before pushing for commitments. In early spring, Tommy suggested to the other leaders they should have a special meeting to be held at the site of the Democratic National Convention. He suggested the leaders needed to take a unified political stand behind a candidate who favored them. The other leaders agreed with him.

The majority of the leaders were more behind Lyndon Johnson than John Kennedy. The reason was plain to see. Senator Johnson was considered a street guy even though he had spent a lifetime in government. He was a guy who knew how to conduct business. He was in tight with the oil companies. And the big oil companies were friends to the Mafia. Oilmen like Clint Murchinson and H. L. Hunt had worked with Carlos Marcello for years. But Senator Kennedy had some supporters from the heads of the Families, also. At one meeting Carlos, Santo, and Sam Giancana got into a shouting match over the role Robert Kennedy would play in John F. Kennedy's administration. Bill Bonanno remembered a comment Joe, Sr. made on a trip to Arizona to speak to his father. Joe, Sr. claimed when John Kennedy was elected, he was going to make Robert an ambassador to Ireland. The Kennedy dissenters weren't convinced.

After another meeting in the Hilton Hotel, Joe, Sr. placed a call to the Mafia leaders who were at the meeting. Tommy Lucchese talked personally to the elder Kennedy. Tommy informed him no decision had been reached. When he hung up the phone, he told the leaders that Joe, Sr. suggested he would make any agreement if it would put his son over the top. Tommy suggested Senator Kennedy should name Senator Johnson as his vice-president. Everyone agreed if he made Senator Johnson his vice-president, they would support him.

After a March 1960 meeting of President Eisenhower's Nation Security Council, the Central Intelligence Agency began preparing for what would become the disastrous Bay of Pigs Invasion. Also during this meeting Vice-President Richard Nixon pressed for more action on the CIA-Mafia plots to overthrow Cuban Premier Fidel Castro. Later in the summer of 1960 some top CIA officials began meeting with Mafia bosses Johnny Roselli and Santo Trafficante, Jr. about assassinating Fidel Castro. In the past the CIA dealt indirectly with a half dozen mobsters through Jimmy Hoffa. The CIA was now dealing directly with Johnny Roselli, Santo Trafficante, Jr., and Sam Giancana.

The November 1960 election was quickly approaching and Vice-President Nixon needed the boost from which overthrowing Fidel Castro would provide. While the CIA plotted removing Castro, Carlos Marcello and Jimmy Hoffa were assisting in Vice-President Nixon's campaign for president. About the time of the first Senator Kennedy and Vice-President Nixon's debate, Robert Kennedy had an informant who witnessed a meeting in New Orleans between Carlos and Jimmy. He gave Jimmy a suitcase filled with $500,000 in cash destined for Vice-President Nixon. This was half of the promised $1,000,000 contribution to the Nixon campaign.

Before the 1960 presidential election, only a few Cuban exiles were being trained by the Central Intelligence Agency. That wasn't nearly enough for even a small invasion. But it was enough to go into Cuba after Fidel was assassinated to help install a new leader. The CIA/Mafia plot failed to assassinate Castro before the 1960 election. After the election, the CIA extended the exile operation which President Eisenhower had authorized in March 1960.

CHAPTER 13

———————————◻———————————

"I'm an idealist without illusions."

John F. Kennedy

By 1960 Francis Gary Powers was already a veteran of many covert aerial operations reconnaissance missions. The U-2 spy plane was able to reach altitude above 70,000 feet. This made it invulnerable to Soviet anti-aircraft weapons at that time. The plane was equipped with a state-of-the-art camera designed to take high resolution photos from the edge of the stratosphere over hostile countries. The Soviet intelligence, especially the KGB had been aware of the U-2 spy plane since 1956, but lacked the ability to launch counter-measures until 1960.

Francis' U-2 plane, which departed from a military airbase in Peshawar, Pakistan and may have received support from the U.S. Air Station at Badaber, was shot down by an S-75 Divina (SA-2 Surface to Air) missile on May 1, 1960, over Sverdlovsk, Mayak, the site of the 1957 Kyshtyrn disaster, was a goal of this mission. He was unable to activate the plane's self-destruct mechanism before he parachuted to the ground and was captured. His U-2 plane had been hit by the first S-75 missile fired. A total of 3 had been launched; one missile hit a MIG-19 jet fighter sent to intercept the U-2, which was unable to reach a high enough altitude. The Soviet pilot, Sergey Safronov, crashed his plane in an unpopulated forest area rather than bailing out and risking his plane crashing into nearby Degtyarsk. Another Soviet aircraft, a newly manufactured Su-9 in transit flight, also attempted to intercept Power's plane. The unarmed Su-9 was directed to ram the U-2. The pilot attempted but missed because of the large differences in speed. When United States Government learned of Francis Gary Powers' disappearance over the Soviet Union, it issued a cover statement claiming a "weather plane" had crashed after its pilot had "difficulties with his oxygen equipment." What CIA officials did not realize was the plane crashed almost fully intact, and the Soviets recovered its equipment.

President Dwight Eisenhower had high hopes for his Crusade of Peace, based upon a successful summit conference in Paris during May 1960, and for a post-summit invitation to Moscow for a grand visit with Soviet Premier Khrushchev. The visit to the Soviet Union was to cap his many triumphant tours of other countries. In preparation for the summit and its theme of worldwide peace and harmony, the White House had directed all aerial surveillance activity (over flights) of Communist territory to cease until further notice and ordered no US military personnel were to become involved in any combat activities, cover or otherwise, during that period. The CIA ignored the orders from President Eisenhower.

The U-2 spy plane came down in Sverdlovsk, halfway to its goal. Francis Gary Powers, alive and well, was captured by the Soviets. This incident destroyed the effectiveness of the summit conference and brought about the cancellation of the invitation to President Eisenhower to visit Moscow. It also ended the President's dream of the Crusade of Peace. The same man who was in charge of the Cuban exile program and the vast over flight program which supported the Khambas. Richard Bissell, Deputy Director of Plans for the CIA, was the man who ran the U-2 program. He was also one of the key authors of the Bay of Pigs invasion operation plans.

CHAPTER 14

— ▢ —

"If art is to nourish the roots of our culture,
society must set the artist free to follow his vision
wherever it takes him."

John F. Kennedy

Lee Oswald originally wanted to stay in Moscow and attend Moscow University. But he was told by Soviet authorities he was being sent to Minsk. With the ordeal in Moscow over, he now had to concentrate on completing his first mission as a CIA agent. Thanks to the Top Secret information he provided the Soviet officials, they set him up in style. Despite a chronic housing shortage, he was given a choice apartment, a luxury unheard of for a young bachelor. Not to mention a foreign bachelor. In addition to his factory pay, he received monetary subsidies from the Red Cross (a Soviet organization entirely separate from the international medical aid organization).

At first he seemed to thrive in his new life. In Minsk, his job was to build prototypes of new models at a radio and television factory, Gorizont (Horizon) Electronics Factory. His job at the factory was thought to have the need for high security clearance. This is exactly what the CIA was hoping the Soviet authorities would do. This gave their agent the chance to gather sensitive information. James Smith, Lee's handler, was hoping the Soviets would try to turn him as a double agent. If they did, then he would have a better chance of gathering valuable information. There was no doubt Lee was set like he was in Russia because of the information he possessed as a radar operator in the United States Marine Corps.

This factory also made military and space electronic components. The KGB kept him under constant surveillance and co-opted most of the people he met. He gave them valuable information which helped them shoot down the U-2 spy plane, but they still didn't trust him. The local KGB office had never had its own American case and they threw themselves into the task, building the lengthy KGB file no. 31451. The file mainly consisted of the mundane account of his daily life.

Lee befriended some college students interested in learning English. As a member of the Gorizont hunting club, he was permitted to own a small .410 shotgun. He went bird hunting with fellow factory employees. His sold his shotgun to a Minsk pawnshop before his departure from the Soviet Union in 1962. He was a popular dinner guest in people's homes and a "man about town" frequently attending the opera, symphony concerts, and the cinema and dating women he met at work. A fellow worker, Pavel Golovachev, spied on him. Not only was he a close friend to Lee, his father was a Red Air Force General, a senior air defense district commander in Siberia. Pavel took many intimate pictures of him at home and at play in Minsk which no doubt were primarily intended for KGB consumption. At the beginning he agreed to spy on Lee because he thought Lee might be an American intelligence officer. Following the KGB instructions Pavel tempted him with information from his father's air defense command. He reported to his superior that Lee wasn't tempted by the information. But what he didn't know was Lee was retaining the information in his mind. When he arrived at his apartment he wrote the information in a secret notebook he kept hidden. When he returned to the United States he turned over several notebooks to his CIA handler. In the end Pavel was convinced he was just who he claimed he was, an American who wanted to experience life in the Soviet Union and write a book about it.

When Lee was with his friends he never talked about the dramatic circumstances of his arrival in Moscow. He never mentioned his suicide attempt or his desire to gain Soviet citizenship. Pavel got the impression his arrival in the Soviet Union hadn't been contentious. He never heard Lee speak badly of the United States; which was odd. Because he supposedly defected to the USSR because he had grown tired of living in the US. Lee refrained from talking about politics in general. If a normal Russian citizen would ask him if life was better in the USA or USSR, he would reply in his opinion there were pros and cons to both places.

CHAPTER 15

---□---

"If we cannot now end our differences at least we can help make the world safe for diversity."

John F. Kennedy

On the night of August 1-2, 1943 Lieutenant Junior Grade John F. Kennedy was at the wheel of his *PT 109* patrol boat. He was patrolling Blackett Strait in the Solomon Islands. Lieutenant Kennedy and his crew were searching for Japanese destroyers who were known to use this corridor of water for a passageway. Without a moon in the sky, the night was pitch black. Without warning a large Japanese destroyer broke through the blackness. It was headed straight for the *PT 109*.

"Watch out! A ship is coming at two o'clock!!" someone yelled at Lt. Kennedy.

Lt. Kennedy quickly spun the wheel to dodge the oncoming destroyer. He wasn't fast enough. The much bigger Japanese destroyer slammed into the *PT 109*. Men, equipment and pieces of the patrol boat flew in every direction. A large strip was torn off the starboard side as the destroyer sliced the smaller boat in half.

"So this is how it feels to be killed," the young lieutenant thought as he was thrown through the cockpit.

After landing hard on his back, Lt. Kennedy tried to shake the cobwebs from his head. He looked around for a moment. He saw pieces of the boat in the water. He tried to move but he felt a sharp pain in his lower back. He slowly stood to his feet. Suddenly the gasoline onboard exploded in the night. Lt. Kennedy found himself on his back once more. He was sprawled out on a section of the boat which was still floating on the water.

Once he could move again, Lt. Kennedy stood gingerly to his feet. He soon found four of his twelve crewmen were also on the floating piece of the boat with him. He looked around once more. He saw burning pieces of his boat scattered in the water. He could hear screaming in the night air. He looked for the source of the screams. It was too dark. He couldn't see who was screaming. Despite reinjuring his back the young lieutenant jumped into the water. If he could help it he would not let any of his men perish. He needed to find his crewmen and get them to safety. After a few minutes of searching, he was able to locate six more of his men. Two were still missing; sadly those two men was never found. In his search, Lt. Kennedy was able to find his badly burned engineer. He convinced his crewmen not to give up. He towed the injured engineer back to the section of the ship on which the other crewmen were standing. Lt. Kennedy and the other crewmen climbed up onto the floating section and collapsed. They waited to be rescued by the *PT*s from the base on Rendova Island which was forty miles away.

Daylight came and noon soon followed but they hadn't been rescued yet. The men abandoned the floating section and decided to take their fate in their own hands. They swam to a small, deserted island, in the midst of larger islands which was occupied with Japanese soldiers. Nine of the crewman held onto a two by six timber and swam to the island. Lt. Kennedy towed the injured engineer by holding a strap from the engineer's life preserver in his teeth. He led the way with his engineer in tow. It took the eleven men four hours to reach the island. Exhausted, the men stumbled onto the island. They managed to duck under some trees just as a Japanese barge floated by the island. They just missed getting spotted by the enemy barge. When early evening came with no rescue, Lt. Kennedy decided he needed to act.

"I don't think a rescue is coming. So I have to go find a way to get us off this island. We will not survive long here just on coconuts. I am going to swim out into the Ferguson Passage. It's about a mile and a half away from here. The *PT*s boats usually patrol in that passage. I'm going to take the lantern with me to help signal the boats. When they pick me up and I will bring them here," said the young lieutenant.

Lt. Kennedy wrapped the lantern in a life jacket. He swam for a half hour. He climbed onto a reef. He rested for a little while and then he swam for another hour. He reached his destination; where he was hoping to intercept one of the patrolling *PT* boats. He treaded water; waiting, hoping to see one of the *PT* boats. After waiting for what seemed like hours, Lt. Kennedy noticed something in the distance. He saw flares of action just pass the Gizo Island. The island was ten miles away from him. He realized the *PT*s had taken a different route that night.

Lt. Kennedy grew tired and he began to worry. He was on the verge of admitting defeat. He continued to tread the water. When he left the island, he had his shoes with him. He dropped his shoes but he continued to hold onto the much heavier lantern. He stopped swimming. It would appear he had ceased to care if he lived or died. His mind went blank but he continued to grip the lantern. As the early morning sky turned from black to gray so did his mind. At about six in the morning, sun broke through the clouds. He looked around and realized he was where he had been when he had noticed the flares beyond Gizo. Renewed strength hit him and he swam back to the island. He stumbled onto the island and collapsed into the arms of his crewman.

"What happened? Where's the rescue boats?" one of his crewmen asked him.

"They took a different route last night," Lt. Kennedy said breathlessly. "Last night I saw flares of action by Gizo."

"What are we going to do?"

"I don't know. We have to survive. Somehow we have to survive," Lt. Kennedy replied.

The explosion from the collision on August 2nd was spotted by an Australian coast watcher, Sub Lieutenant Arthur Reginald Evans. He manned a secret observation post at the top of the Mount Veve volcano on Kolombangara Island. More than 10,000 Japanese troops were stationed below him on the southeast portion. The Navy and its squadron of *PT* boats held a memorial service for the crew of *PT 109* after reports were made of the large explosion. Sub LT. Evans dispatched Solomon Islanders Biuku Gasa and Eroni Kumana in a dugout canoe to look for possible survivors after decoding news the explosion he had witnessed was probably from the lost *PT 109*. The canoes were similar to the ones used for thousands of years in the Pacific by local people from Polynesia and coastal North and South America. They could avoid detection by Japanese ships and aircraft. If, by chance, they were spotted they could claim to be native fishermen.

Lt. Kennedy and his remaining crewmen lived on coconuts while they hoped to be rescued. Gasa and Kumana disobeyed an order by stopping by Nauru to investigate a Japanese destroyer wreckage. They salvaged fuel and food from the wreck. Suddenly they heard someone shouting at them. They fled from the man in their canoe. They didn't know the shouting man was the lieutenant from the missing *PT 109* boat. They fled to the neighboring island where they came upon the rest of the *PT 109* crewmen. Gasa and Kumana turned their Tommy guns on the crewmen. They were scared because the only light skinned people they were expecting to find were Japanese people. The crewmen tried to convince them to lower their weapons. But Gasa and Kumana didn't understand the language the crewmen were speaking. Lt. Kennedy was able somehow to convince the two scared men they were on the same side. The surviving *PT 109* crewmen had been found, but there was a problem. The small canoe wasn't big enough for passengers. Lt. Kennedy decide to carve a message on a coconut for the natives to take back to Sub Lt. Evans. So, he climbed up a tree and pulled down a coconut. He carved this message on the coconut: "*NAURO ISL COMMANDER . . . NATIVE KNOWS POS'IT . . . HE CAN PILOT . . . 11 ALIVE NEED SMALL BOAT . . . KENNEDY*"

The message carved on the coconut was delivered through 65 km of hostile waters patrolled by the Japanese to the nearest Allied base at Rendova. A canoe returned for Lt. Kennedy and took him to the coast watcher to plan a rescue. The *PT 157* commander Lieutenant William Liebenow was able to pick up the survivors.

President-elect John F. Kennedy pulled on a white dress shirt. He turned and looked his wife, Jacqueline. As usual she looked great. She was truly the most beautiful woman he had ever seen. She reached for the strap of his back brace. He winced as she tightened it. She kissed him on the lips as he turned to look in the full length mirror on the wall. She watched him as he slowly buttoned up his shirt.

"How did you sleep last night?" Jacqueline asked.

"Amazingly, I slept good last night. I think that new cocktail of painkillers helped a lot last night."

"A new cocktail? Isn't that dangerous?" she asked.

"It will be fine. Doc knows what he's doing. If it was too harmful, he wouldn't give them to me."

"You looked as if you were in deep thought. What were you thinking about?" she asked him as she sat on the bed.

"I was thinking about August 1943."

"August 1943? You was thinking about the night that Japanese destroyer rammed into your patrol boat? Why?" she questioned him.

"That night has a lot to do with why I am here today."

"How is that?"

"That incident in the South Pacific changed my life in more ways than one. It mainly changed how I viewed war in general," he replied.

"What do you mean?"

"I saw firsthand how war could affect every day people. And when Joe, Jr. was killed during a bombing mission during the war, I witnessed the effect war had on the family of a soldier. I don't see how a war can bring anyone any good. America needs to avoid another world war no matter the cost," he replied as he tied his bowtie.

"So that's the reason you got into politics?"

"No, I got into politics because my father wanted me to get into politics," he said.

"Come on, be honest with me. You are here on your own accord," Jacqueline said as she stood to her feet.

"Ok, in the beginning, my father pushed me towards politics as a career. But I tried to resist him every step of the way. I just wanted to be a journalist or professor or something along that line. In April or May of 1945, I was working as a journalist for the Hearst Press. I attended a conference in San Francisco. It was this conference which founded the United Nations. It was my experience at that conference which made me realize the political arena, whether you really liked it or not, was the place where I personally could do the most to prevent another war. So I entered politics in 1946. In a way you could say I was destined to be here at this moment," he replied as someone knocked on the door.

"Mr. and Mrs. Kennedy, the limousine is ready for you," someone said from the other side of the door.

"Well, we are here now. Jack, let's go re-write the history books," she said as she took his hand.

President John F. Kennedy stepped up to the podium. The weather had cleared enough for the crowd to be fairly large. It had been snowing all night long. The city street crews worked effortlessly to clear the streets so the American people could come and see him deliver his inaugural address. He could feel the warmth of the fire from below the podium. He cleared his throat and began speaking. As the American people listened to him, three men across town also listened with great interest.

Federal Bureau of Investigation Director J. Edgar Hoover, Central Intelligence Agency Director Allen Dulles, and his Deputy Director of Plans Richard Bissell watched from the FBI director's office as the new president gave his Inaugural Address on the television.

"What do you have on this new president?" asked CIA Director Dulles.

"What do you mean?" asked FBI Director Hoover.

"Cut the crap. I know you have the habit of digging up dirt on the incoming president. So, I will ask once more . . ." said Allen.

"I'm not an imbecile. You do not need to repeat any questions asked of me. What I meant was; do you want to know the personal dirt or career?"

"I don't care to know about his personal life. That doesn't interest me. Where does he stand on the war against Communism?" asked the CIA director.

"Well, that's the easier of the two. I think you will have some problems with your little plan in Indochina," FBI Director Hoover commented as he walked to a filing cabinet. He thumbed through the files until he found the one he was looking for. He handed it to Allen. The CIA director opened the file and began to read the contents.

In 1946, United States Representative James Michael Curley decided to become the mayor of Boston. So he vacated his seat in the strong Democratic 10th Congressional district in Massachusetts. On April 22nd, John F. Kennedy announced his candidacy for Congress. Even though the young John Kennedy was seeking just his first term as a Democratic for Congress, his announcement sounded more like a presidential candidate running on a "peace" ticket. In his candidacy announcement he said:

> *"What we do now will shape the history of civilization for many years to come. We have a weary world trying to bind the wounds of a fierce struggle. That is dire enough. What is infinitely far worse is that we have a world which has unleashed the terrible powers of atomic energy. We have a world capable of destroying*

itself. The days which lie ahead are most difficult ones. Above all, day and night, with every ounce of ingenuity and industry we possess, we must work for peace. We must not have another war."

"That was in 1946. Maybe he's changed his mind on this whole world peace thing," suggested the CIA director.

"You could only hope so. He developed an early interest in foreign policy. As a Congressman he toured Europe. He visited Britain, France, Italy, Spain, Yugoslavia and West Germany. When he returned to the United States, he told the Senate Committee on Foreign Relations that the US should maintain its policy of helping to defend Western Europe. But he thought those countries should contribute more to costs of the operation," said J. Edgar.

"Well, at least he doesn't think the United States should foot the entire cost for these countries," said Allen.

"Well, he also argued for increased financial aid to underdeveloped countries," said the FBI director.

"He sounds like a bleeding heart to me," suggested Richard Bissell.

"Oh, it gets better than that. Read this," the FBI director took the file from Allen and he looked for a certain page. Once he found it, J. Edgar handed it to the CIA director.

"No amount of American military assistance in Indochina can conquer an enemy which is everywhere and at the same time nowhere, an enemy of the people, which has the sympathy and covert support of the people," Allen read aloud. "He stated he saw only two peace treaties for Vietnam, 'one granting the Vietnamese people complete independence,' the other 'a tie binding them to the French Union on the basis of full equality'."

"That doesn't sound good," said Richard.

"To those new states whom we welcome to the ranks of the free, we pledge our word that one form of colonial control shall not have passed away merely to be replaced by a far more iron tyranny. We shall not always expect to find them supporting our view. But we shall always hope to find them strongly supporting their own freedom—and to remember that, in the past, those who foolishly sought power by riding the back of the tiger ended up inside," President Kennedy said on the TV.

"No, it doesn't. As a senator he was criticizing the prediction of a United States sponsored French victory over Ho Chi Minh's revolutionary forces in Vietnam. I would say he's threat for your little party in Indochina," said J. Edgar Hoover.

"But the psychological profile we did on him revealed to the analysts that he would be in support of any war efforts we put before him. He's a Cold War warrior, for God's sake," said Allen.

"Well, he did give the go ahead for an invasion of Cuba. That sounds like a change of heart to me," suggested Richard.

> *"Finally, to those nations who would make themselves our adversary, we offer not a pledge but a request: that both sides begin anew the quest for peace, before the dark powers of destruction unleashed by science engulf of humanity in planned or accidental self-destruction,"* the young president pledged before the American people.

"We shall see," commented the FBI director.

"I had him deported," Robert Kennedy said as he walked into the Oval Office.

"I will have to call you back," President Kennedy hung up the phone. He looked at his younger brother, the United States Attorney General. "Bobby, you can't just barge in here. You never know who I am talking to in here."

"Was you talking to one of your many mistresses?"

"No," replied the young president.

"Ok, were you talking to some foreign leader? Or was you talking to one of your military advisers? Or better yet were you talking to our father?"

"No to all those questions, Bobby."

"Then it doesn't matter who you were talking to, because it wasn't important."

"Bobby, just because you're the United States Attorney General and my brother doesn't mean you can barge in here any time you feel the need," said President Kennedy.

"Whatever. Did you hear what I said?"

"Yes, I did hear you. Who are you talking about?"

"Carlos Marcello. I had him deported to Guatemala."

"How the hell did you do that?" asked President Kennedy.

In early 1961, Attorney General Robert Kennedy concentrated on his battles with the Mafia and Jimmy Hoffa. It would become the biggest war on organized crime in the US history. Even though Santo Trafficante, Jr. and Sam Giancana were in his sights, the attorney general had special intentions for New Orleans Mafia boss, Carlos Marcello. He had defied US Immigration authorities for years even though there had been a deportation order. Robert strengthened up the Justice Department's special prosecutors and organized them into Organized Crime and "Get Jimmy" sections. He sent his men to Central America to investigate Carlos' fake Guatemalan birth certificate. The entire time Robert's men were being followed by his private pilot, David Ferrie.

On April 4, 1961, Carlos Marcello and his lawyer went to his required tri-monthly visit, as an alien, to the offices of the Immigration and Naturalization Service. While they were waiting in an office someone opened the door. Carlos and his attorney stood to their feet.

"Carlos Marcello?" asked the young uniformed man at the door.

"Yes."

"You are being deported out of the country."

"What are you talking about? I have been coming to these meetings like I was ordered to do so," said the Mafia boss.

"It's doesn't matter. You are an illegal alien in this country," the Immigration official said as several police officers and FBI agents walked into the office.

One of the police officers pushed Carlos up against the wall and handcuffed him. Another officer did the same to his attorney. They half drug and half pushed Carlos and his lawyer out of the building. They guided Carlos to car waiting outside. His attorney was close behind. Two more cars were parked behind the one the officials pushed the Mafia boss into

"Where the hell are we going?" he asked the driver of the car.

"I believe it's already been explained to you, Mr. Marcello. You are being deported out of the country."

"You can't do this to me. Do you know who I am?" he said as the driver sped away and the other two cars followed closely behind them.

"Yeah, you're an illegal alien."

"I need to make a phone call to my family and my deportation attorney in Washington. What you are doing is illegal," demanded Carlos.

"No, sir. I was told to take you and your attorney there straight to the airport."

"Well, can you at least take me by my house to get some clothes and money for this little vacation the United States Government is sending me on?" asked Carlos.

"No, sir. Once again I was instructed to take you and your lawyer straight to the airport. I am not authorized to make any stops along the way."

When the convoy arrived at the airport it was immediately surrounded by police and Carlos was escorted by a small army of police and immigration officials to an airplane. It took off as soon as he was on board.

Attorney General Robert Kennedy announced publicly that Carlos Marcello had been deported to Guatemala and he was taking full responsibility for the expulsion of the New Orleans Mafia boss. Robert stated he was very happy the Mafia was no longer in the United States. On April 10th, the Internal Revenue Service filed tax liens in excess of $835,000 against Carlos and his wife, which was instigated by Robert.

Carlos Marcello's exile in Central America started off well, but it soon changed for the worse. He was tossed out of Guatemala and was forced to trek through the jungle. During the whole trek he cursed and swore vengeance against Robert F. Kennedy. He was forced to leave Guatemala when the country's president responded to pressure from a major local newspaper. Carlos and his attorney were left at an army camp in the Salvadorian jungle near the Guatemala-Salvador border. They were left at the mercy of the Salvadorian soldiers. Then he and his lawyer were taken by a bus twenty miles into Honduras and thrown from the bus like discarded luggage. They were left to fend for themselves on a hilltop with no signs of civilization. He managed to walk the 17 mile trek to a tiny village, and then another trek through the jungle before they finally reached a small airport. They were still wearing their city clothes. They had little to drink or eat. He found breathing difficult along the mountain top road. He fell down three times, complaining he could go no farther, and he was finished. Once they reached the airport, Carlos fell down a pathless slope. He ended in a burrow, bleeding from thorns, bruised by rocks. He was suffering from severe pain in his side from three broken ribs. He swore revenge on the man he blamed; Attorney General Kennedy. Once at the airport, he was able to secretly reenter the United States with the help of his private pilot, David Ferrie.

CHAPTER 16

"In the long history of the world,
only a few generations have been granted the role
of defending the freedom in its hour of maximum danger.
I do not shrink from this responsibility—I welcome it."

John F. Kennedy

Lee Harvey Oswald soon grew tired of a relatively monotonous Soviet life. The Soviet Union's oppressive bureaucracy made him realize the country was a poorly implemented perversion of Marxist goals. He believed himself to be a pure Marxist. He was ready for his mission to be over and looking for the time he went back to United States. Moreover he had felt unappreciated when he was assigned factory work in Minsk instead of being permitted to study at the University of Moscow as he had requested. He thought the information he provided the KGB would afford him the life of ease in Moscow. He was wrong.

He gradually grew bored with the limited recreation available in Minsk and was stunned when co-worker Ella Germann refused his marriage proposal and then rejected him. He had talked about the two of them going to live in Czechoslovakia or even Yugoslavia, where he thought Communism was more liberal. He also told her he was hiding in Minsk because the US had "hunted" him in Moscow and if he returned to the United States he would be "shot".

It's not clear why Lee told this lie to her. It wasn't in his instructions from his CIA handler. In fact, James Smith had advised him not to get romantically involved with any of the Russian women. It was a known intelligence fact the KGB used women as agents also. Lee knew he was there working as a CIA agent and returning to the US would be no problem. Maybe he was trying to impress her. In fact, while he was saying these things to her he had made his first attempt to write the United States embassy in Moscow about returning to the US. The KGB intercepted the letter and never forwarded it to the embassy.

At a dance in March 1961 Lee met Marina Nikolayevna Prusakova, a troubled 19-year-old pharmacology student from a broken family in Leningrad. She was now living with her aunt and uncle in Minsk. Her uncle was a lumber industry expert in the MVD (Ministry of Interior) with a bureaucratic rank equivalent to colonel. The MVD at the time was analogous with the US departments of Justice and Interior combined. Marina's uncle administered lumbering projects using inmate labor, which by the time of Nikita Khruschev consisted of mostly non-political criminal prisoners.

It was highly suspected by James Smith she was a plant by the KGB. He advised Lee on numerous occasions he was playing with fire by getting involved with her. But he wouldn't listen. Whether or not they were truly in love was unknown. Either way, Lee and Marina married less than a month and a half after they met. Even though he didn't admit it to her, he was on the rebound from his failed relationship with Emma. Marina had a secret of her own, also. She only married him because of his high standard of living and the possibility of immigrating to the United States. She soon became pregnant and gave birth to their daughter June.

According to the CIA plan, Lee never formally renounced his US citizenship and began seeking permission for the three of them to go to the United States. Most of the Russians who knew him during his stay in the Soviet Union recalled him as a boyish, silly and immature youth. He was described by some as shallow, with limited intelligence, a poor and lazy worker but almost all remembered him as sympathetic. He did not drink or smoke, which the Russians found strange. His only vice seemed to be sweets and pastries.

Most Russians who knew him recall once the thrill of meeting an American wore off, Lee was rather dull company with little of interest to say. A shelf in his apartment was filled with books on Marxism but his understanding of it seemed rudimentary. Neighbors who lived directly above him, with windows looking onto his balcony below described him as a rude lout who was frequently heard berating Marina for her apparent lack of cooking and cleaning skills. They claimed she told them he had struck her on occasions.

CHAPTER 17

---□---

"We have the power to make this the best generation of
mankind in the history of the world or make it the last."

John F. Kennedy

The Bay of Pigs Invasion was the first test for the new, young President
John Kennedy. It was a covert operation he had inherited from the prior
administration; the Eisenhower Administration. On March 17, 1960,
President Dwight Eisenhower approved a document prepared by the
5412 Committee at a meeting of the United States National Security
Council (NSC). This committee, which was empowered to direct covert
operations, had approved the limited use of military personnel for Cuban
training.

On August 18, 1960, President Eisenhower approved a budget of $13
million for the operation. By October 31st, most guerilla infiltrations and
supply drops directed by the Central Intelligence Agency into Cuba had
failed. Developments of further guerilla strategies were replaced by plans to
mount an initial amphibious assault, with a minimum of 1,500 men. On
November 18th CIA Director Allen Dulles and Deputy Director of Plans
Richard Bissell first briefed the President-elect John F. Kennedy on the
outline plans. Having experiences in actions such as the 1954 Guatemalan
coup d'état, CIA Director Dulles was confident the CIA was capable of
overthrowing the Cuban government which was led by Prime Minister
Fidel Castro since February 16, 1959.

On November 29, 1960, President Eisenhower met with the heads
of the CIA, Defense, State and Treasury departments to discuss the
new concept. No objections were expressed, and President Eisenhower
approved the plans, with the intentions of persuading President-elect

Kennedy of their merit. On December 8, 1960, Richard Bissell presented outline plans to the Special Group while declining to commit details to written records. Following formal authorization from the White House Special Group, the CIA set out to recruit 300 Cuban exiles for covert training outside the United States. The CIA began in accordance with NSC directives to go to the military for support. An inactive military base in Panama, Fort Gulick, was selected as the initial training site. The CIA put together a small unit to reactivate the base and to provide the highly specialized paramilitary training which the Agency employs for similar units at certain military-covered facilities in the United States. Further development of the plans continued, and on January 4, 1961 they consisted of an intention to carry out a lodgement by 750 men at an undisclosed site in Cuba, supported by considerable air power.

On January 28, 1961, President John F. Kennedy was briefed, together with all the major departments, on the latest Cuban covert plan, code-named *Operation Pluto*. This plan involved 1,500 men to be landed in a ship-borne invasion at Trinidad, Cuba, southeast of Havana, at the foothills of the Escambray Mountains in Sancti Spiritus province. President Kennedy approved the active departments to continue and to report to him their progress. Trinidad had good port facilities; it was closer to many existing counter-revolutionary activities. It had an easily defensible beachhead, and it offered an escape route into the Escambray Mountains.

This covert operation was eventually rejected by the State Department. The CIA went on to propose an alternative plan. On April 4, 1961, President Kennedy approved the Bay of Pigs plan, code named *Operation Zapata*. He approved the plan because it had an airfield which would not need to be extended to handle bomber operations. It was farther away from large groups of civilians than the Trinidad plan. It was also less "noisy" militarily, which would make any future denial of direct United States involvement more plausible. The invasion landing area was changed to beaches bordering the Bahia de Cochinos (Bay of Pigs) in Las Villas Province. The landings were to take place at Playa Giron (code-named Blue Beach), Playa Larga (code-named Red Beach), and Caleta Buena Inlet (code-named Green Beach).

In March1961, the CIA helped Cuban exiles in Miami to create the Cuban Revolutionary Council (CRC). The CRC was chaired by Jose Miro

Cardona, who was the former Prime Minister of Cuba in January 1959. Jose became the de facto leader-in-waiting of the intended post-invasion Cuban government. Prior to the invasion, the CIA supported and supplied various groups with arms and other resources, but they were not included in the invasion plans due to concerns about information security. The concept behind the Bay of Pigs tactical plan was similar to that of the 1956 British-French clandestine attack on Nasser's air force on Egypt, which destroyed his entire combat air force first, making it possible for General Moshe Dayan's Israeli army to dash across the Sinai to the Suez Canal without attacks from the air.

Zapata, the beach on the Bay of Pigs, had been selected on purpose because there was an airstrip there suitable for B-26 operations against Castro's ground forces. It was isolated and could be reached only via causeways or the narrow beach itself. The brigade could take over the airstrip after securing the beachhead, and B-26s flown by Cuban pilots operating from that strip could have overwhelmed any Castro force approaching via the causeways. This tactical plan was predicted upon the total destruction of Castro's entire force of combat-capable aircraft. A second attack was scheduled to knock out Castro's three remaining aircraft at dawn before the brigade hit the beach and alerted Castro's air defense. It was essential those three aircrafts be taken out first.

On April 3, 1961, a bomb attack on militia barracks in Bayamo killed four militia, and wounded eight more. On April 6th, the Hershey Sugar factory in Matanzas was destroyed by sabotage. On April 14, 1961, guerillas fought Cuban government forces near Las Cruces, Montembo, Las Villas, where several government troops were killed and others wounded. Also on April 14th, a Cuban airliner was hijacked and flown to Jacksonville, Florida; resultant confusion then helped discovery of the stage "defection" of a B-26 and pilot at Miami on April 15th.

In April 1960, the CIA began to recruit anti-Castro Cuban exiles in the Miami area. Until July 1960, assessment and training was carried out on Useppa Island and at various other facilities in South Florida. Specialist guerilla training took place at Fort Gulick, Panama and Fort Clayton, Panama. For the increasing ranks of recruits, infantry training was carried out a CIA-run base code-named JMTrax near Retalhuleu in the Sierra Madre on the Pacific coast of Guatemala. The exiles group named themselves Brigade 2506.

In summer 1960, an airfield, (code-named JMMadd) was constructed near Retalhuleu, Guatemala. Gunnery and flight training of Brigade 2506 aircrews were carried out by personnel from Alabama Air National Guard using at least six Douglas B-26 Invaders in the markings of FAG (Fuerza Aerea Guatemalteca), legitimate delivery of those to the FAG being delayed by about six months.

An additional 26 B-26s were obtained from US military stocks, "sanitized" at "Field Three" to obscure their origins, and about 20 of them were converted for offensive operations by removal of defensive armament, standardization of the "eight-gun nose", addition of under wing drop tanks and rocket racks. Paratroop training was at a base nicknamed *Garrapatenango*, near Quetzaltenango, Guatemala. Training for boat handling and amphibious landings took place at Vieques Island, Puerto Rico. Tank training took place at Fort Knox, Kentucky and Fort Benning, Georgia. Underwater demolition and infiltration training took place at Belle Chase near New Orleans. The CIA used Douglas C-54 transports to deliver people, supplies, and arms from Florida at night. Curtiss C-46s were also used for transport between Retalhuleu and the CIA base code named *JMTide*, at Puerto Cabezas, Nicaragua. On April 9th, Brigade 2506 personnel, ships, and aircraft started transferring from Guatemala to Puerto Cabezas, Nicaragua.

In early 1961, Cuba's army possessed Soviet-designed T-34 and IS-2 *Stalin* tanks, SU-100 self-propelled "tank destroyers", 122 mm howitzers, other artillery and small arms, plus Italian 105 mm howitzers. The Cuban air force armed inventory included Douglas B-26 Invader light bombers, Hawkeye Sea Fury fighters and Lockheed T-33 jets, all remaining from the *Fuerza Aerea del Ejercito de Cuba* (FAEC), the Cuban air force of the Batista government.

Anticipating an invasion, Che Guevara stressed the importance of an armed civilian populace, stating "all the Cuban people must become a guerilla army, each and every Cuban must learn to handle and if necessary use firearms in defense of the nation." The Cuban security apparatus knew the invasion was coming, via their secret intelligence network, as well as loose talk by members of the brigade, some of which was heard in Miami, and was repeated in US and foreign newspaper reports.

Nevertheless, days before the invasion, multiple acts of sabotage were carried out, such as the EL Encanto fire, an arson attack in a department store in Havana on April 13th, which killed one shop worker. The Cuban government also had been warned by senior KGB agents Osvaldo Sanchez Cabrera and "Aragon", who died violently before and after the invasion, respectively. The general Cuban population was not well informed, except for CIA-funded Radio Swan. As of May 1960, almost all means of public communication were in the government's hands.

At about 6:00 on April 15, 1961, eight Douglas B-26B Invader bombers in three groups attacked three Cuban airfields at San Antonio de Los Banos and at Ciudad Libertad, both near Havana. The bombers also attacked Antonio Maceo International Airport at Santiago de Cuba. The B-26s had been prepared by the CIA for the Brigade 2506. The bombers had been painted with the markings of the Fuerza Aerea Revolucionaria (FAR), the air force for the Cuban government. They had flown from Puerto Cabezas in Nicaragua. The bombers were flown by Cuban exiles pilots. The purpose of this operation (code named *Operation Puma*) was to destroy most or all of the armed aircraft of the FAR in preparation for the main invasion. At Santiago, the two bombers destroyed a C-47 transport, a PBY Catalina flying boat, two B-26s and a civilian DC-3 plus various other civilian aircraft. At San Antonio, the three bombers destroyed three FAR B-26s, one Sea Fury and one T-33, and one bomber diverted to Grand Cayman due to low usable fuel. At Ciudad Libertad, the three bombers destroyed only non-operational aircraft such as two P-47 Thunderbolts. One of the bombers was damaged by anti-aircraft fire, and ditched north of Cuba. Its companion B-26, also damaged, continued north and landed at Boca Chica field (Naval Air Station Key West) Florida.

About 90 minutes after the eight B-26s had taken off from Puerto Cabezas, another B-26 departed on a deception flight which took it close to Cuba but headed north towards Florida. Like the bomber groups it carried false FAR markings and the same number 933 was painted on at least two of the others. Before the bomber's departure, the cowling from one of the aircraft's two engines was removed the CIA personnel, fired upon, then re-installed to give the false appearance the aircraft had taken ground fire at some point during its flight. At a safe distance north of Cuba, the pilot feathered the engine with the pre-installed bullet holes in the cowling, radioed a mayday and requested immediate permission to land at Miami International airport.

On April 15th at 10:30 AM at the United Nations, the Cuban Foreign Minister Raul Roa tried to accuse the United States of aggressive air attacks against Cuba.

"I assure you that the United States armed forces will not under any conditions intervene in whatever is going on in Cuba. And the United States would do everything in its power to ensure no US citizens would participate in actions against Cuba," said United Nations Ambassador Adlai Stevenson.

"Not intervene in Cuba? What do you call these attacks on Cuba? It was aggressive air attacks by the United States," claimed Raul.

"The attacks were not from the United States armed forces. The attacks were carried out by Cuban defectors. And here is proof," Adlai displayed a UPI wire photo of a B-26 with Cuban markings at Miami airport.

When UN Ambassador Stevenson made his announcement of Cuban defectors being responsible, he was speaking of what he thought was true. He would later learn he had been lied to by the CIA and Secretary of State Dean Rusk. He was embarrassed he had announced a false statement at the United Nations. President Kennedy supported the statement made by Ambassador Stevenson.

"I have emphasized before that this was a struggle of Cuban patriots against a Cuban dictator. While we could not be expected to hide our sympathies, we made it repeatedly clear that the armed forces of this country would not intervene in any way," President Kennedy said when he was asked about the attacks on Cuba.

That night, April 15th, the Nino Diaz group attempted a diversionary landing at a location near Baracoa. Following the air strikes on the morning of April 15th, the FAR managed to prepare for armed action for at least four T-33s, four Sea Furies and five or six B-26s. All three aircrafts were armed with machine guns for air-to air combat and for strafing of ships and ground targets. CIA planners of the invasion didn't know the US-supplied T-33s had been equipped with M-3 machine guns. The three aircrafts also had the ability to carry bombs for attacks against ships and tanks. It was an oversight by the Central Intelligence Agency. The CIA had predicted tens of thousands of Cubans would rise to join the brigade and revolt against Castro. They felt if this happened, then he would either be killed, flee, or surrender. This was the plan. But between the time of President Kennedy's approval at 1:45 pm on Sunday, and the time for the release of the B-26s, the vital airstrike to destroy Castro's three remaining T-33 jets was called off by National Security Adviser McGeorge Bundy.

Late on April 16th, Brigade 2506 invasion fleet converged on "Rendezvous Point Zulu," which was south of Cuba. The fleet, which was labeled "Cuban Expeditionary Force" (CEF), included five 2,400 ton freighter ships chartered by the CIA from the Garcia Line, and subsequently outfitted with anti-aircraft guns. Four of the freighters, *Houston* (code named *Aguja*), *Rio Escondido* (code named *Ballena*), *Caribe*, and *Atlantico* (code named *Tiburon*) were planned to transport 1,400 troops in seven battalions of troops and armaments near the invasion beaches. The fifth freighter, *Lake Charles*, was loaded with follow-up supplies and some *Operation 40* personnel. The freighters sailed under Liberian ensigns. Accompanying them were two LCIs (Landing Craft Infantry) purchased from Zapata Corporation. They were outfitted with heavy armament at Key West. The LCIs were *Blagar* (code named *Marsopa*) and *Barbara J* (code named *Barracuda*) and they were sailing under Nicaraguan ensigns.

The CEF ships were individually escorted (outside visual range) to *Point Zulu* by United States Navy destroyers USS *Bache*, USS *Beale*, USS *Conway*, USS *Convoy*, USS *Eaton*, USS *Murray*, and USS *Waller*. A task force had already assembled off the Cayman Islands, including aircraft carrier USS *Essex* with task force commander Admiral John A. Clark onboard. Helicopter assault carrier USS *Boxer*, destroyers USS *Hank*, USS *John W. Weeks*, USS *Purdy*, USS *Wren*, and submarines USS *Cobbler* and USS *Threadfin* was included in the assembled task force also. Command and control ship USS *Northampton* and carrier USS *Shangri-La* were also reportedly active the Caribbean at the time. USS *San Marcos* was a Landing Ship Dock which carried three LCUs (Landing Craft Utility) and four LCVPs (Landing Craft, Vehicles, Personnel). At *Point Zulu*, the seven CEF ships sailed north without the escorts, except for *San Marcos* which continued until the seven landing craft were unloaded when they reached just outside the 3 mile Cuban territorial limit.

During the night of April 16th, a mock diversionary landing was organized by CIA operatives near Bahia Honda, Pinar del Rio Province. A flotilla of small boats towed rafts containing equipment which broadcasted sounds and other effects of a ship borne invasion landing. This was the source of Cuban reports which briefly lured Fidel Castro away from the Bay of Pigs battlefront area.

On April 17ᵗʰ, at about midnight, the two CIA LCIs *Blagar* and *Barbara J*, each with a CIA "operating officer" and an Underwater Demolition Team (UDT) of five frogmen, entered the Bay of Pigs on the southern coast of Cuba. They headed a force of four transport ships (*Houston, Rio Escondido, Caribe,* and *Atlantico*) carrying about 1,400 Cuban exile ground troops of Brigade 2506, plus tanks and other vehicles in the landing craft. At about 1:00 AM, the *Blagar*, as the battlefield command ship, directed the principal landing at Playa Giron (code named *Blue Beach*), led by the frogmen in rubber boats followed by troops from *Caribe* in small aluminum boats, then LCVPs and LCUs. The *Barbara J*, leading *Houston*, similarly landed troops 35 km further northwest at Playa Larga (code named *Red Beach*), using small fiberglass boats. Unloading troops at night was delayed, due to engine failures and boats damaged by unseen coral reefs. The few militia in the area succeeded in warning Cuban armed forces via radio soon after the first landing, before the invaders overcame their token resistance.

At about 6:30 AM, three FAR Sea Furies, one B-26 and two T-33 jets started attacking those CEF ships still unloading troops. Twenty minutes later *Houston* was damaged by several rockets from a Sea Fury and a T-33. Two hours the captain of *Houston* intentionally beached it on the western side of the bay. About 270 troops had been unloaded, but about 180 survivors struggled onto the shore. These survivors were not able to take part in further action because of the loss of most of their weapons and equipment. At about 7:00, two invading FAL B-26s attacked and sank the Cuban Navy Patrol Escort ship *El Baire* at Nueva Gerona on the Isle of the Pines. They then proceeded to Giron to join two other B-26s to attack Cuban ground troops and provide distraction air cover for the paratroop C-46s and CEF ships under air attack. At about 7:30, five C-46s and one C-54 transport aircraft dropped 177 paratroops from the parachute battalion of Brigade 2506 in an action code named *Operation Falcon*. About 30 men, plus heavy equipment, were dropped south of Australia sugar mill on the road to Palpite and Playa Larga, but the equipment was lost in the swamps, and troops failed to block the road. Other troops were dropped at San Blas at Jocuma between Covadonga and San Blas, and at Horquitas between Yaguaramas and San Blas. Those positions to block the roads were maintained for two days, reinforced by ground troops from Playa Giron. By 9:00, Cuban troops and militia from outside the area had started arriving at Australia sugar mill, Covadonga and Yaguaramas.

Throughout the day they were reinforced with more troops, heavy armor and T-34 tanks carried on flatbed trucks. At about 9:30, FAR Sea Furies and T-33s fired rockets at the *Rio Escondido* and sank it south of Giron.

"The invaders, members of the exiled Cuban revolutionary front have come to destroy the revolution and take away the dignity and rights of men," Premier Fidel Castro announced at about 11:00 over Cuba's nationwide network.

At the same time, the two remaining freighters *Caribe* and *Atlantico*, and the CIA LCIs and LCUs, started retreating south to international waters, but still pursued by FAR aircraft. BY 12:00, hundreds of militia cadets had secured Palpite, and carefully advanced on foot south towards Playa Larga, suffering many casualties during attacks by FAL B-26s. By dusk, other Cuban ground forces were gradually advancing southward from Covadonga and southwest from Yaguaramas toward San Blas, and westward along coastal tracks from Cienfuegos towards Giron, all without heavy weapons or armor. By 4:00 PM, Fidel Castro had arrived had at the central Australia sugar mill, joining Jose Ramon Fernandez whom he had appointed as battlefield commander before dawn that day. At about 9:00 PM, a night strike by three FAL B-26s on San Antonio de Los Banos airfield failed, due to incompetence and bad weather. Two other B-26s had aborted the mission after take-off.

At about 10:30 on April 18th, Cuban troops and militia, supported by tanks, took Playa Larga after Brigade forces had fled towards Giron in the early hours. During the day, Brigade forces retreated to San Blas along the two roads from Covadonga and Yaguaramas. By then, both Fidel Castro and Jose Ramon Fernandez had re-located to that battlefield area. At about 5:00 PM, FAL B-26s attacked a Cuban column of 12 civilian buses leading trucks carrying tanks and other armor, moving southeast between Playa Larga and Punta Perdiz. The vehicles, loaded with civilians, militia, police and soldiers, were attacked with bombs, napalm and rockets, suffering heavy casualties. The six B-26s were piloted by two CIA contract pilots plus four pilots and six navigators from Brigade 2506 air force. The column later re-formed and advanced to Punta Perdiz.

During the night of April 18th, a FAL C-46 delivered arms and equipment to the Giron airstrip occupied by Brigade 2506 ground forces, and took off before daybreak on April 19th. The C-46 also evacuated Matias Farias, the pilot of B-25 serial 935 (code named *Chico Two*) which had been shot down and crash landed at Giron on April 17th. The final air attack mission (code named *Mad Dog Flight*) comprised five B-26s, four of which were manned by American CIA contract air crews and pilots from the Alabama Air National Guard. One FAR Sea Fury and two FAR T-33s shot down two shot down two of these B-26s, killing four American airmen. Sorties were flown to reassure Brigade soldiers and pilots, and to intimidate Cuban government forces without directly engaging in acts of war. Without direct air support, and short of ammunition, Brigade 2506 ground forces retreated to the beaches in the face of considerable onslaught from Cuban government artillery, tanks and infantry. Late on April 19th, destroyers USS *Eaton* and USS *Murray* moved into Cochinos Bay to evacuate retreating Brigade soldiers from beaches, before firing from Cuban army tanks caused Commodore Crutchfield to order a withdrawal.

On April 19, 1961, at least seven Cubans plus two CIA hired US citizens were executed in Pinar del Rio province after a two day trial. Between April and October 1961, hundreds of executions took place in response to the invasion. They took place at various prisons. About 12:02 Brigade 2506 members were captured, of which nine died from asphyxiation during transfer to Havana in a closed truck. In May 1961, Fidel Castro proposed to exchange the surviving Brigade prisoners for 500 large farm tractors valued at $28 million US dollars. On September 8, 1961, 14 Brigade prisoners were convicted of torture, murder and other major crimes committed in Cuban before the invasion, five being executed and nine jailed for 30 years.

On March 29, 1962, 1,179 men were put on trial for treason. On April 7, 1962, all were convicted and sentenced to 30 years in prison. On December 21, 1962, Cuban Prime Minister Fidel Castro and James Donovan, a United States attorney, signed an agreement to exchange 1,113 prisoners for $53 million US dollars in food and medicine. On December 24, 1962, some prisoners were flown to Miami, others following on the ship *African Pilot*, plus about 1,000 family members allowed to leave Cuba. On December 29, 1962, President Kennedy attended a "welcome back" ceremony for the Brigade 2506 veterans at the Orange Bowl in Miami, Florida.

CHAPTER 18

The failed invasion severely embarrassed the Kennedy Administration, and Castro became wary of future United States intervention in Cuba. President Kennedy didn't know where to go from here. He felt he was destined to be in the White House. Ever since his older brother, Joe, Jr., had died this life was laid before him. He didn't want to be a failure. He didn't want the country to think he was weak. He wanted to crawl in a deep dark hole. But his brother, Robert Kennedy, had another suggestion. He felt President Kennedy should hold a press conference and tell the American people that he had failed them and he took full responsibility. Robert felt it was better if his brother just came out and admit he was human and he had failed. President Kennedy agreed with his younger brother.

On April 21, 1961, in a State Department press conference, President Kennedy said:

> *"There's an old saying that victory has a hundred fathers and defeat is an orphan . . . What matters is only one fact, I am the responsible officer of the government."*

Later on that evening President Kennedy sat in the Oval Office thinking about the embarrassing fiasco called the Bay of Pigs invasion. Attorney General Robert Kennedy, and his two closest friends, Kenneth

O'Donnell and Dave Powers sat on the couch near him. These three men was President Kennedy's most trusted advisers in his administration.

"They screwed me," President Kennedy said angrily.

"Are you talking about the Central Intelligence Agency?" asked Dave Powers.

"You're damned right I am talking about the CIA. They lied to me," President Kennedy gingerly stood to his feet.

"You can't blame yourself, Jack," said Robert.

"I have to blame myself! I am the leader of this country! I should have known better than listen to them say how easy this invasion would be!" the president slammed his fist down onto his desk.

"Bobby is right. They made the plan sound foolproof," suggested Kenneth.

"I want to end the Cold War and here they are trying to continue it. I swear I will not be made a fool again," said President Kennedy.

"What are you going to do? Stand up to the all-powerful Central Intelligence Agency?" asked Dave.

"I will have to do just that. The United States needs to be the bearer of a higher standard, but not at the cost of looking like a bully. And if the CIA has their way, the United States will become a worldwide bully," said President Kennedy.

"I am going to be the bad guy here and play devil's advocate. Why didn't you authorize an all-out invasion with the help of the United States military?" asked Dave.

"Are you crazy, Dave?" asked Robert.

"I was worried that if the United States invaded Cuba, then it would be like Pearl Harbor in reverse. It would look like a bigger country picking on a smaller country. And I didn't want that. Plus, I was assured the anti-Castro Cubans on the island would join," replied President Kennedy.

"Well, what's done is done. There's nothing you can do about it now," said Dave.

"They knew from the beginning, I would NOT authorize the use of United States combat forces to aid in the invasion. I realized too late that I had been tricked . . . that I had been drawn in a trap set by the CIA," said the president.

"What do you mean?" asked Kenneth.

"Isn't it plain to see? They assumed he would be forced by circumstances to abandon his earlier announcement of not using the United States combat forces to aid in the invasion," replied Robert.

"The CIA had their vision on how to involve the United States into the Cuban conflict. They never really expected an uprising against the Castro regime when the exiles landed in Cuba. The CIA expected the invaders would establish and secure a beachhead. Once the beachhead was secured they would announce the creation of a counter-revolutionary government. Then they would appeal for aid from the United States and the Organization of American States. The CIA wrongly assumed I would be forced by public opinion to aid the returning patriots," explained President Kennedy.

"Like Dave, said what's done is done. What are you going to do now?" asked Kenneth.

"What would happen if I was to disband the Central Intelligence Agency?" President Kennedy asked almost to himself.

"What are you asking or suggesting? Are you truly asking what I think you are asking?" asked Robert.

"They have too much power. It's not a good idea for a group men to have the power the CIA has," replied President Kennedy.

"That's true, but what can you do?" asked Kenneth.

"I am the President of the United States. I will shatter the Central Intelligence Agency into a thousand pieces and scatter them into the wind. But if I can't dismantle the CIA, then I sure as hell can limit the power they possess. And I think I know exactly how to do it, too," stated the president.

Shortly after the exiles surrendered, President Kennedy formed a Cuban Study Group. The group consisted of General Maxwell Taylor, Attorney General Robert Kennedy, Admiral Arleigh Burke, and CIA Director Allen Dulles. This group's responsibility was to discover what caused the failure of the covert operation he had inherited from the Eisenhower Administration. The group found the failure was due to the lack of early realization of the impossibility of success by covert means, inadequate aircraft, limitations of armaments, pilots and air attacks to attempt plausible deniability, and ultimately, loss of important ships and lack of ammunition. The group also claimed the action of National Security Adviser McGeorge Bundy calling back the air support President

Kennedy had ordered was the primary reason for the failure. As a result of that top-level cancellation, those three T-33 jets shot down 16 brigade B-26s, sank the supply ships offshore, and raked the beach with heavy gunfire. That cancellation of the dawn air strike had created President Kennedy's defeat and brought the whole burden down on the shoulders of the new president. This group of highly intelligent men pinned the primary reason for the failed mission on a call made by National Security Adviser McGeorge Bundy not President John Kennedy. But yet the CIA felt betrayed by President Kennedy. Military adviser General Charles Cabell even went as far as calling him a traitor when he returned to the Pentagon.

President Kennedy knew he had to curtail the power of the CIA. With this in mind, on June 28, 1961 he signed National Security Action Memorandum # 55. It said in full:

> *"I wish to inform the Joint Chiefs of Staff as follows with regard to my views of their relations to me in Cold War operations: I regard the Joint Chiefs of Staff as my principal military advisor responsible both for initiating advice to me and for responding to requests for advice. I expect their advice to come to me direct and unfiltered. The Joint Chiefs of Staff have a responsibility for the defense of the nation in the Cold War similar to that which they have in conventional hostilities. They should know the military and paramilitary forces and resources available to the Department of Defense, verify their readiness, report on their accuracy, and make appropriate recommendations for their expansion and improvement. I look to the Chiefs to contribute dynamic and imaginative leadership in contributing to the success of the military and paramilitary aspects of Cold War programs. I expect the Joint Chiefs of Staff to present the military viewpoint in governmental councils in such a way as to assure that the military factors are clearly understood before decisions are reached. When only the Chairman or a single Chief is present, that officer must represent the Chiefs as a body, taking such preliminary and subsequent actions as may be necessary to assure that he does in fact represent the corporate judgment of the Joint Chiefs of Staff. While I look to the Chiefs to represent the military factor without reserve or hesitation, I regard*

them to be more than military men and expect their help in fitting military requirements into the over-all context of any situation, recognizing that the most difficult problem in Government is to combine all assets in a unified, effective pattern."

Once this memorandum was put into effect, which President Kennedy planned to do after his re-election in 1964, it would change what the CIA had power to do or not do concerning covert operation. It took the responsibility to defend the nation during the Cold War from the CIA and placed it in the hands of his Joint Chiefs of Staff. This pretty much blocked the CIA from being involved with covert operations. This did not make them happy with him. In 1962, President Kennedy moved quickly to cut the CIA budget. He did the same in 1963, aiming for a 20% reduction by 1966.

A few days later President Kennedy sat at his desk in the Oval Office. He slowly stood and walked to a large window. Someone knocked at his office door. He turned and looked at the door. His secretary, Evelyn Lincoln, stuck her head into the doorway.

"You have visitors," she said.

"Show them in," he said as he walked to the front of his desk.

CIA Director Allen Dulles, CIA Deputy Director of Plans Richard Bissell and General Charles Cabell walked into the Oval Office. They had a feeling why the president had asked to see them. They had heard the rumors that their jobs were in danger. Why should their jobs be in danger? If the president had only followed their instructions, then the Bay of Pigs invasion wouldn't had failed. In their opinion President Kennedy's job should be the one that's in danger. In their eyes he had been the one to fail the country not them. They walked over the couch and started to sit down on it.

"Evening, gentlemen. Don't bother to sit down, this won't take long. Richard and General Cabell, this plan was mastered mind by the two of you and it was a total embarrassment for this country and this administration. If this is the kind of work I can expect from the two of you, then this Administration is better off without you. Your services are no longer needed. The both of you are fired, effective immediately. And as for you, Allen, your services are no longer needed either. Effectively immediately. Now, if you don't mind, I need to concentrate on finding your replacements," the president turned and walked away from them.

A little while later, Allen Dulles was in the process of cleaning out his desk at the CIA Headquarters when Richard Helms walked into his office.

"What happened?" asked Richard.

"He fired us."

"Who?"

"That bastard Kennedy, he fired General Cabell, Richard Bissell and myself."

"Can he do that? I mean after all the years you have been here? And after all you have done for this country? Can he just fire you like that?" asked Richard.

"Unfortunately he can. But I am not going down without a fight. I have helped organized coup d'états in other countries, maybe it's time I organize one for this country," Allen Dulles suggested.

"What are you talking about? I can't believe you just said that? Are you talking about the removal of the leader of the United States?"

"Yes, I am. Do not breathe a word of what I am about to say to anyone."

"Yes, sir."

"Kennedy is a Communist disguised as an American. He is going to be the downfall of this country. Not on my watch. I want you and Richard Bissell to get together and devise a foolproof plan to eliminate him. I want you to get in touch with your contacts in the Mafia. They hate the Kennedys as much as anyone else. They will be thrilled to lend a hand," suggested Allen.

After the Bay of Pigs failure, President John Kennedy was worried the American people would see him as being too weak to lead this country. He was afraid the rest of the world would try to take advantage of his appearance of being weak; especially the Soviet Union. Former President Eisenhower told President Kennedy that the failure of Bay of Pigs will push the Soviets to do something they would not normally do. President Kennedy believed and feared the Domino Theory. The Domino Theory was a theory which stated when a country succumbs to Communist then all the other countries around it would fall one after another.

On June 4, 1961, President John Kennedy and Soviet Premier Nikita Khrushchev had a summit conference in Vienna, Austria. The Vienna Summit marked the first time the two leaders would meet face to face. Soviet Premier Nikita Khrushchev had been in power since Josef Stalin had died in 1953. He was determined to prove his apparent superiority over the young and inexperienced American President. The discussions were cordial, unlike the breakdown in the Paris Summit between President Dwight Eisenhower and Premier Khrushchev in 1960. When the two men first met in Vienna, President Kennedy couldn't help but look Premier Khrushchev up and down several times. And he was unable to hide his curiosity about the Soviet leader. The Summit, despite being dominated by discussions over Berlin, covered a wide range of topics. They discussed the position of Laos and the broader conflict in Indochina, nuclear disarmament and ideological musings.

Premier Khrushchev threatened to sign a peace agreement with East Germany which would intrude on Western access to Berlin by turning over control of the access roads and air routes. President Kennedy stood firm on Western access to Berlin; he also placed unprecedented emphasis on the phrase "West Berlin" during the summit and conveyed unstated compliance to Soviet actions in their sector of Berlin, including a possible border closure. Premier Khrushchev told President Kennedy, "*Force will be met by force. If the US wants war, that's its problem. It's up to the US to decide whether there will be war or peace. The decision to sign a peace treaty is firm and irrevocable, and the Soviet Union will sign it in December if the US refuses an interim agreement.*" With this said, President Kennedy replied, "*Then, Mr. Chairman, there will be a war. It will be a cold, long winter.*"

At first the summit was seen as a diplomatic triumph. President Kennedy had refused to allow Soviet pressure to force his hand, or to influence the American policy of containment. He had adequately stalled the Soviet Premier, and made it clear the United States was not willing to compromise on a withdrawal from Berlin. However, after a further review, it appeared to have been a failure. The two leaders became increasingly frustrated at the lack of progress of the negotiations. After the summit, Premier Khrushchev realized he had underestimated the much younger President Kennedy. And President Kennedy felt he had to avoid giving the same impression of weakness which he had demonstrated before the summit, and felt he had demonstrated to Premier Khrushchev during the summit. He later stated Premier Khrushchev, "*beat the hell out of me. It was the worst thing in my life. He savaged me."* Observing President Kennedy's depressed expression at the end of the summit, Premier Khrushchev believed *"he looked not only anxious, but deeply upset . . . I hadn't meant to upset him. I would have liked very much for us to part in a different mood. But there was nothing I could do to help him . . . Politics is a merciless business."*

Late June 5, 1961, on the flight back to Washington the weary President Kennedy tried to relax. He asked his secretary, Evelyn Lincoln, to file the documents he had been working on. As she cleared the table, she noticed a slip of paper had fallen onto the floor. The two lines written on the piece of paper was in the president's handwriting. It was his favorite saying from Abraham Lincoln. It said:

> *"I know there is a God—and I see a storm coming; if he has a place for me, I believe that I am ready."*

CHAPTER 19

———————◻———————

"Leadership and learning are indispensable to each other."

John F. Kennedy

In the summer of 1961, President Kennedy was again getting pressure from his military advisers. This time it was over Berlin. In the summer and fall he struggled with Soviet Premier Khrushchev over the divided Berlin, Germany. His military advisers continued to pressure him into a war. They began to apply pressure on the young president to use nuclear weapons in Berlin. Each time they would request his authorization to use nuclear weapons, he would walk out on the meetings. One of these walk-outs resulted in President Kennedy throwing up his hands and wondering if his advisers were crazy. The advisers, in turn, wondered if he was crazy.

In October 1961, President Kennedy's personal representative in West Berlin, retired General Lucius Clay, tried to escalate the crisis in Berlin to a point where the young president didn't have any other choice but to invade the German town. In August of 1961, Soviet Premier Khrushchev ordered the construction of a wall in Berlin. The next month, General Clay began secret preparations to tear down the wall. He ordered Major General Albert Watson, who was the United States military commandment in West Berlin, to have army engineers build a duplicate section of the Berlin Wall in a forest. United States tanks with bulldozer attachments were used to experiment attacks on the wall. General Bruce Clark learned what General Clay was doing and he put an end to the experiment. General Watson was commander of the United States forces in Europe. Neither of the men discussed what had happened in the forest with the president.

Where President Kennedy wasn't aware of what took place in the Berlin forest, the soviet premier was well informed of what had happened. Soviet spies watched and took pictures of the secret endeavors. Premier Khrushchev assembled a group of advisers to decide what to do if the United States indeed tried an assault on the Berlin Wall. Secretly the Soviet Premier seriously doubted President Kennedy agreed to the secret actions in the forest. He felt the United States president was being undermined.

After a long summer of increasing tensions over Berlin, President Kennedy prepared to give his first speech at the United Nations. The president and Arthur Schlesinger were staying the night at a Manhattan hotel when Arthur agreed to an urgent call from Georgi Bolshakov. Georgi had an urgent message from the Soviet Premier for President Kennedy. The message was Premier Khrushchev was now willing to consider American proposals for a rapprochement on Berlin. He wanted to schedule a summit with President Kennedy as soon as possible. Premier Khrushchev feared a major military incident would spark terrible consequences. President Kennedy sent a message of his own, he was cautiously receptive to Khrushchev's proposal for an early summit on Berlin. But first there should be a demonstration of Soviet good faith in Laos. In his eyes Berlin and Laos were linked.

On October 27th, 10 American M-48 tanks, with bulldozers mounted on the lead tanks, forced their way to Checkpoint Charlie at the center of the Berlin Wall. Ten Soviet tanks met the American tanks at the wall. Soon twenty more Soviet tanks appeared as reinforcements. And shortly thereafter twenty United States tanks moved into reinforcement positions. The American and Soviets tanks faced off with each other. They trained their long barreled guns on each other. For a total of sixteen hours the confrontation continued. If the US tanks advanced on the wall, the Soviet tanks were ordered to fire on the American tanks.

"What is Khrushchev thinking?" President Kennedy asked his brother.

"I don't know, Jack. I don't know what Khrushchev is thinking."

"I thought Khrushchev wanted to settle this situation in Berlin.," said President Kennedy.

"Well, Jack, to be honest our boys over there isn't helping to send a picture that we want to resolve the Berlin issue."

President Kennedy leaned back in his rocking chair. Robert was sitting on the white couch in the Oval Office. He had just received the report on what had happened in Berlin. He couldn't believe what the US military was trying to start in Berlin. He was wanting a peaceful end to the confrontation, but it appeared they were trying to push the issue to a breaking point. President Kennedy stuck a lit cigar in his mouth as he thought about the next step to take.

"I got to get a message to Khrushchev. Bobby, can you use your back channels and get a message to him?" asked the president.

"Sure. What do you want the message to say?"

"Tell Premier Khrushchev that if he would withdraw his tanks within 24 hours after getting this message, then the US will withdraw our tanks thirty minutes later," President Kennedy said.

"Are you sure? Do you think our boys will listen to you?"

"Yes, I'm sure. They have to listen to reason. And no one needs to know about this message, ok?"

"Sure thing, Jack," said Bobby.

The following morning the Soviet tanks retreated. Thirty minutes later the American tanks did the same. Premier Khrushchev agreed to taking the first steps in the retreat because he knew of the pressures being applied on President Kennedy. The military advisors of President Kennedy were starting to see his action as a threat to the survival of the nation. They also saw his growing connection to the Soviet premier as treacherous.

Something else had taken place during the Berlin Crisis to which President Kennedy's military advisors wasn't aware. He and Soviet Premier Khrushchev had started communicating secretly. The Soviet Premier's advisers were not aware of this communication either. The communication with Premier Khruschev was one of the few things President Kennedy was able to keep hidden from his presidential advisers. This communication with the Soviet Premier is exactly what his military advisers didn't want to happen.

In 1960, President Eisenhower and Soviet Premier Khrushchev were discussing a possible peace treaty. If a peace treaty was successful, then the Cold War would end before the CIA had a chance to launch their secret war in Indochina which would lead to the Vietnam War. The Central Intelligence Agency intervened in this possible peace talk with President Eisenhower and Premier Khrushchev by planting a spy in Russia. This spy was Lee Harvey Oswald and he was armed with Top Secret information about the CIA U-2 spy plane. Premier Khruschev became aware of the spy plane when they were finally able to shoot it down. Khrushchev was convinced President Eisenhower was behind the U-2 spy plane's flights over his country. The problem with that thought was, President Eisenhower was not aware of the flights of the U-2 spy plane. The spy plane operation was directly headed by Deputy Director of Plans Richard Bissell. When the Russians shot down Powers' spy plane, the result was the end of the peace talk between the two leaders. This was proof the CIA was willing to go to any lengths to avoid peace between the United States and the Soviet Union. Now they needed to take steps to avoid peace talk with the new president and the Soviet Premier.

Premier Khrushchev sent his first private letter to the young president on September 29, 1961. It was wrapped in a newspaper and it was brought to President Kennedy's press secretary, Pierre Salinger. It was delivered at a New York hotel by Soviet "newspaper editor" and KGB agent Georgi Bolshakov. In the letter the Soviet Premier wrote:

> *"Dear Mr. President, at present I am on the shore of the Black Sea . . . This is indeed a wonderful place. As a former Naval officer you would surely appreciate the merits of these surroundings, the beauty of the sea and the grandeur of the Caucasian mountains. Under this bright southern sun it is even somehow hard to believe that there still exist problems in the world which, due to lack of solutions, cast a sinister shadow on peaceful life, on the future of millions of people."*

In the letter Premier Khrushchev expressed his regret over the Vienna Summit. He wrote he had given great thought to the development of international events since their meeting in Vienna, and had decided to approach the American president with a letter. The Soviet leader felt the whole world had hopefully expected their meeting would have a soothing effect, would turn relations between the two countries into the correct channel and promote the adoption of decisions which would give the peoples confidence that at last peace on earth would be secured. He wrote, *"To my regret—and, I believe, to yours—this did not happen."*

*"My thoughts have more than once returned to our meeting
in Vienna. I remember you emphasized that you did not want to
proceed towards war and favored living in peace with our country
while competing in the peaceful domain. And thought subsequent
events did not proceed in the way that could be desired, I thought it
might be useful in a purely informal and personal way to approach
you and share some of my ideas. If you do not agree with me you
can consider that this letter did not exist while naturally I, for
my part, will not use this correspondence in my public statements.
After all only in confidential correspondence can you say what you
think without a backward glance at the press, at the journalists,"*
Soviet Premier Khrushchev wrote to President Kennedy.

The first letter Premier Khrushchev wrote to President Kennedy was
twenty-six pages long. He talked about politics, particularly Berlin, and
the civil war in Laos. He compared his and President Kennedy's situation
with *"Noah's Ark where both the 'clean' and the 'unclean' found sanctuary.
But regardless who lists himself with the 'clean' and who is considered to be
'unclean,' they are all equally interested in one thing and that is that the
Ark should successfully continue its cruise. And we have no other alternative;
either we should live in peace and cooperation so that the Ark maintains its
buoyancy, or else it sinks."*

On October 16, 1961, President Kennedy responded in private to
Premier Khrushchev. He was at Hyannis Port, his own place of retreat
beside the ocean. He wrote:

*"My family has had a home here overlooking the Atlantic
for many years . . . So this is an ideal place for me to spend my
weekends during the summer and fall, to relax, to think, to devote
my time to major tasks instead of constant appointments, telephone
calls and details. Thus, I know how you feel about the spot on the
Black Sea from which your letter was written, for I value my own
opportunities to get a clearer and quieter perspective away from the
din of Washington . . . Certainly you are correct in emphasizing
that this correspondence must be kept wholly private, not to be
hinted at in public statements, much less disclosed to the press and
give us each a chance to address the other in frank, realistic and
fundamental terms. Neither of us is going to convert the other to*

a new social, economic, political point of view. Neither of us will be induced by a letter to desert or subvert his own cause. So these letters can be free from the polemics of the 'cold war' debate . . . I like very much your analogy of Noah's Ark, with both the 'clean' and the 'unclean' determined that it stay afloat. Whatever our differences, our collaboration to keep the peace is as urgent—if not more urgent—than our collaboration to win the last world war."

Even after a year of corresponding in private letters, President Kennedy and Soviet Premier Khrushchev hadn't ironed out their differences. The Cuban Missile Crisis was evident of that. The Soviet Premier felt betrayed by President Kennedy because of his intention to invade Cuba again. And the American President in turn felt betrayed by Premier Khrushchev when he placed missiles in Cuba.

CHAPTER 20

"Let every nation know, whether it wishes us well
or ill, that we shall pay any price, bear any burden, meet any
hardship, support any friend, oppose any foe to assure the
survival and success of liberty."

John F. Kennedy

President John Kennedy realized the plan for the Bay of Pigs was set up to fail unless he agreed to send military air support to aid the Cuban exiles. He didn't fall for it and he accepted defeat. He pushed the Bay of Pigs invasion fiasco out of his mind and began to concentrate on Laos. CIA Deputy Director of Plans Richard Helms tried to plot a way to force President Kennedy into action in Laos. One night he discussed such a plot with former CIA operative Colonel Edward Lansdale and Air Force General Curtis LeMay. They sat in Richard's office away from President Kennedy and the other advisers so they could speak in private.

"Well, Kennedy chickened out on calling for air support in the Bay of Pigs. Do you think he will do the same with Laos?" Richard Helms asked them.

"We have to apply pressure on him to force him to invade Laos," suggested General LeMay.

"Let me and my men go down there stir up a hell of a mess. That would force him to intervene in Laos," said Colonel Lansdale.

"He wouldn't fall for that. General LeMay, work with the other military advisers on devising a plan for Laos. We can't let Laos go in the way Cuba did," suggested Richard.

"Good deal, sir," General LeMay stood to his feet and left the deputy director's office.

Colonel Lansdale also stood to his feet, but the deputy director of plans motioned him to wait for a moment. Once the Air Force General had exited the office, the colonel sat down in the chair.

"Have you had a chance to work on the operation I gave you?" asked Richard.

"I don't like the president any more than the next guy, but don't you think it's a little early to be thinking of a coup?"

"To be honest? No, I don't think it's too early," replied Richard.

"Christ, Richard, Kennedy has only been in the White House a few months. I think we should give him a little more time to learn to play ball," suggested General LeMay.

"He shouldn't even be in the White House. If his father hadn't intervene, Dick would be in the White House. And if Nixon was president we wouldn't have been embarrassed in Cuba."

"Do you think he's that much of a threat to the United States?"

"Who knows? Just get the operation started, have a plan in place just in case," said Richard.

In the beginning, the Joint Chiefs of Staff asked for 40,000 troops to be deployed to Laos. They raised that number to 60,000 by the end of March. They raised that number once more to 140,000 by the end of April. Each time President Kennedy balked at their suggestions.

"I don't think Laos is that big of deal to continue to send troops there," President Kennedy said to his military advisors in a meeting in his Oval Officer.

"I think we should go into Laos with the intention of winning the war there," suggested Army General George H. Decker.

"How do you suggest that?" asked President Kennedy.

"I think we should bomb Hanoi and possibly China," replied the Army General.

President Kennedy grew impatient with the advice his advisers was giving him about Laos. He soon backed away from the entire idea of troops in Laos. He questioned his advisers closely and he exposed holes in their plans. After the Bay of Pigs failure and the hard push for intervention in Laos, President Kennedy began to lose confidence in his Joint Chiefs of Staff. One day he discussed his military experts' advice with Retired General Douglas MacArthur. The retired general gave the president advice which he wouldn't soon forget. In fact whenever the discussion about

South Asia arose, President Kennedy would repeat the advice to his own advisers. Retired General MacArthur told the young president, *"Anyone wanting to commit American ground forces to the mainland of Asia should have his head examined."*

On August 29, 1961, on the recommendation of his military, CIA, and State Department advisers, President John Kennedy agreed to raise the number of United States advisers in Laos to five hundred and to go ahead with the equipping of two thousand of the members of the Hmong tribe "Meo". This increased the number of Laotian men recruited into the CIA's covert army to eleven thousand. President Kennedy believed he was supporting an indigenous group of people who were profoundly opposed to their land's occupation by the Pathet Lao army. He was trying to hold on to enough ground, through some effective resistance to the Pathet Lao advance, to leave something for Averell Harriman to negotiate with in Geneva toward a neutralist government.

President Kennedy was playing right into the CIA's hands. The CIA was more than willing to manipulate his policy to benefit their favorite Laotian strongman, General Phoumi Nosavan. He knew of this dangerous game he was playing. With this in mind, President Kennedy moved ahead in strengthening the CIA-"Meo" army, so as to stem a Communist takeover in Laos, while at the same time trying by other means to rein in the CIA. This gave them the opportunity not only to strengthen General Phoumi's hand but also to encourage Phoumi to undercut the president's neutralist policy. Phoumi was happy to oblige.

While President Kennedy's military advisers pressure him to intervene in Laos, the Central Intelligence Agency secretly plotted against Fidel Castro. The Cuban Project, also called *Operation Mongoose*, was a program of the Central Intelligence Agency. *Operation Mongoose* was a covert operations developed during the early years of President Kennedy's Administration. On November 30, 1961 aggressive covert operations against the communist government of Fidel Castro in Cuba were authorized by President Kennedy. The operation was led by Air Force Colonel Edward Lansdale and went into effect after the failed Bay of Pigs Invasion. *Operation Mongoose* was a secret program of propaganda, psychological warfare, and sabotage against Cuba to remove the communists from power; which was a prime focus of the Kennedy administration. A document from the United

States Department of State confirmed the project aimed to "help Cuba overthrow the Communist regime"; including its leader Fidel Castro and it aimed "for a revolt which can take place in Cuba by October 1962". United States policy makers also wanted to see "a new government with which the United States can live in peace".

After the Cuban Revolution, and the rise of Communism under Castro, the United States government was determined to undercut the integrity of the socialist revolution and install in its place a government more in line with US philosophy. A special committee was formed to search for ways to overthrow Castro when the Bay of Pigs Invasion failed. The committee became part of the Kennedy imperative to keep a tough line on communism especially as it, Cuba, was the nearest communist country. The operation was based on the estimation of the United States Government that coercion inside Cuba was severe and the regime was serving as a spearhead for allied communist movements elsewhere in the Americas. It was further believed repressive measures within Cuba, together with the seeming failure of the government's socialist economic policies, had resulted in an atmosphere among the Cuban people which made a resistance program a distinct possibility at that moment. As such, the United States designed the covert plan to fuel a growing anti-regime spirit to provoke an overthrow of the government or assassination attempts on Castro.

The United States Department of Defense and the Joint Chiefs of Staff saw the project's ultimate objective was to provide adequate justification for a United States military intervention in Cuba. They requested the Secretary of Defense Robert McNamara assign them responsibility for the project, but Attorney General Robert Kennedy retained effective control. The reason for this was because President Kennedy didn't trust the CIA. He was still working on either dismantling them or reducing their power. The failure of the Bay of Pigs Invasion was still fresh on his mind.

Operation Mongoose was led by Colonel Edward Lansdale in the Defense Department and William King Harvey at the CIA. Colonel Lansdale was chosen due to his experience with counter-insurgency in the Philippines during the Huk Rebellion, and also due to his experience supporting the Diem regime in Vietnam. Thirty-three plans were considered under the Cuban Project, some of which were carried out. The plans varied in efficacy and intention, from propagandistic purposes to effective disruption of the

Cuban government and economy. Plans included the use of American Green Berets, destruction of Cuban sugar crops, and mining of harbors.

Operation Mongoose **was** a complete failure because Fidel Castro remained in control even after the operation was cancelled. Some of the plots which came about from the operation were ridiculous and borderline stupid. The men involved with *Operation Mongoose* were some of the most intelligent men in the country. But you couldn't tell it by some of the plots which resulted from the operation.

A group of men sat at a table in office used for meetings at the CIA headquarters. Very few people knew about this office. At the head of the table was Deputy Director of Plans Richard Helms. Around the table were Colonel Sheffield Edwards, Director of the Office of Security and the Chief of Operational Support Division of the Office of Security James O'Connell, Colonel Edward Lansdale, David Atlee Phillips, Sam Giancana, Santo Trafficante, Jr., and Johnny Roselli. They were discussing possible plots against Fidel Castro.

"We need to remove Castro by killing him," suggested Santo.

"I think that's a little extreme. What if you try to discredit him in the eyes of the Cuban people," said James.

"How would that result in removing Castro?" asked Johnny Roselli.

"What about contaminating the air of the radio where he normally broadcasted his speeches?" suggested James.

"That's interesting. How would we accomplish that?" asked Richard.

"We would use an aerosol spray of a chemical which produced reactions similar to those of lysergic acid (LSD)," said James.

"What would that do?" asked Colonel Lansdale.

"Well, that drug would cause Castro to flip and trip on the air. He would make a fool of himself through hallucinogen-inspired ranting," replied James.

"That's crazy. It would never work," said Sam.

"What about them damned cigars of Fidel's," Robert Maheu said as he walked into the office. Robert was the original contact between the CIA and the Mafia.

"You took the words out of my mouth," Sidney Gottlieb, of the CIA Technical Services Division, said as he entered the office behind Robert.

The two men apologized for being late as they sat of the table. Both Robert and Robert already had connections to the CIA plots to assassinate

Castro. In March 1960, President Dwight Eisenhower approved a CIA plan to remove Fidel Castro. The plan involved a budget of $13 million to train a paramilitary force outside Cuba for guerilla action. The strategy was organized by Richard Bissell and Richard Helms. Sidney was asked to come up with proposals which would undermine Castro's popularity with the Cuban people. Plans included a scheme to contaminate Castro's shoes with thallium which was believed would cause the hair in his beard fall out. On March 12, 1961, William King Harvey arranged for CIA operative, James O'Connell to meet Sam Giancana, Santo Trafficante, Jr., Johnny Roselli, and Robert Maheu at the Fontainebleau Hotel. During the meeting, James gave poison pills and $10,000 to Johnny to be used against Fidel Castro.

"What are you suggesting about the cigars?" asked Richard Helms.

"We could prepare a box of cigars which had been treated with some sort of chemical. The cigars would be intended to produce temporary personality disorientation. The idea is to somehow arrange to have Castro smoke one of the cigars before making a speech. After smoking one of the contaminated cigars he would make a public spectacle of himself," replied James.

"Are you serious?" asked Johnny.

"Come on, guys, you are supposed to be some of the most intelligent men in the country. We need to get serious about removing Castro," suggested Santo.

"I think the plan involving dusting Castro's shoes with thallium powder should be taken serious," said James.

"Ok, tell us more about it," said Richard.

"When Castro makes a trip outside of Cuba, he normally sets his shoes outside his room to be shined. We could take his shoes and dust them with thallium powder. As I stated before the powder would cause his beard to fall out. We've even tested it out on animals."

"Is that the best you can come up with?" asked Robert Maheu.

"I think embarrassing Castro will not be enough. He has to be removed permanently," said Colonel Lansdale.

"I agree. That's why we have decided to enlist the help of the Mafia. Hence, the reason Santo, Johnny and Sam is present at this meeting. I think we need to hit Castro and make it look like a gang-like drive by shooting," said Richard.

"That won't work either," suggested Sam.

"Well, enlighten me then, Mr. Giancana. Why wouldn't that work?" asked Richard.

"It wouldn't work because it would be too hard to recruit assassins when their chances of survival and escape would be slim to none. I have suggested to James about using a lethal pill which could be slipped into Castro's drink by a Cuban contact of Santo," said Sam.

"Why haven't I been told about this plan? I told everyone all plans need to go through me first," Richard asked James.

"Well, because when a test was run on the lethal pills, they didn't dissolve in a glass of water. We conducted a test on guinea pigs and monkeys to make sure the pills were lethal. The pigs survived, but the monkeys didn't. It was decided the guinea pigs survived because they had a higher intolerance to the toxins. Even then we decided to go ahead with the plan," replied James.

"Without my authority?" asked Richard.

"Yes, we didn't think we had time to waste," answered James.

"Well, what went wrong?" asked Richard.

"Sir?" asked James.

"Well, apparently the plan failed or we wouldn't be sitting here. What caused the plan to fail?" asked Richard.

"The botulinus pills were concealed in a pin and delivered to Johnny Roselli. He gave the pills to Santo Trafficante, Jr., here, who delivered them to Juan Ortga in Cuba. Juan was supposed to use the pills to poison Castro. The plan failed because he was fired from his position in the Cuban Prime Minister's office and he fled to Florida," answered James.

"Well, I have to report to the attorney general on the progress of the plots. We will meet again in a few weeks," Richard stood to his feet and left the office.

In December 1961, approximately six months before Lee Oswald left the Soviet Union, the KGB reported he had manufactured a pipe bomb using parts he took home from the factory's metal shop and filled with gunpowder from ammunition for his shotgun. The KGB at the time became concerned when an assassination attempt was made on the life of Soviet Premier Khrushchev several weeks later on a visit to a Minsk area resort. (The details of the Khrushchev assassination attempt are still classified.) He discarded the pipe bomb into the trash where the KGB recovered it.

This incident with the pipe bomb almost blew his cover. The CIA officials who were over the Oswald operation almost cut him loose from the Central Intelligence Agency. They were convinced he had become a liability, maybe even a loose cannon. They felt he was a danger not only to himself, but also the United States. James Smith, Lee's handler, was able to convince his superiors they needed to bring him home to the United States. He needed to be debriefed and then they could decide if his services were still needed in the Central Intelligence Agency.

What the CIA officials didn't realized was, Lee had learned he was under KGB observation. He informed James he knew the Soviets were watching his every move. He became worried and feared for his life. He was terrified that the Soviets would try to kill him. He was convinced the Soviets would never let him and his family leave the Soviet Union. It was James who suggested he make the pipe bomb to hasten the Soviets into issuing him an exit visa.

On December 25, 1961, within a few weeks of the incident, exit visas for Lee and Marina were approved. But the Oswald's departure was delayed by a further six months because US authorities were reluctant to approve Marina's entry into the US. They were still having trouble verifying whether or not she was an agent.

CHAPTER 21

———————□———————

"Let the word go forth this time and place,
to friend and foe alike, that the torch has been passed to a
new generation of Americans—born in this century, tempered
by war, disciplined by a hard and bitter peace."

John F. Kennedy

In 1962, President John Kennedy began secret negotiations with Fidel Castro through New York attorney James Donovan. Bill Mason, from Attorney General Robert Kennedy's office and James had negotiated the return of the Bay of Pigs prisoners. In April 1963, they returned to Cuba for more negotiations. These negotiations opened the door for a possible normal relations between the United States and Castro's Cuba. These talks of normal relations with Castro weren't happy news for the CIA.

Colonel Edward Lansdale walked into Deputy Director of Plans Richard Helms' office. He sat down in a chair across from the deputy director. Richard was on the phone, so Colonel Lansdale waited patiently. A few minutes later he hung up the phone. Richard pulled out a folder from one of the drawers in his desk. He opened it and set it on his desktop.

"Have you heard the latest on our president?" he asked the colonel.

"If you are talking about his mistresses, then I don't have time for this," Colonel Lansdale started to stand to his feet.

"No, I am not talking about his mistresses. What I have learned affects you and the CIA," said Richard.

"What are you talking about?"

"I have information that President Kennedy has started 'secret' negotiations with Fidel Castro," he said.

"If you are talking about the release of the Bay of Pigs prisoners, then I already know about this. I actually agree with him on that."

"No, the information I have received is he is using an attorney from New York as a go-between with Castro. And these talks don't just involve the Bay of Pig prisoners, but what I am told is the talks involved a possible rapprochement with Castro," stated Richard.

"What? Are you serious? He is in talks with the enemy?"

"I am deadly serious. First he screwed us on the Bay of Pigs invasion, now he is trying to screw us in Cuba completely with these secret talks with Castro," said Richard.

"I thought the president and the attorney general was as hell bent as the CIA in getting rid of Castro?" asked the colonel.

"Well, apparently he's not."

"I am telling you, this president is dangerous for this country. I don't think he has this country's best interest in mind as he runs this country into the ground. I suspect he might be soft on Communism. We tried to pressure him to invade Berlin and Laos, but he refused. What about when it comes time for us to get involved in Indochina? What's he going to do about that?" asked the colonel.

"I believe he will try to screw us then, too."

"Is the CIA still plotting to assassinate Fidel?" asked Colonel Lansdale.

"Yes we are. And as far as Indochina, I don't think he will be around to screw that up for us."

"What are you talking about?" asked Colonel Lansdale.

"I can't say a whole lot right now. Just know there's an operation in the early talks. And it deals with removing President Kennedy from office," said Richard Helms.

CHAPTER 22

━━━━━━━━━━ ▫ ━━━━━━━━━━

*"As we express our gratitude we must never forget
that the highest appreciation is not to utter words,
but to live by them."*

John F. Kennedy

On June 1, 1962, after nearly a year of paperwork and waiting, the young Oswald family left the Soviet Union for the United States. Having started his teen years as a lonely troubled truant in New York, Lee Oswald had been brought back by his mother to New Orleans, where he developed numerous friendships and acquaintances during his high school years. He did likewise in the Marines but led his most active social life in the Soviet Union where he had a number of girlfriends, married, fathered a child, formed social bonds, went on picnics and hunting trips, to parties, to dinners in people's homes, dances and moved among a broad range of people. However, after returning to the United States in 1962 he would have few friends or acquaintances other than George de Mohrenschildt. He had become disillusioned and isolated even from his own family. He would eventually separate from his wife, Marina, and their infant daughter, living alone in distant rooming houses. There are periods in the final months of his life during which his movements and activities have remained undocumented. Some observers have remarked during the last year of his life, he appeared to change physically, rapidly balding and appearing to age significantly beyond his twenty-four years.

When Lee Oswald returned to the United States on June 13, 1962 he was welcomed with open arms by the American officials. The United States made no move to prosecute him for treason. In fact the United

States Embassy loaned him the money to return to the United States. By the order of the United States government Lee and his wife was met after they disembarked from the ocean liner *Maasdam*. The Oswalds were greeted at the dock by a representative of the Traveler's Aid Society. At this time the representative was the secretary-general of the American Friends of the Anti-Bolshevik Nations, which was an anti-communist organization with extensive intelligence connections.

Once Lee was back in the United States, Marina and he settled in the Dallas/Fort Worth area. He attempted to write his memoir and commentary on Soviet life. It was a small manuscript called *The Collective*. He soon gave up the idea but his search for literary feedback put him in touch with the area's close-knit community of anti-Communist Russian émigrés. While merely tolerating the belligerent and arrogant Lee Oswald, they sympathized with his wife, partly because she was in a foreign country with no knowledge of English, which her husband refused to teach her, and because he had begun to beat her. Although they eventually abandoned Marina when she made no sign of leaving him, he had found an unlikely best friend in the well-educated and worldly petroleum geologist George de Mohrenschildt.

George de Mohrenschildt was born April 17, 1911 in Mozyr in Tsarist, Russia near the border of Poland. His wealthy father, an anti-Communist, was arrested and put in prison by the Bolsheviks shortly after the Russian Revolution. After being sentenced to life as an exile in Siberia, he managed to escape with his family to Poland during the 1920's. George graduated from a military academy in 1931. While a young man he left Poland and spent time traveling around Europe. George claimed he was involved in a pro-Nazi plot to kill Joseph Stalin. He received the equivalent of a doctor of science of international commerce from the University of Liege in 1938.

When George immigrated to the United States in 1938, British Intelligence reportedly notified the United States government they suspected he was working for German intelligence. He was placed under FBI surveillance for a short time. He went to work for Shumaker Company in New York. He worked for Pierre Fraiss, who had connections with French intelligence and was engaged in gathering information about people engaged in "pro-German" activities. These activities included

Nazi bidding for United States oil leases before the United States became involved in the war.

He spent the summer of 1938 with his older brother Dmitri on Long Island, New York. He became acquainted with the Bouvier family, including a young Jacqueline Bouvier, the future Mrs. John F. Kennedy. He became a close friend to Jacqueline's aunt. In 1939, he went work for Humble Oil which was co-founded by Prescott Bush. Prescott was former President George W. Bush's grandfather. It was also at this time he met George H.W. Bush.

From 1939 to 1941, George dabbled in the insurance business, but failed to pass the broker's examination. When the United States entered World War II, his application to join to the Office Strategic Services was rejected because it was alleged he was a Nazi espionage agent. After the war he moved to Venezuela where he worked for Pantepec Oil, a company owned by the family of William F. Buckley. In 1949 he became a United States citizen. In 1950 he launched an oil investment firm with Edward Hooker with offices in New York City, Denver, and Abilene. In 1952 he settled in Dallas, Texas and took a job with oilman Clint Murchinson as a petroleum geologist. He became a respected member of the Russian émigré community in Dallas, teaching at a local college. He joined the Dallas Petroleum Club and became a regular at Council on World Affairs meetings, a right wing organization established by Neil Mallon. He also joined the Texas Crusade for Freedom.

In 1957 he met J. Walton Moore, a CIA agent of the Domestic Contacts Division. The two men had several meetings over next few years. George worked for various oil companies as a geologist and traveling throughout the Americas with his fourth wife. He was an active member of 2 CIA Proprietary Organizations: The Dallas Council on World Affairs and The Crusade for a Free Europe.

George de Mohrenschildt was introduced to Lee Oswald and his Russian wife, Marina in the summer of 1962 in Fort Worth, Texas. He had heard of the Oswalds from one of the Russian-speaking group of émigrés in the Dallas-Fort Worth area. Early in the summer of 1962 he had heard of the unusual couple. He heard the man was supposedly an ex-marine, and an unfriendly and eccentric character, which had gone to Russia and brought back with him a Russian wife. George and his wife befriended them, tried to help them as best they could, and introduced them to the Russian community in Dallas. Shortly after being introduced to Lee and Marina, George met with J. Walton Moore to discuss Lee.

"I am aware of Lee's defection to Russia and then back home to the United States. Is it safe for a man with my connections to the Central Intelligence Agency to assist Lee and his Russian wife, Marina?" asked George.

"It's ok. Lee is also connected to the CIA," claimed J. Walton.

"How connected is he to CIA?"

"Now, George, you should know I can't answer that question. Just know he recently completed an important mission over in the Soviet Union. In fact he was brought to Dallas and to your attention for a purpose."

"And what purpose is that?" George asked him.

"We are not sure yet. His handler for his mission was James Smith. We want you to be his handler here in Dallas."

"What do you want me to do?"

"We are not sure what we want to do with Lee. Just know he's ok, a bit of a lunatic. Just keep him close to you for the moment. We will let you know what we decide to do with Mr. Oswald," said J. Walton Moore.

CHAPTER 23

———————————□———————————

"A child miseducated is a child lost."

John F. Kennedy

In Early 1962, Soviet Premier Nikita Khrushchev was convinced, through persuasion from his military advisors, that the failed Bay of Pigs was just the beginning of the United States interfering with Cuban affairs. To defend Cuba from the threat of another United States invasion, Khrushchev and his military advisors came up with the idea of installing missiles with nuclear heads in Cuba. The idea was to install the missiles with the United States learning of the missiles before they could do anything about it. Khrushchev reasoned: *"The main thing was that the installation of our missiles in Cuba would have equalized what the West likes to call 'the balance of power.' The Americans had surrounded our country with military bases and threatened us with nuclear weapons, and now they would learn just what it feels like to have enemy missiles pointing at you."*

In May 1962, Soviet Premier Nikita Khrushchev was persuaded to the idea of countering the United States' growing lead in developing and deploying strategic missiles by placing Soviet intermediate-range nuclear missiles in Cuba. Premier Khrushchev was reacting in part to the Jupiter intermediate-range ballistic missiles which the United States had installed in Turkey during April 1962. From the beginning, the Soviet's operation entailed elaborate denial and deception. All of the planning and preparation for transporting and deploying the missiles were carried out in the utmost secrecy. Only a very few were told the exact nature of the mission. Even the troops detailed for the mission were given misdirection instructions. The troops were told they were headed for a cold region and outfitted with ski boots, fleece-lined parkas, and other winter equipment. The Soviet code name, *Operation Anadyr*, was also the name of a river flowing into the Bering Sea, the name of the capital of Chukotsky District, and a bomber base in the far eastern region. All these were meant to conceal the program from both internal and external audiences.

In early 1962, a group of Soviet military and missile construction specialists accompanied an agricultural delegation to Havana. They obtained a meeting with Cuban leader Fidel Castro. The Cuban leadership had a strong expectation the United States would invade Cuba again and they enthusiastically approved the idea of installing nuclear missiles in Cuba. Specialists in missile construction under the disguise of "machine operators," "irrigation specialists" arrived in July. Marshal Sergei Biryuzov, chief of the Soviet Rocket Forces, led a survey team which visited Cuba. He informed Premier Khrushchev the missiles would be concealed and camouflaged by the palm trees.

Like Castro, Soviet Premier Khrushchev felt a United States invasion of Cuba was imminent, and to lose Cuba would do great harm to communist cause, especially in Latin America. Soviet Premier Khrushchev wanted to confront the Americans with more than words and he felt the logical answer was nuclear missiles. The Soviets maintained their tight secrecy, writing their plans longhand, which was approved by Rodion Malinovsky on July 4th and Khrushchev on July 7th. The Soviet leadership believed, based on their perception of President Kennedy's lack of confidence during the Bay of Pigs Invasion, he would avoid confrontation and accept the missiles without taking action against them. On September 7th, Soviet Ambassador Anatoly Dobrynin assured United States Ambassador to the United Nations Adlai Stevenson that the USSR was supplying only defensive weapons to Cuba. The Soviets continued their deceptive plans to conceal their actions in Cuba. They repeatedly denied the weapons being brought into Cuba were offensive in nature.

On September 11TH, the Soviet Union publicly warned a United States attack on Cuba or on Soviet ships carrying supplies to the island would mean war. Also on September 11th, the Soviet News Agency TASS announced the Soviet Union had no need or intention to introduce offensive nuclear missiles into Cuba. On October 13th, Soviet Ambassador Dobrynin was questioned by former Undersecretary of State Chester Bowles about whether the Soviets plan to put offensive weapons in Cuba.

He denied any such plans. And again on October 17th, Soviet embassy official Georgy Bolshakov brought President Kennedy a "personal message" from Khrushchev reassuring him *under no circumstances would surface-to-surface missiles be sent to Cuba.*"

As early as August 1962, the United States suspected the Soviets of building missiles facilities in Cuba. During that month, its intelligence services gathered information about sightings by ground observers of Russian-built MiG-21 fighters and Il-28 light bombers. U-2 spy planes found S-75 Dvina surface-to-air missile sites at eight different locations. Central Intelligence Agency John McCone was suspicious. On August 10th, he wrote a memo to President Kennedy in which he guessed the Soviets were preparing to introduce ballistic missiles in Cuba. On August 31st, Senator Kenneth Keating warned on the Senate floor the Soviet Union may be constructing a missile base in Cuba. It's possible he received his information from Cuban exiles in Florida.

Air Force General Curtis LeMay presented a pre-invasion bombing plan to President Kennedy in September, while spy flights and minor military harassment from US forces at Guantanamo Bay Naval Base was the subject of continual Cuban diplomatic complaints to the United States government.

The first consignment of R-12 missiles arrived on the night of September 8th, followed by a second on September 16th. The R-12 was the first operational intermediate-range ballistic missile, the first missile ever mass-produced, and the first Soviet missile deployed with thermonuclear warhead. It was a single-stage, road-transportable, surface-launched, storable propellant fueled missile which could deliver a megaton-class nuclear weapon. The Soviet were building nine sites—six for R-12 medium-range missiles with an effective range of 1,200 miles and three for R-14 intermediate-range ballistic missiles with a maximum range of 2,800 miles.

On October 7th, Cuban President Osvaldo Dorticos spoke at the United Nations General Assembly: "*If we are attacked, we will defend ourselves. I repeat we have sufficient means with which to defend ourselves; we have indeed our inevitable weapons, the weapons, which we would have preferred not to acquire, and which we do not wish to employ.*"

The missiles in Cuba allowed the Soviets to effectively target almost the entire continental United States. The planned arsenal was forty missile launchers. The Cuban populace readily noticed the arrival and deployment of the missiles and hundred reports reached Miami. United States intelligence received countless reports, most of which could be dismissed as describing defensive missiles. Only five of the reports concerned the analysts. The reports described large trucks passing through towns at night carrying very long canvas-covered cylindrical objects which could not make turns through towns without backing up and maneuvering. Defensive missiles could make those turns. These reports could not be satisfactorily explained.

Despite the increasing evidence of military build-up on Cuba, no U-2 flights were made over Cuba from September 5th until October 14th. The first problem which caused the pause in reconnaissance flights took place on August 30th. An Air Force Strategic Air Command U-2 flew over Sakhalin Island in the Far East by mistake. The Soviets lodged a protest and the United States apologized. Nine days later, a Taiwanese operated U-2 was lost over western China. US officials were worried one of the Cuban or Soviet SAMs in Cuba might shoot down a CIA U-2, initiating another international incident. At the end of September, Navy reconnaissance aircraft photographed the Soviet ship *Kasimov* with large crates on its deck the size and shape of Il-28 light bombers.

On October 12th the administration decided to transfer the Cuban U-2 reconnaissance missions to the Air Force. In the event another U-2 was shot down, they thought a cover story involving Air Force flights would be easier to explain than CIA flights. There was also some evidence which the Department of Defense and the Air Force lobbied to get responsibility for the Cuban flights. When the reconnaissance missions were re-authorized on October 8th, weather kept the planes grounded. The United States first obtained photographic evidence of the missiles on October 14th when a U-2 flight piloted by Major Richard Heyser took 928 pictures, capturing images of what turned out to be an SS-4 construction site at San Cristobal, Pinar del Rio Province, in western Cuba.

On October 15th, the CIA's National Photographic Intelligence Center reviewed the U-2 photographs and identified objects which they interpreted as medium range ballistic missiles. That evening, the CIA notified the Department of State and at 8:30PM, National Security Adviser McGeorge Bundy elected to wait until morning to tell the president. Secretary of Defense Robert McNamara was briefed at midnight.

The next morning, McGeorge met with President Kennedy and showed him the U-2 photographs and briefed him on the CIA's analysis of the images. At 6:30PM, President Kennedy convened a meeting of the nine members of the National Security Council and five other key advisers, in a group he formally named the Executive Committee of National Security Council (EXCOMM).

The United States had no plan in place because US intelligence had been convinced the Soviets would never install nuclear missiles in Cuba. The EXCOMM quickly discussed several possible courses of action, including:

1. No action.
2. Diplomacy: Use diplomatic pressure to get the Soviet Union to remove the missiles.
3. Warning: Send a message to Castro to warn him of the grave danger he, and Cuba were in.
4. Blockade: Use the United States Navy to block any missiles from arriving in Cuba.
5. Air strike: Use United States Air Force to attack all known missiles sites.
6. Invasion: Full force invasion of Cuba and overthrow of Castro.

"I think a full-scale attack and invasion is the only solution," suggested Air Forces General Curtis LeMay.

"What will be the Soviets reaction to a United States invasion of Cuba?" asked President Kennedy.

"I don't believe they will stop us from conquering Cuba," replied the Air Force general.

"I think you are wrong in your belief, general. If we attack Cuba, then it would signal to the Soviets to go and ahead and attack Berlin. Our allies would look at the United States as trigger-happy cowboys who lost Berlin to the Soviets because we couldn't resolve the Cuban situation in a peaceful manner. No, I think an invasion needs to be our last possible option," said President Kennedy.

On October 18TH, President Kennedy met with Soviet Minister of Foreign Affairs, Andrei Gromyko, who claimed the weapons were for defensive purposes only. Not wanting to expose what he already knew, and wanting to avoid panicking the American public, the President did not reveal he was already aware of the missile build-up.

That evening President Kennedy held another meeting with his military advisors. They once again discussed their options in dealing with the missiles in Cuba. His advisors continued to pressure him into authorizing an air strike and an invasion of Cuba. But he resisted the pressure they were applying on him. After the meeting, he sat at his desk in the Oval Office. He reached into his desk and activated a recording device he used to record his personal thoughts on events he faced in his presidency.

"We held another meeting about the Soviet missiles sighted in Cuba. It would appear that the opinions moved away from an air strike and towards a military blockade of Cuba as the meeting evolved. Former Secretary of State Dean Acheson was an advocate of the air strike. But former Secretary of Defense Robert Lovett is a supporter of the blockade. My National Security Adviser McGeorge Bundy has urged the United States to avoid playing the Soviet game and take no military action at all while waiting for a Soviet response in Berlin. I agreed. There will be no declaration of war but rather a limited blockade for a limited purpose. It's been suggested that I continue with my political speeches to maintain a cover that we are not aware of the missiles in Cuba. I will do this until the weekend," President Kennedy said and then turned off the recorder. He picked up a cigar and lit it. He leaned back in his chair. He continued to sit there in deep thought until late in the night.

By October 19th, frequent U-2 spy flights showed four operational missile sites. As part of the blockade, the US military was put on high alert to enforce the blockade and to be ready to invade Cuba at a moment's notice. The 1st Armored Division was sent to Georgia, and five army divisions were alerted for maximal action. The Strategic Air Command (SAC) distributed its shorter-ranged B-47 Stratojet medium bombers to civilian airports and sent aloft its B-52 Stratofortress heavy bombers.

President John Kennedy secretly recorded his White House meetings in the Oval Office. Very few people were aware of the hidden recording devices situated in certain places throughout the Oval Office. His meeting with his military advisors during the Cuban Missile Crisis was one of those meetings he secretly recorded. One of the meetings he recorded was his meeting with the Joint Chiefs of Staff on October 19, 1962.

"This blockade and political action is almost as bad as the as the appeasement in Munich. I just don't see any other solution except direct military intervention right now," suggested Air Force Chief of Staff General Curtis LeMay.

President Kennedy didn't reply to General LeMay's comment. The Joint Chiefs held their breath as they waited for the president to speak. The Navy, Army, and Marine Corps Chiefs of Staff argued for quick military action of bombing and invading Cuba.

"The Joint Chiefs of Staff have agreed on the air strikes along with the blockade. But I am concerned about the political impact especially on our allies. And it's possible that all the sites will probably not be destroyed during an air strike," suggested Joint Chiefs of Staff Chairman General Maxwell Taylor.

"I think a blockade and political talk would be considered by a lot of our friends and neutrals as being a pretty weak response to this. And I'm sure a lot of our own citizens would feel that way, too. In other words, you're in a pretty bad fix at the present time," suggested General LeMay.

"What did you say?" questioned the young president.

"I said, you're in a pretty bad fix."

"Well, if you haven't noticed, you're in that fix with me, personally," said President Kennedy.

The meeting continued. The president pushed the Chiefs for further information. General LeMay tried to pressure President Kennedy into authorizing a massive attack on Soviet missiles, Cuban air defenses, and all communications systems.

"What do you think the Soviet's reprisal would be if we were to launch an attack?" President Kennedy asked General LeMay.

"Well, sir, I don't believe they would do anything in return if we were to attack them," replied the Air Force general.

"I would have to agree with General LeMay," said Admiral George Anderson.

"You can't be serious. They can't let us take out, I mean after their statements. They can't let us take out their missiles, kill a lot of Russians, and not do . . . not do anything. I mean, what would we do if they attacked us?" asked President Kennedy.

"I am serious. I don't believe the Soviets will strike back at us," said General LeMay.

"Well, it's my belief that we issue an order for air strike on Cuba that the Soviet Union will indeed respond. But it will be against Berlin. The air strike will give the Russians a clear line to take Berlin, the way they took Hungary after the 1956 Suez invasion. I think that an air strike would neutralize the missiles but would likely force the Soviet Union to take Berlin. This leaves me with only one alternative which is to fire nuclear weapons. That is a hell of an alternative to begin a nuclear exchange. I don't think we have any satisfactory alternatives. The thing is this problem isn't just about Cuba, but also Berlin. If it was only Cuba, then it would be easy. But if we do nothing, we will have problems in Berlin anyway, so we have to do something," said President Kennedy.

"Well, Mr. President the blockade and the political talks without accompanying military action will lead to war. I believe the Soviets will not take Berlin if we act in Cuba. But if we don't act in Cuba, then they sure as hell will take Berlin. I just don't see any other solution except direct military intervention right now. We are wasting time, Mr. President," General LeMay argued forcefully.

When the meeting was over, President Kennedy discussed the meeting with his aide and close friend, Dave Powers. "Can you imagine General LeMay saying a thing like that? These brass hats have one great advantage in their favor. If we listen to them, and do what they want us to do, none of us will be alive later to tell them that they were wrong."

CHAPTER 24

---□---

"Change is the law of life. And those who look only
to past or present are certain to miss the future."

John F. Kennedy

Two Operational Plans (OPLAN) were considered. OPLAN 316 envisioned a full invasion of Cuba by Army and Marine units supported by the Navy following Air Force and naval airstrikes. However, Army units in the United States would have had trouble fielding mechanized and logistical assets, while the United States Navy could not supply sufficient amphibious shipping to transport even a modest armored contingent from the Army. OPLAN 312, mainly and Air Force and Navy carrier operation, was designed with enough flexibility to do anything from engaging individual missile sites to providing air support for OPLAN 316's ground forces.

President Kennedy met with members of EXCOMM and other top advisers throughout October 21st, considering two remaining options: an air strike primarily against the Cuban missile sites, or a naval blockade of Cuba. A full-scale invasion was not the administration's first option, but something had to be done. Secretary of Defense McNamara supported the naval blockade as a strong but limited military action which left the United States in control. According to international law a blockade is an act of war, but the Kennedy Administration did not think the Soviet Union would be provoked to attack by a mere blockade. Once President Kennedy learned that an air strike would result in 10,000-20,000 casualties and that another U-2 flight discovered bombers and cruise missiles sites along Cuba's northern shores, he agreed on a naval blockade of Cuba. He requested that the press be informed to hold the story of the missiles in Cuba until he had a chance to address the nation.

On October 22nd at 3:00PM, President Kennedy formally established EXCOMM with National Security Action Memorandum (NSAM) 196. At 5:00PM, he met with Congressional leaders who contentiously opposed a blockade and demanded a stronger response. That night he spoke to nation and revealed for the first time, to the American public, the existence of Soviet missiles in Cuba. He stated:

> "... This Government, as promised, has maintained the closest surveillance of the Soviet Military buildup on the island of Cuba. Within the past week, unmistakable evidence has established the fact that a series of offensive missile sites is now in preparation on that imprisoned island. The purpose of these bases can be none other than to provide a nuclear strike capability against the Western Hemisphere. Upon receiving the first preliminary hard information of this nature last Tuesday morning at 9am, I directed that our surveillance be stepped up. And having now confirmed and completed our evaluation of the evidence and our decision on a course of action, this Government feels obliged to report this new crisis to you in fullest detail . . . The size of this undertaking makes clear that it has been planned for some months. Yet only last month, after I had made clear the distinction between any introduction of ground-to-ground missiles and the existence of defensive anti-aircraft missiles, the Soviet Government publicly stated on September 11th, and I quote, 'the armaments and military equipment sent to Cuba are designed exclusively for defensive purposes,' that, and I quote the Soviet Government, 'there is no need for the Soviet Government to shift its weapons . . . for a retaliatory blow to any other country, for instance Cuba,' and that, and I quoted their government, 'the Soviet Union has so powerful rockers to carry these nuclear warheads that there is no need to search for sites for them beyond the boundaries of the Soviet Union.' That statement was false . . . Neither the United States of America nor the world community of nations can tolerate deliberate deception and offensive threats on the part of any nation, large or small. We no longer live in a world where only the actual firing of weapons represents a sufficient challenge to a nation's security

to constitute maximum peril. Nuclear weapons are so destructive and ballistic missiles so swift, that any substantially increased possibility of their use or any sudden change in their deployment may well be regarded as a definite threat to peace . . . Acting, therefore, in the defense of our own security and of the entire Western Hemisphere . . . I have directed that the following initial steps be taken immediately: First: To halt this offensive buildup, a strict quarantine on all offensive military equipment under shipment to Cuba is being initiated. All ships of any kind bound for Cuba from whatever nation or port will, if found to contain cargoes of offensive weapons, be turned back. This quarantine will be extended, if needed, to other types of cargo and carriers. We are not at this time, however, denying the necessities of life as the Soviets attempted to do in their Berlin blockade of 1948. Second: I have directed the continued and increased close surveillance of Cuba and its military buildup . . . Should these offensive military preparations continue, thus increasing the threat to the hemisphere, further action will be justified. I have directed the Armed Forces to prepare for any eventualities; and I trust that in the interest of both the Cuban people and the Soviet technicians at the sites, the hazards to all concerned in continuing this threat will be recognized. Third: It shall be the policy of this Nation to regard any nuclear missile launched from Cuba against any nation in the Western Hemisphere as an attack by the Soviet Union on the United States, requiring a full retaliatory response upon the Soviet Union. Fourth: As a necessary military precaution, I have reinforced our base at Guantanamo, evacuated today the dependents of our personnel there, and ordered additional military units to be on a standby alert basis. Fifth: We are calling tonight for an immediate meeting of the Organ of Consultation under the Organization of American States, to consider this threat to hemispheric security . . . Sixth: Under the Charter of the United Nations, we are asking tonight that an emergency meeting of the Security Council be convoked without delay to take action against this latest Soviet threat to world peace. Our resolution will call for the prompt dismantling and withdrawal of all offensive weapons in Cuba, under the supervision of U.N. observers, before the quarantine can be lifted. Seventh and finally: I call upon Chairman Khrushchev to halt and eliminate this clandestine, reckless and provocative threat to world peace and to stable relations between our two nations. I call upon him further to abandon this course of world domination, and to join in an historic effort to end the perilous arms race and to transform the history of man. He has an opportunity now to move the world back from the abyss of destruction—by returning to his government's own words that it had no need to station missiles outside its own territory, and withdrawing these weapons from Cuba—by refraining from any action which will widen or deepen the present crisis—and then by participating in a search for peaceful and permanent solutions . . ."

In Moscow, Ambassador Kohler briefed Soviet Premier Khrushchev on the pending blockade and President Kennedy's speech to the nation. Ambassadors around the world gave advance notice to non-Eastern Bloc leaders. Before the speech, United States delegations met with Canadian Prime Minister John Diefenbaker, British Prime Minister Harold Macmillan, West German Chancellor Konrad Adenaur, and French President Charles de Gaulle to brief them on the United States intelligence and their proposed response. All were supported of the US position. During the speech a directive went out to all US forces worldwide placing them on DEFCON 3. The heavy cruiser USS *Newport News* was designated flagship for the quarantine, with the USS *Leary* as *Newport News'* destroyer escort.

On October 23rd, the EXCOMM members met to review the latest intelligence from Cuba and the proclamation and implementation of the quarantine. Attorney General Robert Kennedy grew angry over not discovering the Soviet missiles sooner in Cuba.

"How the hell did we not know about these missiles until now? Jack, this is pretty much the case of the farmer shutting the barn door after the horse has escaped," said Robert Kennedy.

"How are we going to handle the press on this situation in Cuba?" asked President Kennedy.

"Well, I think specific reporters should be briefed by specific EXCOMM members on a strictly off-the-record basis," suggested presidential aide Kenneth O'Donnell.

"You know, that a ship carrying offensive weapons will have to be stopped and perhaps disabled," suggested Secretary of Defense McNamara.

"I don't think it will come to that. I think the Soviets will likely turn around such ships on their own to avoid a confrontation," said President Kennedy.

"Can we get back to my question? Why didn't we know about these missiles sooner? How did we let this happen?" asked an irritated Robert.

"Bobby, the only way the placement of the missiles could have been prevented would have been by invading Cuba six months or one, two or even three years ago. What we are doing is throwing down a card on the table in a game which we don't know the ending of," replied President Kennedy.

"We need to have plans ready for destroying any SAM site which shoots down a U-2 spy plane," suggested Secretary of Defense McNamara.

"I agree, and that same time when we take out the SAM site the United States should announce that if another plane is brought down all the SAM sites will be destroyed," said the young president.

"Mr. President, may I suggest that you delegate the authority to order an air strike against a SAM to Secretary of Defense McNamara," requested McGeorge Bundy.

"Ok, but there must be absolute verification that the plane was brought down by hostile military action and not the result of an accident," said President Kennedy.

A cable drafted by George Ball, on October 23rd, was sent to the US Ambassador in Turkey and the US Ambassador to NATO which notified them that they were considering making an offer to withdraw what the United States knew to be nearly obsolete missiles from Italy and Turkey in exchange for the Soviet's withdrawal of missiles in Cuba. Turkish officials replied that they would resent any trade offer which involved the removal of the US missile stationed in their country. Two days later, on the morning of October 25th, journalist Walter Lippmann proposed the same thing in his syndicated column. Fidel Castro reaffirmed Cuba's right to self-defense and said that all of its weapons were defensive and Cuba would not allow an inspection.

Three days after President Kennedy's speech, the Chinese *People's Daily* announced that about 650,000,000 Chinese men and women were standing by Cuba. In Germany, newspapers supported the United States' response, contrasting it with the weak American action in the region during the preceding months. They also expressed some fear that the Soviets might strike back against Berlin. In France the crisis made the front page of all the daily newspaper. On October 24th, an editorial in *Le Monde* expressed doubt concerning the CIA's photographic evidence of the missile sites. Two days later, they accepted the photographic proof of the missiles; after a visit by a high-ranking CIA agent.

On the morning of October 24th, Robert Kennedy and President Kennedy sat in the Oval Office alone. They were waiting on the start of the next EXCOMM meeting. They discussed the strategic situation in Cuba and its political implications.

"Jack, General Lucius Clay has offered to return to Berlin. But I think it would be a bad idea to concentrate on Berlin at this time," said Robert.

"You're right. Tell General Taylor to tell General Clay to stand by for the next few days, but not to go at this moment. I wonder what would have happened to me if I had taken immediate action in response to the Soviet missiles in Cuba."

"I think there would have been no choice. You would have been impeached," answered Robert.

"That's what I think. I would have been impeached."

"You could not have done less and your judgment is now supported by our allies," said Robert.

A few minutes later the rest of the members of EXCOMM entered the Oval Office for the scheduled meeting. They continued to review the impact of latest intelligence on the quarantine, world reaction, negotiations at the United Nations and possible developments in Berlin. After reviewing new reconnaissance photos of Cuba, they began discussing the need of dispersing planes at Florida bases in the event of attacks by MiGs based in Cuba.

"This quarantine can be a dangerous situation," commented Robert McNamara.

"What do you mean?" asked President Kennedy.

"Well, these Soviet ships which are traveling to Cuba, you can be sure, will be shadowed by Soviet submarines. And I am almost certain that these subs will have nuclear-tipped torpedoes onboard," replied the Secretary of Defense.

"Well, what will happen if a US destroyer tried to board and search a ship and is then sunk by a Soviet submarine?" When no one answered him, the president said, "I think we ought to wait on boarding today. We don't want to have the first thing we attack a Soviet sub. I'd much rather have it being a merchant ship. I also think we should put Russian speaking personnel on all the ships at the quarantine line."

"That has already been done," said McGeorge.

"The latest intelligence suggests that many Soviet ships are turning around," said General Taylor.

"It seems to me we want to give that ship a chance to turn around. We don't want the word to go out from Moscow to turn around and then suddenly we sink their ship. So I would think we ought to wait to see if the ship continues on its course in view of this other intelligence," said President Kennedy.

On the evening of October 24th, the Soviet news agency Telgrafnoe Agentstvo Sovetskogo Soyuza (TASS) broadcast a telegram from Soviet Premier Khrushchev to President Kennedy, in which he warned that the United States' pirate action would lead to war. This telegram was followed by a telegram from the Soviet leader to the American president in which Soviet Premier Khrushchev stated, "*If you coolly weigh the situation which has developed, not giving way to passions, you will understand that the Soviet Union cannot fail to reject the arbitrary demands of the United States*" and that the Soviet Union views the blockade as "*an aggression*" and their ships will be instructed to ignore it.

Also on October 24th at 5:00pm, President Kennedy met with the Congressional leaders. They discussed the using of intelligence data in public briefings. They reviewed potential implications of actions in and near Cuba on the status Berlin.

"I think we should discuss the uncertainty of the Soviets about how this will play out due to the intense reaction of the United States. I want to bring to your attention a statement from Khrushchev in which he stated that the USSR will not take rash steps despite 'unjustified' actions by the United States," said Secretary Dean Rusk.

"Khrushchev has made a public request for a summit with the United States to find a solution to this crisis," said Senate minority leader Everett Dirksen.

"I think a summit at this time would be useless," said President Kennedy.

The United States requested an emergency meeting of the United Nations Security Council on October 25th. During this meeting UN Ambassador Adlai Stevenson, in a loud resounding voice, confronted Soviet Ambassador Valerian Zorin. Ambassador Stevenson tried to persuade the Soviet Ambassador to admit the existence of Soviet missiles in Cuba. But Soviet Ambassador Zorin refused to answer. The next day at 10:00 pm, the United States raised the readiness level of SAC forces to DEFCON 2. B-52 bombers were sent to different locations and were ready to take off on fifteen minutes notice. One-eighth of SAC's 1,436 bombers were put on airborne alert, 145 intercontinental ballistic missiles stood on ready alert. Air Defense Command (ADC) redeployed 161 nuclear-armed interceptors to 16 dispersal fields within nine hours with one-third maintaining 15-minute alert status. Twenty-three nuclear-armed B-52s were sent to orbit points within striking distance of the Soviet Union. The movement of these B-52s was to prove to the Soviet Union that the United States was serious about the missile sites in Cuba.

By October 22nd, Tactical Air Command (TAC) had 511 fighters with supporting tanks and recon aircraft deployed to face Cuba on a one hour alert status. TAC and the Military Air Transport Service had some problems. The concentration of aircraft in Florida strained command and support echelons. They faced critical low personnel in security, armaments, and communications. The absence of initial authorization for war reserve stocks of conventional munitions forced TAC to search for extra munitions. The lack of airlifts assets to support a major airborne drop necessitated the call-up of 24 Reserve squadrons.

October 25th, President Kennedy responded to Premier Khrushchev's telegram, stating that the United States was forced into action after receiving repeated assurances that no offensive missiles were being placed in Cuba, and that when these assurances proved to be false, the deployment required responses "*I have announced . . . I hope that your government will take necessary action to permit a restoration of the earlier situation.*"

At 10:00am on October 25th, the EXCOMM met to discuss the movement of *Bucharest* and other Soviet ships towards the quarantine and possible United States response.

"What happened with the Soviet ship *Bucharest*?" asked President Kennedy.

"Well, it was hailed and it was determined that it was not carrying prohibited items. It is being shadowed by a US destroyer. We must decide whether or not the ship should be boarded. I recommend establishing a pattern of aerial surveillance which would look like an air attack so that surprise could be maintained as long as possible if an attack is eventually ordered," said Secretary of Defense McNamara.

"If we let the *Bucharest* pass through the quarantine, then what will be the political ramifications? I think it might be worth giving the Soviets sufficient grace to get its instruction clear or for the United Nations to reach an agreement. The whole problem is to make a judgment based on Khrushchev's message to me last night and the efforts at the UN. What impression will they get if we let the *Bucharest* through the quarantine? What is the advantage of letting this one pass?" asked President Kennedy.

"I think the advantage is to avoid a shooting incident over a ship that is not carrying offensive weapons. I don't think we have weakened the forceful position that will lead to removal of the missile by letting the *Bucharest* through the quarantine," replied the secretary of defense.

"I think the quarantine has already been successful since the Soviet Union has already turned back fourteen ships presumably carrying offensive weapons. But, we have got to face up to the fact we're going to have to grab a Russian ship. We just need to decide whether it is better for that to be today or tomorrow," said President Kennedy.

"There is nothing in your speech requires you to stop any ship, even if it is found to contain offensive cargo we deem unacceptable. The way in which we define this is our business," said McGeorge Bundy.

"We also need to decide when is the right time to lift the quarantine," said Robert McNamara.

"I think we could lift the quarantine if the UN provides guarantees that no new offensive weapons would be introduced. I think that would make us seem less negative than if we say we don't lift under any circumstances," said President Kennedy.

"I think the real issue is the removal of existing missiles not the introduction of new ones. I believe the quarantine shouldn't be lifted without removal of the missiles," said Secretary of Defense McNamara.

"The plan being discussed at UN would put UN guarantees against new missiles into place as a substitute for the quarantine for only 2-3 weeks while negotiations continue for a permanent solution involving complete removal," said Secretary of State Dean Rusk.

"I don't see any way to get those weapons out of Cuba, never have thought we would get them out of Cuba, without the application of substantial force. The force we can apply is economic force and military force," said the secretary of defense.

"Well, this UN proposal puts us in a reasonable stance," said the president.

"I have read Khrushchev's letter from October 24th and I think the Soviet Union is preparing for a resistance by force—that is—forcing us to take forceful action," said former ambassador to Moscow Llewellyn Thompson.

"What will we do in the next 24 hours if there is no Soviet ship carrying offensive weapons which can be intercepted and construction of the missile sites also continues. I recommend spending the rest of the day planning the escalation of the quarantine," said Robert McNamara.

"Well, the purpose of the quarantine is not to stop the delivery of the weapons since they are already there. I fear that we will have a showdown with the Russians of one kind or another. We don't want to precipitate an incident. This is not the appropriate time to blow up a ship," said President Kennedy.

Later that day, at 5:43 pm, the commander of the blockade effort ordered the USS *Kennedy* to intercept and board the Lebanese freighter *Marucla*. This took place the next day, and the *Marucla* was cleared through the blockade after its cargo was checked. At 5:00 pm, William Clements announced that the missiles in Cuba were still actively being installed. A CIA report verified there had been no slow down on the missile installation. In response, President Kennedy issued Security Action Memorandum 199, which authorized the loading of nuclear weapons onto aircrafts under the command of SACEUR, which had the duty of carrying out first air strikes against the Soviet Union. During the day, the Soviets responded to the blockade by turning back 14 ships presumably carrying offensive weapons.

The next morning, the members of the EXCOMM informed President Kennedy they believed only an invasion would remove the missiles in Cuba. But he persuaded them to give the matter more time and continued with both military and diplomatic pressure. They agreed and he ordered the low-level flights over the island to be increased from two per day to once every two hours. He also ordered a crash program to institute a new civil government in Cuba if an invasion went ahead. At this point, the crisis was unfortunately at a stalemate. The Soviet Union had shown no indication that they would back down and had made several comments to the contrary. The United States had no reason to believe otherwise and was in the early stages of preparing for an invasion, along with a nuclear strike on the Soviet Union in case it responded with its military. And a military response by the Soviet Union was deeply assumed by the United States.

CHAPTER 25

—□—

"Let us never negotiate out of fear
but let us never fear to negotiate"

John F. Kennedy

On October 26th at 1:00pm, John Scali of ABC News had lunch with Aleksandr Fomin at Fomin's request.

"It appears that war between our countries is about break out," commented Aleksandr.

"It would appear so. I don't think President Kennedy is going to back off from an invasion of Cuba."

"Well, a war is the last thing we want. Could you use your contacts to talk to your high-level friends at the State Department to see if the United States would be interested in a diplomatic solution?" asked Aleksandr.

"Really, well, your men are the one who started installing missiles in Cuba. But that seems to be beside the point. What are you suggesting?"

"Maybe the language of the deal from Soviet Union would contain an assurance from us to remove from the missiles under an UN inspection and that Castro would publicly announce that he would not accept such weapons in the future," suggested Aleksandr.

"What do you want from us?"

"We want a public announcement from President Kennedy stating the United States will never invade Cuba," said Aleksandr.

"I will see what I can do," said John Scali.

The United States responded by asking the Brazilian government to pass a message to Fidel Castro that they would be unlikely to invade if the missiles were removed. At 6:00pm, the State Department started receiving a message which appeared to be written personally by Soviet Premier

Khrushchev. The long letter took several minutes to arrive, and it took translators additional time to translate and transcribe it. It read in part:

> *"Mr. President, we and you ought not now to pull on the ends of the rope in which you have tied the knot of war, because the more the two of us pull, the tighter that knot will be tied. And a moment may come when that knot will be tied so tight that even he who tied it will not have the strength to untie it, and then it will be necessary to cut that knot, and what that would mean is not for me to explain to you, because you yourself understand perfectly of what terrible forces our countries dispose. Consequently, if there is no intention to tighten that knot and thereby to doom the world to the catastrophe of thermonuclear war, then let us not only relax the forces pulling on the ends of the rope, let us take measures to untie that knot. We are ready for this . . ."*

Attorney General Robert Kennedy described the letter as very long and emotional. The Soviet Premier stressed the basic outline which had been stated to John Scali earlier that day. *"I propose: we, for our part, will declare that our ships bound for Cuba are not carrying any armaments. You will declare that the United States will not invade Cuba with its troops and will not support any other forces which might intend to invade Cuba. Then the necessity of the presence of our military specialists in Cuba will disappear."* At 6:45 pm, the report of Aleksandr Fomin's offer to John Scali was heard. It was decided the offer was to serve as an introduction to Premier Khrushchev's letter. The letter was considered official and accurate.

Che Guevara considered a direct aggression towards Cuba by the United States would mean nuclear war. He felt the United States would lose a nuclear war. Fidel Castro was convinced an invasion of Cuba by the United States was soon at hand. On October 26th, he sent a telegram to Premier Khrushchev which appeared to call for a pre-emptive nuclear strike on the United States. He also ordered all anti-aircraft weapons in Cuba to fire on any US aircraft. In the past they had been ordered only to fire on groups of two or more US aircraft.

At 6:00am on October 27th, the CIA delivered a memo reporting three of the four missiles sites at San Cristobal and the two sites at Sagua la Grande appeared to be fully operational. They also reported the Cuban military continued to organize for action, although they were under order not to initiate action unless attacked. At 9:00am, Radio Moscow began broadcasting a message from Soviet Premier Khrushchev. Contrary to the letter of the night before, the message offered a new trade, that the missiles in Cuba would be removed in exchange for the removal of the Jupiter missiles from Italy and Turkey. At 10:00am, the executive committee met again to discuss the situation and came to the conclusion that the change in the message was due to internal debate between Premier Khrushchev and other party officials in the Kremlin. Secretary of Defense Robert McNamara noted in the meeting that another tanker, *Grozny*, was about 600 miles out and should be intercepted. He explained that the United States had not made the Soviet Union aware of the blockade line and suggested relaying this information to them through U Thant at the United Nations. At 11:03am, a new message began to arrive from Premier Khrushchev. The message read in part:

> "*You are disturbed over Cuba. You say that this disturbs you because it is ninety-nine miles by sea from the coast of the United States of America. But . . . you have placed destructive missiles weapons, which you call offensive, in Italy and Turkey, literally next to us . . . I therefore make this proposal: We are willing to remove from Cuba the means which you regard as offensive . . . Your representatives will make a declaration to the effect that the United States . . . will remove its analogous means from Turkey . . . and after that, persons entrusted by the United Nations Security Council could inspect on the spot the fulfillment of the pledges made . . .*"

Throughout the crisis, Turkey had repeatedly stated that it would be upset if the Jupiter missiles were removed. Italy's Prime Minister Fanfani offered allow withdrawal of the missiles deployed in Apulia as a bargaining chip. The Soviets were not aware the US regarded the Jupiter missiles as obsolete and already supplanted by the Polaris nuclear ballistics submarine missiles.

On the morning of October 27th, a U-2F piloted by USAF Major Rudolf Anderson departed its forward operating location at McCoy AFB, Florida, and at approximately 12:00pm. The aircraft was struck by an S-75 Divina SAM missile launched from Cuba. The aircraft was shot down and Anderson was killed. The stress in negotiations between the

US and the USSR intensified, and only much later was it learned that the decision to fire the missile was made locally by an undetermined Soviet commander. Later that day, at about 3:41pm, several US Navy RF-8A Crusader aircraft on low-level photoreconnaissance missions were fired upon, and one was hit by a 37 mm shell but managed to return to base. At 4:00 pm, President Kennedy recalled members of EXCOMM to the White House and ordered that a message immediately be sent to U Thant asking the Soviets to stop work on the missiles while negotiations were carried out. During this meeting, General Maxwell Taylor delivered the news that the U-2 had been shot down. President Kennedy had stated earlier he would order an attack on such sites if fire upon, but he decided not to act unless another attack was made.

Emissaries sent by both President Kennedy and Soviet Premier Khrushchev agreed to meet at the Yenching Palace Chinese restaurant in the Cleveland Park neighborhood of Washington, D.C. on the evening of October 27th. President Kennedy suggested that they take the Soviet Premier's offer to trade away the missiles. Unknown to most members of EXCOMM, Robert Kennedy had been meeting with the Soviet Ambassador in Washington to discover whether or not these intentions were true. The EXCOMM was generally against the proposal because it would undermine NATO's authority, and the Turkish government had repeatedly stated it was against any such deal. As the meeting progressed, a new plan emerged and President Kennedy was slowly persuaded. The new plan called for him to ignore the latest message and instead to return to Premier Khrushchev's earlier one. He was hesitant at first. He felt the Soviet leader would no longer accept the deal because a new one had been offered. Llewellyn Thompson argued that Premier Khrushchev might accept it anyway. White House Special Counselor and Advisor Ted Sorenson and Robert Kennedy left the meeting and returned 45 minutes later with a draft letter to this effect. President Kennedy made several changes, had it typed and sent it.

After the EXCOMM meeting, a smaller meeting continued in the Oval Office. The group argued that the letter should be underscored with an oral message to Ambassador Dobrynin stating that if the missiles were not withdrawn, military action would be used to remove them. Secretary of State Dean Rusk added one proviso, that no part of the language of the deal would mention Turkey, but there would be an understanding that the missiles would be removed voluntarily in the immediate aftermath. President Kennedy agreed and the message was sent.

Aleksandr Fomin and John Scali met once more.

"Why were the two letters from Premier Khrushchev so different?

"They were different because of poor communications."

"Poor communications? Your claim isn't very credible. We believe it is a stinking double cross. I am here to tell you that an invasion of Cuba is only hours away," suggested John.

"It wasn't a double cross. I was instructed to tell you that a response to the United States message from Chairman Khrushchev was expected shortly. Please tell your States Department that no treachery was intended on our part."

"I'm not sure anyone at the State Department would believe me. But I will deliver your message to the appropriate people," said John.

Within the US establishment, it was well understood that ignoring the second offer and returning to the first one put the Soviet Premier in a bad position. Military preparations continued and all active duty Air Force personnel were recalled to their bases for possible actions. The letter drafted earlier that day was delivered around 8 pm. It read in part:

> "*As I read your letter, the key elements of your proposals—which seemed generally acceptable as I understand them—are as follows: 1) You would agree to remove these weapons systems from Cuba under appropriate United Nations observation and supervision; and undertake with suitable safe-guards, to halt the further introductions of such weapons systems into Cuba. 2) We, on our part, would agree—upon the establishment of adequate arrangements through the United Nations, to ensure the carrying out and continuation of these commitments (a) to remove promptly the quarantine measures now in effect and (b) to give assurances against the invasion of Cuba.*" The letter was also released directly to the press to ensure it would not be delayed.

With the letter delivered, a deal was on the table. The Kennedy Administration had little expectation the deal would be accepted. Plans were drawn up for air strikes on the missile sites as well as other economic targets. At 12:12am on October 27th, the United States informed its NATO allies that "*the situation was growing shorter . . . the United States may find it necessary within a very short time in its interest and that of its fellow nations in the Western Hemisphere to take whatever military action may be necessary*" A report from the CIA, that morning, that all the missiles in Cuba were now ready for action added stress in the White House.

Later that day, the US Navy dropped a series of depth charges on a Soviet submarine at the blockade line. They were not aware the sub was armed with a nuclear-tipped torpedo with orders which allowed it to be used if the submarine was damaged in the hull by depth charges or surface fire. On that same day, A U-2 spy plane made an accidental, unauthorized ninety minute over flight of the Soviet Union's eastern coast. The Soviets scrambled MiG fighters from Wrangel Island and in response the Americans sent F-102 fighters armed with nuclear air-to-air missiles over the Bering Sea.

After much deliberation between the Soviet Union and the United States, President Kennedy secretly agreed to remove all missiles set in southern Italy and in Turkey in exchange Soviet Premier Khrushchev removing all missiles in Cuba.

At 9am on October 28th, a new message from Premier Khrushchev was broadcasted on Radio Moscow. He stated, "*the Soviet government, in addition to previously issued instructions on the cessation of further work at the building sites for the weapons, has issued a new order on the dismantling of the weapons which you describe as offensive and their crating and return to the Soviet Union.*"

President Kennedy immediately responded, issuing a statement calling the letter "*an important and constructive contribution to peace.*" He continued this in a formal letter which read in part:

> "*I consider my letter to you of October twenty-seventh and your reply of today as firm undertakings on the part of both our governments which should be promptly carried out . . . The US will make a statement in the framework of the Security Council in reference to Cuba as follows: it will declare that the United States of America will respect the inviolability of Cuban borders and not permit our territory to be used as a bridgehead for the invasion of Cuba, and will restrain those who would plan to carry*

an aggression against Cuba, either from US territory or from the
territory of other countries neighboring to Cuba."

The Soviet publicly balked at the United States demands, but in secret back-channel communications initiated a proposal to resolve the crisis. The confrontation ended on October 28, 1962, when President Kennedy and United Nations Secretary General U Thant reached a public and secret agreement with Premier Khrushchev. Publicly, the Soviets would dismantle their offensive weapons in Cuba and return them to the Soviet Union, subject to United Nations verification, in exchange for a United States public declaration and agreement never to invade Cuba. Secretly, the U.S. agreed it would dismantle all United States built Thor and Jupiter IRBMs deployed in Europe and Turkey.

Only two weeks after the agreement, the Soviets had removed the missile systems and their support equipment, loading them onto eight Soviet ships from November 5-9. A month later, on December 5 and 6, the Soviet Il-28 bombers were loaded onto three Soviet ships and shipped back to Russia. The quarantine was formally over on November 20, 1962. Eleven months after the agreement, all American weapons were deactivated by September 1963. An additional outcome of the negotiations was the creation of the Hotline Agreement and the Moscow-Washington hotline, a direct communications link between Moscow and Washington, D.C.

One has to wonder how the Cuban Missile Crisis would have ended if Attorney General Robert Kennedy hadn't intervened. There was no doubt he played a vital role in helping President Kennedy reach a peaceful solution in the missile crisis. Secretly Robert met privately with Soviet Ambassador Anatoly Dobrynin.

> *"The President is in a grave situation and he does not know*
> *how to get out of it. We are under severe stress. In fact we are under*
> *pressure from our military to use force against Cuba. We want*
> *to ask you, Mr. Dobrynin, to pass President Kennedy's message*
> *to Chairman Khrushchev through unofficial channels. Even*
> *though the President himself is very much against starting a war*
> *over Cuba, an irreversible chain of events could occur against his*
> *will. That is why the President is appealing directly to Chairman*
> *Khrushchev for his help in liquidating this conflict. If the situation*

continues much longer, the President is not sure the military will not overthrow him and seize power," Robert told Soviet Ambassador Anatoly Dobrynin.

It's never been proven the meeting between Robert Kennedy and the Soviet ambassador was what ended the missile crisis. But it wasn't long after that meeting the Soviet Premier made the startling announcement he was withdrawing the missiles from Cuba.

What especially moved Soviet Premier Khrushchev to help President Kennedy by withdrawing the Soviet missiles from Cuba was Ambassador Anatoly Dobrynin's description of his meeting with Attorney General Robert Kennedy. The president's brother was exhausted. Dobrynin could see from Robert Kennedy's eyes he hadn't slept for days. Robert told him the president *"didn't know how to resolve the situation. The military is putting great pressure on him, insisting on military actions against Cuba and the President is in a very difficult position . . . Even if he doesn't want or desire a war, something irreversible could occur against his will. That is why the President is asking for help to solve this problem."*

Once again President Kennedy's action appeared weak in the eyes of the CIA and his military advisers. They believed the United States had the perfect chance to invade Cuba and continue the "Cold War". What they didn't know was the stipulation of the missile withdrawal left them an open invitation to invade Cuba. Soviet Premier Khruschev agreed to remove the missiles if President Kennedy agreed not to invade Cuba. President Kennedy agreed not to invade Cuba as long as Fidel Castro would agree to a United Nations inspection of the missile sites. If Castro didn't agree to the inspection, then the agreement not to invade Cuba would be void. And of course Castro refused to allow the UN inspectors in Cuba.

CHAPTER 26

─────────■─────────

"If a freed society cannot help the many who are poor,
it cannot save the few who are rich."

John F. Kennedy

One month after the Cuban Missile Crisis, the Joint Chiefs of Staff pushed for a buildup in United States strategic forces to a disarming first-strike capability. On November 20, 1962, they sent a memorandum to Secretary of Defense Robert McNamara stating: "The Joint Chiefs of Staff consider that a first-strike capability is both feasible and desirable . . ."

Robert, reflecting what he knew was President John Kennedy's position, wrote the president on the same day about the challenge they faced. He wrote:

> *"It has become clear to me that the Air Force proposals, both for the RS-70 [Bomber] and for the rest of their Strategic Retaliatory Forces, are based on the objective of achieving first-strike capability."*

He told President Kennedy what was at issue with the Air Force was whether United States forces should attempt to achieve a capability to start a thermonuclear war in which the resulting damage to ourselves and our Allies could be consider acceptable on some reasonable definition of the term. The secretary of defense said he believed a first-strike capability should be rejected as a U.S. policy objective, and the United States should not augment its forces for a first-strike capability.

In the fall of 1962, Edward Becker, who was a private investigator, met with Carlos Marcello and his longtime associates. Carlos pulled out an expensive bottle of scotch and poured a round of scotch. The conversation wandered on different subjects for a few hours.

"That Robert Kennedy really messed up when he had you deported, huh?" asked Edward.

"Livarsi na pietra di la scarpa!" Carlos exclaimed as he jumped to his feet. This was an old Sicilian oath meaning "*Take the stone out of my shoe!*" Edward looked at his friend for a moment.

"Don't worry about that Robert. He's going to be taken care of," claimed the Mafia boss.

"If you are talking about killing Robert Kennedy, then you are out of your mind. If you have the United States Attorney General murdered, then you would be in a hell of a lot of trouble," said Edward.

"I am not talking about killing Bobby. If you cut off the tail of a dog it will still bite you. But if you get the head off then it will cease to bother you," remarked Carlos Marcello.

Edward realized his friend was referring to Bobby as the tail and the president as the head of the dog. Meaning if he had Bobby killed then President Kennedy would come after him. But if he had President Kennedy killed, then Bobby would lose his power to come after the Mafia. Carlos quickly changed the subject. The Kennedy brothers were never mentioned again.

Deputy Director of Plans Richard Helms walked into his living room. He wanted this meeting to take place away from Langley. He chose the privacy of his home. This meeting, in his opinion dealt with the National Security of the United States. He stepped through the living room into his dining room. He took his place at the head of the table.

"I am glad everyone was able to make it tonight," said Richard.

"Has this covert operation been given a go?" asked Air Force General Curtis LeMay.

"Yes, it has. President Kennedy needs to be removed," replied Richard.

"Who all knows about this operation?" asked Colonel Edward Lansdale.

"Just the people sitting at this table knows," answered Richard.

"Good, the less that knows, better the chance we will have containing any possible leaks," said Colonel Lansdale.

"That's what I am thinking," said Richard.

"Where will it take place? I think outside the United States would be best," suggested General LeMay.

"Well, with the presence of Santo Trafficante, Sam Giancana, Johnny Roselli, and Carlos Marcello should tell you we have narrowed it down to 3 locations; Chicago, Tampa Bay, and Dallas. Once we have decided we will let you know," answered Richard.

"Why these three locations?" asked General LeMay.

"Because these three cities are controlled by these men. It will be easier to control what the local authorities investigates," said Richard.

"I think we should provide the snipers," said Sam.

"The thought hadn't crossed my mind. But that's a good idea so none of our agents will be implicated in the hit," said Richard.

"Actually that wasn't my thinking at all. I want us the provide the snipers because I know they won't miss," said Sam.

"Also, I think a patsy, a fall guy, should be used to avoid any of our guys being implicated in the assassination," suggested Carlos.

"That idea has already been put into motion," said Richard. "Well, if no one has any questions that will be for now"

Richard stood to his feet. He watched as everyone left and he sat down at the table once more. He heard a door opened and he listened as someone made their way to the dining room. He didn't have to look to see who it was. He was expecting this visit. He didn't say a word as Vice-President Lyndon B. Johnson sat at his table.

"I want the coup d'état to take place in Texas," said Lyndon.

"Fine. We will need to find a way to satisfy Sam and Santo."

"Leave that to me," said Lyndon.

In the fall of 1962, New York lawyer James Donovan secretly represented President Kennedy and Robert Kennedy in negotiations with Fidel Castro for the release of the Bay of Pigs prisoners. During these negotiations, James and Castro became friends. He made a return trip to Cuba in January 1963. Rene Vallejo, Castro's aide and physician raised a new possibility which James reported to United States intelligence officials.

"What do you think about re-establishing diplomatic relations between Cuba and the United States?" Rene asked James Donovan as he about to board his flight back to the United States.

"I think it would worth discussing further with the president."

"Why don't you see about returning to Cuba. We can discuss the future of Cuba and international relations in general," Rene offered him.

President Kennedy took careful note of this development and tried to smooth the way for further dialogue with Castro. In a March 14, 1962 memorandum, Robert Kennedy unsuccessfully urged the president to move against Castro: "*I would not like it said a year from now that we could have had this internal breakup in Cuba but we just did not set the stage for it.*" When he didn't receive a response from the president, on March 26th he wrote his brother once again in frustration: "*Do you think there was any merit to my last memo? . . . In any case, is there anything further on this matter?*" While President Kennedy was being silent towards his brother's queries on anti-Castro schemes, he himself was turning towards a new approach to Castro.

On March 19th, the CIA sponsored Cuban exile group Alpha 66 announced at a Washington press conference it had raided a Soviet "fortress" and ship in Cuba, causing a dozen casualties and serious damage. Alpha 66 was one of the commando teams maintained by the giant CIA station in Miami, "JM/WAVE," for its attacks on Cuba. Alpha 66 exile leader Antonio Veciana claimed the purpose of the CIA-initiated attack on the Soviet vessel in Cuban waters was to publicly embarrass President Kennedy and force him to move against Castro. Antonio's CIA adviser was a man who used the cover name "Maurice Bishop." Antonio claimed "*Bishop kept saying President Kennedy would have to be forced to make a decision, and the only way was to put him up against the wall.*" So Maurice targeted Soviet ships to create another Soviet-American crisis.

The Alpha 66 raid was only the beginning. It was followed up eight days later by another Cuban exile attack which damaged a Soviet freighter in a Cuban port. The JM/WAVE chief of operations coordinating these efforts to force President Kennedy's hand against Castro was the CIA's David Sanchez Morales, a longtime co-worker of David Atlee Bishop.

The Cuban exile attacks prompted a Soviet protest in Washington. Premier Khruschev naturally held President Kennedy responsible for refugee gunboats which the CIA was running out of Miami. The CIA's tactic was forcing the president to choose between the militant Cold War politics of a Miami exile community manipulated by the CIA and the almost indefinable politics which President Kennedy was developing with the Soviet Premier. Instead of backing Alpha 66, he ordered a government crackdown on all Miami exile raids into Cuba. In doing so, he enlisted the help of his brother.

On March 31st, Robert Kennedy's Justice Department took its first step in implementing a policy of preventing Cuba refugees from using United States territory to organize or launch raids against Cuba. The Justice Department ordered eighteen Cubans in the Miami area, who were already involved in raids, to confine their movements to Dade County under the threat of arrest or deportation. One of them was Alpha 66 leader Antonio Veciana. Within a week, the Coast Guard in Florida, working in concert with British officials in the Bahamas, seized a series of Cuban rebel boats and arrested their commando groups before they could attack Soviet ships near Cuba.

By enforcing President Kennedy's new policy, the Justice Department and the Coast Guard were restraining a covert arm of the Central Intelligence Agency from drawing the United States into a war with Cuba. Premier Fidel Castro responded with evident surprise by saying President Kennedy's curtailment of the hit-and-run raids was "a step forward toward reduction of the dangers of crisis and war." The Florida refugee groups subsidized by the CIA exploded with bitterness charging the Kennedy Administration with engaging in "coexistence" with the Castro regime.

While the United States and British forces continued to round up anti-Castro rebels and boats, Dr. Jose Miro Cardona resigned in protest to the shift in the US policy. Dr. Cardona was the head of the Cuban Revolutionary Council (CRC). The CRC had been created by the US government prior to the Bay of Pigs as a provisional Cuban government to seize power when Castro was overthrown. It also served as an umbrella organization for the variety of Miami exile groups.

With rebel raiders under arrest and government funding for exile army suddenly drying up, forcing them to disperse, Dr. Cardona saw the handwriting on the wall and the initials beneath it was: "JFK". The Florida exile community united behind Dr. Cardona and against the president whom they now saw as an ally of Castro.

CHAPTER 27

"Those who make peaceful revolution impossible
will make violent revolution inevitable"

John F. Kennedy

In Dallas Lee Harvey Oswald accepted a job with the Leslie Welding Company but disliked the work and quit after three months. He then found a position at the graphic arts firm of Jaggars-Chiles-Stovall as a photo print trainee. The company had been cited as doing classified work for the United States government which included typesetting for maps. He used the photographic and typesetting equipment to create falsified identification documents, including some in the name of an alias he created, Alex J. Hidell. His co-workers and supervisors eventually grew frustrated with his inefficiency, lack of precision, inattention and rudeness to others. His rudeness had reached the point where fistfights had threatened to break out. After six months his supervisor finally terminated him after seeing him reading a Russian magazine (*Krokodil*) in the cafeteria. Shortly after losing his job, Lee's CIA handler, James Smith, had a meeting with his superior, David Atlee Phillips. They discussed Lee's future with the Central Intelligence Agency.

"How is it possible your agent keeps losing jobs the Agency set up for him?" asked David.

"I don't know."

"I don't think he is fit to be an agent for the CIA anymore. He has become a liability now," stated David.

"Well, what do you suggest we do?"

"We have to remove him," said David.

"What do you have in mind?"

"General Edwin Walker is making a little too much noise in Dallas. I want you to attempt to assassinate him and lay the blame at Lee's feet."

"How do you want it done?" asked James.

"While Lee was working at Jaggars-Chiles-Stovall he created a fake identification in the name of Alex J. Hidell."

"Really? He used my cover name? What the hell is he planning?" asked James.

"I don't know. But you need to use it against him. I want you to mail order a revolver and a rifle in that fake name. Your choice in what type of guns. Make sure the rifle and revolver is delivered at Lee's post office box. Then I want you to attempt to assassinate General Walker and stash the rifle and revolver in Lee's house."

"Twice you said 'attempt to assassinate'. Are you not ordering a hit on General Walker?" questioned James.

"No, this isn't about the retired general. Lee can't shoot worth a damn, so if you actually shoot and kill General Walker, then it might be a hard sell that Lee shot him. You have to miss to make it appear Lee pulled the trigger. I am told that the CIA is working on a covert operation which may need a fall guy. He has been tapped as that fall guy."

"I will make it happen," James stood to his feet and walked out of David's office.

General Edwin Walker was an outspoken anti-communist, segregationist and a member of the John Birch Society. He had been the commanding officer of the Army's 24th Infantry Division based in West Germany under NATO supreme command. He was relieved of his command in 1961 by President Kennedy for distributing right-wing literature to his troops. General Walker resigned from the service and returned to his native Texas. General Walker ran in the six person Democratic gubernatorial primary in 1962 but lost to John Connally, who went on to win the race.

When he came to Lee's attention in February 1963 the general was making front-page news with an evangelist partner in an anti-Communist tour called *Operation Midnight Ride*. This was the start of setting Lee up as the assassin the CIA's covert operation to eliminate John F. Kennedy as president. By setting Lee up as the assassin, the CIA would accomplish numerous goals. They were making it appear Lee was pro-Communist, and they would make it appear Castro and Khrushchev was behind the assassination. If their covert operation was successful, then the CIA and the military would have their excuse to invade Cuba and bombing the Soviet Union.

"I don't understand what the reason for assassinating General Walker is. He seems harmless enough," said Lee.

"Sometimes the reason is not for the agent to know. You will learn in your career as an agent for Agency is you don't question your mission," replied James Smith, his handler.

Under the direction of James, Lee put Edwin Walker under surveillance, taking pictures of the general's home and nearby railroad tracks. Everything was set except he didn't own a rifle. Once again, James instructed him on how to buy a rifle.

"You want me to order a rifle through the mail?" asked Lee.

"Yes, you didn't have a problem ordering a revolver through the mail in January."

"How . . ."

"How did I know you ordered a revolver through the mail using your alias Alex J. Hidell?"

"Yes, how did you know? I thought I covered my tracks well," said Lee.

"Please, don't forget the fact I also work for the Agency. And you using a silly little alias isn't going to throw me off your trail. I want you to order a rifle in the same manner."

"Wouldn't it be easier for me to buy a rifle at a local gun store using my alias? It wouldn't be so easily traced back to me," suggested Lee.

"No, I want it to be done the way you ordered the revolver in January."

"Ok, I will do it that way," said Lee.

Lee planned the assassination for April 10th, ten days after he was fired from Jaggars-Chiles-Stovall. He chose a Wednesday evening since the neighborhood would be relatively crowded because of services in a church adjacent to Edwin Walker home: he would not stand out and could mingle with the crowds if necessary to make his escape. He left a note in Russian for Marina with instructions for her to follow should he be caught. In the letter he revealed everything he ever done with the CIA. General Edwin Walker was sitting at a desk in his dining room when Lee fired at him from less than a hundred feet away. He survived only because the bullet struck the wooden frame of the window, which deflected its path. The general was injured in the forearm by bullet fragments.

CHAPTER 28

———————————□———————————

"A nation that is afraid to let its people judge the truth and
falsehood in an open market is a nation
that is afraid of its people."

John F. Kennedy

President John F. Kennedy wrote Soviet Premier Khrushchev on April
11, 1963, explaining to his Cold War counterpart a policy chosen partly
on Khrushchev's behalf which was already beginning to cost him dearly.
In his letter President Kennedy said he was "*aware of the tensions unduly
created by recent private attacks on your ships in Caribbean waters; and we
are taking action to halt those attacks which are in violation of our laws, and
obtaining the support of the British Government in preventing the use of their
Caribbean islands for this purpose. The efforts of this Government to reduce
tensions have, as you know, aroused much criticism from certain quarters of
this country. But neither criticism nor the opposition of any sector of our society
will be allowed to determine the policy of this Government. In particular, I
have neither the intention nor the desire to invade Cuba.*"

 One weekend in the spring of 1963, Carlos Marcello was at his lodge
with friends from the old Sicilian family in New Orleans. He was drinking
a glass of scotch in the kitchen when one of the friends mentioned an
article he had read.

 "I read an article in a magazine which stated the Supreme Court was
going to uphold your deportation order. What are you going to do?"

 Carlos began to choke, spitting out his scotch onto the floor. After he
recovered, Carlos formed the southern Italian symbol of "the horn" with

his left hand. He held the ancient symbol of hatred and revenge above his head.

"Don't worry, man, about that Bobby Kennedy. We are going to take care of him," stated Carlos.

"Are you going to give it to Bobby?" asked a close family friend.

"What good would that do? You hit Bobby and his brother calls out the National Guard. No, you got to hit the top man and what happens with the next top man," said Carlos.

"Are you talking about Lyndon Johnson?"

"Yes, Vice-President Johnson doesn't like Bobby Kennedy. Sure as I stand here something awful is going to happen to John Kennedy," claimed Carlos.

In early April, James Donovan returned to Cuba to negotiate the release of more prisoners. In the meantime, the Central Intelligence Agency had been at work on a plan to assassinate Fidel Castro, through his negotiating friend, James. He was unaware of the CIA's intention to use him to double cross President Kennedy and Fidel Castro. A plan was devised to have him present a contaminated skin diving suit to Fidel as a gift. With James acting on the request of President Kennedy, the CIA kept in the dark about the dive suit being contaminated. The technique involved dusting the inside of the suit with a fungus which would produce a disabling and chronic skin disease (Madura foot) and contaminating the breathing apparatus with tubercle bacilli.

This plan was abandoned because he had already given a skin diving suit to Fidel as a gift. By trying to use James Donovan as an unwitting participant in Fidel's murder, the CIA knew it was also setting up the authority he represented, President Kennedy. If this plan had succeeded, then President Kennedy would have been blamed for Fidel's easily traceable death. This would put to end, Fidel's life, President Kennedy's creditability, and the hope of a Cuban-American dialogue.

On April 13, 1963, three days after Lee Harvey Oswald's attempt on the life of conservative activist General Edwin Walker, George de Mohrenschildt and his wife visited the Oswald's apartment. George, aware of his dislike for the general, joked with Lee about how it was possible he missed the general. Lee and Marina looked at each other but said nothing. Jeanne de Mohrenschildt later noticed a rifle leaning against a wall in a room which served as Lee's study. She told her husband about the rifle and he asked him about it. Lee claimed it was for target shooting.

In June 1963, George and his wife moved to Haiti, where he and other investors had set up an industrial development enterprise whose work was to include conducting a geological survey of Haiti to plot out oil and geological resources on the island. He was set up with this job in Haiti in payment for directing Lee to making contact with his new CIA babysitters, the Paines. Then they moved back to Dallas in 1967.

"I have a new mission for you," James Smith told him shortly after his failed assassination attempt on General Edwin Walker.

"You are giving me another mission after I failed on succeeding with the last mission."

"Don't worry about that."

"What is the new mission?" asked Lee.

"I need you to move to New Orleans."

"Ok, that's easy enough. What do you want me to do once I get there?" asked Lee.

"We have reason to believe some anti-Castro exiles are planning to assassinate President John F. Kennedy."

"Yes, I have heard several of the Cuban exiles weren't happy with the outcome of the Bay of Pigs invasion. And they are angry that he didn't invade Cuba last year when he had the chance. But are they angry enough to attempt to assassinate the president?" asked Lee.

"I am afraid so. Have you heard of the Fair Play for Cuba Committee?"

"Yes, I have. It's an organization which favors Fidel Castro, right?" replied Lee.

"Yes, you're right. It's an organization which demonstrates against any US-sponsored action against Cuba and Castro. Well, I want you to use the cover of starting a chapter in New Orleans and try to infiltrate the anti-Castro organization in New Orleans. You should start by making connect with Guy Banister and David Ferrie."

"Can I ask why me?" asked Lee.

"The Agency wants you to do it because of your background in the Soviet Union. The organization would accept you quicker than any other agent we have in the Agency."

"You want me to make connect with a Guy Banister and David Ferrie? Who are they?" questioned Lee.

"They are the leading anti-Castro activists in New Orleans. They also helped trained some of the anti-Castro Cuban exiles which was involved in the Bay of Pigs invasion. And they also helped run guns for FBI."

"What do you know about Guy Banister?" asked Lee. James opened a folder and began to read.

"Guy was born in Monroe, Louisiana. He worked for the Monroe Police Department before joining the Office of Naval Intelligence during World War II. In 1934 he joined the Federal Bureau of Investigations. He was originally based in Indianapolis, later he was transferred to New York City. While at the New York office he was involved in the investigation of the American Communist Party. Eventually he was promoted to the Special Agent in Charge in Chicago. One of his associates was Robert Maheu, who served as a liaison between the CIA and the Mafia regarding various assassination plots against Fidel Castro. He retired from the FBI in 1954. He returned to Louisiana and in January 1955 he became the Assistant Superintendent of the New Orleans Police Department. He was given the task of investigating organized crime and corruption within the police force. On the campus of Tulane University and LSU he ran a network of informants collecting information on 'communist' activities. He submitted reports of his finding to the FBI through contacts. In March 1957 he was suspended for pulling out his gun in public and threatening a waiter. After leaving the police department, he started his own private detective agency called Guy Banister Associates, Inc. at 531 Lafayette Street on the ground floor of the Newman Building. Around the corner but located in the same building, with a different entrance was the address 544 Camp Street. The building housed militant Anti-Castro groups: The Cuban Revolutionary Council (from October 1961-February 1962), Sergio Aracha Smith's Crusade to Free Cuba Committee."

"David Ferrie? That names sounds familiar. Why?" asked Lee.

"It should sound familiar to you. He was over your Civil Air Patrol when you was 15," his handler opened another folder and began to read, "David obtained a pilot's license and began teaching aeronautics at Cleveland's Benedictine High School. He was fired for several infractions including taking boys to a house of prostitution. In 1951 he moved to New Orleans where he worked as a pilot for Eastern Air Lines. He was fired in August 1961 after being arrested twice on morals charges. He was involved with the Civil Air Patrol in several ways: started as a Senior Member (adult member) with the 5th Cleveland Squadron at Hopkins Airport in 1947. When he moved to New Orleans he transferred to the New Orleans Cadet Squadron at Lake Front Airport. He served as an instructor, later as the Commander. He was asked to be a guest aerospace educating instructor at a smaller squadron at Moisant Airport. In March 1958, a former cadet-turned commander invited him back to the New Orleans Cadet Squadron. He served unofficially for a time and was reinstated as Executive Officer in September 1959. In September 1960, he started his own unofficial squadron called the Metairie Falcon Cadet Squadron. He was a 'rapid' anti-communist. He often accused previous presidential administrations of being 'sell outs' to communism. By early 1961, David was working with right wing Cuban exile Sergio Aracha Smith. Sergio was head of the CIA backed Cuban Democratic Revolutionary Front in New Orleans. David became his partner in counterrevolutionary activities. In July 1961, he gave an anti-Kennedy speech before the New Orleans Chapter of the Military Order of World War. His topic was the Presidential Administration and the Bay of Pigs invasion 'fiasco.' In his speech, he attacked President Kennedy for not providing air support to the Cuban exiles. His tirade was so offensive he was asked to leave the podium."

"Is that him?" Lee pointed at a picture in the file.

"Yes, that's David Ferrie."

"I think I remember him. He looks a bit like a freak," commented Lee.

"Yes, well, don't underestimate him. David Ferrie is very dangerous."

"I will be careful. I will leave for New Orleans as soon as possible," said Lee.

On April 25, 1963, Lee Oswald moved to New Orleans. Marina and their young daughter moved in with Ruth Paine. With the failure of the assassination of General Edwin Walker still fresh on their minds, the CIA once again pushed for the removal as Lee as an agent. But James Smith came to his rescue once more. They decided to send him to New Orleans on a new mission. He would act as a pro-Castro trying to infiltrate the anti-Castro organizations. What he didn't know was the CIA operation to eliminate John F. Kennedy as president had already began. And New Orleans would play a significant part in the CIA covert operation.

When Lee arrived at the bus station in New Orleans, he called his Uncle Charles and Aunt Lillian Murret. He asked them if he could stay with them while he sought employment. Two days later on April 26, 1963, he began his search for employment. The Louisiana Labor Department sent him out for several interviews; however, the CIA had already had a job set up for him. He just had to go through the motions of looking for employment.

CHAPTER 29

*"As we express our gratitude, we must never forget
that the highest appreciation is not to utter words,
but to live by them."*

John F. Kennedy

In late April 1963 at James Donovan's recommendation, Fidel Castro granted ABC reporter Lisa Howard an interview. On her return from Cuba, Lisa innocently briefed the CIA in detail on Castro's surprising openness toward President John F. Kennedy. She reported when she asked Castro how a rapprochement between the United States and Cuba could be achieved, Castro said, "*steps were already being taken.*" When she pressed Castro further, he said, nodding towards President Kennedy's initiative, he considered "*the U.S. limitation on exile raids to be a proper step toward accommodation.*" She concluded from the ten-hour interview Castro was looking for a way to reach a rapprochement with the United States Government. She said Castro also indicated, however, if a rapprochement was wanted, then President John Kennedy would have to make the first move.

Each of these Castro overtures for a new United States-Cuban relationship was noted word for word in a secret CIA memorandum written on May 1, 1963 by the CIA Deputy Director of Plans Richard Helms. It was addressed to CIA Director John McCone. A scribbled "*P saw*" on the upper right-hand side of the document indicates it was read also by the president. The Central Intelligence Agency tried to block the door which could be seen opening through Lisa Howard's interview. CIA Director McCone argued her approach to Cuba would leak and compromise a number of CIA operations against Castro. In a May 2nd memorandum to National Security Adviser McGeorge Bundy, CIA Director McCone urged the Lisa Howard report be handled in the most limited and sensitive manner and that no active steps be taken on the rapprochement matter at this time.

On May 9, 1963, Lee Oswald rented an apartment at 4905 Magazine Street. The neighborhood was somewhat on the seedy side. He was caught numerous times putting his trash in neighbors' garbage cans. He was seen doing this to garbage cans up and down his road by his landlady, Mrs. Jesse Garner. Why would a normal person place his trash in his neighbor's trash can? Was he acting under the direction of his CIA handler? Was he attempting to cover his tracks from whomever could be tailing him? Maybe he was just being rude and throwing his trash in his neighbor's garbage cans because he wasn't a very good neighbor.

On May 10, 1963, Lee started work at the William B. Reily Coffee Company at 640 Magazine Street. His job was oiling coffee grinding equipment for $1.50 an hour. This job was the employment the CIA had arranged for Lee once he arrived in New Orleans. The Reily Company was known for its international connections. The owner, William B. Reily, was a wealthy supporter of the CIA-sponsored Cuban Revolutionary Council.

Reily's Coffee Company had long been part of the CIA's New Orleans network. The Reily Coffee Company was located at the center of the United States intelligence community in New Orleans, close by the offices of the CIA, FBI, Secret Service, and Office of Naval Intelligence (ONI). Directly across the street from Naval Intelligence and Secret Service was another office. It was the office of the detective agency of former FBI agent Guy Banister.

Guy Banister Associates functioned more as a covert-action center for United States intelligence agency than it did as a detective agency. Guy's office helped supply munitions for CIA operations ranging from the Bay of Pigs to the Cuban exile attacks designed to ensnare President Kennedy. Guns and ammunition littered the office. CIA paramilitaries checked in with Guy on their way to and from nearby anti-Castro training camps. He was known as a bagman for the CIA and running guns to the Alpha 66 in Miami.

The reason for Lee working at his office was so Guy could keep an eye on him. The CIA didn't trust Lee could actually complete his so-called mission in New Orleans to success. They were sure he would do something to blow his cover. And as a result blow the cover for the CIA's covert operation to assassinate President Kennedy. Guy was a long time intelligence man and he could be trusted to guide Lee in his mission.

Shortly after Lee started working at the Reilly Coffee Company; Ruth Paine drove Marina and her daughter to New Orleans on May 11, 1963. The next day he had his and his family's mail forwarded from Post Office Box 2915 in Dallas to 4907 Magazine Street in New Orleans. Again, this was to cover his tracks just in case his cover got comprised. But who exactly was he afraid of finding him? By this time he had gained the attention of the Federal Bureau of Investigation. He knew the FBI was watching his every move in Dallas. What would be the reason for the FBI to have Lee under surveillance if he was a contract agent for the CIA? They were worried that while he was in Russia, the Soviets might have turned him. Normally the FBI didn't know what the CIA was doing and vice versa. They didn't know he was a paid employee of the CIA. In fact, there's evidence suggesting the FBI didn't know of this little fact until just before President Kennedy was assassinated.

On May 26, 1963, Lee requested membership in the Fair Play for Cuba Committee. He wrote:

"Dear Sirs: I am requesting formal membership in your organization. In the past I have received from you pamphlets, both bought by me and given to me by you. Now that I live in New Orleans I have been thinking about renting a small office at my own expense for the purpose of forming an F.P.C.C. branch here in New Orleans. Could you give me a charter? Also, I would like information on buying pamphlets in large lots, as well as blank Fair Play for Cuba Committee applications also a picture of Fidel, suitable for framing would be a welcome touch. Office down here rent for $30 a month and if I had a steady flow of literature I would be glad to take the expense. Of course I work and could not supervise the office at all times but I'm sure I could get some volunteers to do it. I am not saying this project would be a roaring success, but I am willing to try, an office, literature, and getting people to know who you are the fundamentals of the F.P.C.C. as far as I can see so here's hoping to hear from you."

V.T. Lee, the National Chairman of Fair Play for Cuba Committee sent samples of literature to Lee, but he never authorized him to open a chapter of the Fair Play for Cuba Committee in New Orleans, nor did he supply him with funds to support his activities there. On May 29, 1963, V. T. Lee responded to his letter. He stated a search of the files of the Fair Play for Cuba Committee indicated there was little interest in the organization in the Louisiana area, but "we are certainly not adverse to a small chapter."

V.T. Lee thought the New Orleans chapter should have had twice as many members as the number needed to conduct a legal executive board for the Chapter. If Lee Oswald attracted enough members, he would be granted a charter. V.T. Lee advised him, however, not to open a public office since "we do have a serious and often violent opposition . . . the lunatic fringe." V.T. Lee advised him to open a post office box instead.

CHAPTER 30

—▯—

"Geography has made us neighbors.
History has made us friends. Economics has made us
partners, and necessity has made us allies. Those whom God
has so joined together, let no man put asunder."

John F. Kennedy

On June 10, 1963, President John F. Kennedy left no doubt in his military advisers' mind where he stood when it came to the Cold War. On this date he proposed an end to the Cold War in a speech at American University. In this speech he reached out to Soviet Premier Khrushchev. At the same it widened the gap between President Kennedy and his military advisers. With his speech to the university, he introduced his most important concern; world peace.

". . . What kind of peace do I mean? What kind of peace do we seek? Not a Pax Americana enforced on the world by American weapons of war. Not the peace of the grave or the security of the slave. I am talking about genuine peace, the kind of peace that makes life on earth worth living, the kind that enables men and nations to grow and to hope and to build a better life for their children—not merely peace for Americans but peace for all men and women—not merely peace in our time but peace for all time. Every graduate of this school, every thoughtful citizen who despairs of war and wishes to bring peace, should begin by looking inward—by examining his own attitude toward the possibilities of peace, toward the Soviet Union, toward the course of the Cold War and toward freedom and peace here at home . . ."

President Kennedy rejected the idea of the United States forcing their type of peace on the people around the world. He felt the United States could bring the world together in ways other than by force. This rejection was an act of resistance to the military-industrial complex. The military-industrial complex depended on the United States ability to enforcing a Pax Americana on the world through invasions and threats of war. The Pax Americana, which policed by the Pentagon, was considered as the only means of defeating the spread of Communism. By rejecting the idea of a Pax Americana President Kennedy was rejecting the very foundation of the Cold War.

In early June 1963, Marina Oswald received a letter from the Soviet Embassy regarding her failure to follow through on her visa request. In her three-page handwritten response, she apologized for not answering the two previous letters she had received from the Soviet Embassy earlier. And explained to the Embassy she was expecting her second child in October 1963; her relationship with Lee seemed to have improved; and her husband agreed to return to the USSR with her and the children. She wrote Lee now expressed a "sincere desire" to return with her and she earnestly begged for Chief of the Consular Section Reznichenko's assistance.

> She wrote: *"There is not much that is encouraging for us here and nothing to hold us. I would not be able to work for the time being, even if I did find work. And my husband is often unemployed. It is very difficult for us to live here. We have no money to enable me to come to the Embassy, even to pay for hospital and other expenses connected with the birth of a child."*

Lee, using the name Lee Osborne, printed handbills reading "Hands off Cuba," as well as application forms and membership cards for the New Orleans branch of the Fair Play for Cuba Committee. Some of these leaflets were stamped with his actual name and home address; others were stamped with the name "A. Hidell P.O. Box 30061."

On June 11, 1963, Lee opened Post Office Box 30061 in New Orleans. A. Hidell and Marina Oswald were authorized to receive mail through the box. His application listed his address as 657 French Street (Charles and Lillian Murret lived at 757 French Street) rather than 4905

Magazine Street. Once again this might have been a feeble attempt by him to keep his location unknown. For a short time it worked, but the FBI soon discovered he was in New Orleans. About five days later, he distributed handbills and other material uneventfully in the vicinity of the USS *Wasp*, which was berthed in New Orleans.

Sometime in June 1963, Lee wrote V.T. Lee again:

> "*I was glad to receive your advice concerning my try at starting a New Orleans F.P.C.C. chapter. I hope you won't be too disapproving at my innovations but I do think they are necessary for this area. As per your advice, I have a taken a P.O. Box (no 30061) against your advice I have decided to take an office from the very beginning. As you see from the circulars I had jumped the gun on the charter business but I don't think it's too important, you may think the circular is too proactive, but I want it to attract attention, even if it's the attention of the lunatic fringe. I had 2000 of them run off. The major change in tactics you can see from the small membership blank, in that I will charge $1.00 a month dues for the New Orleans chapter only, and I intend to issue N.O.F.P.C.C. membership cards also. This is without recourse to the $5.00 annual national F.P.C.C. for every New Orleans chapter member who remains a dues paying member for 5 months in any year. It just that people I am approaching will not pay 5 dollars all at once to a committee in New York which they cannot see with their own eyes. But they may pay a dollar a month to their own chapter, after having received their membership card from my hand to theirs. Also I think such a dues system binds the members closer to the F.P.C.C.*"

On June 29, 1963, J. Edgar Hoover received a letter from Rafael Aznarz Costea: "*Attached hereto please find a pamphlet given to me by a young American that was at Canal Street with a big advice "HANDS OFF CUBA" you know that is a communist slogan against the United States. I argued with him and called him a communist, but you know they denied belong to the party.*"

Lee could not have invented members of the New Orleans Chapter of the Fair Play for Cuba Committee then sent their names to V.T. Lee without having risked detection. Instead, he circumvented the rules of the Fair Play for Cuba Committee, by having his own membership cards printed. He still intended to open an office of the Fair Play for Cuba Committee in New Orleans.

The Fair Play for Cuba Committee was a national organization and Lee set out on his own initiative as a one-member New Orleans chapter, spending $22.73 on 1000 flyers, 500 membership applications and 300 membership cards. He asked Marina to sign the name "A. Hidell" as chapter president on one card.

As instructed by his CIA hander, on June 24, 1963, Lee applied for a new passport; he received it the following day. He listed his occupation as photographer, and stated he planned to travel to England, France, Germany, Holland, USSR, Finland, Italy, and Poland. It was unusual for someone like him to get another visa this quickly. When he defected to the Soviet Union and returned, he should have been put on a "watch list". When someone entered the United States and was considered a national security threat, they were put on the "watch list". If he was on a "watch list", then he wouldn't have received another exit visa. Again this was proof he had help in his actions.

Someone had to make sure he wasn't on the "watch list". Who better to assure this than the CIA? They wanted to make sure it would appear he was trying to defect again. Before the State Department issued or renewed a passport, it checked the name of the applicant against its lockout card file. The State Department had issued a refusal sheet on Lee after he defected. In addition, a lookout card for Lee should have been prepared in June 1962, when he received a repatriation loan. These additional refusal sheets and lookout cards disappeared or were never prepared. This was the work of the Soviet section of the CIA. They didn't want anything to interfere with Lee getting another passport.

CHAPTER 31

——————□——————

"History is a relentless master. It has no present,
only the past rushing into the future. To try to hold fast
is to be swept aside."

John F. Kennedy

On June 27, 1963, the FBI office in New York sent the FBI office in Dallas two copies of a photograph of Lee Harvey Oswald's name on the mailing list of the Fair Play for Cuba Committee. It was received by the Dallas Office on July 1, 1963, and initiated into file by Special Agent James Hosty. On June 27, 1963, Special Agent Hosty was advised by the New York FBI his Subject (Lee Oswald) was living in New Orleans. It was at this time the CIA became aware the FBI was also interested in him.

On June 28, 1963, Special Agent Hosty asked the New Orleans FBI to determine Lee's address and activities, and asked to take partial responsibility for the case, because he was now in its area. Special Agent Hosty explained: "*After it was determined that the Subjects had left Dallas, the lead to determine Oswald's employment from Marina Oswald appeared unnecessary at the time. The Subjects were not active in any subversive organizations and had done nothing to arouse any undue interest. The sole purpose of the investigation at this time was to locate and interview Marina Oswald.*"

Basically, the FBI was saying they weren't interested in Lee, they were interested in Marina. Why? Well, because FBI Director J. Edgar Hoover was a hardliner who was severely against Communism. Throughout his career J. Edgar had numerous people deported for suspicion of Communism. It was quite possible he believed she was a KGB agent spying on the United

States. This could explain his interest in her. For now she was a person of interest to question.

On July 1, 1963, Lee sent a letter to the Soviet Embassy asking the Embassy to rush an entrance visa for his wife; additionally, he requested his visa be considered separately: *"Please rush the entrance visa for the return of Soviet citizen, Marina Oswald. She is going to have a baby in October; therefore you must grant the entrance visa and make transportation arrangements before then. As for my return entrance visa please consider it separately."*

Although he had Marina write to the Soviet Embassy in Washington, D.C. about the possibility of returning to the Soviet Union, he was still disillusioned with USSR. The action of Marina in New Orleans, which was directed by James Smith, was needed to make it appear he wasn't really interested in returning to the Soviet Union. The CIA needed Lee to appear as if his Marxist hopes had become pinned on Fidel Castro and Cuba. Through the instructions from the CIA he soon became a vocal pro-Castro advocate.

On July 5, 1963, Marina Oswald wrote to the Soviet Embassy seeking the *"results of the replies to my appeals with regard to the departure of our family to the USSR . . ."* Possession of a Soviet visa meant the Cuba government would automatically issue its holder a transit visa, and you could stop in Cuba en route to the USSR. Marina believed this was why he wanted the visa. It was all to give the public the impression he was pro-Castro and he wanted to go back to Russia.

Lee's inability to keep gainful employment appeared once more. On July 19, 1963 Lee was fired from his job at the Reilly Coffee Company by Emmett Barbe. Emmett had grown tired of his lame excuses of where he was when Emmett was looking for him. He thought Lee was leaving the premises while he was supposed to be working. One of his job was he had to clean the roasters at night. He would clean the front row but he wouldn't clean the back row. When Emmett asked him about that, he gave him some more excuses so he fired him. The Central Intelligence Agency had set up this job for him, but they had failed to tell his employers. The CIA didn't tell his employers he was a CIA agent, he left his place of employment numerous times to meet with his handler. They failed to tell his employer, because they needed him to lose another job. This would play into their loner portrait they were painting of him.

During Lee Oswald's period of intense activity on behalf of the Fair Play for Cuba Committee, he lectured at the Jesuit House of Studies in Mobile Alabama on July 27, 1963, at the request of his cousin who was studying there. This is an example of some of that lecture:

> *"The Communist Party of the United States has betrayed itself! It has turned itself in the traditional lever of a foreign power to overthrow the Government of the United States; not in the name of freedom of high ideals, but in the servile conformity to the wishes of the Soviet Union and in anticipation of Soviet Russia's complete domination of the American Continent . . . There can be no sympathy for those who have turned the idea of communism into a vile curse for western man . . . The communist movement in the U.S. personalized by the Communist Party U.S.A. had turn itself into a 'valuable gold coin' of the Kremlin. It has failed to denounce any actions of the Soviet Government when similar actions on the part of the U.S. Government bring pious protest . . . In order to free the hesitating and justifiably uncertain future activist for the work ahead we must remove that obstacle which has so efficiently retarded him, namely the devotion of Communist Party, U.S.A. to the Soviet Union, Soviet Government, and Soviet Communist International Movement. It is readily foreseeable that a coming economic, political and military crisis, internal or external, will bring about the final destruction of the Capitalist system, assuming this, we can see how preparation in a special party could safeguard an independent course of action after the debacle, an American course steadfastly, opposed to intervention by outside, relatively stable foreign powers, no matter from where they come, but in particular, and if necessary, violently opposed to Soviet intervention . . . The emplacement of a separate, democratic pure Communist society is our goal, but one with Union-communes, democratic socializing of production and without regard to the apart of Marxist Communist by other powers. The right of the private personal property, religious tolerance and Freedom of*

*Travel (which have all been violated under Russian 'Communist'
rule) must be strictly observed . . ."*

Now think about this lecture for a second or two. Lee was supposed to
be portraying a hard pro-Castro advocate. His true feelings and views on
Communism came out in this lecture. He denounced the Communist in
his speech to the Jesuits as a tool of Soviet imperialism, yet he subscribed
to *The Worker*, the organ of the Communist Party of the United States,
and two months later, he offered his services to the Communist Party. He
attacked Soviet Communism at the same time he applied for a Soviet visa.
His ideal activist would emerge after an economic crisis, just as Hitler did
in Nazi Germany, and become part of a "special party" of those opposed
to Soviet intervention. He was willing to enlist disenchanted members
of the Socialist Party. He cited the Minutemen as a group who would be
active after the military debacle of the United States. He portrayed the
Minutemen as "redefending their own backyards," a noble purpose. His
politics made little sense. He said he was alarmed about Soviet "domination
of the American continent," yet he supported Fidel Castro's Cuba, which
had been widely regarded as Moscow's "stepping stone" to the American
continent since 1961. He was aware of the close relationship between
Russia and Cuba. He mentioned Cuba only once in his speech. This made
no sense in light of his intensive Fair Play for Cuba Committee activity
at the time. Lee made efforts to start a branch of the Fair Play for Cuba
Committee in New Orleans.

It was almost as if he didn't know what he really believed in. It was as if he
was confused about what he actually stood for. His little anti-Communism
lecture angered the officials who were involved in his cover. This lecture
represented his true feelings about Russia and Communism. If this lecture
got in the hands of the wrong people it might've blown his cover. It
would have been made clear he wasn't really interested in Cuba, Russia,
or Communism. But, at the same time, he might have given the lecture
to appear he was anti-Castro so he could infiltrate those anti-Castro
organizations in New Orleans like he was instructed to do. Well, if he
was walking on a thin line to blowing his "CIA cover", then he just about
stepped over it in a letter he wrote to the National Chairman of the Fair
Play for Cuba Committee.

On August 1,1963 (the envelope was postmarked for August 4, 1963), in another letter Lee Oswald wrote V.T. Lee he stated he had rented an office as planned, but it was closed down three days later. He said the renters claimed "they said something about remodeling." He claimed by working out of a Post Office Box and by using street demonstrations and some circular work he had sustained a great deal of interest but no new members. He claimed through efforts of some "cuban-exial gusanos" during a street demonstration he was attacked and they were officially cautioned by the police. He stated the incident robbed him of what support he had.

This confrontation would be well documented. Lee was handing out his pro-Castro leaflets and a couple of anti-Castro exiles jumped him and they were arrested. The problem came when he wrote V.T. and discussed this confrontation. In the letter he wrote about an incident which had not happened yet. Police report failed to reflect any activity on his part prior to August 9, 1963, except for the uneventful distribution of literature at the Dumaine Street wharf in June 1963. He wrote about his fight with Cuban exiles before it took place.

How was this possible? How could Lee write about a confrontation which hadn't happened yet? It's because the fight had been planned before it happened. The fight was the work of action between Cuban exile Carlos Bringuier and Lee Harvey Oswald. Its purpose was to attract media, police and FBI attention to Lee and the New Orleans Chapter of the Fair Play for Cuba Committee, in order to establish connection with the Cubans which would allow him to travel to Cuba. It's quite possible this doesn't make sense to the people who knew Carlos was head of the anti-Castro organization Lee was trying to infiltrate. Why would he work with a supposedly pro-Castro person to infiltrate his organization? Well, maybe a little background on just who was Carlos Bringuier may help at this time.

On May 4, 1960, Carlos Bringuier left Cuba for Guatemala, and then for Argentina. He entered the United States on February 8, 1961, and arrived in New Orleans on February 18th. It's in New Orleans where he became associated with the Cuban Revolutionary Front. His first job in New Orleans was with the California Redwood Produce Company. He lasted just two days. On April 1, 1961, he became a self-employed peddler with his brother-in-law, Rolando Pelaez. They bought clothing and radios at wholesale price and went aboard ships to sell the same items. On October 1, 1962, he opened the Casa Roca clothing store and has been working there since. He was also associated with another man with connections with the Central Intelligence Agency; Howard Hunt. Years later he would claim he didn't know Howard.

Howard and Carlos were connected to the Cuban Revolutionary Front and the Cuban Revolutionary Council. Howard described himself as being involved in the propaganda efforts of the Cuban Revolutionary Council. Carlos described himself as the secretary of press of propaganda of the Cuban Revolutionary Council. Carlos' brother, Juan Felipe Bringuier, was a member of the 2506 Brigade and was captured during the Bay of Pigs Invasion. Howard and Carlos held many similar ideas. Both felt President Kennedy was going to replace Fidel Castro with leftist Manolo Ray. Carlos termed this Operation Judas.

In the late spring of 1961, three Directorio Revoltionaire Estudiantil (DRE) leaders escaped from Cuba and arrived in Miami, where they immediately offered the Cuban Revolutionary Front their services. The DRE was rendered an affiliate of the Cuban Revolutionary Front and Cuban Revolutionary Council. DRE leaders and members were supplied with weapons and money. By November 1961, Fidel Castro had driven the DRE groups operating inside Cuba underground. The DRE withdrew from the Cuban Revolutionary Council in March 1962. Juan Manuel Salvat headed a raid on Havana in August 1962, which proved embarrassing to United States authorities. The Miami-based DRE was shelling Havana from boats. These attacks were brought to the attention of Attorney General Robert F. Kennedy. After a warning from the Justice Department, the DRE distributed leaflets which accused President Kennedy of abandoning it. It warned it would continue to attack Cuba, since the Bay of Pigs had culminated in treachery.

On August 25, 1962, the DRE almost assassinated Castro when it attacked the Sierra Maestre Hotel in Havana. Two speedboats fired 30 rounds of 20-millimeter cannon shells of which 28 hit the hotel. Two rounds went wild and hit the Blanquita Theater, where Castro was watching a Charlie Chaplin movie. Castro was enraged and claimed it was a CIA attempt on his life. The DRE leaders were brought to Washington, and were applauded by Deputy Director of Plans Richard Helms. Despite political differences, the DRE began working closely with Alpha 66 at this time. After the October 1962 Cuban missile crisis, the Kennedy

Administration curtailed the activities of the DRE, although it was apparently moving closer to assassinating Castro.

In April 1963, President Kennedy prohibited DRE and Cuban Revolutionary Council exile leaders from leaving the United States. In New Orleans, Carlos Bringuier, the DRE leader, proclaimed his group would continue efforts to liberate Cuba despite United States action to stop raids originating from US soil.

DRE was conceived, created and funded by the Central Intelligence Agency. Former CIA agent Howard Hunt claimed the DRE was run for the CIA by David Atlee Phillips. David was the same man behind the scenes who as "Maurice Bishop" had directed the Alpha 66 raids designed to push President Kennedy into war with Cuba.

To the arresting officers the fight between Lee and Carlos looked staged. The reason the fight appeared to be staged was because it was, well, staged. Carlos worked for the CIA and he was a devout anti-Castro Cuban. He felt President Kennedy had betrayed the Cubans during the Bay of Pigs invasions and the Cuban Missile Crisis. He was willing to do whatever he had to demonstrate his hatred for President Kennedy. He was contacted by James Smith to set up the scuffle on Canal Street. The purpose of the demonstration with Lee was to draw the attention of media to the fact he was pro-Castro. The demonstration was a success.

CHAPTER 32

———————◻———————

"If anyone is crazy enough to want to kill a president of the United States, he can do it. All he must be prepared to do is give his life for the president's."

John F. Kennedy

On August 5, 1963, Marina Oswald received word from the Soviet Embassy in Washington that her request for a visa had been forwarded to Moscow for processing. Vitaly Alekseevich Gerasimov, who signed the letter, advised her as soon as the Embassy received a reply she would be notified. Gerasimov was known to be a member of the KGB. The New Orleans FBI investigated and had finally located Lee Oswald, learning his address and of his former employee. Also, on August 5, 1963, he initiated contact with Carlos Bringuier at the Casa Roca clothing store at 107 Decatur Street.

"Are you Carlos Bringuier?" asked Lee.

"Yes, I am. How can I help you?"

"My name is Lee Oswald. I am here to offer my services to the DRE delegate of New Orleans."

"I'm sorry. What are you talking about?" Carlos glared at him.

"Aren't you the leader of the DRE delegate for New Orleans?"

"I wouldn't call myself the leader. But, yes, I am involved with the DRE delegates here in New Orleans. Again, what can I do for you?"

"I am a former Marine and I am offering services in the capacity of a military trainer. I speak both Russian and Spanish."

The conversation drew the attention of two young anti-Castro Americans, Vance Blalock and Philip Geraci. They were there collecting for the DRE organization. They listened closely as Lee continued to talk to Carlos.

"What part does the DRE organization play in the main anti-Castro movement in Florida?" asked Lee.

Before Carlos could answer his question, Lee spoke once again, "While I was in the Marines I had training in guerilla warfare."

Carlos couldn't believe what this American man was saying. He told them how to blow up bridges, derail trains, make zip guns, and make homemade gunpowder. He told them to put powder charges at each end of the bridge from the foundation to where it meets the suspension part, and to blow that part up and the center part of the bridge would collapse. Carlos was immediately suspicious of him. He told him to deal directly with the Military Section of the DRE in Miami. He was concerned because Lee knew about the LaCombe, Louisiana, training camp. He was also concerned because Lee had mentioned he wanted to help train anti-Castro guerrillas. He was worried about infiltrators, because one of his brothers-in-laws was a Castro double agent. Shortly after he left Carlos' office, a couple of CIA agents paid him a visit. They explained to him what the situation was with Lee Oswald. They offered him money to stage a fight with Lee while he was handing out pro-Castro leaflets.

Carlos wasn't aware of the assassination plot against President Kennedy. He was just informed that the CIA was maneuvering certain people around to make it appear a pro-Castro individual would have a demonstration against the president. He was informed in not so many words that Lee Oswald was a key person in that plot. He was informed that Lee was going to be the fall guy in the demonstration against President Kennedy. And Carlos was more than willing to work in a demonstration against the president.

On August 6, 1963, Lee returned to Carlos Bringuier's store, and left his Marine training manual with his brother-in-law. On Friday August 9, 1963, Carlos was informed an unidentified man was carrying a pro-Castro sign and handing out literature on Canal Street. Lee had contacted, by phone, Major Presley J. Trosclair, Intelligence Unit Commander of the New Orleans Police Department, to secure a picketing permit. Major Trosclair told him to contact his attorney concerning his picket permit request. Carlos and two of his friends confronted the unidentified man. Carlos recognized the man as Lee and realized he had tried to infiltrate his group. And he had remembered what the CIA agents had told him a few days before. Lee was also privately filmed passing out fliers in front of the International Trade Mart with two "volunteers" he had hired for $2 at the unemployment office. The police came and arrested all participants.

Lee waited in the interrogation room of the New Orleans Police Department. Officers Horace J. Austin and Warren Roberts walked into the room. Each officer sat in a chair across from him.

"What is your name?" asked Officer Austin.

"My name is Lee Harvey Oswald."

"Do you have any identification on you?" asked Officer Austin.

Lee pulled out his wallet. He handed the officers his National Membership card for the Fair Play for Cuba Committee. Officer Austin looked at it. He noticed it was stamped as being issued on May 28, 1963. The president's name on the card was V.T. Lee. He also handed them a local membership card. Officer Roberts looked at this card. He noticed it was stamped as being issued on June 6, 1963. The name of the president of the local chapter was A. J. Hidell. Lee presented his Social Security card, which he hadn't signed. And he presented his US Marine Discharge Card. He failed to tell the officers his discharge had been changed from honorable to dishonorable because of his defection to Russia.

"What did you do while you were in the Marine Corps?" asked Officer Austin.

"I did mechanic work in the Marine Corps," replied Lee.

"Where do you work now?" asked Officer Roberts.

"I am presently unemployed and have been for the past three weeks."

"Tell us what happened?" suggested Officer Austin.

"Okay. I talked to a Major Trosclair about getting a permit for the Fair Play for Cuba Committee. He advised me to consult my attorney."

"Did you consult your attorney about getting a permit?" asked Officer Austin.

"No, sir, I didn't. The two Cubans walked up to me while I was handing out leaflets. They snatched the papers, ripped them up and threw the pieces in the street. They started yelling at me that I was a communist and it was at this time when the officers from the first district came up and a crowd gathered around us," said Lee.

Lee had inadvertently given them a piece of paper, with Russian writing on it, when he gave them his membership cards. The police reported the existence of this piece of paper to the FBI. The New Orleans police was concerned he might have been a Russian spy disguised as an organizer for the Fair Play for Cuba Committee. Despite this, the FBI didn't step up their investigation of him and the New Orleans Chapter of the Fair Play for Cuba Committee. It would appear he had dodged a bullet in blowing his cover for the CIA. Before the New Orleans police could alert the FBI about Lee, he requested a meeting with the FBI. He was interviewed by Special Agent John Lester Quigley, on Saturday August 10, 1963.

"Are you the member of the Fair Play for Cuban Committee?" asked Agent Quigley.

"Yes, I am."

"What is the function of the Fair Play for Cuba Committee?" asked the FBI agent.

"It is my understanding that the theme of the Committee was to prevent the United States from invading or attacking Cuba or interfering in the political affairs of Cuba."

"Is this committee a communist-controlled group?" asked Agent Quigley.

"No, sir. The Fair Play for Cuba Committee is not a communist-controlled group. An inquiry in New Orleans developed the fact there apparently was a New Orleans Fair Play for Cuba Committee chapter."

"What are the names of the members of the committee?" he asked.

"I don't know their names."

"Where are the other members' offices located?"

"I do not know," he handed the agent his National Membership card. It was signed by National President V.T. Lee.

"A short time after that I received in the mail a white card which shows I am member of the New Orleans chapter of the Fair Play for Cuba Committee," he handed the agent his local membership card.

Agent Quigley noticed the membership card was signed by an A.J. Hidell. He saw the number 33 in the lower right hand corner. He asked Lee about the number.

"It's my membership number. I receive a monthly circular of the committee through the mail. The circular is about seven pages long."

"What is the name of the publication?"

"I don't remember the name of the publication," Lee replied. "After receiving my membership card I spoke to Alek Hidell on the telephone on several occasions."

"What did you and Alek discussed during these phone calls?"

"He would discuss general matters of our mutual interest in connection with committee business. And sometimes he would inform me of a scheduled meeting," Lee answered.

"Have you ever met this Alek Hidell?"

"No. He had a telephone but it is discontinued," he answered.

"What was his telephone number?"

"I can't remember what the number was," said Lee.

"How many committee meetings have you attended?"

"Two," he replied.

"How many other members attended those meetings? And what were their names?"

"At each of the meetings there were about five different individuals. At each of these meetings the persons present were different. I don't know the last name of any of these individuals, I was only introduced to them by their first name," said Lee.

"Well, what was the members' first name?"

"I don't remember their first names, either," he answered.

"What was discussed during the meetings?"

"At the meetings the general conversation dealt with Cuba, and the latest news on the internal affairs of Cuba. On one occasion I held a committee meeting at my home," said Lee.

"How did you get word to the other members about the committee meeting you held at your home?"

Lee looked at the agent for a moment. He continued speaking without answering the question. "On August 7, 1963 I received a note through the mail from Alek. He asked me if I had the time would I mind distributing some Fair Play for Cuba Committee literature in the downtown area of New Orleans. He knew I was not working and probably had time."

"How much did you get paid to do this?"

"I didn't get paid to distribute the literature. I was doing it as a patriotic duty," answered Lee.

Lee told Special Agent Quigley he made up a sandwich-board sign reading "VIVA FIDEL" and had leaflets, membership applications and several pamphlets entitled, "The Crime against Cuba," with him that day. Special Agent Quigley's copy of the pamphlets did not carry the 544 Camp Street stamp, unlike the copy seized by the New Orleans Police. Lee's application for membership in the Fair Play for Cuba Committee was very professionally laid out and contained no spelling errors. His story was filled with lies. He didn't mention his defection, he claimed his wife was American, and he said his membership number in the New Orleans Chapter was 33, which implied the Chapter had at least 33 members.

Special Agent Warren C. DeBrueys was in charge of investigating the Fair Play for Cuba Committee. Special Agent Quigley's report was turned over to him. The FBI had been unable to locate a chapter for the Fair Play for Cuba Committee in New Orleans, yet Lee could readily join this shady organization, which sporadically met in cells of five, where no one knew anyone else's names. The organizer, A.J. Hidell did not appear at meetings, and could be reached only by telephone; which according to Lee it was discontinued. A check of FBI records would immediately have indicated to Special Agent DeBrueys that Lee was a defector, with a dishonorable discharge from the Marines, who married a Russian woman. That would have rendered him more suspicious of Lee and the Fair Play for Cuba Committee. A shady organization of this nature had to be infiltrated. The FBI investigation of A.J. Hidell, the Fair Play for Cuba Committee, and Oswald was not increased.

Lee spent the night in jail. On August 10, 1963, Lee telephoned the Murrets and asked for their help in arranging bail. He was released after Charles Murret got his business partner, Emile Bruneau, to intervene. Emile had close ties to New Orleans Mafia boss, Carlos Marcello. Lee pleaded guilty to disturbing the peace and was fined $10 on August 12, 1963. The anti-Castro Cubans had not been charged.

To the normal person it would have seemed a little strange the anti-Castro Cubans weren't charged in the disturbance. By all accounts they were the instigators. Maybe it was feared if Carlos was charged, then maybe it would reveal the CIA had set up the confrontation. If it was revealed the CIA had set up the confrontation, then the whole assassination plot would be revealed. So surely someone from the CIA placed a call to the New Orleans Police Department and made arrangements for the anti-Castro Cubans not to be charged.

CHAPTER 33

"Khrushchev reminds me of the tiger hunter who has picked
a place on the wall to hang the tiger's skin long before he has
caught the tiger. This tiger has other ideas."

John F. Kennedy

ON AUGUST 12, 1963, Lee Oswald wrote another letter to V.T. Lee.

*"Continuing my efforts on behalf of the F.P.C.C. in New
Orleans, I find that I have incurred its displeasure of the Cuban
exile 'worms' here. I was attacked by three of them as the copy of the
enclosed summons indicates I was fined ten dollars and the three
Cubans were not fined because of 'lack of evidence' as the judge
said. I am very glad I am stirring things up and shall continue to
do so. The incident was given considerable coverage in the press
and local TV news broadcast. I'm sure it will all be to the good of
the Fair Play for Cuba Committee."*

During the incident with Carlos Bringuier, Lee encountered Frank
Bartes. After Bringuier and Oswald were arrested in the street scuffle,
Bartes appeared in court with Bringuier on August 12, 1963. During the
hearing, Lee sat in the section of the courtroom reserved for "Negros."
The news media surrounded him hoping for a statement after the bail
hearing. Frank engaged in an argument with Lee and the news media.
Bartes claimed he spoke to an FBI agent that day and warned them Lee
was dangerous.

On August 16, 1963, Lee was again observed distributing pro-Castro
literature. He hired two men from a local employment agency. On August

20, 1963, the New Orleans FBI Office received a letter from Jesse Core, the FBI contact at the International Trade Mart. The letter contained one of Lee's "The Crime against Cuba" leaflets which was stamped FPCC 544 Camp Street New Orleans, La. No investigation was conducted. Carlos Quiroga who was a member of the Cuban Revolutionary Front was also a FBI informant. He was acquainted with Carlos Bringuier. He knew about the arrest of Bringuier and two other Cubans along with Lee.

On August 16, 1963, Carlos Quiroga was seated in Thompson's Restaurant when the representative of Puerto Rico, who had an office at the International Trade Mart, showed him the Fair Play for Cuba Committee leaflets. He told Carlos Quiroga the handbills were being passed out in front of International Trade Mart. Carlos Quiroga notified the police, but the police arrived too late, and the person passing out handbills had left. He drove to the address listed on the handbill. When Lee saw Carlos was Cuban, he said, *"Don't hit me. If you are coming as friend come in."* He met with Lee for about an hour. Lee told him Fidel Castro was not a dictator; all the Cuban exiles were criminals; he hated Anastasio Somoza and believed he should be eliminated; if the United States invaded Cuba, he would fight with Fidel Castro. He said Lee claimed to be a student of language at Tulane University and to be the delegate for the Fair Play for Cuba Committee in New Orleans. He wanted Carlos Quiroga to join the FPCC. Lee gave him a membership application. Carlos Quiroga contacted Lt. Branch Martello of the New Orleans Police Department and offered to infiltrate the Fair Play for Cuba Committee, but he received no encouragement, and so he took no further action.

On August 17, 1963, William Stuckey visited Lee at his apartment to invite him to appear on his radio program. William's preliminary interview lasted 32 minutes. He condensed it down to five minutes. The condensed tape of Lee was broadcasted on William Stuckey's radio program, Latin American Post. That same day, 1963. Lee wrote his last letter to V.T. Lee. He wrote, *"Since I last wrote you about my arrest and fine in New Orleans for distributing literature for the F.P.C.C. things have been moving pretty fast. On August 8, 1963, I organized an F.P.C.C. demonstration of three people. This demonstration was given considerable coverage by WDSU-TV Channel 6, and also by our Channel 4 T.V. station. Due to that I was invited by Bill Stuckey to appear on his T.V. show called 'Latin American Focus' at 7:30 P.M. Saturday's on WDSU-Channel. After this 15 minute interview, which was filmed on magnetic type at 4:00 P.M. for rebroadcast at 7:30. I was flooded with callers and invitations to debate, as well as people interested in joining the F.P.C.C. New Orleans branch. That than is what has happened up to this day and hour. You can I think be happy with the developing situation here in New Orleans . . . I would, however, like to ask you to rush some more literature particularly the white sheet 'Truth about Cuba' regarding government restrictions on travel, as I am quickly running out."*

Lee characterized himself as a highly successful political activist who had received television coverage. He had been on the radio. His interview was condensed and he was heard for less than five minutes on August 17, 1963. He had only one caller, an agent of Carlos Bringuier. It wasn't much but it was going as the CIA had planned. Lee was getting exposure as being pro-Castro.

William Stuckey wanted to air the Lee Oswald tape in its entirety, and suggested this to the station manager. The station manager asked him to arrange a debate during which Lee's pro-Castro views could be countered by others. Lee's second appearance on William's radio show took place on August 21, 1963. He was part of a debate. It was Lee versus Carlos Bringuier and Edward Scannell Butler, who headed the Information Council of Americas. William described the Information Council of Americas as an "*anti-communist propaganda organization.*" Its principal activity was to take tape-recorded interviews with Cuban refugees and distribute these tapes to radio stations throughout Latin America. William described Lee and Carlos' dialogue as unreal. Carlos was an obnoxious, loudmouth who would have been hostile to Lee; assuming they were not in collusion.

The reason for the lack of animosity between Lee and Carlos was a result of the fact both men deeply admired each other and no real hostility existed. Carlos knew the purpose of the debate was to further establish Lee as the leader of the Fair Play for Cuba Committee in New Orleans. He also knew Lee could not have possibly furthered the case of Cuba, because he was a former defector to the Soviet Union. No other leaders of the Fair Play for Cuba Committee had similar backgrounds. When asked if the Fair Play for Cuba Committee was controlled by the Communist Party, Lee never responded; instead he said the Senate Subcommittee had investigated the Fair Play for Cuba Committee found no connection between the two organizations.

Lee was unfamiliar with the leadership of the Fair Play for Cuba Committee, although he claimed to be the Secretary of the New Orleans Chapter. The only name he knew was V. T. Lee, with whom he corresponded. Lee linked the British democratic socialists who sponsored socialized medicine with Marxism. This was a right-wing operation. When Lee was accused of being a KGB agent, he merely confirmed his opponent's beliefs by saying he was aware the building was at 11 Kuznetskow Street. Carlos brought up President John F. Kennedy and got Lee to admit he was against him and the CIA. This was the second and last time Oswald mentioned the initials CIA. When he first mentioned it, he called it, "*the now-defunct CIA.*" The Cubans and Fair Play for Cuba Committee leadership were convinced despite the replacement of Allen Dulles by John McCone as the Director of the Central Intelligence Agency; the CIA continued to conspire against them. A right-wing who believed the CIA had been hamstrung by President Kennedy, would have called it "*now-defunct.*" The Louisiana training camp referred to by Carlos Bringuier in relation to Lee was organized by the Christian Democratic Movement in June 1963. The Christian Democratic Movement and the DRE worked together.

In early September, Lee Harvey Oswald met Central Intelligence Agent David Atlee Phillips in the busy lobby of downtown office building in Dallas. Alpha 66 leader Antonio Veciana, who worked for years under Phillips and knew him by his code name "Maurice Bishop," witnessed the Dallas scene. As soon as Veciana walked into the lobby he saw Phillips standing in the corner of the lobby talking to a pale, slight and soft-featured young man. Phillips ended his conversation with the young man shortly after Veciana had arrived. The three of them walked out of the lobby onto the busy sidewalk. Phillips and the young man stopped behind Veciana for a moment, and had additional words. Then the young man motioned farewell and walked away. Phillips immediately turned to Veciana and began a discussion of the current activities of the Alpha 66 as they walked into a nearby coffee shop. He never spoke to Veciana about the young man and Veciana never asked.

Also in September 1963, in a safe house in Sao Paulo, Brazil, CIA case workers met with Rolando Cubella. He was a minister within the Cuban government. Two years earlier, he had come to the attention of the Central Intelligence Agency because he had claimed to have become disillusioned with Castro and wanted to defect to the United States. He was a former commander with Castro's army, a hero of the revolution, and a close friend of Fidel Castro. Rolando would be a great asset to the CIA if he was to defect to the US. He could offer great Intel on the intentions of the Castro regime. But instead of Rolando defecting to the US, the CIA had him stay where he was in Cuba. They were hoping he could provide them with valuable information on Castro. Some CIA case workers went to the meeting with him hoping he had some good information for them. He informed them he was interested in the complete overthrow of the Castro regime. He considered the assassination of Fidel Castro was vital to the success of a regime overthrow. He stated he was willing to undertake the inside job, if he had the support of United States government. Rolando's offer was relayed to the CIA headquarters on September 7th. The offer was directed to the Special Affairs Staff (SAS). The SAS was the CIA division which was responsible for all covert operations against Cuba. It was headed by Desmond Fitzgerald, who was a personal friend of Robert Kennedy. This division had agents stationed throughout the world. It even had its own station in Miami, JMWAVE Station. The mission of this station was to overthrow the Castro regime.

On the same day the CIA case workers were talking with Rolando, Castro permitted a private interview with Daniel Harker, a reporter for the Associated Press. In this interview Castro warned against United States leaders using terrorist plans to eliminate Cuban leaders.

> "I will tell you that Cuba is prepared to answer in kind. United States leaders should think if they are aiding terrorist plans to eliminate Cuban leaders, they themselves will not be safe. And I feel the CIA is involved with these plans to eliminate the Cuban leaders," said Castro.

The CIA counterintelligence staff was struck by the coincidence of Castro issuing his warning at the very same time the CIA case workers were talking to Rolando. This gave the CIA some concern Rolando may in fact be a double agent sent over to see what the intentions of the Kennedy Administration was towards Castro. The SAS chief warned Desmond Fitzgerald that Rolando's true intentions were not clear and he disapproved of the operation concerning him.

Castro's threat against the United States leaders had been considered and evaluated by the Kennedy Administration. The CIA's covert operation against Cuba was under the direct supervision of a Special Group in the National Security Council, directed by Robert Kennedy and General Maxwell Taylor. This Special Group was designated as a special committee comprised of Desmond Fitzgerald and a representative of both the Attorney General and the Secretary of State to weigh the risks involved in proceeding with covert operation against Cuba. On September 12th the committee met at 2:30PM at the Department of State. The committee concluded if Castro was to retaliate that it be at a low level. It was assumed the possibility of an attack against US officials as unlikely. Desmond informed the SAS case officials to tell Rolando his proposal was being considered at the highest levels.

CHAPTER 34

——◻——

"Let both sides seek to invoke the wonders of science instead
of its terrors. Together let us explore the stars, conquer the
deserts, eradicate disease, tap the ocean depths, and encourage
the arts and commerce."

John F. Kennedy

ON SEPTEMBER 20TH, President John Kennedy went to New York to
address the United Nations General Assembly. He took the opportunity
to return to the theme of his American University address—pursuing a
strategy of peace through a step-by-step process.

*"Peace is a daily, a weekly, a monthly process, gradually
changing opinions, slowly eroding old barriers, quietly building
new structures. And however undramatic the pursuit of peace, that
pursuit must go on,"* President Kennedy said.

*"Today we must have reached a pause in the cold war—but
that is not a lasting peace. A test ban treaty is a milestone—but
it is not the millennium. We have not been released from our
obligations—we have been given an opportunity. And if we fail
to make the most of this moment and this momentum—if we
convert our new-found hopes and understandings into new walls
and weapons of hostility—if this pause in the cold war merely leads
to its renewal and not its end—then the indictment of posterity
will rightly point its finger at us all. But if we can stretch this
pause into a period of cooperation—if both sides can now gain new
confidence and experience in concrete collaborations for peace—if*

we can now be as bold and farsighted in the control of deadly weapons as we have been in their creation—then surely this first small step can be the start of a long and fruitful journey. I would say to the leaders of the Soviet Union, and to their people, that if either of our countries is to be fully secure, we need a much better weapon than the H-bomb—a weapon better than ballistic missiles or nuclear submarines—and that better weapon is peaceful cooperation," President Kennedy continued.

At the UN General Assembly, President Kennedy met privately with Ambassador Adlai Stevenson. They discussed the possibility of a Kennedy-Castro dialogue.

"Adlai, tell William Atwood to go ahead and make discreet contact with Dr. Carlos Lechuga (Cuba's United Nations Ambassador). Tell him to go ahead and explore a possible dialogue with Castro," suggested President Kennedy.

"To be honest, Mr. President, I don't think a dialogue with Fidel Castro is possible at this point in time," said Ambassador Stevenson.

"Why do you think that?"

"Well, Mr. Kennedy, unfortunately the Central Intelligence Agency is still in charge of Cuba," Ambassador Stevenson replied.

"I don't care, Adlai. I believe the time is right to begin talking with Castro," said President Kennedy. He knew the danger of him once again going against the CIA, but he was determined to do things his way.

"Mr. Helms, Colonel Lansdale is on the phone for you," said the secretary of Richard Helms.

"Colonel, how are you today?" Richard asked as he picked up his phone.

"I am going make this call short. Have the locations been decided?"

"Yes, Chicago, Tamp Bay and Dallas. I want you to have plans for all three cities. I don't know when he is going to those cities yet. But I want you to be ready on a moment notice, okay?" asked Richard.

"We will be. I am going to use three sniper teams for each city. Each team for each city will be different. I have a fall guy lined for Chicago and Tampa Bay. But I don't have one for Dallas."

"Who do you have for Chicago and Tampa Bay?" questioned the deputy director of plans.

"Thomas Arthur Valle in Chicago and a right-wing extremist, Joseph Milteer, in Tampa Bay. But like, I said, I don't have anyone for Dallas. I don't think it will come down to getting someone for the Dallas. We should get him in Chicago or Tampa Bay."

"The hit is being planned for Dallas. Chicago and Tampa Bay is just test runs for Dallas."

"Well, I will have to find the perfect fall guy for Dallas," said the colonel.

"Don't worry about that. It's being taken care of. Just make sure when it goes down in Dallas that it's perfectly executed," Richard said as he hung up the phone.

CHAPTER 35

———————— ❑ ————————

"No one has been barred on account of his race from fighting
or dying for America, there are no white or colored signs on
the foxholes or graveyards of battle."

John F. Kennedy

RICHARD CASE NAGELL walked into a bank in El Paso, Texas, on September 20, 1963, and calmly fired two shots from a Colt .45 pistol into a plaster wall just below the bank's ceiling. He then went outside and waited in his car until a police officer came to arrest him. When questioned by the FBI, Nagell made only one statement: *"I would rather be arrested than commit murder and treason."*

Richard Case Nagell had been a United States Army counterintelligence officer from 1955 to 1959. He was assigned to Field Operations Intelligence (FOI), which he later described as *"a covert extension of CIA policy and activity designed to conceal the true nature of CIA objectives."* During his FOI orientations at Far East Headquarters in Japan, Nagell was familiarized with *"simple intricate weapons to be used in assassinations."* He was also *"advised that in event I was apprehended, killed, or compromised during the performance of my illegal FOI duties, the Department of the Army would publicly disclaim any knowledge of or connection with such duties, exercising its right of plausible denial."*

In the late fifties while stationed in Japan, Richard began his Army/CIA role as a double agent in liaison with Soviet intelligence. In Tokyo, his path converged with that of counterintelligence agent Lee Harvey Oswald. Both men worked in a counterintelligence operation with the code name "Hidell," which Oswald later used as part of his alias, "Alek James Hidell." As a continuing double agent in 1963, Richard was working with Soviet intelligence in Mexico City. He was reporting back to the CIA, in an operation directed by the chief of the Cuban Task Force, Desmond FitzGerald. Richard was assigned by the KGB to monitor Lee Harvey Oswald in the United States after Oswald returned from Russia. He became involved in New Orleans and Texas with Oswald and two Cuban exiles in what he saw as a "large" operation to kill President Kennedy. The Cubans were known by their "war names" of "Angel" and "Leopoldo." He claimed Angel and Leopoldo were connected with a violence-prone faction of a CIA-financed group operating in Mexico City and elsewhere. He claimed the CIA-financed group was the Alpha 66.

In September 1963, Richard was ordered by the KGB to convince Lee he was being set up by Angel and Leopoldo as the assassination patsy—or if that failed, to murder him in Mexico City and then take up residence abroad. The Soviets wanted to save President Kennedy by eliminating the scenario's patsy, and to keep them from becoming scapegoats themselves. He met with Lee in New Orleans. He warned Lee that Leopoldo and Angel were manipulating him. He was evasive and unresponsive to Richard's appeals he quit the assassination plot.

By that time Richard had lost contact with his CIA case worker under Desmond FitzGerald. Rather than carry out the KGB orders to kill Lee Oswald, he sent FBI Director J. Edgar Hoover a registered letter on September 17th warning of the president's impending assassination, spelling out what he knew of it. Having put his warning on record, Richard then decided to remove himself from any possible role in the assassination plot. He therefore did his bank escapade in El Paso on September 20th, to place himself in federal custody rather *than commit murder and treason."* He was convicted of armed robbery and served four and a half years in prison.

IN COLLABORATION WITH William Attwood, Lisa Howard organized a party at her New York apartment on September 23rd to serve as the pretext and social cover for a first conversation between William Attwood and Dr. Carlos Lechuga.

"What are the chances of the Cuban government allowing me to come to Havana? Would you say the chances of me coming to Havana to discuss a possible rapprochement between Washington and Cuba were about fifty-fifty?" William asked Dr. Lechuga.

"Well, I think with the current United States policy, President Kennedy's recent address at American University and the nuclear test ban treaty present one aspect of a possible rapprochement between the United States and the Cuban government. I think you would agree these decisions are heading in the right direction," said Dr. Lechuga.

"Well, I can't help but agree with you on that. But at the same time we have that damned CIA and their saboteurs in Cuba and the spy planes flying over Cuba isn't helping the possibility of a rapprochement. It's actually created an absurd situation," said William Atwood.

"Yes, the Central Intelligence Agency isn't helping the matter at all," said Carlos Lechuga.

"Well, I will tell you what President Kennedy has confessed a time or two in private conversation with his true close advisers. He has said he didn't know how he was going to change United States policy on Cuba. He also said neither the United States nor Cuba could change it overnight because of the prestige involved. He confessed something had to be done about it and a start had to be made," said William.

The next day, on September 24th, William Attwood met Robert Kennedy in Washington and reported on his first meeting with Carlos Lechuga.

"I need to go to Cuba and discuss the idea of a rapprochement," William suggested to the attorney general.

"I don't know. I think if you took a trip to Cuba, it would be too risky. There are too many loose lips around Washington. And these lips would be happy to see my brother fail. If you took a trip to Cuba, then it's bound to leak out. It would provoke accusations of appeasement. And we definitely don't need that right now," said Robert.

"Sir, that may be true, but we can't sit around and not do anything. I think Premier Castro is willing to talk about a rapprochement. At least that's the feeling I get."

"If Fidel is really interested, then he would agree to meet somewhere else other than in Cuba; perhaps at the United Nations," suggested Robert Kennedy.

"What do you think we should do, then?"

"I think you should continue pursuing the matter with Carlos Lechuga," replied the attorney general.

Three days later William Attwood met once again with Carlos Lechuga at the United Nations Delegates Lounge.

"I talked to Attorney General Robert Kennedy about what we discussed a couple of days ago. He believes it would be too risky for me to go down to Cuba. And I would have to agree with him. As a United States government official it would be difficult to go to Cuba and it not leak out to the wrong people," said William.

"Yes, I could see where that might cause a problem. What do you or the attorney general suggest?"

"If Fidel Castro or a personal emissary had something to tell us, then we are prepared to meet him and listen wherever else would be convenient," suggested William.

"I will pass this information onto Havana," Carlos agreed.

After three weeks without a reply from Havana, with William Attwood's approval, Lisa Howard began phoning Rene Vallejo, Castro's aide and confidant, who favored a United States-Cuban dialogue. She doubted the message from Lechuga had ever gotten past the Cuban Foreign Office. She wanted to make sure through Vallejo that Castro himself knew there was a United States official ready to talk with him.

IN THE LAST week of September 1963, Silvia Odio, a twenty-six-year-old Cuban immigrant living in Dallas, was visited at her apartment door in the early evening by three strange men. Her seventeen year old sister, Annie, who had come to babysit for Silvia's children, answered the door and spoke with the men first.

"Is Silvia Odio in?" asked a Cuban man.

"Yes, she's getting ready to go out for the evening. I'll go get her," Annie said as she turned away from them.

"I'm Silvia Odio. How can I help you?" Silvia asked as she walked up to the three men.

"My name is Leopoldo and this is Angelo. And this is our gringo American friend Leon Oswald. We are Cuban exiles, can we talk to you for a moment?" the Cuban spoke in Spanish.

Two of the men looked Latin and spoke rapidly in Spanish. To Silvia the American seemed unable to follow the Spanish. Yet the third man's silent presence for a few minutes at her door would traumatize her future.

"Sure."

"We are members of JURE (Junta Revolucionaria Cubana). We are very good friends with your father, Amador. We know he is being held in a Cuban prison. We also knew Manolo Ray," said Leopoldo.

"The JURE's leader? My father worked closely with him," she said uneasily.

Carrying out the tradition of her parents, Silvia had also become a JURE activist. She was working with their friend, Manolo Ray, at raising funds for JURE. That made her not only an opponent of Castro but, in a more immediate context, an outsider in the Dallas community and a problem to the CIA. Most anti-Castro activists and their CIA sponsors regarded JURE, with its platform in support of economic justice and agrarian reform, as "Fidelism without Fidel." For anti-Castro organizers, JURE's democratic socialism had too much in common with the enemy.

CIA organizers of the Bay of Pigs invasion even suspected JURE founder, Manolo Ray, Castro's recently resigned Minister of Public Works, was a Cuban agent. He was a critic of the CIA's role in the invasion before it happened. Perhaps his greatest liability in the eyes of the CIA was his favored-Cuban-activist status with President Kennedy and his brother Robert. His leftist convictions, which alienated him from the exile community and the CIA, were what moved the Kennedys to overrule the agency and insist on his inclusion in the coalition of exile leaders.

In July 1963, Manolo's defensiveness among the exiles for him being a Kennedy ally only made matters worse. He told a presumably anti-Kennedy Cuban that he thought CIA agents *were more dangerous than the Kennedy Administration.* He waded into still deeper water by adding, *"The Kennedy Administration would end but CIA agents always stayed, and their memory was longer than the memory of elephants and they never forgot or forgave."*

The CIA's tensions with Manolo Ray and JURE provided the backdrop to visit known JURE activist Silvia Odio by "JURE members" Leopoldo and Angel—and, most significantly, their friend Leon Oswald. The CIA saw Manolo Ray and JURE too closely related to a president who had become a national security risk. The encounter at Silvia Odio's door would link the man portrayed as Kennedy's assassin-to-be with a group the CIA wanted to contaminate.

"We came to see you because we wanted you to meet this American. Leon Oswald is very much interested in the Cuban cause," said Leopoldo.

Silvia would remember the American vividly. He himself told her his name was Leon Oswald. She noticed he stood between the two Cubans just inside the vestibule, less than three feet away from her. While Leopoldo talked on quickly, Leon just *"kept smiling most of the time,"* with the bright overhead lights shining down on his face. *"He had a special grin,"* she claimed, *"a kind of funny smile."*

"We just came directly from New Orleans," said Leopoldo.

Silvia noticed the three men appeared *"tired, unkempt, and unshaven, as if they had just come from a long trip."*

"We are about to go on another trip," said Leopoldo. Silvia had the feeling she was being deliberately told about this unspecified trip.

"The purpose of this visit is we want to ask your help in raising funds for JURE. Would you write for us some very nice letters in English as appeals to local businessmen?" asked Leopoldo.

Silvia offered little comment, making no commitment. As the strained conversation ended, Leopoldo gave her the impression he would contact her again. From her window Silvia watched the two Cubans and their American friend get in their car and drive away.

When Silvia got home from work a night or two later, she received a phone call from Leopoldo.

"What do you think of the American?" asked Leopoldo.

"I don't think anything," she replied.

"You know, our idea is to introduce him to the underground in Cuba because he is great, he is kind of nuts. He told us Cubans don't have any guts, because President Kennedy should have been assassinated after the Bay of Pigs, and some Cubans should have done that, because he was the one that was holding the freedom of Cuba actually."

Silvia was getting upset with the conversation, but Leopoldo continued telling her what the American, "Leon Oswald," supposedly said.

"And he said, 'It is so easy to do.' He has told us," Leopoldo swore in Spanish, emphasizing Leon's point about how easy it was to kill President Kennedy. "The American had been a Marine and was an expert shot. He was kind of loco. Angel, Leon and I are about to leave on a trip. We would like to see you again when we returned to Dallas," He hung up, Silvia never heard from him again.

Three days later Silvia wrote to her father in prison about the visit of the three strangers, saying two had called themselves friends of his. He wrote back that he knew none of the men, and that she should not get involved with any of them.

CHAPTER 36

—————————◻—————————

"Our most basic common link is that we all inhabit this
planet. We all breathe the same air. We all cherish our
children's future. And we are all mortal."

John F. Kennedy

Lee Harvey Oswald crossed the border into Mexico at Nuevo Laredo,
Texas on a Continental Trailways bus. He had a strange feeling about
this mission his CIA handler had him on in New Orleans. Marina had
been asking about going back to Russia. She missed her homeland and
her family. Maybe this was the perfect time for him to defect back to the
Soviet Union. But this time maybe he could actually enjoy it without
the pressure of working for the United States Government. He didn't
understand the point of going to see that Silvia woman before he traveled
to Dallas. But the two Cuban agents he was traveling with said it was
vital that he was with them that night. He needed a way to get to Russia.
They advised him to go to the Cuba and Russian Embassy in to Mexico.
So before returning to Dallas, Lee made a quick trip, unbeknownst to the
CIA, to Mexico.

While traveling on the Continental Trailways bus, Lee had a
conversation with one of the passengers, John McFarland, a doctor from
Liverpool, England, while riding on the bus.

"I am on my way to Cuba. I have to go by way of Mexico since it was
illegal to travel there from the United States," stated Lee.

"What did you do in New Orleans?" asked John McFarland.

"I had been a Secretary of the New Orleans branch of the Fair Play for
Cuba Committee."

"Why do you want to go to Cuba?" asked the Liverpool doctor.

"To see Castro, if I could," replied Lee.

Lee's bus arrived in Mexico City at 10AM on September 27th. He walked four blocks to the Hotel Comercio. He registered under the alias O. H. Lee. He was given a room on the third floor at $1.28 a night. He then walked two miles to the Soviet and Cuban embassies. He, first, went to the Soviet embassy to start the necessary paperwork for his visa. Lee spoke briefly with Valery Kostikov.

"I am seeking a visa to the Soviet Union," said Lee.

"You need to talk to Oleg Nechiporenko," he directed Lee to Oleg's office.

"How can I help you?" Oleg asked as Lee sat in a chair in his office.

"I am requesting an immediate visa to the Soviet Union."

"We do not handle request for travel to the Soviet Union. You need to go to our embassy in Washington, D.C. But I can make an exception for you and send your papers to Moscow. But the answer to your request will be made to your permanent residence. But it will take at the very least four months," explained Oleg.

Lee leaned into his face and shouted, "This won't do for me! This is not my case! For me, it's all going to end in tragedy!" Oleg showed him out of the compound. Then he walked to the Cuban embassy. He was interviewed by Silvia Duran.

"How can I help you?" asked Silvia.

"I want to travel through Cuba on my way to the Soviet Union. I plan to resettle in Odessa with my wife."

"Do you know anyone in Cuba?" she asked him.

"I am a friend of the Cuban revolution."

He presented the documentary evidence he had prepared to showcase his pro-Castro activities. These papers included the record of his arrest, contacts with the Communist and Socialist parties, and even the records he had taken from Jaggars-Chiles-Stovall. Silvia strongly supported Castro even though she was a Mexican citizen. She was impressed with his credentials. On his visa application she wrote: *"The applicant states that he is a member of the American Communist Party and Secretary in New Orleans of the Fair Play for Cuba Committee. He displayed documents in proof of his membership in the two aforementioned organizations . . ."* She wrote down his address and phone number.

She was a little suspicious of him. She felt the American was too eager in displaying his leftist credentials such as: membership cards for the Fair

Play for Cuba Committee, and the American Communist Party, old Soviet documents, a newspaper clipping on his arrest in New Orleans, a photo of him being escorted by a policeman on each arm which Duran thought looked phony. She also knew belonging to the Communist Party was illegal in Mexico in 1963. For that reason, a Communist would normally travel in the country with only a passport. Yet here was Lee carrying items which could result in him being arrested. She told Lee he lacked the photographs he needed for his visa application. Lee, again, walked to the Soviet and then returned to the Cuban embassy that same afternoon. He had the photographs she had requested.

"I have the photographs you asked for," said Lee.

"I see, but your visa still can't be processed."

"And why the hell not?" demanded Lee.

"You first need an entry visa into the Soviet Union."

"Well, that shouldn't be a problem. I use to live there. Call the Soviet embassy," he suggested.

She called the Soviet embassy. They informed her it would take four or five months before they could issue him a visa. And still he may need permission from Moscow. When she relayed the message to Lee, he became angry. He demanded to see a higher ranked Cuban official. He met with the consul, Eusebio Azque, briefly. After an exchange of heated words, he refused to expedite Lee's visa so he could leave immediately for Havana. His efforts on behalf of the Fair Play for Cuba Committee were not important enough to the Cuban revolution to gain him the special treatment he demanded. Lee stormed out of the embassy.

Lee returned to the Cuban embassy the next day even though it was Saturday. After a brief meeting with the Cuban officials Lee walked back to the Soviet embassy. He suggested that maybe the Soviet embassy in Washington, D.C. might be able to resolve the situation. After he left the embassy, the Soviet officials cabled the KGB center in Moscow. They requested information on whether or not should Lee be granted an immediate visa.

Lee returned to the Soviet embassy on Monday morning. He renewed his request for a quick visa to the Soviet Union. Lee became even more agitated than he had on Saturday, referring to FBI surveillance and persecution. He took a revolver from his jacket pocket, placed it on the table, and said, "*See? This is what I must now carry to protect my life.*" The Soviet officials carefully took the gun and removed its bullets. They told him once again they could not give him a quick visa. They offered him instead the necessary forms to be filled out. He didn't take them. Oleg Nechiporenko joined the three men as their conversation was ending. For the second time, he accompanied a depressed Lee Oswald to the gate of the embassy, this time with Lee's returned revolver and its loose bullets stuck back in his jacket pocket. Nechiporenko and the other officials immediately prepared a report on his two embassy visits which they cabled to Moscow Center.

On Tuesday, October 1st, Lee returned to the Cuban Embassy to make a final attempt to get his visa. As requested by Lee, Silvia called the Soviet Embassy and handed the receiver to him. He spoke in Russian to a Soviet guard. He wanted to know if a telegram had arrived from the Soviet Embassy about his visa. The guard wasn't familiar with the case so he suggested Lee returned to the Soviet Embassy.

Later on that same day, Pedro Gutierrez, a credit investigator for a Mexican department store, saw Lee leaving the Cuban Embassy in the company of a tall Cuban man and the both of them got into a car. That night Lee was seen in the hotel with two dark-skinned Cubans. Early the next morning he checked out of the hotel and hailed a taxi. At 8:30AM he caught the Transporte del Norte bus for Texas.

The CIA's plan for Lee Harvey Oswald was working to perfection. At first they panicked when he went to Mexico City. But they realized the fact he was applying for Cuban and Soviet visas could be used as evidence of his attempting to gain asylum in Communist countries. Lee didn't realize it but by traveling to Mexico City, the scenario there laid the foundation for blaming the president's upcoming murder on Cuba and USSR, thereby providing the rationale in its aftermath for an invasion of Cuba and a possible nuclear attack on Russia.

The CIA knew Lee wouldn't be able to get a visa to travel to Cuba. But it didn't matter, because everything was going according to their plans. Once President Kennedy was assassinated, this trip would help solidify their story Lee was a pro-Castro nut. And it would give the CIA and the military leaders just what they wanted: the authorization to invade Cuba and the go ahead to bomb the Soviet Union. But the fact the CIA wasn't aware or prepared for Lee's trip to Mexico City would become obvious to investigators of President Kennedy's murder.

The Central Intelligence Agency's Mexico City Station kept a close watch on activities at the Cuban and Soviet Consulates. Agents had set up hidden observation points across the street which took pictures of visitors to the two consulates. The Agency had also wiretapped the phones at both the Cuban and Soviet Consulates. The CIA had front-row surveillance seats for what transpired there.

On October 9, 1963, CIA headquarters received a cable from its Mexico City Station about an October 1st phone call to the Soviet Consulate which had been wiretapped, taped, transcribed, and translated from Russian to English. The call came from *"an American male who spoke broken Russian"* and who *"said his name (was) Lee Oswald."* The man who said he was Oswald stated he had been at the Soviet Embassy on September 30th when he spoke with a consul he believed was Valery Vladimirovich Kostikov. He asked *"if there (was) anything new re telegram to Washington."* The Soviet guard who answered the phone said nothing had been received yet, but the request had been sent. He then hung up.

Valery Vladimirovich Kostikov was well known to the Central Intelligence Agency and the Federal Bureau of Investigation as the KGB agent in Mexico City who directed Division 13. Division 13 was the KGB department for terrorism, sabotage, and assassination. Given the notoriety Kostikov in the United States intelligence circles, it is remarkable that when CIA headquarters cabled the State Department, the FBI, and the Navy on October 10th to relay the wiretapped information it had received on Lee Oswald the day before, the cable made no reference to his specific connection to Kostikov. What were they hiding?

CHAPTER 37

---◻---

"Sure it's a big job; but I don't know anyone
who can do it better than I can."

John F. Kennedy

In the meantime, an impatient President John F. Kennedy had decided to create his own back channel to communicate with Fidel Castro, just as he had done with Nikita Khrushchev. On October 24th, President Kennedy was interviewed at the White House by French journalist Jean Daniel. He granted the interview as a perfect way for him to communicate informally with Castro, through pointed remarks which Jean would inevitably share with his next interview subject. Jean realized President Kennedy, who asked to see him, again right after he saw Castro, wanted to know Castro's response. The president was making Daniel his unofficial envoy to the Cuban prime minister.

> *"From the beginning I personally followed the development of these events (in Cuba) with mounting concern. There are few subjects to which I have devoted more painstaking attention . . . Here is what I believe. I believe that there is no country in the world, including all the African regions, including any and all the countries under colonial domination, where economic colonization, humiliation and exploitation were worse than in Cuba, in part owing to my country's policies during the Batista regime . . . I approved the proclamation which Fidel Castro made in the Sierra Maestra, which he justifiably called for justice and especially yearned Cuba of corruption. I will go even further: to some extent it is as though Batista was the incarnation of a number of sins on*

the part of the United States. Now we shall have to pay for those sins. In the matter of the Batista regime, I am in the agreement with the first Cuban revolutionaries. That is perfectly clear. But it is also clear that the problem has ceased to be a Cuban one, and has become international—that is, it has become a Soviet problem . . . I know that through (Castro's) fault—either his 'will to independence' his madness or Communism—the world was on the verge of nuclear war in October 1962. The Russians understood this very well, at least after our reaction; but so far as Fidel Castro is concerned, I must say I don't know whether he realizes this, or if he even cares about it. The continuation of the blockade (against Cuba) depends on the continuation of subversive activities", said President Kennedy.

When briefing President Kennedy, President Dwight Eisenhower emphasized the communist threat in Southeast Asia as a requiring priority. He considered Laos to be "the cork in the bottle" in regards in the regional threat. In March 1961, President Kennedy voiced a change in policy from supporting a "free' Laos to a "neutral" Laos, indicating privately Vietnam, not Laos, should be deemed America's tripwire for communism's spread in the area.

On April 20, 1961, President Kennedy still upset over the failure in Cuba; he accepted the counterinsurgency program for Vietnam. He directed Deputy Secretary of Defense Roswell Gilpatric to make recommendations for a series of actions to prevent the Communist domination of the government of Vietnam. By the end of April, a revised counterinsurgency program had been submitted to President Kennedy. He wasted no time in implementing many of its recommendations. The first troop movement, the deployment of a four hundred man Special Forces group to South Vietnam, was made to accelerate the training of the South Vietnamese army. In May 1961, he dispatched Lyndon Johnson to meet with South Vietnam's President Ngo Dinh Diem. Lyndon assured President Diem of more aid in molding a fighting force which could resist the Communists. President Kennedy announced a change of policy from support to partnership with the South Vietnam president in defeat of communism in South Vietnam.

Initially President Kennedy followed President Eisenhower's lead by using limited military action to fight the North Vietnamese communist forces led by Ho Chi Minh. Proclaiming a fight against the spread of communism, President Kennedy enacted policies providing political, economic, and military support for the unstable French-installed South Vietnamese government, which included sending 16,000 military advisers and United States Special Forces to the area. President Kennedy also agreed to the use of free-fire zones, napalm, defoliants and jet planes. Late in 1961, the Viet Cong began assuming a predominant presence, initially seizing the provincial capital of Phuoc Vinh. The Kennedy Administration increased military support, but the South Vietnamese military was unable to make headway against the pro-independence Viet-Minh and Viet Cong forces.

In April 1963, President Kennedy expressed his assessment of the situation in Vietnam at the time: *"We don't have a prayer of staying in Vietnam. Those people hate us. They are going to throw our asses out of there at any point. But I can't give up that territory to the Communists and get the American people to re-elect me."*

By July 1963, President Kennedy faced a crisis in Vietnam. The Administration's response was to assist in the coup d'état of the president of South Vietnam, Ngo Dinh Diem. On August 21st, just as the new United States Ambassador Henry Cabot Lodge arrived, Ngo Dinh Diem, and his brother Ngo Dinh Nhu ordered South Vietnam forces, funded and trained by the CIA, into the temples to quell Buddhist demonstrations. The crackdowns heightened expectations of a coup d'état to remove Diem with (or perhaps by) his brother, Nhu. Henry Cabot Lodge was instructed to try to get Diem and Nhu to step down and out of the country. Diem would not listen to him.

Cable 243 (DEPTEL 23) dated August 24th followed, declaring: Washington would no longer tolerate Nhu's actions and Henry Cabot Lodge was ordered to pressure Diem to remove his brother. If Diem refused, the Americans would explore alternative leadership. Henry Cabot Lodge replied to this contradictory cable, saying the only workable option was to get the South Vietnam generals to overthrow Diem and Nhu, as originally planned. At week's end, President Kennedy learned from Henry Cabot Lodge the Diem government might, due to France's assistance to Nhu, be dealing secretly with the Communists—and might ask the Americans to leave. Orders were sent to Saigon and throughout Washington to "destroy all coup cables".

In September, at a White House meeting, symbolic of very different ongoing appraisals of Vietnam, President Kennedy was given updated assessments after personal inspections on the ground by the Department of Defense, General Victor Krulak, and State Department, Joseph Mendenhall. General Krulak said the military fight against the communists was progressing and being won. While Joseph stated the country was civilly being lost to any United States influence. President Kennedy reacted by saying, "*Did you two gentlemen visit the same country?*" He was unaware the two men were at such odds that they did not speak on the return flight.

In October 1963, President Kennedy appointed Defense Secretary Robert McNamara and General Maxwell Taylor to a Vietnam mission in another effort to synchronize the information and formulation of policy. The stated objective of the McNamara-Taylor mission was to emphasize the importance of getting to the bottom of the differences in reporting from US representatives in Vietnam. In meeting with McNamara, Taylor, and Lodge, Diem again refused to agree to governing measures insisted upon by the United States, helping to dispel McNamara's previous optimism of Diem. Taylor and McNamara were also enlightened by Vietnam's V.P. Nguyen Tho (choice of many to succeed Diem should a coup occur), who in detailed terms obliterated Taylor's information that the military was succeeding in the countryside. The Mission report, after it had been through the NSC, nevertheless retained, at President Kennedy's insistence, a recommended schedule for troop withdrawals: 1,000 by year's end and complete withdrawal in 1965, something the NSC considered strategical fantasy. The final report also portrayed military progress, an increasingly unpopular Diem-led government, not vulnerable to a coup, albeit possible internal assassination.

In late October, intelligence wires again reported a coup of the Diem government was afoot. The source, Duong Van Minh a/k/a "Big Minh" wanted to know the position of the United States. President Kennedy's instruction to Henry Cabot Lodge was to offer covert assistant to the coup, excluding assassination, but to ensure deniability by the United States. Later that month as the coup became imminent, President Kennedy ordered all cables routed through him, and a policy of "control and cut out" was initiated—to insure presidential control of United States responses, while cutting him out of the paper trail.

South Vietnam's Buddhist majority had long been discontented with Diem's strong favoritism towards Catholics. Public servants and army officers had long been promoted on the basis of religious preference, and government contracts, American aid, business favors and tax concessions were preferentially given to Catholics. The Catholic Church was the largest landowner in the country, and its holdings were exempt from land reform. In the countryside, Catholics were *de facto* exempt from performing corvee labor and in some rural areas; Catholic priests led private armies against Buddhist villages. Discontent with Diem and Nhu exploded into mass protest during the summer of 1963 when nine Buddhists died at the hand of Diem's army and police on Vesak, the birthday of Gautama Buddha.

In May 1963, a law against the flying of religious flags was selectively invoked; the Buddhist flag was banned from display on Vesak while the Vatican flag was displayed to celebrate the anniversary of the consecration of Archbishop Ngo Dinh Thuc, Diem's brother. The Buddhists defied the ban and a protest was ended when government forces opened fire. With Diem remaining intransigent in the face of escalating Buddhist demands for religious equality, sections of society began calling for his removal from power.

The key turning point came shortly after midnight on August 21, when Nhu's Special Forces raided and vandalized Buddhist pagodas across the country, arresting thousands of monks and causing a death toll estimated to be in the hundreds. Numerous coup plans had been explored by the army before, but the plotters intensified their activities with increased confidence after the administration of President Kennedy authorized the U.S. embassy to explore the possibility of a leadership change.

On September 2, 1963, President Kennedy was interviewed by television anchorman Walter Cronkite, who said, "Mr. President, the only hot war we've got running at the moment is of course the war in Vietnam, and we have our difficulties there quite obviously."

"I don't think that unless a greater effort is made by the government to win popular support that the war can be won out there. In the final analysis, it is their war. They are the ones who have to win or lose it. We can help them, we can give them equipment, we can send our men out there as advisers, but they have to win it, the people of Vietnam, against the Communists," replied President Kennedy.

President Kennedy was losing control of his government. In early September, he discovered another key decision related to a coup had been made without his knowledge. At a White House meeting the president was discussing whether or not to cut off the Commodity Import Program which propped up South Vietnam's economy. It was a far-reaching decision. The United AID, David Bell, made a casual comment which stopped the discussion.

"There's no point in talking about cutting off commodity aid. I've already cut it off," said David Bell.

"You've done what?" asked President Kennedy.

"Cut off commodity aid," David replied.

"Who the hell told you to that?" asked President Kennedy.

"No one, it's an automatic policy. We do it whenever we have differences with a client government," said David Bell.

President Kennedy shook his head in dismay. "My God, do you know what you've done?"

By having AID cut off the Commodity Import Program, the Central Intelligence Agency made it almost impossible for President Kennedy to avoid a coup in South Vietnam. The aid cutoff was a designated signal for a coup. In late August, the CIA had agreed with the plotting South Vietnamese general that just such a cut in economic aid would be the United States government's green light to the generals for a coup.

On August 29th, at a top-secret meeting in Vietnam approved by Henry Cabot Lodge, the CIA's Lucien Conein had asked coup leader General Duong Van Minh point blank, "What would you consider a sign that the American government does indeed intend to support you generals in a coup?"

Minh answered, "Let the United States suspend economic aid to the Diem government."

It was twelve days later when David Bell told President Kennedy at the White House he had in fact already cut off commodity aid to Diem. The CIA had thereby sent a signal to the generals to prepare a coup. The aid cutoff was the official confirmation that the United States government supported the generals' plot.

Given the accomplished fact of the aid cutoff, President Kennedy was left with the choice of either relieving that economic pressure on Diem, which would be taken as President Kennedy's consent to Diem's repression of the Buddhists, or allowing the suspension of aid to take its gradual toll on the South Vietnamese economy and government—thus proceeding step by step toward a coup. President Kennedy's slender hope was the gradual impact of the aid cutoff, combined with a genuine effort at dialogue with Diem, could still persuade Diem to lift his repression of the Buddhists in time to avoid a coup. The moment even seemed ripe for a change in Diem, who surprised his critics by deciding to invite a United Nations fact-finding mission to South Vietnam to investigate the Buddhists crisis.

CHAPTER 38

———————□———————

"The basic problems facing the world today
are not susceptible to a military solution."

John F. Kennedy

In the early summer, President Kennedy had kept his military and CIA advisers out of his discussions on Vietnam. During the early part of President Kennedy's final summer in office, he consulted on Vietnam with just a few advisers in the State Department and White House, thereby leaving out representatives of the Defense Department, the Joint Chiefs of Staff, and the CIA. By leaving the Pentagon and the CIA out of the Vietnam loop, President Kennedy wasn't fooling them. They knew he planned to withdraw from Vietnam. At the Pentagon, the Joint Chiefs of Staff were dragging their heels on the Vietnam withdrawal plan. President Kennedy knew his key ally in the Pentagon was his loyal civilian bureaucrat Secretary of Defense Robert McNamara. However, McNamara's power on his behalf was hedged in by the noncooperation of the top brass. He had been stalled by his generals for a full year from getting the Vietnam withdrawal President Kennedy wanted drawn up. When the Pacific Command did finally come up with a plan in May 1963, McNamara had to reject its timeline as at least a year too slow. After the Defense Secretary ordered an expedited plan, the Joint Chiefs balked again. The chiefs used the Buddhist crisis as a rationale for bogging down Robert McNamara's May order that a specific plan be prepared for the withdrawal of one thousand military personnel by the end of 1963. On August 20th, the chiefs wrote to McNamara that *"until political and religious tensions now confronting the Government of Vietnam have eased," "no US units should be withdrawn from the Republic of Vietnam."* The chiefs argued, for the same reason, that "*the final decision to implement the withdrawal plan should be withheld until late October.*" They now wanted any decision on a withdrawal put on hold until late October. Pushed by his recognition of the war's futility and its rising death toll, President Kennedy had waited long enough to begin withdrawing from Vietnam. Although pressured by the Pentagon for a bigger war and by the State Department for a CIA-aided coup, the president decided to authorize a troop withdrawal, while continuing to hold off a coup.

In the fall of 1963, while Lee Harvey Oswald was being redirected to Dallas, Texas, President John Kennedy was trying to begin his withdrawal from Vietnam. He was being obstructed by military officials—and by his own support of a coup d'état against the South Vietnamese government. On August 24th, President Kennedy was in Hyannis Port for the weekend. During this weekend Roger Hilsman, working with Averell Harriman and President Kennedy's aide Michael Forrestal, drafted an urgent telegram to newly appointed Saigon ambassador Henry Cabot Lodge. The telegram authorized United States support of a looming coup by rebel South Vietnamese generals, if Diem refused to remove from power his brother Nhu and sister-in-law Madame Nhu.

Ngo Dinh Nhu seemed to be taking over the Saigon government. His ever more violent repression of the Buddhists, together with Madame Nhu's statements applauding Buddhists immolations, had outraged Vietnamese and American public opinion. When President Kennedy was urged by Michael Forrestal in Washington to endorse the telegram because all his advisers had done so, the president said to go ahead and send it. Then the generals backed down from the coup. However, in a hasty policy decision which President Kennedy soon regretted but never reversed, he had put the government on record as being in conditional support of a coup—after giving South Vietnam President Diem plenty of chances to remove the Nhus. After the telegram, Henry Cabot Lodge cabled back to the State Department the following: "*Believe that chances of Diem meeting our demands are virtually nil. At same time, by making them we give Nhu chance to forestall or block action by military. Risk, we believe, is not worth taking, with Nhu in control of combat forces in Saigon. Therefore, propose we go straight to Generals with our demands, without informing Diem.*"

The State Department agreed at once to Vietnam Ambassador Lodge's downward revision of an already disastrous directive. In Hyannis Port, President Kennedy was informed after the fact by Michael Forrestal that Acting Secretary of State James Ball, Averell Harriman, and Roger Hilsman had approved Lodge's "modifications" that now gave Diem no opportunity at all to forestall a coup.

Through longtime CIA operative in Vietnam Colonel Lucien Conein, Ambassador Lodge maintained regular contacts with the generals. Conein had known most of the coup generals for years, ever since he conducted the CIA's sabotage operations against Viet Minh in the mid-fifties under the direction of Colonel Edward Lansdale. Henry Cabot Lodge was continually frustrated over the next two months that he could not, even though Lucien urging, get the generals to stage a coup sooner. President Kennedy, on the other hand, continued to hope Diem might still somehow back away from his repressive policies and remove the Nhus, who seemed to be the force behind them. Through Secretary of State Dean Rusk, the president repeatedly urged Lodge to explore such alternatives with Diem.

On August 28th, Rusk wired Lodge: "*We have concurred until now in your belief that nothing should be said to Diem, but changing circumstances, including his probable knowledge that something is afoot, lead us to ask again if you see value in one last man-to-man effort to persuade him to govern himself and decisively to eliminate political influences of Nhus.*"

Lodge rejected Rusk suggestion: "*I believe that such a step has no chance of getting the desired result and would have the very serious effect of being regarded by the Generals as a sign of American indecision and delay; I believe this is a risk which we should not run.*" Lodge lectured the Secretary of State that removing the Nhus "*surely cannot be done by working through Diem. In fact Diem will oppose it . . . The best chance of doing it is by the Generals taking over the government lock, stock, and barrel.*" President Kennedy had another objective in mind in his 11th hour efforts to appeal to Diem, an objective he realized Henry Cabot Lodge was not going to facilitate. He wanted to save President Diem's life. To the Cold War establishment, Ngo Dinh Diem was becoming disposable. Washington's Cold War leaders had been divided for some time over the merits of retaining Diem as their client "democratic" head of state for the Vietnam War. It was becoming obvious that Diem, an incompetent despot, had to go. President Kennedy was under mounting pressure from the more liberal side of his government, the State Department, to end Diem's flagrantly authoritarian rule by a coup.

Central Intelligence Agency's Deputy Director of Plans Richard Helms was asked by Averell Harriman to approve the August 24th telegram to Lodge since CIA Director John McCone (a Diem supporter) was out of town. He did so without hesitation. It was the CIA's career tactician Helms, not President Kennedy's appointee John McCone, who was running the Agency's covert operations. Central Intelligence Agency Director John McCone was a figurehead out of the CIA's covert action loop. Richard felt no need to seek out John McCone's judgment when it came to the CIA's endorsing a coup in South Vietnam. "*It's about time we bit this bullet,*" he commented to Averell Harriman. This was in direct conflict with what CIA Director McCone would say to President Kennedy on his return to Washington. But it was the deputy director of plans who was literally calling the CIA's shots, not McCone.

On September 19, 1963, Henry Cabot Lodge sent a telegram to President Kennedy rejecting once again the president's suggestion that the ambassador "*resume dialogue*" with Diem and Nhu (a dialogue never really begun). He told President Kennedy that such a dialogue was hopeless: "*Frankly, I see no opportunity at all for substantive changes.*" He continued to think his silence was better than dialogue: "*There are signs that Diem-Nhu is somewhat bothered by my silence.*" By this time President Kennedy had realized that he could not rely on his newly appointed ambassador to carry out his wishes. For this reason President Kennedy chose to send Robert McNamara and General Maxwell Taylor, two coup opponents, to Vietnam to assess the situation and meet with President Diem. The McNamara-Taylor mission stalled the forward progress of Lodge's coup-making with the CIA and the generals. President Kennedy's purpose was being undermined at the same time by a letter sent surreptitiously to Lodge by Roger Hilsman, principal author of the August 24th telegram.

CHAPTER 39

―◻―

"The cost of freedom is always high, but Americans
have always paid it. And one path we shall never choose, and
that is the path of surrender, or submission."

John F. Kennedy

Once Lee Harvey Oswald was back in Dallas, he spent a night in the
YMCA. Then he moved to a rooming house on North Marsalis Street
in the Oak Cliff Section. One week later, he changed his residence once
again to a rooming house at North Beckley Street. He registered under the
alias O. H. Lee. Marina at this time was still staying with Ruth Paine. He
didn't want Marina telling anyone where he was staying.

One late night in September a man who resembled Lee Harvey
Oswald asked Malcolm H. Price, Jr for help in adjusting his scope on his
rifle at the Sports Drome Rifle Range in Dallas. It was just about dusk
when Malcolm turned on his car headlights on a target at the rifle range,
so he could adjust the man's scope. After he zeroed in the rifle, "Lee" used
it to fire three shots into a bull's eye on the target illuminating by the car's
headlights. Malcolm would see the same man practicing with his rifle in
late October at the Sports Drome, and again in November not long before
President Kennedy's assassination. The CIA hired this "Lee Oswald" look
alike to showcase he was honing his shooting skills in the weeks before
President Kennedy was assassinated. But what they failed to realize at the
time was Lee's handler had lost contact with him. They were sure he was
in Dallas, but when in reality he was in Mexico City trying to get a visa to
the Soviet Union through the Cuban and Russian Embassy. They would
have to explain how Lee could be in two places at once. To be able to
explain this feat, the CIA hired a man to call the embassies in Mexico City

and make them believe he was Lee. They even had him go down to the embassies so the surveillance team could take pictures of him. The reason for this little charade was to make it appear that Lee really didn't go to Mexico City but had been in Dallas all that time.

When Robert McNamara and Maxwell Taylor returned from their trip to Vietnam on October 2ⁿᵈ, President Kennedy already knew the recommendation of the report they delivered to him. They had originally come from the president himself. While McNamara and Taylor were gathering information in Vietnam, they cabled the data back to General Victor Krulak's Pentagon office. His editorial and stenographic team worked twenty-four hours a day to put together the fact-finding trip's report. General Krulak went regularly to the White House to confer confidentially with John and Robert Kennedy. There President Kennedy and his brother dictated to him the recommendation of the *"McNamara-Taylor Report."* When the secretaries finished typing up the report in General Krulak's office, it was then bound in a leather cover flown to Hawaii, and placed in the hands of McNamara and Taylor on their way back from Vietnam. They read the report on their flight to Washington, and presented it to President Kennedy at the White House on the morning of October 2ⁿᵈ. The president accepted its recommendations, most significantly one for the withdrawal of one thousand military personnel by the end of the year.

President Kennedy convened a National Security Council (NSC) meeting on the evening of October 2ⁿᵈ, to discuss the McNamara-Taylor Report. The majority of NSC members were opposed to the withdrawal. The president himself hesitated over the critical phrase *by the end of this year* as a preface to the sentence, *The U.S. program for training Vietnamese should have progressed to the point where 1,000 U.S. military personnel can be withdrawn.*

"You know, if we are not able to take this action by the end of the year, we will be accused of being overoptimistic," said President Kennedy.

"It will meet the view of Senator Fulbright and others that we are bogged down forever in Vietnam. It reveals that we have a withdrawal plan," suggested Robert McNamara.

"Okay, I will agree to that as long as the time limits were presented as a part of the report. It cannot be viewed as a prediction of mine," said President Kennedy.

President Kennedy then bypassed the National Security Council majority and endorsed the report's withdrawal recommendations which had come from himself.

"Mr. President, I suggest you announce the plan to withdraw from Vietnam as soon as possible," said the secretary of defense.

"You're right, Robert, by announcing the withdrawal plan publicly will pretty much set it in concrete," said President Kennedy.

Nine days later President Kennedy signed NSAM 263, therefore making official governmental policy the McNamara-Taylor recommendations for the withdrawal of "*1,000 U.S. military personnel by the end of 1963*" and "*by the end of 1965 . . . the bulk of U.S. personnel.*" That 1963 withdrawal, together with President Kennedy's plan to withdraw the majority of the United States personnel in Vietnam by the end of 1965, became official government policy on October 11, 1963, in the president's National Security Action Memorandum (NSAM) Number 263. President Kennedy sensed the CIA and the military would now try to cut the political ground out from under his withdrawal plans by changing their reports from good to bad.

Henry Cabot Lodge devoted the bulk of his October 7, 1963 telegram to documenting the most basic reason why he thought Diem and his dominant brother had to be removed from power at any cost. It was not the Buddhists crisis but something more worrisome: "*Nhu says in effect that he can and would like to get along without the Americans. He only wants some helicopter units and some money. But he definitely does not want American military personnel who, he says, are absolutely incapable of fighting a guerilla war.*"

The bottom line for Henry was President Diem and Nhu were dangerously close to doing what they had been threatening to do for months—asking the United States government to withdraw its forces from Vietnam. He concluded his rebuttal to President Kennedy by making an ominous connection between a withdrawal request and a coup: "*we should consider a request to withdrawal as a growing possibility. The beginning of withdrawal might trigger off a coup.*"

The South Vietnam ambassador had President Kennedy in a corner. At the very moment when President Kennedy was quietly ordering the beginning of his own United States withdrawal from Vietnam, Henry was warning him that the request for a withdrawal by Diem and Nhu could trigger a coup in Saigon which he was facilitating. In his efforts to gain control of his own government on a Vietnam policy, President Kennedy found himself in another struggle with the CIA. When he was blocked by a CIA front, AID, President Kennedy was experiencing one effect of the way in which the CIA had established its invisible control over Vietnam.

It was also during this time Marina was staying with Ruth Paine. Lee moved into a boarding house under the alias of O.H. Lee. Their second daughter was born while she was living with Ruth. Marina helped with the housework and Ruth's Russian studies while he visited on the weekends. Even though Lee lived in a boarding house, he stored some of his items in Ruth's garage. On October 31, 1963, FBI agent, James Hosty visited Ruth and Marina to discover where Lee was living. That was the excuse he used to talk to Marina, in actuality he was more interested in interviewing Marina. The FBI was still intent on learning whether or not she was a KGB agent. He spoke to both Ruth and Marina about Lee. When Lee heard about the visit he went to the FBI office in Dallas. When he was told James was at lunch, Lee left him a note in an envelope. The content of the envelope has remained a mystery. A receptionist working at the Dallas FBI office claimed it included a threat to *"blow up the FBI and the Dallas Police Department if you don't stop bothering my wife."* James Hosty claimed it said *"If you have anything you want to learn about me, come talk to me directly. If you don't cease bothering my wife, I will take appropriate action and report this to the proper authorities."* And then there were some conspiracy theorists who believe Lee was a FBI informant all this time. They claimed Lee was actually warning the FBI about the plot the assassinate President Kennedy in Dallas.

CHAPTER 40

—▢—

"The courage of life is often a less dramatic spectacle than
the courage of a final moment; but it is no less a magnificent
mixture of triumph and tragedy."

John F. Kennedy

Lee Oswald wasn't the only one with CIA connection. Ruth Paine's father
had been employed by the CIA for International Development. It was
regarded by many as a source of cover for the CIA. Her brother-in-law was
employed by the same agency in the Washington, D.C. area. It was also
a popular belief that Ruth was employed by the CIA to "babysit" Marina
while Lee continued to work towards the completion of his current
mission for the CIA.

On October 9, 1963, one week before Lee Harvey Oswald began
his job at the Texas School Book Depository Building, an FBI official
in Washington, D.C., disconnected him from a federal alarm system
which was about to identify him as a threat to national security. The FBI
man's name was Marvin Gheesling. He was a supervisor in the Soviet
espionage section at FBI headquarters. His timing was remarkable. Four
years earlier, in November 1959 shortly after he told the United States
Embassy in Moscow he would give military secrets to the Soviet Union,
the FBI issued a FLASH on him. A "Wanted Notice Card" was sent
throughout the Bureau stating that anyone who received information or
an inquiry on him should notify the Espionage Section, Division 5. By its
FLASH the FBI had sent out a security watch on him which covered all
its offices. When Marvin Gheesling cancelled Lee's FLASH, he effectively
silenced the national security alarm which was just about to sound from

an incoming CIA report on his activities in Mexico City. Had the FBI alarm sounded, he would have been placed on the Security Index, drawing critical law enforcement attention to him prior to President Kennedy's visit to Dallas.

President Kennedy wanted to save South Vietnam President Diem's life from the looming general's coup which had picked up a steamrolling momentum not only in South Vietnam (with Henry Cabot Lodge pushing it) but also from opposite sides of the United States government in Washington. As a senator, John Kennedy, like Mike Mansfield, had helped bring Diem to power in South Vietnam. Regardless of Diem's downward path since then, President Kennedy did not want to see him killed in a coup, especially one he was condoning. Because he was surrounded by people he couldn't trust, President Kennedy called in an old friend to help him try to save Diem's life.

Torby Macdonald had been President Kennedy's closest friend at Harvard. Just like President Kennedy, Torby was Irish Catholic, a second son, an athlete, and an avid reader. Torby was at his side through severe illnesses at Harvard. Both men had sharp wits. In turn they became political comrades in Washington. He was elected as a Massachusetts member of the House of Representatives in 1954, with Senator Kennedy's support. When Kennedy was elected President, Torby remained his closest friend in Congress. Torby Macdonald, perhaps the man President Kennedy trusted most after Robert Kennedy, was who he turned to in the fall of 1963 to help him try and save the life of Ngo Diem.

President Kennedy commissioned Torby to go to Saigon to appeal personally to Diem on behalf of the president. He was to bypass the CIA, the State Department, and Henry Cabot Lodge, in order to make an urgent personal appeal to the South Vietnamese president to take the steps necessary to save his life. Torby would fly in and out of Saigon on military, not civilian, planes to maintain as much secrecy as possible. He needed to show the South Vietnam president that the American president still maintained a lingering support for Diem. Torby's preparations for his mission and the trip itself were carried out in total secrecy, with no known written records.

Torby Macdonald met with President Diem. He represented President Kennedy's personal plea to Diem to remove the Nhus from power and he himself take refuge in the American Embassy in Saigon. Macdonald warned Diem: "*They're going to kill you. You've got to get out of here temporarily to seek sanctuary in the American Embassy and you must get rid of your sister-in-law and your brother.*" Diem would not budge.

On October 14, 1963, at the suggestion of a neighbor, Ruth Paine phoned the Texas School Book Depository and was told there was a job opening. She informed Lee. He was interviewed the following day at the TSBD and started to work there on October 16, 1963. On October 15, 1963, Robert Adams of the Texas Employment Commission phoned the Paine residence with a much better job prospect for Lee. He spoke with someone at the Paine residence about being prepared to give Lee a referral for permanent employment as a baggage or cargo handler at Trans Texas Airways, for a salary $100 per month higher than what was offered by the Book Depository's only temporary job. Robert learned from the person who answered the phone that Lee was not there. He left a message with that person that Lee should contact him at the Commission. Robert called the Paine residence about the higher-paying job again the next morning. He learned from the person who answered the phone that Lee was not there and he had already obtained employment at the Texas School Book Depository. He accordingly cancelled Lee as a referral for the more lucrative job.

Toward the end of October, Rolando Cubella made an extraordinary demand of the Central Intelligence Agency. Before he would go ahead with his proposed plan to eliminate Fidel Castro, he wanted an assurance from the Attorney General that the Kennedy Administration would actively support him in this operation. Forgoing the objection of his superior, Desmond Fitzgerald decided to meet with Rolando. He acted as a "personal representative" of Robert Kennedy. This meeting risked compromising President Kennedy. But in his opinion the risk was outweighed by the gains in advancing the removal of Fidel Castro. The meeting took place on October 29th. He assured Rolando that once the coup had succeeded and Castro had been removed from power, the Kennedy Administration would be fully prepared to aid and support the new government. Rolando asked the delivery of specific weapons. He wanted a rifle with telescopic sights and a means of delivering a poison injection without detection. About two weeks later, Desmond arranged a further "signal" for Rolando and his followers in Cuba. He claimed he wrote a section of a speech President

Kennedy was set to deliver in Miami on November 18th. The passaged described the Castro government as a "small band of conspirators" which "once removed," would ensure United States assistance to the Cuban nation. The day after President Kennedy delivered this "signal," Desmond ordered the case officer to arrange another meeting with Rolando. At this meeting the specifics of his operation would be discussed. Rolando agreed to postpone his scheduled return to Cuba if the meeting could take place in Paris on November 22nd.

On October 29TH, after a week of leaving phone messages for Lisa Howard, Castro's aide Rene Vallejo finally reached Howard at her home.

"Fidel Castro is just as eager as he was during your visit in April to improve relations with the United States," said Rene.

"That's good to hear," said Lisa.

"The only thing is, it is impossible for Fidel Castro to leave Cuba to go to the United Nations or anywhere else to talk with a Kennedy representative."

"That's okay because I have been authorized to tell you that there is now a United States official who has been authorized to listen to Castro," said Lisa.

"I will relay that message to Castro and then I will call you back."

At the same time as the generals were confirming their plot in Saigon, the FBI was discovering a plot to assassinate President Kennedy in Chicago three days later—within hours of the time Diem would be assassinated. On October 30, 1963, the agents at the Chicago Secret Service office were told of the Chicago plot by Special Agent in Charge Maurice Martineau. His announcement to the Chicago Secret Service agents about a plot against President Kennedy came in the context of their preparations for the president's arrival at O'Hara Airport three days later on Saturday, November 2, 1963 at 11:40 AM. On Saturday afternoon, President Kennedy was scheduled to attend the Army-Air Force football game at Soldier Field.

At 9:00 AM Wednesday morning, Maurice Martineau told the agents that the FBI had learned from an informant that four snipers planned to shoot President Kennedy with high-powered rifles. Their ambush was set to happen along the route of the presidential motorcade, as it came in from O'Hara down the Northwest Expressway and into the Loop on Saturday morning.

The FBI reported that, *"the suspects were rightwing para-military fanatics."* The assassination *"would probably be attempted at one of the Northwest Expressway overpasses."* They knew this from an informant named "Lee." The following day, the landlady at a boarding house on the North Side independently provided further information. Four men were renting rooms from her. She had seen four rifles with telescopic sights in one of the men's rooms, together with a newspaper sketch of the president's route. She called the FBI. The FBI told Maurice that everything was now up to the Secret Service. James Rowley, head of the Secret Service in Washington, confirmed to him that J. Edgar Hoover had passed the buck. It was the Secret Service's jurisdiction. The FBI would do nothing to investigate or stop the plot against President Kennedy. Maurice set up a twenty-four hour surveillance of the men's boarding house. He passed out to his agents four photos of the men allegedly involved in the plot. The stakeout reached a quick climax on Thursday night, October 31st, at the same time as halfway around the world rebel tanks and troops were preparing to move through the streets of Saigon toward the presidential palace.

In Chicago, Secret Service agent J. Lloyd Stocks, while in his car, spotted two of the suspects driving. He followed them. When the men drove into an alley behind their rooming house, he did, too. He discovered too late that the alley was a dead end. The men had turned their car around and were on their way back out. As their car squeezed past his car his car radio blared out a message from Maurice Martineau. The startled men looked his way, and then drove off quickly. He reported back to Maurice that he'd blown the surveillance. Maurice ordered the two men be taken into custody immediately. They were seized and brought to the Secret Service headquarters early Friday morning. Through the early morning hours, Stocks questioned one of the two men, while his fellow agent Robert Motto questioned the other. The two suspects, who have remained unknown to this day, stonewalled the questions. In the meantime, their two reported collaborators remained at large. President Kennedy was due to arrive the next day for his motorcade through the streets of Chicago.

Rene Vallejo called Lisa Howard, again on October 31st. He told her, *"Castro would very much like to talk to the United States official anytime*

and appreciated the importance of discretion to all concerned." The key
Castro's comment was the phrase *"to all concerned."* At this point Castro,
like President Kennedy and Khrushchev, was circumventing his own
government in order to talk with the enemy. Castro, too, was struggling
to transcend his Cold War ideology for the sake of peace. Like President
Kennedy and Premier Khrushchev, he had to walk softly.

Lisa Howard reported the Vallejo calls to William Attwood, who in
turned relayed the information to the White House. On November 5th,
he met with President Kennedy's National Security Adviser, McGeorge
Bundy, and Gordon Chase of the National Security Council staff. He
filled them in on Castro's eagerness to facilitate a dialogue with President
Kennedy.

At 11:30 on November 1, Generals Duong Van Minh, the Presidential
Military Adviser, and Tran Van Don, Army Chief of Staff, led a coup
against President Ngo Dinh Diem, assisted by mutinous ARVN officers.
The rebels carefully devised plans to neutralize loyalist officers to prevent
them from saving President Diem. Unbeknownst to Diem, General Ton
That Dinh, the supposed loyalist who commanded the ARVN III Corps
which surrounded the Saigon area, had allied himself with the plotters of
the coup. The second of Diem's most trusted loyalist generals was Huynh
Van Cao, who commanded the IV Corps in the Mekong Delta. Diem
and Nhu were aware of the coup plan, and Nhu responded by planning
a counter-coup, which he called *Operation Bravo*. This plan involved
Dinh and Colonel Le Quang Tung, the loyalist commander of the Special
Forces, staging a phony rebellion before their forces crushed the uprising
to reaffirm the power of the Ngo family.

Unaware Dinh was plotting against him, President Diem allowed Dinh
to organize troops as he saw fit, and Dinh transferred the command of the
Seventh Division from Cao's IV Corps to his own III Corps. This allowed
Colonel Nguyen Huu Co, Dinh's deputy, to take command of the 7th
Division based at My Tho. The transfer allowed the rebels to completely
encircle the capital and denied Cao the opportunity of storming Saigon
and protecting Diem, as he had done during the previous coup attempt
in 1960. Minh and Don had invited senior Saigon based officers to a
meeting at Tan Son Nhut Air Base, the headquarters of the Joint General
Staff (JGS), on the pretext of routine business. Instead, they announced
a coup was underway, with only a few, including Tung, refusing to join.

Tung was later forced at gunpoint to order his loyalist Special Forces to surrender. The coup went smoothly as the rebels quickly captured all key installations in Saigon and sealed incoming roads to prevent loyalist forces from entering. This left only the Presidential Guard to defend Gia Long Palace. The rebels attacked government and loyalist army buildings but delayed the attack on the palace, hoping Diem would resign and accept the offer of safe passage and exile. Diem refused, vowing to reassert his control. After sunset, the 7th Division of Colonel Nguyen Van Thieu, who later became the nation's president, led an assault on Gia Long Palace and it fell by daybreak.

On November 1, 1963, at the same time as the Chicago plot was unraveling, a man bought ammunition for his rifle in a strange way at Morgan's Gun Shop in Fort Worth, Texas. A witness, Dewey Bradford, later told the Federal Bureau Investigations the man was *"rude and impertinent."* The man made an enduring impression on the gun shop's other customer's, as he seemed to have intended. He made a point of telling Bradford he had been in the Marine Corps, a detail which fit Lee Harvey Oswald's background.

CHAPTER 41

———————————————◻︎———————————————

"The great enemy of the truth is very often
not the lie, deliberate, contrived and dishonest, but the
myth, persistent, persuasive and unrealistic."

John F. Kennedy

IN THE EARLY morning of November 2, President Diem agreed to surrender. The ARVN officers had intended to exile Diem and Nhu, having promised the Ngo brothers safe passage out of the country. At 06:00, just before dawn, the officers held a meeting at JGS headquarters to discuss the fate of the Ngo brothers. According to Lucien Conein, the US Army officer and CIA operative who was the American liaison with the coup, most of the officers, including Minh, wanted Diem to have an "honorable retirement" from office, followed by exile. Not all of the senior officers attended the meeting, with Don having already left to make arrangements for the arrival of Diem and Nhu at JGS headquarters. General Nguyen Ngoc Le, a former police chief under Diem in the mid-1950s, strongly lobbied for Diem's execution. There was no formal vote taken at the meeting, and Le attracted only minority support. One general was reported to have said "*To kill weeds, you must pull them up at the roots.*" Lucien reported that the generals had never indicated assassination was in their minds, since an orderly transition of power was a high priority in achieving their ultimate aim of gaining international recognition.

Minh and Don asked Lucien to secure an American aircraft to take the brothers out of the country. Two days earlier, U.S. Ambassador to Vietnam, Henry Cabot Lodge, Jr., had alerted Washington such a request was likely and recommended Saigon as the departure point. This request put the Kennedy administration in a difficult position, as the provision of an airplane would publicly tie it to the coup. When Lucien telephoned David Smith, the acting chief of the Saigon CIA station, there was a ten minute wait. The U.S. government would not allow the aircraft to land in any country, unless that state was willing to grant asylum to Diem. The United States did not want Diem and Nhu to form a government in exile. But at the same time they wanted the brothers far away from Vietnam. Assistant Secretary of State Roger Hilsman had written in August that he believed the brothers should not be allowed to remain in Southeast Asia close to Vietnam. He believed they would plot to regain power in South Vietnam. He felt that if the generals did in fact decided to exile Diem, then he should sent outside of Southeast Asia. Unconditional surrender should be the terms for the Ngo family since it will otherwise seek to outmaneuver both the coups forces and the U.S. If the family is taken alive, the Nhus should be banished to France or any other country willing to receive them. Diem should be treated as the generals wished.

After surrendering, President Diem called Henry Cabot Lodge and spoke to the American ambassador for the last time. Lodge did not report the conversation to Washington, so it was widely assumed the pair last spoke on the previous afternoon when the coup was just starting. When the South Vietnam president called, the United States Ambassador placed the call on hold and then walked away. Upon his return, the ambassador offered Diem and Nhu asylum, but would not arrange for transportation to the Philippines until the next day. This contradicted his earlier offer of asylum the previous day when he implored President Diem to not resist the coup. Henry Lodge placed the call on hold in order to inform Lucien Conein where the brothers were so the generals could capture them. Lucien had phoned the embassy early on the same morning to inquire about the generals' request for a plane to transport the brothers out of Saigon. One of Henry's staff told him the plane would have to go directly to the faraway asylum-offering country, so the brothers could not disembark at a nearby stopover country and stay there to stage a counter-coup. He was told the nearest plane which was capable of such a long range flight was in Guam, and it would take twenty-four hours to make the necessary arrangements. Minh was astounded and told him the generals could not hold Diem for that long of a period. Lucien did not suspect a deliberate delay by the American embassy.

In the meantime, Minh left the JGS headquarters and travelled to Gia Long Palace in a sedan with his aide and bodyguard, Captain Nguyen Van

Nhung. Minh had also dispatched an M-113 armored personnel carrier and four jeeps to Gia Long to transport Diem and Nhu back to JGS headquarters. While Minh was on the way to supervise the takeover of the palace, Generals Don, Tran Thien Khiem and Le Van Kim prepared the army headquarters for Diem's arrival and the ceremonial handover of power to the junta. Diem's pictures were taken down and his statue was covered up. A large table covered with green felt was brought in with the intention of seating Diem for the handover to Minh and Vice President Nguyen Ngoc Tho, who was to become the civilian Prime Minister during a nationally televised event witnessed by international media. Diem and Nhu would then ask the generals to be granted exile and asylum in a foreign country, which would be granted. The brothers were then to be held in a secure place at JGS headquarters while awaiting deportation. Minh arrived at the palace at 08:00 in full military ceremonial uniform to supervise the arrest of Diem and Nhu for the surrender ceremony.

Minh instead arrived to find the brothers were not in the palace. In anticipation of a coup, they had ordered the construction of three separate tunnels leading from Gia Long to remote areas outside the palace. Around 8:00 on the night of the coup, with only the Presidential Guard to defend them against mutinous infantry and armor units, Diem and Nhu hurriedly packed American banknotes into a briefcase. They escaped through one of the tunnels with two loyalists: Cao Xuan Vy, the head of Nhu's Republican Youth, and Air Force Lieutenant Do Tho, Diem's aide. Tho was the nephew of Colonel Do Mau, the director of military security and a participant in the coup plot. After the coup, General Paul Harkins, the head of the U.S. presence in Vietnam, inspected the tunnel and noted that the tunnel went so far down that he didn't want to go down the tunnel to turn around and walk back up it. The brothers emerged in a wooded area in a park near the Cercle Sportif, the city's upper class sporting club, where they were picked up by a waiting Land Rover. Ellen Hammer disputes the tunnel escape, asserting the Ngo brothers simply walked out of the building, which was not yet under siege. Ellen claimed the brothers walked past the tennis courts and left the palace grounds through a small gate at Le Thanh Ton Street and entered the car.

The loyalists travelled through narrow back streets in order to evade rebel checkpoints and changed vehicles to a black Citroen sedan. After leaving the palace, Nhu was reported to have suggested to Diem that they should split up, arguing this would enhance their chances of survival. Nhu proposed one of them travel to the Mekong Delta to join Cao's IV Corps, while the other would travel to the II Corps of General Nguyen Khanh in the Central Highlands. Nhu felt the rebel generals would not dare to kill one of them while the other was free, in case the surviving brother was to regain power. Diem turned down Nhu, reasoning that his brother couldn't leave him alone because they hated him too much. President Diem feared they would kill his brother. He wanted Nhu to stay with him so he could protect him. Another version of the story stated that South Vietnam president told his brother that they been together for the last few years and that they couldn't separate at this critical time in their life. Nhu agreed to stay together until the end.

The loyalists reached the home of Ma Tuyen in the Chinese business district of Cholon. Ma Tuyen was a Chinese merchant and friend who were reported to be Nhu's main contact with the Chinese syndicates which controlled the opium trade. The brothers sought asylum from the embassy of the Republic of China, but were turned down and stayed in Ma Tuyen's house as they appealed to ARVN loyalists and attempted to negotiate with the coup leaders. Nhu's secret agents had fitted the home with a direct phone line to the palace, so the insurgent generals believed the brothers were still besieged inside Gia Long. Neither the rebels nor the loyalist Presidential Guard had any idea that at 21:00 they were about to fight for an empty building, leading to futile deaths. Minh was reported to be mortified when he realized Diem and Nhu had escaped in the middle of the night. After Minh had ordered the rebels to search the areas known to have been frequented by the Ngo family, Colonel Pham Ngoc Thao was informed by a captured Presidential Guard officer that the brothers had escaped through the tunnels to a refuge in Cholon. Thao was told by Khiem, his superior, to find and prevent Diem from being killed. When Thao arrived at Ma Tuyen's house, he phoned his superiors. Diem and Nhu overheard him and fled to the nearby Catholic Church of St. Francis Xavier. Tho drove them to the church which they had frequented over the years. Lieutenant Tho died a few months later in a plane crash, but his diary was not found until 1970. Tho recorded Diem's words as they left the house of Ma Tuyen as being *"I don't know whether I will live or die and I don't care, but tell Nguyen Khanh that I have great affection for him and he should avenge me"*. Soon after the early morning mass celebrating All Souls' Day, the congregation emptied from the building. The Ngo brothers walked through the shady courtyard and into the building wearing dark gray suits. It was speculated they were recognized by an informant while they walked through the yard. Inside the church, the brothers prayed and received Communion.

A few minutes later, just after 10:00, an armored personnel carrier and two jeeps entered the narrow alcove housing the church building. Lieutenant Tho had earlier urged Diem to surrender, saying he was sure his uncle Mau, along with Dinh and Khiem, would guarantee their safety. Tho wrote in his diary afterwards that "*I consider myself responsible for having led them to their death*". The convoy was led by General Mai Huu Xuan and consisted of Colonels Nguyen Van Quan and Duong Ngoc Lam. Quan was the deputy of Minh and Lam was the Commander of Diem's Civil Guard. Lam had joined the coup once a rebel victory seemed assured. Two more officers made up the convoy: Major Duong Hieu Nghia and Captain Nguyen Van Nhung. Nhung was Minh's bodyguard. President Diem requested the convoy stop at the palace so he could gather personal items before being exiled. Xuan turned him down, clinically stating his orders were to take Diem and Nhu directly to headquarters. Nhu expressed disgust that they were to be transported in an APC, asking "*You use such a vehicle to drive the president?*" Lam assured them the armor was for their own protection. Xuan said it was selected to protect them from the extremists who wanted to harm them. Xuan ordered the brothers' hands be tied behind their backs before shoving them into the carrier. One officer asked to shoot Nhu, but Xuan turned him down.

After the arrest, Nhung and Nghia sat with the brothers in the APC, and the convoy departed for Tan Son Nhut. Before the convoy had departed for the church, Minh was reported to have gestured to Nhung with two fingers. This was taken to be an order to kill both brothers. The convoy stopped at a railroad crossing on the return trip, where by all accounts the brothers were assassinated. An investigation by Don later determined that Nghia had shot the brothers at point-blank range with a semi-automatic firearm and Nhung sprayed them with bullets before repeatedly stabbing the bodies with a knife. Nghia gave his account of what occurred during the journey back to the military headquarters: "*As we rode back to the Joint General Staff headquarters, Diem sat silently, but Nhu and Captain Nhung began to insult each other. I don't know who started it. The name-calling grew passionate. The captain had hated Nhu before. Now he was charged with emotion.*" Nghia said when the convoy reached a train crossing, "*Nhung lunged at Nhu with a bayonet and stabbed him again and again, maybe fifteen or twenty times. Still in a rage, he turned to Diem, took out his revolver and shot him in the head. Then he looked back at Nhu, who was lying on the floor, twitching. He put a bullet into his head too. Neither Diem nor Nhu ever defended themselves. Their hands were tied."* At the time of their deaths, Diem was 62 and Nhu 53 years old.

CHAPTER 42

"The greater our knowledge increases the more
our ignorance unfolds."

John F. Kennedy

In mid-afternoon on November 2, 1963, a man who resembled Lee Harvey Oswald walked into the Downtown Lincoln-Mercury showroom near Dealey Plaza in Dallas. He told car salesman Albert Guy Bogard he was interested in buying a red Mercury Comet. He told Albert he didn't have any money then for a down payment, but he had some money coming in within two or three weeks and would pay cash for the car. He accepted Albert's invitation to test drive a red Comet. He then gave the salesman a memorable ride accelerating the car to speeds up to 75 and 85 miles an hour on a Stemmons Freeway route which coincided with the scheduled route of President Kennedy's motorcade twenty days later. Back in the showroom, the increasingly flamboyant young man became bitter that Albert's fellow salesman, Eugene M. Wilson, tried to sell him the Comet on the spot but he said he needed a credit rating. The man then said provocatively, "*Maybe I'm going to have to go back to Russia to buy a car.*" This was once again the work of the Central Intelligence Agency in an attempt to frame Lee for the murder of the president. What they didn't realize was that Lee didn't have a driver's license nor did he even know how to drive. Anyone who knew him, knew there was no possible way Lee would be out shopping around for a car. But the CIA didn't care. They were going to go "all out" to set up the image of Lee Oswald as a Pro-Communist nut.

While most of the Chicago Secret Service agents were scrambling to locate and arrest all four members of the sniper team before the president's Saturday, November 2, 1963, arrival, two agents were acting on another threat. The Secret Service office had also received a tip that Thomas Arthur Vallee, an alienated ex-Marine, had threatened to kill President Kennedy in Chicago. Thomas Arthur Vallee was quickly identified from intelligence sources as an ex-Marine who was a "disaffiliated member of the John Birch Society," a far right organization obsessed with Communist subversion in the United States. He was also described as a loner, a paranoid schizophrenic, and a gun collector. The two Secret Service agents who were surveilling him broke into his rented North Side room in his absence. They found an M-1 rifle, a carbine rifle, and twenty-five hundred rounds of ammunition. The agents had seen enough. On Friday, November 1st, they phoned the Chicago Police Department captain Robert Linsky, requesting twenty-four hour surveillance on Thomas. They requested that Thomas needed to be brought in for questioning. Two experienced Chicago Police officers, Daniel Groth and Peter Schurla, were assigned the task. After watching Thomas for hours, the officers arrested him on Saturday, November 2 at 9:10 AM, two and a half hours before President Kennedy was due at O'Hara Airport. They stopped his car at the corner of West Wilson and North Damen Avenue. They stopped him as he was turning south toward the president's motorcade route. The pretense for the arrest was an improper turn signal. When the police officers found a hunting knife lying on his front seat, they also charged him with carrying a concealed weapon. They, also, found three hundred rounds of ammunition.

The officers first took Thomas Vallee to the Secret Service headquarters. There he was questioned by Special Agent in Charge Maurice Martineau behind closed doors in his office. The police then took Vallee to a Chicago jail. They had succeeded in bringing him in before President Kennedy's visit to Chicago. But as they may have known already from intelligence sources, he was no isolated threat but a pawn being moved in a much larger game.

The first clue to Thomas Arthur Vallee's connection with intelligence agencies was in the New York license plate on the 1962 Ford Falcon he was driving: 31-10RF. A few days after President Kennedy's assassination, NBC News in Chicago learned about Thomas' arrest on the same day President Kennedy had been scheduled to come to Chicago. Luke Christopher

Hester, an NBC Chicago employee, asked his father-in-law, Hugh Larkin, a retired New York Police officer, to check on Thomas' license plate. Larkin asked his old friends in the New York Police Department if they would run a background check on it. They came back to Larkin saying the license plate information was "frozen" and that "only the FBI could obtain this information." NBC News got no further. The registration for the license plate for the car Thomas Arthur Vallee was driving at the time of his arrest was classified—restricted to U.S. intelligence agencies. The similarities between Thomas and the eventual accused assassin Lee Harvey Oswald was unreal.

Thomas Arthur Vallee had grown up as a middle child between his two sisters, Margaret, two years older, and Mary, three years younger. Their French Canadian family lived in a German-Irish neighborhood in the northwest part of Chicago. Mary's strongest memory of her brother was of him always wanting to be a Marine like his older cousin, Mike. At the age of fifteen, Thomas realized his dream. He ran away from home, lied about his age, and joined the Marine Corps. He was wounded in the Korean War when a mortar shell exploded near him. He suffered a concussion that would affect him the rest of his life. An FBI teletype on him the week after President Kennedy's assassination stated that the schizophrenic ex-Marine had a prior history of mental commitment, "*allegedly has a metal plate in his scalp*," and "*received complete disability from the Veteran's Administration.*"

After Thomas was discharged from the Marine Corps at the age of nineteen in November 1952, he used his money to buy a new car. A few days later, he got drunk in a neighborhood bar and then wrecked the car in an accident. He suffered another serious head injury and was in a coma for a couple of months. His father stayed by his bed. When Thomas finally regained consciousness, he had to go through a complete rehabilitation program, learning all over how to walk, talk, and hold a knife and fork. Soon after he returned home, while he was regaining the basic skills of living, his father died of a heart attack. An uncle accused Thomas of driving his father to death by his errant behavior. Mary said her brother felt deeply guilty about her father's death. She claimed after Thomas' accident he was never the same again.

In spite of his shaky health, Thomas reenlisted for a second term in the Marines in February 1955. It was another unsettling experience.

His Marine Corps medical records noted he was usually nervous and he was prone to fits of excitement with the inability to talk to anyone. His medical also stated he was very hyper-active and did not get along with the other Marines in his barracks. After giving Vallee an extensive psychiatric evaluation, the Marines honorably discharged him in September 1956 for a physical disability diagnosed as "Schizophrenic Reaction, Paranoid Type #3003, Moderate, and Chronic." His military records show further that a Naval Speed Letter to the Navy's Bureau of Medicine and Surgery on August 6, 1956, requested a bed for him in a Veteran's Administration Hospital near Chicago for an indefinite length of time. Thomas Vallee told investigative reporter Edwin Black that he had been assigned by the Marines to a U-2 base in Japan, Camp Otsu. While there he came under the control of the Central Intelligence Agency, which commanded the U-2, just as Lee Oswald would come under the CIA's control as a radar operator at another CIA U-2 base in Japan. He also told Black that he later worked with the CIA at a camp near Levittown, Long Island, helping to train Cuban exiles to assassinate Fidel Castro.

In August 1963 as Lee Oswald was preparing to move from New Orleans back to Dallas, Thomas Vallee moved from New York City back to Chicago. Just as Lee got a job in a warehouse right over President Kennedy's future motorcade route in Dallas, Thomas also got a job in a warehouse right over President Kennedy's future motorcade route in Chicago. Like Lee in Dallas, Thomas found employment as a printer. He was hired by IPP Litho-Plate, located at 625 West Jackson Boulevard in Chicago. His location at IPP Litho-Plate actually gave him a nearer, clearer view of the November 2nd, Chicago motorcade than Lee's supposedly sniper's nest did of the November 22nd Dallas motorcade. Lee's job was on the sixth floor. Thomas' work site was three floors lower. Thomas' location in the warehouse put him in the culpable position of having an unimpeded shot at the president passing directly below him. At the same time, the unidentified snipers in the Chicago plot could have shot President Kennedy from hidden vantage points and then escaped, leaving him to take the blame. This was clearly a "dry run" for the CIA's covert operation in Dallas. There was never any real intent on assassinating President Kennedy in Chicago. The plot in Chicago was the CIA's way of working of any "bugs" in their operation planned for Dallas, Texas on November 22nd. Nothing could stand in their way operating the first ever coup d'état on American soil.

Thomas Arthur Vallee had two people in particular to thank for him not becoming the scapegoat in a presidential assassination that almost occurred beneath his Chicago workplace. Lieutenant Berkley Moyland, a member of the Chicago Police Department, was the first intervening angel who saved him from suffering what would soon become Lee's fate. In the fall of 1963, Lieutenant Moyland had the habit of eating at a cafeteria on Wilson Avenue in Chicago, where he knew the manager. One day in late October, the manager alerted the Lieutenant Moyland, who was dressed in plainclothes, to a regular customer who had been making threatening remarks about President Kennedy, who was due to visit Chicago within the week. The manager told him when the threatening customer usually came in. The police lieutenant decided to wait for him at the appropriate time. When the manager indicated that this was the man, the lieutenant took his tray over to Thomas' table, sat down with him, and engaged him in conversation. Lieutenant Moyland sized him up quickly and came to the conclusion that Thomas had a damaged imbalanced personality. Lieutenant Moyland also realized he probably had weapons in his possession, as would soon be confirmed. He told the man firmly that nothing good could come from the remarks he was making about President Kennedy. After leaving the cafeteria, Lieutenant Moyland phoned the Secret Service with a warning about Thomas Vallee. He was told that the Secret Service would take care of the situation. As a result of the tip, Thomas was investigated and placed under police surveillance. However, it was not Lieutenant Moyland but an FBI informant named "Lee" whose alert disrupted the more critical four-man rifle team which represented the real threat to President Kennedy, and thus to potential patsy Vallee as well. The "Lee" informant was actually Lee Oswald's handler. He was directed to leak information concerning an assassination plot in Chicago. Once again, there was no real threat of an assassination in Chicago, but it had to appear there was one. The CIA needed to know if there was any area of their covert operation which needed to be improved upon.

Lieutenant Moyland was phoned back by an official in the Treasury Department, which with jurisdiction over the Secret Service, who committed him to the absolute silence on the matter which he almost took to his grave. The Treasury Department official gave the police officer stringent orders. He said: "*Don't write anything about it. Don't tell anybody about it. Just forget about it.*"

CHAPTER 43

—————————◻—————————

"The problems of the world
cannot possibly be solved by skeptics or cynics whose horizons
are limited by the obvious realities. We need men who can
dream of things that never were."

John F. Kennedy

On Saturday November 2, at 9:35 AM, President Kennedy held a meeting at the White House with his principal advisers on Vietnam. As the meeting began the fate of Diem and Nhu was unknown. Michael Forrestal walked in with a telegram. He handed it to the president. It was from Ambassador Henry Cabot Lodge. The message was that *"Diem and Nhu were both dead, and the coup leaders were claiming their deaths to be suicide."* Despite what the message said, President Kennedy, instantly, knew they must have been murdered. General Maxwell Taylor watched President Kennedy leap to his feet and rushed from the room with a look of shock and dismay on his face. President Kennedy had always insisted Ngo Diem must never suffer more than exile and had been led to believe or had persuaded himself a change in the South Vietnam government could be carried without bloodshed.

Shortly after midnight on November 2nd in Washington, the CIA sent word to the White House that Diem and Nhu were dead, allegedly due to suicide. Vietnam Radio had announced their deaths by poison, and they had committed suicide while prisoners in an APC transporting them to Tan Son Nhut. Unclear and contradictory stories abounded. General Paul Harkins reported the suicides had occurred either by gunshot or by a grenade wrestled from the belt of an ARVN officer who was standing guard. Minh tried to explain the discrepancy by saying *"Due to an inadvertence, there was a gun inside the vehicle. It was with this gun that they committed suicide.*" President Kennedy later penned a memo, lamenting the assassination was "*particularly abhorrent*" and blaming himself for approving Cable 243, which authorized Henry Cabot Lodge to explore coup options in the wake of Nhu's attacks on the Buddhists pagodas. Forrestal said "*It shook him personally . . . bothered him as a moral and religious matter. It shook his confidence, I think, in the kind of advice he was getting about South Vietnam.*" When President Kennedy was consoled by a friend who told him he need not feel sorry for the Ngo brothers he replied "*No. They were in a difficult position. They did the best they could for their country.*"

At the last possible moment at 10:15AM on Saturday November 2, 1963, White House Press Secretary Pierre Salinger announced that President Kennedy's trip to Chicago had been cancelled. The decision to call off his trip was made so late that the press plane had already taken off for Chicago. Pierre said to the media left behind: "*The President is not going to the football game.*" Chicago Secret Service agents knew that another reason for the last second cancellation was the warning they had given the White House: Two snipers with high-powered rifles were thought to be waiting along the president's parade route. Three other potential assassins were already in custody or about to be arrested: the two suspected snipers being held at the Secret Service office, and Thomas Arthur Vallee, who was being followed by the Chicago Police. The time at which Thomas Arthur Vallee was arrested, 9:10 AM Central Time (10:10 AM Eastern Time), by Chicago Police intelligence officers Daniel Groth and Peter Schurla, is important. The press announcement of the Chicago trip's cancellation was made at 10:15 AM Eastern (9:15 AM Central), even a quick decision to cancel the trip would have been made at least ten minutes before the public announcement—with government authorities therefore being aware of the trip's cancellation by about 10:00 AM Eastern (9:00 AM Central).

The purpose of the two intelligence-connected officers was not to restrain Thomas but to shadow him until the president was actually shot. For success of the assassination plot, the scapegoat had to remain free—and did remain free—so as long as President Kennedy was still coming to Chicago and could be shot there. If the officer's purpose was, as claimed, "*to get Vallee off the street*" and protect the president, why was

Vallee's arrest put off until after authorities knew President Kennedy was no longer coming to Chicago? It's apparent the local authorities were not aware that this a "practice" run for the real plot in Dallas.

Although the failed Chicago plot was hushed up, Thomas Arthur Vallee still became a minor scapegoat. He was the only person arrested in Chicago who was ever identified publicly. He was scapegoated as a threat to the president a month after his arrest and twelve days after President Kennedy's assassination in Dallas. On December 3rd, an article appeared in the *Chicago American* on his November 2nd arrest, "*Cops Seize Gun-Toting Kennedy Foe.*" The unnamed detectives who disclosed his arrest characterized him as a gun-toting loner who had expressed violent anti-Kennedy remarks before President was assassinated in Dallas. A similar article on his arrest, drawing on unidentified federal agents, appeared in the *Chicago Daily News* on the same day. The anonymous police detectives and federal agents who informed the media after Dallas of his arrest in Chicago one month earlier never mentioned the Secret Service's detention and questioning of the two suspected snipers. After November 2, 1963, they and their two unapprehended comrades in arm vanished without a trace of their existence. There had to appear that there was a real threat in Chicago. This was why the plot wasn't revealed until after President Kennedy was assassinated in Dallas. A vital question remained unanswered once the plot in Chicago was revealed. Why was the Secret Service and the local authorities, in Chicago, able to stop an apparent assassination plot in Chicago but couldn't stop the plot in Dallas? Because it never intended for President Kennedy to die in Chicago. President Kennedy needed to die in Dallas, Texas. Even though there would also be a so-called assassination attempt in Tampa Bay, Florida, it also served as a fine tuning operation for the plot in Dallas. President Kennedy had to die in Dallas for one reason; Carlos Marcello controlled Dallas. Carlos wanted, needed, revenge for the embarrassment Robert Kennedy caused him in April 1961.

President Kennedy's reaction to the news of Diem's death did not draw sympathy from his entire administration. Some believed he should not have supported the coup because they were uncontrollable, assassination was always a possibility. President Kennedy was skeptical about the story and suspected a double assassination had taken place. He reasoned the Catholic Ngo brothers would not have taken their own lives, but Roger Hilsman rationalized the possibility of suicide by asserting

Diem and Nhu would have interpreted the coup as Armageddon. The Americans soon became aware of the true reasons for the deaths of Diem and Nhu. President Kennedy was shocked by the deaths and to find out afterwards Minh had asked the CIA field office to secure safe passage out of the country for Diem and Nhu, but was told 24 hours was needed to get a plane. Minh responded he could not hold them that long and thus handed them a death sentence. Initially after the news of the coup, there was renewed confidence in America and South Vietnam; now the war might truly be won. McGeorge Bundy drafted a National Security Action Memo to present to President Kennedy upon his return from Dallas. It reiterated United States resolve to fight communism in Vietnam, with both military and economic aid at a higher level, including operations in Laos and Cambodia.

President Kennedy blamed the CIA for manipulation, and in this case, assassination. In his anger at the CIA's behind-the-scenes role in the deaths of Diem and Nhu, he said to his friend Senator George Smathers, "*I've got to do something about those bastards . . . they should be stripped of their exorbitant power.*" Before leaving for Dallas, President Kennedy told Mike Forrestal that after the start of 1964, he wanted an in depth study done on every possible option, which included a withdrawal option. He wanted to review the options completely from top to bottom. President Kennedy had grown tired of the CIA's controlled war in South Vietnam.

CHAPTER 44

—————————□—————————

"The very word 'secrecy' is repugnant
in a free and open society; and we are as a people inherently
and historically opposed to secret societies, to secret oaths,
and to secret proceedings."

John F. Kennedy

Two months before President Kennedy's assassination he was given another "Net Evaluation Subcommittee Report" on preemptive war planning. This time around, President Kennedy was prepared by two years of struggle with his military commanders for what he was about to hear. After he heard the Net Subcommittee Report from General Maxwell Taylor, President Kennedy engaged in a cat-and-mouse game with his generals. He opened the discussion with a question whose premise was the first-strike strategy he knew they wanted in place.

"Even if we attacked the USSR first, would the loss to the United States be acceptable to our political leaders?" asked President Kennedy.

"Yes, I believe the loss would be acceptable. Even if we preempt, surviving Soviet capability is sufficient to produce an acceptable loss in the United States," replied Air Force General Leon Johnson.

President Kennedy appeared to have been relieved by General Johnson's response. The window of opportunity for a "successful" U.S. preemptive strike on the Soviets by his generals had apparently closed. The USSR had by now deployed too many missiles in hardened underground silos for superior United States forces to be able to destroy with a retaliatory force in a first strike. That meant President Kennedy's military command could not pressure him with the same urgency for a preemptive strike. He decided to press his advantage.

"Are we then in fact in a period of nuclear stalemate?" President Kennedy asked General Johnson.

"I believe we are in fact in a nuclear stalemate," admitted General Johnson.

"Really? I read the statement in this morning's paper by the Air Force Association recommending a nuclear superiority. What do they mean by nuclear superiority versus nuclear stalemate. How could you get superiority?" asked the president.

"Well, Mr. President, this is how I see it. I believe the members of the Committee of the Air Force Association which drafted the resolution did not have the facts as brought out in the report being presented at this time. In fact, I believe it would be impossible for us to achieve nuclear superiority," General Johnson said carefully, like he was measuring his words.

"Even if we spend $80 billion more for shelters and increased weapons systems than we are now spending, we would still have at least 30 million casualties in the United States in the 1968 time period, even if we made the first strike against the USSR," Secretary of Defense Robert McNamara stated.

"Those fatality figures are much higher than I heard recently in Omaha. As I recall, Strategic Air Command estimated that if we preempted, then we would have 12 million casualties. Why do we need as much as we got? Charles De Gaulle believes even the small nuclear force he is planning will be big enough to cause unacceptable damage to the USSR," said President Kennedy.

"Well, Mr. President we could bring down the number of casualties by undertaking additional weapons programs," claimed General Johnson.

"Doesn't that just get us into overkill?" asked President Kennedy.

"No, sir. We can cut down United States losses if we knock out more Soviet missiles by having more United States missiles and more accurate United States missiles. The more Soviet missiles we can destroy the less the loss to us," countered General Johnson.

The National Security Council had once again reached the point of blandly considering the killing of 140 million Soviet citizens in a United States effort to beat their leaders to the nuclear punch. This time President Kennedy did not walk out on his military commanders. He continued to probe their preemptive-war planning. He wanted to know as much as he could, for a purpose far different from theirs. His purpose was in terms of people, as opposed to their purpose which were in terms of missiles, was how to keep such a slaughter from ever happening.

"There is no way of launching a no-alert attack against the USSR which would be acceptable. No such attack, according to the calculations, could be carried out without 30 million United States fatalities. This is an obviously unacceptable number. The President deserves an answer to his question as to why we have to have so large a force," said Secretary of Defense Robert McNamara.

The painfully obvious answer was the Joint Chiefs wanted to be able to preempt the Soviets. President Kennedy, on the other hand, saw such an option as a danger within his own government.

"The answer lies in the fact that there are many uncertainties in the equations presented in today's report," Defense Secretary McNamara was caught between his president and his military chiefs. He tried to explain away their conflict.

"Why does the Soviet Union have a smaller force than the United States? Maybe the United States might want to follow their example rather than vice versa," suggested the young president.

"Well, the Soviets might think they have enough to deter the United States from attacking them. I would be very disturbed if the President considered this report as indication that we could reduce our forces and not continue to increase those programmed. If a reduction should take place, the relative position of the United States and Soviets would become less in our favor," said General Johnson.

"I understand," replied President Kennedy. "Preemption is not possible for us. This is a valuable conclusion growing out of an excellent report. This argues in favor of a conventional force."

"I have concluded from the calculations that we could fight a limited war using nuclear weapons without fear that the Soviets would reply by going to an all-out war," disagreed General Johnson.

"What about the case of preempting today with the Soviets in a low state of alert?" asked President Kennedy.

"In the studies I have had done, I have not found a situation in which a preempt during a low-alert condition would be advantageous," suggested Robert McNamara.

None of President Kennedy's other advisers offered an opinion in response to his question about a United States preemptive strike at that particular time. The explicit assumption of the first Net Report was "*a surprise attack in late 1963, preceded by a period of heightened tensions.*"

The focus of that first-strike scenario corresponded to the Kennedy assassination scenario. When President Kennedy was murdered in 1963, the Soviet Union had been set up as the major scapegoat in the plot. If the tactic had been successful in scapegoating the Russians for the crime of the century, there is little doubt it would have resulted in "*a period of heightened tensions*" between the United States and the Soviet Union. Those who designed the plot to kill President Kennedy were familiar with our national security state. Their attempt to scapegoat the Soviet's for the president's murder reflected one side of the secret struggle between President Kennedy and his military leaders over a preemptive strike against the Soviet Union. The assassins' purpose seems to have encompassed not only killing a president determined to make peace with the enemy but also by using his murder as the starting point for a possible nuclear first strike against the same enemy.

On November 11, 1963, Rene Vallejo called Lisa Howard again on behalf of Fidel Castro to reiterate their "*appreciation of the need for security.*" He said Castro would go along with any arrangements President Kennedy's representatives wanted to make. He was again willing to provide a plane, if that would be helpful. On November 12th, after hearing William Attwood's report, McGeorge Bundy said that before a meeting with Castro himself there should be a preliminary talk with Rene at the United Nations to find out specifically what Castro wanted to talk about. On November 14th, Lisa Howard relayed this information to Rene, who said he would discuss it with Castro. Lisa called Rene Vallejo again seven days later. This time William Attwood was present and she handed him the phone. At the other end of the line Fidel Castro was listening in on the Vallejo-Attwood conversation.

"Can you come to New York for a possible preliminary meeting?" asked William.

"I cannot come to New York at this time. But, I assure you, we will send instructions to Carlos Lechuga on what to propose and discuss with you as far as an agenda for a later meeting with Premier Castro."

"I will wait for your call," William said as he hung up the phone.

With this conversation the stage was being set, four days before Dallas, for the beginning of a Kennedy-Castro dialogue on United States-Cuba relations. After the death of President Kennedy, Lyndon Johnson stopped any dialogue between the White House and Fidel Castro, who kept seeking it.

CHAPTER 45

—◻—

"The world is very different now.
For man holds in his mortal the power to abolish all forms
of human poverty, and all forms of human life."

John F. Kennedy

Garland G. Slack saw a man who was firing his rifle at the Sports Drome on November 10th and November 17th. On November 17th, after Garland put up his own target for shooting, the man turned his rifle and repeatedly fired on Garland's target When he objected strenuously, the man gave him a look, which Garland claimed he would never forget. He claimed later that the man resembled Lee Harvey Oswald. This man at the firing range was another CIA placement for Lee. They continued to work on the fabricated story of Lee being a Pro-Communist lone nut that was toning up on his sniper abilities.

Lee Oswald had established a ritual of weekend visits to Irving arriving on Friday afternoon and returning to Dallas on Monday morning with a fellow employee by the name of Wesley Frazier, who lived near Ruth Paine. On Friday November 15th, Marina suggested Lee remained in Dallas because the house would be crowded because of a birthday party for Ruth's daughter. On Monday, November 18th, Lee and Marina quarreled bitterly during a telephone conversation. She learned for the first time he was living at the boarding house under a false name.

The CIA felt the "dry run", in Chicago, for the assassination plot was successful. But they needed to test it one more time before President Kennedy's fatal trip to Dallas. They would get their chance on November

18, 1963 in Tampa Bay, Florida. The CIA used the fact President Kennedy's Administration was keeping the assassination plot in Chicago a complete secret to their advantage. If a story about the assassination plot in Chicago broke in the media, then the security around the president would have tighten and their chance to remove President Kennedy would disappear. But as with any government sponsored operations there were leaks. One such leak came out on November 9th.

A right-wing extremist, Joseph Milteer told a Miami police informant about a possible plot to assassinate President Kennedy with high powered rifle. Without Joseph's knowledge, his conversation was taped by the informant. The tape was given to the Secret Service and the FBI on November 12th. Miami police intelligence officers met with the Secret Service and gave them a transcript of the taped conversation with Joseph Milteer.

"The security around the president will be tight. How could a sniper possibly get to the President of the United States?" the informant asked Joseph Milteer.

"That's easy. The sniper could be stationed in a tall building along the motorcade route," replied Joseph.

"I guess that makes sense. But how could the sniper get away? Because it won't be hard to tell where the shots came from? Surely, the authorities will be able to get to him before the sniper could escape."

"True. Like any other good law enforcement agencies, the Tampa Bay authorities wouldn't leave any stone unturned when President Kennedy is assassinated. In order to divert attention from the real snipers, it would be made sure the authorities would pick up somebody within hours after the assassination," answered Joseph.

"What about the rifle?"

"What do you mean?" asked Joseph.

"I mean, how would the sniper get the rifle into an office building? No one is going to let just anyone walk into a building, much less a building overlooking the presidential motorcade route, with a high power rifle."

"See, the rifles can be broken down to get into the office building. Once the sniper was in place, then the rifle could be assembled," Joseph claimed.

"Would just one sniper be used?"

"At least two will be used. One sniper will be stationed in an office building while another one will placed in a hotel room," answered Joseph.

President Kennedy's motorcade in Tampa Bay was scheduled to go from MacDill Air Force Base to Al Lopez Field, to downtown Tampa Bay. From there it would go to the National Guard Armory, then to the International Inn, and finally back to MacDill Air Force Base. It was the longest presidential motorcade President Kennedy would take in the United States. The Secret Service was concerned about the Floridian Hotel. It was the tallest building at the time in Tampa Bay and the presidential motorcade would make a hard left turn in front of it. This would slow the motorcade down in front of a tall, brick building with several unguarded windows. The Tampa Bay authorities sent men to several offices to look through some bank buildings on the presidential motorcade route. The officers were looking for anything unusual and would leave an officer posted in the building for security purposes. But they couldn't do the same for the Floridian Hotel. The hotel had a great view overlooking the motorcade route and would be packed with visitors waiting to catch a glimpse of the president, so providing security in the hotel would be difficult. But aside from the multiple windows in the hotel, the Tampa Bay authorities was also concerned about luggage containing possible weapons. The authorities had to lean on the hotel employees to inform them if they notices anything suspicious at the hotel.

President Kennedy was briefed by the Secret Service that he was in danger in Tampa Bay. But President Kennedy was in a difficult position. It was too soon after cancelling his scheduled motorcade in Chicago for him to take the chance and cancel another scheduled motorcade. He didn't want to appear weak on a day he needed to show strength and confidence. Cancelling another scheduled motorcade was an option President Kennedy couldn't consider. It was suggested he used the bubble-top for the limousine. President Kennedy knew the bubble-top wasn't bullet-proof so it wouldn't be of any use to him anyway to avoid a sniper fire. So he agreed to the scheduled motorcade as planned without the bubble-top.

After President Kennedy made the first stop on the motorcade at the MacDill Air Force Base, the Secret Service and other agencies tried to ensure his safety on the motorcade through downtown Tampa Bay. The Miami Secret Service office had William Somersett, the police informant who taped Joseph Milteer's conversation, call Joseph's Georgian home. They wanted to make sure he wasn't in Tampa Bay. He was indeed in Georgia, not in Tampa Bay. The police and military units controlled the underpasses along the motorcade route while the Tampa Bay Sheriff

Department secured the rooftops of numerous tall buildings along the route in the downtown and suburban areas. The motorcade was scheduled to last forty minutes and the motorcade would make the hard left turn in front of the Floridian Hotel at about 2:30pm before crossing a bridge on its way to the Armory. President Kennedy survived the motorcade in Tampa Bay to deliver his speeches at the Armory and then at the International Inn.

Having taken the step of approving the secret talks with Fidel Castro, during the final week of his life President Kennedy sent a hopeful message to the Cuban premier. It came in his November 18th address in Miami to the Inter-American Press Association. William Attwood said he was told by Arthur Schlesinger, Jr., who co-authored Kennedy's speech, that the speech was the intention of the president to help signal to Fidel that a rapprochement was possible if he stopped during the Kremlin work in Latin America. In his speech on November 18th, President Kennedy first emphasized the Alliance for Progress did, "*not dictate to any nation how to organize its economic life. Every nation is free to shape its own economic institutions in accordance with its own national needs and will.*" President Kennedy then issued a challenge and a promise to Fidel Castro. He said that "*a small band of conspirators*" had made "*Cuba a victim of foreign imperialism, an instrument of the policy of others, a weapon in an effort dictated by external powers to subvert the other American Republic. This, and this alone, divides us. As long as this is true, nothing is possible. Without it, everything is possible. Once this barrier is removed, we will be ready and anxious to work with the Cuban people in pursuit of those progressive goals which a few short years ago stirred their hopes and the sympathy of many people throughout the hemisphere.*" President Kennedy's final message to Castro was a promise that if he stopped what he regarded as Cuba's covert action in support of Soviet policies in Latin America, the "*everything was possible*" between the United States and Cuba.

At a White House meeting on the evening of Tuesday, November 19th, President Kennedy's next to last night in Washington, he said he was willing to visit the developing nation of Indonesia the following spring. President Kennedy was thereby endorsing a line-standing invitation from President Sukarno, the fiery Indonesian leader. Sukarno was notorious in Washington for his anti-American rhetoric and militant third world nationalism. Although Sukarno said he was a neutralist in terms of the Cold War, United States analysts saw him favoring Soviet policies, as shown by his acceptance of Soviet military aid to Indonesia. President Kennedy's openness to Sukarno and the nonaligned movement he represented once again placed the president in direct conflict with the Central Intelligence Agency. The CIA's Deputy Director for Plans Richard Bissell wrote to President Kennedy's National Security Adviser McGeorge Bundy in March 1961, *"Indonesia's growing vulnerability to communism stems from the distinctive bias of Sukarno's global orientation, as well as from his domestic policies . . . That his dictatorship may possibly endure as long as he lives strikes us as the crux of the Indonesian problem."* What did this mean? Simple, The Central Intelligence Agency wanted Sukarno dead.

The CIA's coup plotting against Sukarno became public during the Eisenhower Administration. In the fall of 1956, the CIA's then-Deputy Director of Plans Frank Wisner, said to his Far East division chief, *"I think it's time we held Sukarno's feet to the fire."* The Agency then fomented a 1957-58 army rebellion in Indonesia, supplied armed shipments to the rebels, and even used a fleet of camouflaged CIA planes to bomb Sukarno's government troops. The CIA's covert role was exposed after one of its hired pilots, Allen Pope, bombed a church and a central market killing many civilians. He was shot down and identified as a CIA employee. Sukarno freed him from a death sentence four years later in response to a personal appeal by Robert Kennedy. This appeal came from the Attorney General when he visited Indonesia on the behalf of his brother, thereby strengthening the bonds Sukarno felt with both Kennedys.

Unlike the Central Intelligence Agency, President Kennedy wanted to work with Sukarno, not kill or overthrow him. In 1961-62, President Kennedy brokered an agreement between Indonesia and its former colonial master, the Netherlands, on the eve of war between them. President Kennedy's peaceful resolution of the Indonesian-Dutch crisis through the United Nations ceded the contested area of West Irian (West New Guinea) from the Netherlands to Indonesia, giving the people of West Irian the option by 1969 of leaving Indonesia. The CIA felt President Kennedy was thereby aiding and abetting the enemy. President Kennedy looked at the situation not through the CIA's eyes, but instead through Sukarno's eyes. He said, *"When you consider things like CIA's support to the 1958 rebellion, Sukarno's frequently anti-American attitude is understandable."* Through his empathy with an apparent ideological opponent, President Kennedy was able to acknowledge the truth behind Sukarno's words, and establish a mutual respect with and prevent Indonesia and the Netherlands from going to war.

At the same time, President Kennedy diplomatically resolved the Indonesian-Netherlands conflict, the president encountered the CIA's plots against Sukarno by issuing his National Security Action Memorandum 179 on August 19, 1962. Addressing NSAM 179 to the heads of the State Department, Defense Department, CIA, AID, and the United States Information Agency, President Kennedy ordered them to take a positive approach to Indonesia. He stated, *"With a peaceful settlement of the West Irian dispute now in prospect, I would like to see us capitalize on the US role in promoting this settlement to move toward a new and better relationship with Indonesia. I gather that with this issue resolved the Indonesians too would like to move in this direction, and will be presenting us with numerous requests. To seize this opportunity, will all agencies concerned please review their programs for Indonesia and assess what further measures might be useful. I have in mind the possibility of expanded civic action, military aid, and economic stabilization and development programs, as well as diplomatic initiatives. The Department of State is requested to pull together all relevant agency proposals in a plan of action and submit it to me no later than September 15th."*

The CIA's deep-seated opposition to President Kennedy's openness to Sukarno arose from something more basic than Cold War ideology. Indonesia was rich in natural resources. If its natural resources were developed, Indonesia would become the third or fourth richest nation in the world. United States corporations were determined to exploit Indonesia for their own profits, whereas Sukarno was busy protecting the wealth of his country for the people by expropriating all foreign holdings. With the corporation-friendly Dutch out of the picture thanks to President Kennedy's diplomacy, Sukarno could now block foreign control of West Irian resources as well.

CHAPTER 46

―❑―

"The world knows that America will never start a war.
This generation of Americans has had enough of war
and hate . . . we want to build a world of peace where
the weak are secure and the strong are just."

John F. Kennedy

On Wednesday morning, November 20, 1963, a car with three people in it drove into Red Bird Air Field, on the outskirts of Dallas. The car parked in front of the office of American Aviation Company, a private airline. A heavy-set young man and a young woman got out of the car and entered the office, leaving a second young man sitting in the right front passenger seat. The man and the woman spoke with American Aviation owner, Wayne January, who rented out small planes.

"How can I help you today?" Wayne asked the couple.

"We want to rent a Cessna 310 on the afternoon of Friday, November 22nd," said the man.

"What we your destination be?" Wayne asked.

"We will be heading to the Yucatan Peninsula in Southeast Mexico, near Cuba."

"I see," commented Wayne.

"We just got a couple of questions about the plane. How far will it go without refueling? And what is the speed of the plane?"

Wayne became suspicious of the odd couple. He knew from experience people didn't ask those kinds of questions when they chartered a plane. He decided not to rent the Cessna to the couple. He said later that he suspected from their questions that they might have had in mind hijacking the plane to Cuba, just east of the Yucatan Peninsula. That may have been exactly what they wanted him to believe. As the couple left his office, expressing irritation at his rejection of their deal, Wayne was curious as to why the other man hadn't come in with them. He took a good look at the man sitting in the front passenger seat. Once again it was a CIA placement that resembled Lee Oswald.

The placing of Lee Harvey Oswald at the Red Bird Air Field was nothing more than a ruse in a scene being played out by the couple. The couple was nightclub owner Jack Ruby and one of his dancers. They were hired to go to the air field with the Lee Oswald look alike by the CIA. The scene was designed once again to implicate him. Red Bird Air Field was located just five miles south of Lee's apartment, a short drive away on the freeway connection. The apparent purpose of the plane-chartering scene, two days before the assassination, was to identify him with a covert plan to fly to Cuba right after President Kennedy's murder.

On the night of Wednesday, November 20, 1963, Louisiana State Police Lieutenant Francis Fruge was called to Moosa Memorial Hospital in Eunice, Louisiana. Once there he was given custody of Rose Cheramie, a heroin addict who was experiencing withdrawal symptoms. One of two men with whom she was traveling had thrown her out of the Silver Slipper Lounge in Eunice earlier that evening. While staggering in the parking lot she had been hit by a car, suffering minor abrasions. Lieutenant Fruge took her in an ambulance to East Louisiana State Hospital in Jackson for treatment of her withdrawal symptoms. During the two hour trip, she responded to his questions.

"What happened at the Silver Slipper Lounge?"

"I was thrown out of the lounge and then I was hit by a car," she replied.

"Who threw you out of the lounge, the owner maybe?"

"No, it was one of the men I was traveling with," she said.

"Where are you coming from?" he asked.

"We are coming from Miami."

"Where were you headed to before stopping at the lounge in Eunice?" he questioned her.

"We were headed to Dallas, Texas."

"What business did you and your companions have in Dallas?" asked Lieutenant Fruge.

"We're going to kill President Kennedy when he comes to Dallas in a few days."

"What did you just say?" he was hoping he didn't hear what he thought he heard. *Did she just say there was a plot to murder President Kennedy in Dallas*, he thought to himself.

"Well, we are going to Dallas for a number of things. One we, are to pick up some money. Two, we are to pick up my baby. And three, we are to kill Kennedy."

She has to be in a drug induced fantasy. Surely, she doesn't mean what she is saying, he thought to himself.

At the East Louisiana State Hospital on November 21st, Rose Cheramie said again, this time to hospital staff members, that President Kennedy was about to be killed in Dallas, Texas.

The story the CIA told Lee was the CIA and Secret Service was going to simulate an assassination attempt on President Kennedy while he was in Dallas, Texas. In the 1963, Dallas was known as a violent city. It was also possible the CIA told him there might be a chance someone would actually try to harm the president in some way. He was to keep his eyes open for any possible sightings of anti-Castro Cuban exiles in Dealey Plaza. The minute he saw someone he suspected was an anti-Castro Cuban then he was to connect his CIA handler. After the demonstration was over then he was to meet his handler at the Texas Theater for a de-briefing. He didn't know how everything was going to unfold on November 22nd; he wanted to see his family one last time. Some of the higher CIA officials wasn't too keen on the idea of him visiting his family a day early. But it turned out to be perfect for their plot. Because the CIA could claim Lee went to Ruth's house a day earlier to get the rifle.

When Lee arrived at the Paine's residence Marina and Ruth was surprised to see him since it was a Thursday night. They thought he had returned to make up for Monday's quarrel. Later that evening, when Ruth had finished cleaning the kitchen, she went to the garage and noticed the light was still burning. She was certain she had not left it on. The following morning Lee left while Marina was still in the bed feeding their baby girl. She didn't see him leave, nor did Ruth. He left his wedding ring and his wallet which contained $170 on the dresser drawer in their bedroom. In all the times he had visited Marina and the girls at the Paine's, he had never left any amount of money for her. In Lee's mind, he wasn't sure if the day would end as according to the CIA's plan.

After leaving the Paine's house, Lee walked over to the home of Wesley Frazier. He was carrying a brown package with him. He placed the package in the back seat and then he climbed into the car waiting for his fellow employee. Soon Wesley joined him in the car. After starting the car, Wesley turned around so he could watch as he was backing up the car. He noticed the brown package in the back seat.

"What is that brown package?" asked Wesley.

"It's curtain rods."

"That's right. You did tell me that's why you wanted to go see your wife a day earlier," Wesley said as he pulled the car into the street.

Julia Ann Mercer was a twenty-three year old employee of Automat Distributors in Dallas, Texas. At about 11 AM on Friday, November 22, 1963, she drove into Dealey Plaza. It was an hour and a half before the presidential motorcade would pass through. While Julia's car was stalled by heavy traffic in what would soon become a killing zone, her attention was drawn to a green pickup truck parked up on the curb to her right. As she watched, a man walked around to the back of the pickup truck. He reached in and pulled out a rifle case wrapped in paper. The man carried what appeared to be a rifle up a slope. She looked up at the bridge which formed an arch over the street ahead of her. Three police officers were standing talking beside a motorcycle. She wondered why they took no interest in the man carrying the rifle up the hill.

She eased her car forward, until she was parallel to a second man who was driving the truck. The driver turned his head, looking straight into her eyes. She noticed the man had a round face. He turned his head away, and then he looked back at her. Their eyes locked again. Two days later, while watching television, she recognized the driver of the truck. On her TV, Julia watched the driver of the truck shoot Lee Harvey Oswald. The driver of the truck was Jack Ruby. After she drove away from Dealey Plaza, Julia stopped to eat at a favorite restaurant. She told friends there about the man she saw carrying the rifle up the hill. She guessed he had to be a member of the Secret Service. "*The Secret Service is not very secret*," she told her friends.

Upon leaving the restaurant, she continued her drive to work when a police car pulled her over. Two officers who had overheard her at the restaurant said she was needed for questioning in Dallas. President Kennedy was shot in Dealey Plaza, where she had seen the man with the rifle. For several hours that afternoon and the next morning, Julia was questioned by the Dallas police and the FBI. If Julia Ann Mercer had reported what she had seen an hour before the assassination, then the assassins might've been in a bind they couldn't get out of.

The planners for the covert operation in Dallas needed to meet one more time. So they scheduled for a meeting at a nearby hotel room on November 21, 1963. Just about everybody who was in involved with the operation was at the meeting. CIA Deputy Director of Plans Richard Helms, General Edward Lansdale, former CIA Director Allen Dulles and former Deputy Director Charles Cabell represented the government involvement. Sam Giancana, Santo Trafficante, Carlos Marcello, Johnny Roselli, and Jack Ruby represented the Mafia involvement. Local involvement included mayor Earle Cabell, Marion Baker, and J. D. Tippit. Everyone was sitting at the table in the hotel suite.

"First of all, I have to say Chicago and Tampa Bay was a success," said Richard.

"What do you mean it was a success?" Sam asked.

"If it was such a success, then what are we doing here discussing tomorrow?" asked Santo.

"It was never intended for the operation to take place in Chicago or Tampa," replied General Lansdale.

"What are you talking about?" Sam asked.

"With an operation of this magnitude we had to be sure everything would go as according to the plan. Hence the try runs in Chicago and Tampa," replied Allen.

"Tonight, we are going to finalize the plan and make sure everyone is positive of their responsibilities in this operation," said the deputy director of plans.

"Johnny, did you take the assassins to the location for the crossfire on the motorcade route?" asked Charles.

"Yes, and they agreed that the location is perfect. They have picked out their spots from where they shoot on the motorcade," replied Johnny.

"Speaking on the assassins, where are they?" asked Richard.

"I have them in a safe house just outside of Dallas," answered Carlos.

"Ok. After the final shot, we need to make sure Lee doesn't escape the Texas School Book Depository Building. Marion, you will be in the motorcade, right?" asked General Lansdale.

"Yes, sir."

"Okay, as soon as the final shot is fired I want to head straight for the Texas School Book Depository Building. I don't care what the other officers are doing. I want to go into the Texas School Book Building. According to my reports, Lee should be on his lunch on the second floor. You will go the break room where you will meet him face to face. I want you to pull your service revolver, shove it in his gut and fire one shot," said General Lansdale.

"Yes, sir."

"We will have enough evidence linking Lee to the assassination that your shooting will be ruled as justifiable. With the commotion of the assassination of Kennedy and Oswald, the assassins will make their escape to the Love Field. From there David Ferrie will fly them out of the country," said Edward.

"Where is David Ferrie?" asked Richard.

"He got tied up in New Orleans, but he will be at the airport tomorrow," replied Carlos.

"What will happen if Lee happens to get out of the building before I get there," asked Marion.

"That's where Officer Tippit, here, comes in. He will be patrolling near the boarding room where Lee is staying. He will shoot and kill Lee if need be," replied General Lansdale

"The local and the FBI will investigate the assassination. But we have tied up all the loose ends and whatever evidence they discover will put the smoke gun at Lee Harvey Oswald," said Richard.

"Men, this son of a bitch, cannot be allowed to leave Dallas alive," said Carlos Marcello.

CHAPTER 47

———————◻———————

"There are risks and costs to action. But they are far less than
the long range risks of comfortable inaction."

John F. Kennedy

On Friday, November 22, 1963, at 11: 40 AM, President John F. Kennedy,
his wife Jacqueline, and the rest of presidential entourage arrived at Love
Field in Dallas, Texas, aboard Air Force One after a very short flight from
nearby Carswell Air Force Base in Fort Worth. The motorcade cars had
been lined up in a certain order since earlier that morning. The original
schedule was for the president to proceed in a long motorcade from Love
Field through downtown Dallas, and end at the Dallas Business and Trade
Mart. The motorcade was scheduled to enter Dealey Plaza at 12:10 PM,
followed by a 12:15 arrival at the Dallas Business and Trade Mart so
President Kennedy would deliver a speech and share in a steak luncheon
with Dallas government, business, religious, and civic leaders and their
spouses. Invitations were sent out and specified a 1:00 PM start to the
luncheon while Secret Service Agent Winston Lawson told Chief Jesse
Curry after arriving at Love Field and leaving at 11:30 the 38-45 minute
trip would get them to the Trade Mart on time. Air Force One touched
down at 11:39 AM and did not leave Love Field until about fifteen minutes
later. Dallas' three television stations were given separate assignments.
Bob Walker of WFAA-TV 8 (ABC) was providing live coverage of the
President's arrival at Love Field. KRLD-TV 4 (CBS) with Eddie Barker
was set up at the Trade Mart for President Kennedy's luncheon speech.
WBAP-TV 5 (NBC), being a Dallas/Fort Worth network based in Fort
Worth, had done live coverage of the President's breakfast speech in Fort

Worth earlier that day. On hand to report the arrival on radio was Joe Long of KLIF 1190.

The Presidential motorcade vehicles and personnel were as followed:

The lead car, an unmarked white Ford:

Dallas Police Chief Jesse Curry (driver)
Secret Service Agent Winston Lawson (right front)
Dallas County Sheriff Bill Decker (left rear)
Secret Service Agent Forrest Sorrels (right rear)

President limousine, a 1961 Lincoln Continental code named SS-100-X:

Secret Service Agent William Greer (driver)
Advance Agent and Special Agent In Charge Roy Kellerman (right front)
Nellie Connally (left middle)
Governor John Connally (right middle)
First Lady Jacqueline Kennedy (left rear)
President John F. Kennedy (right rear)

Presidential follow-up car, a convertible code named "Halfback":

Secret Service Agent Sam Kinney (driver)
ATSAIC Emory Roberts (right front)
Secret Service Agent Clint Hill (left front running board)
Secret Service Agent Bill McIntyre (left rear running board)
Secret Service Agent Jack Ready (right front running board)
Secret Service Agent Paul Landis (right rear running board)
Presidential aide Kenneth O'Donnell (left middle)
Presidential aide David Powers (right middle)
Secret Service Agent George Hickey (left rear)
Secret Service Agent Glen Bennett (right rear)

Vice Presidential limousine, a convertible:

Dallas Policeman Hurchel Jacks (driver)
Secret Service Agent Rufus Youngblood (right front)

Senator Ralph Yarborough (left rear)
Second Lady Bird Johnson (middle rear)
Vice-President Lyndon B. Johnson (right rear)

Vice Presidential follow-up car, a hardtop code named "Varsity":

A Texas state policeman (driver)
Vice Presidential aide Cliff Carter (front middle)
Secret Service Agent Jerry Kivett (right front)
Secret Service Agent Woody Taylor (left rear)
Secret Service Agent Lem Johns (right rear)

Press pool car, (on loan from the telephone company)

Telephone company employee (driver)
Malcolm Kilduff White House assistant press secretary (right front)
Merriman Smith, UPI (middle front)
Jack Bell, AP (left rear)
Robert Baskin, *The Dallas Morning News* (middle rear)
Bob Clark, ABC (right rear)

Press Car:

Bob Jackson, *The Dallas Times Herald*
Tom Dillard, *The Dallas Morning News*
Mel Couch: WFAA-TV.

The route scheduled to be driven was as follows: left turn from the south end of Love Field to West Mockingbird Lane, right on Lemmon Avenue, right at the "Y" on Turtle Creek Blvd., straight on Cedar Springs Road, left on North Harwood Street, right on Main Street, right on Houston Street, sharp left on Elm Street, through Triple Underpass, right turn up ramp to North Stemmons Freeway, to Dallas Trade Mart at 2100 North Stemmons. The original route had the motorcade continue straight onto Main instead of turning onto Houston, but it was discovered Elm Street provided the only direct link from Dealey Plaza to the Stemmons Freeway, so the route was altered. As President Kennedy's limousine left Love Field airport, two Secret Service Agents was stationed at each side at the rear. As the presidential limousine began to pull away, a man stands up in the second following car. He pointed and said something to the agent running behind President Kennedy. The agent threw up his hands in confusion and walked to the next car and climbed into it. Why was this agent called away from the presidential limousine? The simple answer was because President Kennedy didn't like the agents to get in between the crowd and him. The presidential motorcade began its route without incident, stopping twice so President Kennedy could shake hands with some Catholic nuns.

Ike Altgens was an American photographer and field reporter for the Associated Press based in Dallas, Texas. He had been employed by the Associated Press for nearly 26 years when he was assigned on November 22, 1963 to photograph the motorcade that would take President Kennedy from Love Field to the Dallas Trade Mart. He asked to go to the railroad overcrossing known to the locals as the "triple overpass" or "triple underpass" to take pictures. He was denied access to the overcrossing by uniformed officers; he took up position in Dealey Plaza instead. He took seven snapshots that day. The first picture was the Presidential limousine as it turned from Main Street onto Houston Street. He ran across the grass, roughly east to west, toward the south curb along Elm Street, and stopped across from the Plaza's north colonnade.

Lee Bowers, Jr. was operating the Union Terminal Company's two-story interlocking tower, overlooking the parking lot just north of the grassy knoll and west of the Texas School Book Depository Building. He had an unobstructed view of the rear of the concrete pergola and the stockade fence atop the knoll. He saw four men in the area: one or two uniform parking lot attendants, one of whom he knew; and two men standing 10 to 15 feet apart near the Triple Underpass, who did not appear to know each other. One was *"middle-aged, or slightly older, fairly heavy-set, in a white shirt, fairly dark trousers"* and the other was *"younger man, about mid-twenties, in either plaid shirt or plaid coat or jacket."*

Infantryman Gordon Arnold was on leave in Dallas after he had completed his basic training. He brought a movie camera with him to Dealey Plaza to film the presidential motorcade. He looked around for the best vantage point of the parade. His eyes found the railroad bridge over the triple overpass. He was convinced it would give him the best point of view to the presidential motorcade. In order to reach the bridge,

Gordon walked behind the fence on top of the grassy knoll. A man dressed in civilian clothes blocked his way. He noticed the man was wearing a sidearm.

"No one should be back here behind the fence," the man said to Gordon.

"What authority do you have to tell me no one should be behind the fence?" asked Gordon.

"I'm with the Secret Service. I don't want anyone up here," he flashed a badge at Gordon.

"Ok," Gordon said as he started walking back along the fence.

Gordon moved back along the fence. He could sense the man was following him. He stopped halfway along the fence. He looked over the fence through his camera. This was clearly the perfect place to film the motorcade. The man walked up to Gordon again.

"I thought I told you to get out of this area. It is off limits to the public," he told Gordon.

"Fine," replied Gordon.

Gordon walked along the rest of the fence. He stepped around the fence to the top of the grassy knoll. A few minutes later, the presidential limousine approached Elm Street. He began filming the presidential motorcade. He stood with his back to the fence which was three feet behind him. He would soon find himself in the line of fire.

Charles Brehm and his five year old son, Joe, were standing in the Dealey Plaza north infield grass, a few feet south of the south curb of Elm Street, across the street from the Dealey Plaza grassy knoll. When the Presidential limousine turned from Main Street onto the Houston Street, Charles and his son watched from that intersection's northwest side. After watching the turn, they ran quickly northwestward across the north infield grass towards the south curb of Elm Street to catch another glimpse of President Kennedy.

Howard Brennan watched the presidential motorcade from a concrete retaining wall at the southwest corner of Elm and Houston streets in Dealey Plaza, where he had a clear view of the south side of the Texas School Book Depository Building. He arrived about 12:23 p.m., and while watching for the motorcade, he looked up and saw a man appear at an open window at the southeast corner of the sixth floor, 120 feet from him. He watched as the man left the window "*a couple of times.*"

Orville Nix worked for the General Services Administration as an air conditioning engineer in the former Terminal Annex building on the south side of Dealey Plaza. He filmed the motorcade with an 8mm movie camera, first from the southwest corner of Main and Houston streets, then from the south side of Main Street 50 feet west of Houston, then from a point about another 50 feet west.

James Tague had been driving to downtown Dallas to have lunch with his girlfriend (and future wife) when he came upon a traffic jam due to the presidential motorcade. He stopped his car, got out of it, and stood by Dealey Plaza, at the south curb of Main Street, 520 feet southwest of the Texas School Book Depository Building. He was a few feet east of the eastern edge of the triple overpass railroad bridge, when he saw the Presidential limousine.

Marie Muchmore was an employee of "Justin McCarty Dress Manufacturer" which was four blocks south of the Texas School Book Depository Building. She was in Dealey Plaza with five other employees, including Wilma Bond, who had a still camera. She set up her 8mm Keystone movie camera near the northwest corner of Main Street and Houston Street and waited for president's arrival. She began filming the presidential motorcade with her movie camera from her initial location near the northwest corner of Main Street and Houston Street as the motorcade turned onto Houston Street into Dealey Plaza. She then turned and walked with Wilma several yards northwestward to again film the President's limousine as it went down Elm Street.

S.M. Holland worked as the Signal Supervisor for Union Terminal Railroad. About 11:00 o'clock, a couple of policeman and a plainclothesman came up on top of the triple underpass. He knew that some fellow employees would be up there and he knew that was the route of the motorcade. So he left his office and walked up to the underpass to talk to the policemen. They asked him to come back up there during the motorcade and identify people that were supposed to be on that overpass. He spoke to the 2 police officers but not the plainclothes officer. He returned to the underpass around a quarter to twelve. He identified each person that came up there that worked at the Union Terminal. He noticed two Dallas Police Officers were on the triple overpass also. He saw about 12 people on the triple overpass at the time the motorcade came through the Dealey Plaza.

At 12:29 pm the presidential limousine entered Dealey Plaza after a 90 degree right turn from Main Street onto Houston Street. The presidential motorcade then made the 120 degree left turn directly in front of the Texas School Book Depository Building. As the presidential limousine turned from Houston onto Elm Street, President Kennedy began to wave to the people of the right of the motorcade. Charles Brehm and his son were standing close to the south curb directly across the street from Bill Newman, Gayle Newman and their sons, about 20 feet northeast from Jean Hill and Mary Ann Moorman.

Ike Altgens snapped his first photograph when he heard a "burst of noise that he thought was firecrackers." The presidential limousine was approaching Charles and his son and the limousine was only 30 feet away when his son then started to wave to President Kennedy. President Kennedy started to wave back when a loud sound rang through the air. Some witnesses claimed that it sounded like a firecracker. But to those familiar with rifles knew what it was; a rifle shot. The first shot was fired by Charles Nicolette from the third floor window of the Dal-Tex building. It missed the motorcade entirely. Howard Brennan heard the shot and looked up. He thought someone had thrown a firecracker from the Texas School Book Depository Building. He saw a man in the sixth floor window with a rifle taking aim. James Chaney was a Dallas police motorcycle presidential escort riding only ten to fifteen away President Kennedy (slightly behind and to the right). He heard the first shot it sounded like a motorcycle backfire. He looked to his left and saw President Kennedy look back over his left shoulder. William Greer, the driver of the presidential limousine, tapped the brakes slowing the limousine to almost a walking pace. He turned to look back at the president. Secret Service Agent Clint Hill was riding in the car which was immediately behind the presidential limousine. As soon as he heard the first shot, he jumped out and began running to overtake the moving car in front of him.

Governor Connally turned to his right because he recognized right away what the sound was. He couldn't see the president, so he turned to his left. Johnny Roselli, who was stationed behind the fence on the grassy knoll, took aim and fired the second shot. It hit President Kennedy in the throat. His mouth opened in a shocked expression and his hands clenched into fists. As President Kennedy reached for his throat, the First Lady noticed something was wrong with her husband. Governor Connally caught a glimpse of President Kennedy reaching for his throat when Lucien Sarti stationed on the sixth floor of the Texas School Book Depository Building fired a shot. This was the first shot fired from the sixth floor of the TSBD. The shot hit President in the back throwing him forward. Charles Brehm could see the President's face pretty well; the President was seated, but was leaning forward when he stiffened. Secret Service Agent Roy Kellerman turned his entire body to view President Kennedy at a time when the president showed distress. He turned back around to face forward in a relaxed position, which he maintained as the remaining shots are fired into the president and the limousine sped from the scene.

Shortly after third shot, Charles fired his second shot. This shot hit Governor Connally in the upper right back located just behind his right armpit. Four inches of his right fifth chest rib was shattered. The bullet exited his chest causing a two-and-a-half inch sized sucking-air chest wound. The bullet then entered his right arm's wrist bone fracturing it into seven pieces, and then it lodged in his upper left thigh. James Chaney didn't see the president get hit, but he saw Governor John Connally's shirt erupt in blood. Lucien fired his second shot and missed the motorcade. It hit a concrete curb where a piece of shard struck James Tague. When the President's limousine was about 15 feet to 25 feet from Charles Brehm, he heard another shot. Just as Ike Altgens was preparing for another snapshot along Elm Street, when he heard a blast he recognized as gunfire and he saw President Kennedy get hit in the head.

Johnny fired his second shot just as Lucien fired his third shot. Both shots struck President Kennedy in the head almost at the same time. Charles Brehm watched President Kennedy's hair fly up and he saw bits of brain and bone fly in the air and then roll over to his side. Then he watched as President slumped all the way down. He grabbed his son and threw him to ground and fell on top him. Howard Brennan looked up once more at the sixth floor window. He saw the man resting against the left window sill, with the rifle shouldered to his right shoulder, holding the gun with his left hand and taking aim and fired his last shot. After a few seconds Howard saw the man draw back the rifle back from the window. He watched the man paused for another second as though to assure himself that he hit his mark, and then he disappeared.

As the blood, brains, and skull pieces splattered the limousine, Mrs. Kennedy screamed and she began to climb onto the back of the limousine. Just as she retrieved a piece of her slain husband's head Agent Clint Hill jumped onto the back of the limousine. He grabbed a small handrail on the left rear of the trunk which was normally used by bodyguards to stabilize them while standing on small platforms on the rear bumper. He grabbed the handrail less than two seconds after the fatal shot to President Kennedy. The presidential limousine driver then accelerated, causing the car to slip away from Clint, who was in the midst of trying to leap on it. He succeeded in regaining his footing and jumped on to the back of the quickly accelerating vehicle. He pushed the First Lady back into her seat as the motorcade sped away. Agent Hill shielded her and the dying president. The First Lady cried, "*I have his brains in my hand!*" He looked at the president and he noticed the right rear portion of his head was missing. He saw President Kennedy's brain was exposed. He saw blood and bits of brain all over the entire rear portion of the limousine. He looked at the First Lady and noticed she was completely covered with blood.

Ike Altgens recovered enough to take his final picture of the limousine showing the First Lady on the vehicle's trunk as Secret Service agent Clint Hill was climbing on behind her. James Chaney's police uniform was splattered with blood and President Kennedy's head matter. The limousine driver and the police motorcade turned on their sirens and raced at full speed to Parkland Hospital. The motorcade arrived at the hospital at about 12:38pm. When the shooting ended in Dealey Plaza, Gordon Arnold was still lying on the ground. He was too scared to move. Two of the shots sounded like they had come from behind him. He was afraid if he stood to his feet, then he would be in the line of fire of the assassin. Suddenly he felt someone give him a sharp kick. He looked up at who was kicking him. A policeman was standing beside him.

"Get up," demanded the policeman.

As Gordon stood to his feet, a second policeman walked up to them. He was crying and shaking. He was holding a long gun which he was pointing nervously at Gordon. The two officers demanded the film he took of the motorcade. He tossed the camera to the first policeman. The officer opened the camera and pulled out the film. And then he threw the camera back to Gordon. The two police officers left quickly with his film. He never saw his film again.

CHAPTER 48

———————◻———————

*"Ask not what your country can do for you,
ask what you can do for your country."*

John F. Kennedy

The conspirators against President Kennedy controlled the crime scene at Dealey Plaza from the beginning. When witnesses instinctively stormed the grassy knoll to chase a shooter who was clearly behind the fence at the top, they immediately encountered men in plainclothes who identified themselves as Secret Service agents. These men facilitated and covered up the escape of the triggermen. After President Kennedy was shot, Dallas Police Officer Joe Marshall Smith was one of the first people to rush up the grassy knoll and behind its stockade fence. As he reached the top, Joe smelled gunpowder. When he encountered a man in the parking lot behind the fence he pulled his pistol from his holster. Joe realized he didn't know who he was looking for so he put his pistol back in the holster. As he did this, the man Joe saw flashed a Secret Service badge at him. Officer Smith had seen Secret Service credentials before and he was satisfied that the man was a Secret Service agent. Officer Smith turned and walked away. But something didn't seem right to him.

From Dallas, local listeners of KLIF Radio were listening to *The Rex Jones Show* when they received the first bulletin at about 12:39pm. A "bulletin alert" sounder faded in during the song "I Have A Boyfriend" by The Chiffons. The song was stopped and newscaster Gary Delaune made the first announcement over the bulletin signal:

"This KLIF Bulletin from Dallas: Three shots reportedly fired at the motorcade of President Kennedy today near downtown

section. KLIF News is checking out the report, we will have further reports, stay tuned."

Dallas' ABC television affiliate WFAA was airing a local lifestyle program, *The Julie Benell Show*, at the time. At 12:45pm, the station abruptly cut from the prerecorded program to news director Jay Watson in the studio, who had been at Dealey Plaza and ran back to the station following the incident. He said:

> *"Good afternoon, ladies and gentlemen. You'll excuse the fact that I am out of breath, but about 10 or 15 minutes ago a tragic thing from all indications at this point as happened in the city of Dallas. Let me quote to you this and I'll . . . you'll excuse me if I'm out of breath. A bulletin, this is from the United Press from Dallas: President Kennedy and Governor John Connally have been cut down by assassin's bullets in downtown Dallas."*

Four minutes following ABC's radio bulletin, CBS was the first to break the news over television at 12:40 pm. The network interrupted its live broadcast of *As the World Turns* with a "CBS News Bulletin" bumper slide and Walter Cronkite filed an audio-only report over it as no camera was available at the time:

> *"Here is bulletin from CBS News. In Dallas, Texas, three shots were fired at President Kennedy's motorcade in downtown Dallas. The first reports say that President Kennedy was been seriously wounded by this shooting. More details just arrived. These details about the same as previously: President Kennedy shot today just as his motorcade left downtown Dallas. Mrs. Kennedy jumped up and grabbed Mr. Kennedy, she called, 'Oh, no!' the motorcade sped on. United Press says that the wounds for President Kennedy perhaps could be fatal. Repeating, a bulletin from CBA News, President Kennedy has been shot by a would-be assassin in Dallas, Texas. Stay tuned to CBS News for further details."*

While the assassins were shooting at President Kennedy, Lee Oswald was walking down the stairs in the Texas School Book Depository Building. It was his lunch break so he was heading to the break room. He passed a couple of female employees as he casually descended down to the second floor. He sat in the break room and ate his lunch. He had no idea President Kennedy had just been shot. He stood and walked to the coke machine and bought a coke. As he turned to face the exit, he came face to face with a Dallas Police Officer.

Officer Marion Baker thought the first shot he heard as he approached the Texas School Book Depository and the Dallas Textile Building had originated from the building in front of him or possibly the one to his right. He jumped the curb with his motorcycle. He jumped off his bike and ran to the Texas School Book Depository Building. He ran into Roy Truly, the superintendent of the Texas School Book Depository and who directed the officer to the stairs. In the second floor lunchroom, he came face to face with Lee Oswald. He pulled out his pistol and shoved it into Lee's gut. Just as he about to pull the trigger, Lee's boss stormed into the break room. He identified Lee as an employee. Officer Baker noticed Lee appeared completely calm, cool, and normal. Lee was not out of breath and was not sweating. The TSBD secretary saw Lee as he crossed through the second floor business office carrying a soda bottle. He left the TSBD at approximately 12:33pm through the front door.

At about 12:40 pm, Lee boarded a city bus by pounding on the door in the middle of a block, but when heavy traffic had slowed the bus to a halt he requested a bus transfer from the driver. He took a taxicab a few blocks beyond his rooming house at 1026 North Beckley Avenue then walked back there to retrieve his revolver and beige jacket at about 1:00 pm and moments later left the house. As he was getting his jacket and revolver, a Dallas police squad car pulled up to the curb. The driver honked the horn twice and then it pulled away from the curb. He lingered briefly at a bus stop across the street from his rooming house, and then began walking. While he was on the bus he had overheard someone say shots had been fired at the presidential motorcade. He knew he needed to head to Texas Theater to meet up with his handler.

Soon after the shooting several witnesses ran up to the grassy knoll, while some police officers ran to the Texas School Book Depository Building. Officer Luke Mooney was one of those police officers. He was the first one to search the 6th floor of the Texas School Book Depository Building. He didn't see anyone so he searched the 7th floor, and then he went back down to the 6th floor. He went to the far corner and found a cubby hole which had been constructed of cartons. Inside the cubby hole were three more boxes arranged as to be a rest for a rifle. On one of these cartons was half eaten piece of chicken. He saw the expended shells on the floor. He called out the window for Sheriff Bill Decker and Captain Will Fritz to send up the Crime Lab Officers. He then continued to search the 6th floor. He heard Deputy Sheriff Eugene Boone yell he found a rifle near the staircase between some rows of cartons. Office Seymour Weitzman stepped onto the sixth floor just as Deputy Sheriff Boone discovered the murder weapon. He was standing with Roger Craig when he first saw the rifle. He was regarded as a weapons expert. He initially described it as a 7.65 German Mauser. Eugene Boone also identified the rifle as a German Mauser.

Officer J. D. Tippit heard the general description of the alleged shooter which was broadcast over the police radio at 12:45 pm. He started patrolling in the general area where Lee lived. He saw two men standing near the corner of Patton Avenue and 10th Street. He noticed one of the men resembled Lee and pulled up to talk to him through his patrol car window. Officer Tippit then got out of his car and began walking towards the two men. Without warning, one of the men began shooting at Officer Tippit. Then the other man began shooting also. Four of the shots hit Officer Tippit, killing him instantly in view of several witnesses. One of the men reloaded his revolver as he walked away, throwing the empty shell casings into some bushes. At least a dozen people witnessed the shooting. A cab driver hiding behind his taxi cab heard the man who resembled Lee mutter 'poor dumb cop' or 'poor damn cop' as he walked away. Lee look alike then broke into a run, still holding the pistol in his hand. Moments later, he dropped his jacket in a parking lot. Officer Tippit's service revolver was found under his body, out of its holster.

While Officer Tippit was getting shot up by two strangers Lee was headed to Texas Theater. A few minutes later, Lee ducked into the entrance alcove of Hardy's Shoe Store on Jefferson Street to avoid passing police cars, then snuck into the nearby Texas Theater without paying while the ticket attendant, Julie Postal, was distracted. The shoe store's manager, Johnny Calvin Brewer, saw all of this, followed him and alerted the theater's ticket clerk, who phoned police. Once inside, he changed seats several times. The police quickly arrived and poured into the theater as the lights were turned on. Officer M.N. McDonald approached him sitting near the rear and ordered him to stand. Lee stood to his feet. He didn't know what was going on when he first saw the officers enter the theater. But as they approached him, it became all too clear. He had been set up. He had been set up by the CIA and his handler.

"Well, it's all over now," he said as he punched Officer McDonald

Lee drew his revolver. He pulled the trigger but the revolver misfired. Officer McDonald briefly struggled with Lee before other officers subdued and arrested him at 1:50 pm.

"I don't know why you are treating me this way. The only thing I have done is carry a pistol into a movie theater," said Lee.

"I don't see why you handcuffed me," he said as Officer McDonald handcuffed him.

"When we take you outside, do you want us to cover your face," asked one of the officers.

"Why should I hide my face? I haven't done anything to be ashamed of. I want a lawyer," he said.

As the officers stepped outside of the theater, a large crowd had gathered. They began yelling and shouting for Lee's death.

"I am not resisting arrest. I didn't kill anybody. I haven't shot anybody. I protest this police brutality. I am a victim. What is this all about?" he asked as he was pushed into the squad car where he continued to complain about his arrest.

"What is this all about? I know my rights," said Lee.

"As if you hadn't heard, a police officer was killed," said Officer McDonald.

"A police officer was killed? I hear they burn for murder. Well, they say it just takes a second to die."

"Do you know why we arrested you?"

"All I did was carry a gun into a theater," he replied.

"I found a Selective Service card in the name of Hidell in your wallet. Is that your name?"

"No, Hidell is not my real name. I have been in the Marine Corps and I have a dishonorable discharge. And I went to Russia," said Lee.

"Have you ever been in trouble with the law before today?"

"I had some trouble with police in New Orleans for passing out pro-Castro literature. Why are you treating me this way? I am not being handled right. I demand my rights," he said. The rest of the way they rode in silence.

CHAPTER 49

—————————————◻—————————————

"There is always inequality in life. Some men
are killed in a war and some men are wounded and some
men never leave the country. Life is unfair."

John F. Kennedy

A little while after the assassination some Dallas police officer pulled into the driveway of Ruth Paine's house. As they walked up to the porch, Ruth came to the door. She told them,

"I've been expecting you all. Well, I've been expecting you to come out. Come right in."

While officers searched Ruth's garage, Lee was taken to the Dallas Police Department. He wasn't handled like a normal prisoner. He was questioned at length several times. The interrogators failed to record any of the interrogation. Most of the interrogating was handled by Captain Fritz and FBI agent James Bookhout.

Silvia Odio heard about President Kennedy's assassination on the radio on her way back to work from lunch. Although the radio made no mention yet of Lee Oswald, Silvia thought immediately of the three men's visit to her apartment and what Leopoldo said on the phone about Leon's remarks on killing President Kennedy. She felt a deep sense of fear. She began saying to herself, "*Leon did it! Leon did it!*" While everyone was being sent home from Silvia's workplace, she became more terrified. As she was walking to her car, she fainted. She woke up in the hospital. When Silvia's sister, Annie, first saw Lee on television that afternoon, she thought, "*My God, I know this guy from somewhere!*" She kept asking herself where she'd seen him. Her sister Serita called to tell her that their sister had fainted at work and was in the hospital. She immediately went to the hospital. When Annie visited Silvia, she told her she knew she'd seen the guy on the TV who'd shot President Kennedy, but she didn't know where. Silvia began to cry. She asked Annie if she remembered the three men who had visited her apartment. Then Annie realized she'd not only seen him but had spoken with him at the door. Silvia told her of Leopoldo's follow-up phone call about his threats against the president. Annie, too, became deeply frightened. Silvia by now had also seen television pictures of the presumed assassin. She was certain Lee Harvey Oswald was identical to the "Leon Oswald" who had stood at her door under the light between the two Cubans.

At Parkland Hospital, a Roman Catholic priest was summoned to perform the last rites for President Kennedy. Dr. M.O. Perry II, assistant professor of surgery at UT Southwestern and vascular surgeon on the Parkland Hospital staff was the first to treat President Kennedy. He performed a tracheotomy, followed by a cardiopulmonary resuscitation performed with another surgeon. Other doctors and surgeons who together worked frantically to save the President's life, but his wounds were too great. At 1:00pm, after all the heart activity has ceased, and after the priest administered the last rites, President Kennedy was pronounced dead. Personnel at Parkland Hospital Trauma Room #1, who treated President Kennedy, observed that, the President's condition was 'moribund,' meaning he had no chance of survival upon arrival at the hospital. Although President Kennedy was pronounced dead at 1:00pm, the official announcement would not come for another half-hour. Immediately after receiving word of the president's death, acting White House press secretary Malcolm Kilduff entered the room where Vice-President Johnson and his wife were sitting. He approached them slowly.

"Mr. President," Malcolm said as Mrs. Johnson let out a short scream. "President Kennedy is dead."

"Oh, God!" exclaimed Lyndon.

"Do you want me to make a public announcement about President Kennedy's death?"

"No, I don't want the announcement to be made until after I have left Parkland," said the new president.

A few minutes after 2:00pm, and after a ten to fifteen minutes confrontation between cursing and weapons-brandishing Secret Service agents and doctors, President Kennedy's body was removed from Parkland Hospital and taken to Air Force One. The removal of the president's body was illegal. In 1963 it was not a federal crime to kill the president, so the assassination of President Kennedy was considered a state crime. The body was considered to be within the Texas jurisdiction. The body was not supposed to be removed without undergoing a forensic examination by the Dallas coroner. Since the Secret Service removed President Kennedy's body before the forensic examination, they broke a Texas state law.

Immediately after President Kennedy's assassination, Lieutenant Francis Fruge called the hospital, telling them not to release Rose Cheramie until he could question her further. When he does so on Monday, November 25th, Rose Cheramie described the two men driving with her from Miami to Dallas as either Cubans or Italians. Lieutenant Fruge would later testify before the House Select Committee on Assassinations that Cheramie had told him, "*The men were going to kill Kennedy* [in Dallas] *and she was going to check in the Rice Hotel* [in Houston], *where reservations were already made for her, and pick up 10 kilos of heroin from a seaman coming into Galveston. She was to pick up the money for the dope from a man who was holding her baby. She would then take the dope to Mexico.*"

The police checked on parts of her story with Nathan Durham, the Chief Customs Agent in the Texas region which included Galveston. He confirmed that the ship with the seaman that she said had the heroin was about to dock in Galveston. The seaman was on it. The police checked on the man holding the money and Rose's baby. He was identified as a suspected dealer in drug traffic. Working with her, the police and customs agents tried to follow and trap the seaman when he disembarked from his ship in Galveston, but the man eluded them. Colonel Morgan of the Louisiana State Police called Captain Will Fritz of the Dallas Police to tell him about her prediction of the assassination, the confirmed parts of her story, and that the Chief Customs Agent in Houston was holding her for further questioning. When Morgan hung up from his conversations with Fritz, he turned to the other officers in the room and said, "*They don't want her. They're not interested.*" By that time Lee had been captured, jailed, and shot to death by Jack Ruby. The Dallas police wanted no further witnesses to the president's assassination. The Chief Customs Agent called FBI agents to pass on the information received from her. The FBI said it also did not want to talk to her. As Rose Cheramie's story was being confirmed, she also told Lieutenant Fruge she used to work for Jack Ruby, as a stripper at his nightclub. She said as a result of her employment by Jack, she knew Lee Harvey Oswald. She was not only a witness participant in President Kennedy's assassination traveling to Dallas but also to Jack and Lee knowing each other. She said she knew that two of them had an intimate relationship "*for years*." After Dallas and federal investigative authorities refused to question her, the Chief Customs Agent released her in Houston, and she disappeared.

Once back at *Air Force One*, and only after Mrs. Kennedy and President Kennedy's body had also returned to the plane, Lyndon Johnson was sworn in by Sarah T. Hughes as the 36th President of the United States of America at 2:38pm. At about 5:00pm *Air Force One* arrived at Andrews Air Force Base near Washington D.C. After President Kennedy's brother, Robert Kennedy, boarded the plane, Kennedy's casket was removed from the rear entrance and loaded into a light gray US Navy ambulance for its transport to the Bethesda Naval Hospital for an autopsy and mortician's preparations. When Jackie Kennedy stepped off the plane with her brother-in-law, her pink suit and legs were still stained with her husband's blood. All that long afternoon and into the early morning hours of the nest day, she objected to leaving her husband's body, except for the swearing in of Lyndon Johnson. She also refused to change out of her blood-stained suit because she wanted the world to see what "they" had done to her husband. Shortly after the ambulance with the casket and Mrs. Kennedy departed, President Johnson and the First Lady exited *Air Force One*. They were led to a podium clustered with microphones where Lyndon Johnson made his first official statement as President of the United States:

"This is a sad time for all people. We have suffered a loss that cannot be weighed. For me, it is a deep personal tragedy. I know the world shares the sorrow that Mrs. Kennedy and her family bear. I will do my best; that is all I can do. I ask for your help and God's."

CHAPTER 50

———————— ❑ ————————

"Those who dare to fail miserably can achieve greatly."

John F. Kennedy

FBI Agent James Bookhout was on leave when President Kennedy made his trip to Dallas. He was requested to come to the office to handle some expedited dictation in a particular case. When he was done, James went the Mercantile National Bank where he transacted some personal business. When he left the bank, James realized the motorcade would be passing soon. He couldn't observe the motorcade clearly because of the size of the crowd on the sidewalk. As he was crossing the street James heard several police sirens on squad cars heading the direction of the county courthouse. As he crossed the street a citizen with a transistor radio told him shots had been fired at the presidential motorcade. James then headed towards the FBI office, he saw 2 agents coming from the direction of the FBI office. He was told to go to the homicide and robbery Bureau of Dallas Police Department. Upon arriving at the Dallas Police Department he called his office. He was told to maintain liaison with the homicide and robbery bureau. At the Dallas Police Department he heard the report about Officer Tippit being shot. Captain Fritz hadn't returned to Dallas Police Department yet. Soon after Captain Fritz returned to the Dallas Police Department, Lee was apprehended at the Texas Theatre. Information was passed onto Captain Fritz about the name of the suspect they apprehended in the Tippit shooting. Captain Fritz stated the suspect was who they were looking for in connection to the killing of President Kennedy. James didn't realize the FBI had been watching Lee so he didn't know much about him. Captain Fritz told him Lee was employed at Texas School Book Depository and he had ascertained Lee had left after the shooting. James was present when they brought Lee into the Dallas Police Department. He noticed Lee was struggling as the officers led him to Captain Fritz's office.

Special Agent James reported to his office the suspect had been brought into the police department. SAC Shanklin advised him to be in the office with James Hosty while he was interrogated. James Bookhout went into Captain Fritz's office about 5 or 10 minutes after the interrogation had started. He noticed Lee was arrogant and argumentative during the interrogation.

"What is your name?" asked Captain Fritz.

"My name is Lee Harvey Oswald."

"Where do you work?"

"I work at the Texas School Book Depository Building," he replied.

"Have you ever lived in Russia?"

"I lived in Minsk and Moscow. I worked in a factory. I liked everything over there except the weather," he said.

"Are you married?"

"Yes, I have a wife and two daughters," he replied.

"Where do you live? What is your address?"

"My address is 1026 North Beckley, Dallas, Texas," he replied.

"Was this in your wallet?" Captain Fritz placed a Select Service card down in front of Lee.

"Yes, that was in my wallet"

"Whose name is on the card?"

"Alex J. Hidell," replied Lee.

"Is this your signature?" asked Captain Fritz.

Lee wouldn't reply to the question.

"You have been to my home two or three times talking to my wife," Lee said to FBI Agent James Hosty. "I don't appreciate your coming out there when I wasn't there. Why did you use unfair tactics while you interviewed my wife last month?"

"Have you ever been to Mexico City?" Agent Hosty asked Lee.

"No, I have never been to Mexico City. But I have been to Tijuana with a friend when I was in the Marines. Please take the handcuffs from behind me, behind my back," he asked the captain.

"Are you a member of the Fair Play for Cuban Committee?" asked Captain Fritz.

"Yes. I am the secretary of the New Orleans branch."

"Who are the officers in Fair Play for Cuba Committee?" asked Agent Hosty.

"I don't want to discuss that matter further."

"Have you ever seen a rifle at the Texas School Book Depository Building?"

"Yes, I observed a rifle at work on November 20th. Mr. Roy Truly, my supervisor, displayed the rifle to individuals in his officer on the first floor," he replied.

"Have you ever owned a rifle?"

"I never owned a rifle myself," he replied.

"When you were in the Marines what did you score on the shooting range when you had to qualify?" asked Captain Fritz. Lee didn't answer the question.

"Why did you use the name O. H. Lee at the residence of 1026 North Beckley?" asked the captain.

"The landlady was old. She thought my last name was Lee."

"Were you at the Texas School Book Depository today?" questioned the captain.

"Yes, of course, I was present in the Texas School Book Depository Building today. I have been employed there since October 15th."

"What kind of access do you have at the Depository?" asked Captain Fritz.

"As a laborer, I have access to the entire building."

"Where in the building did you normally work?" questioned Captain Fritz.

"My usual place of work is on the first floor. But, I frequently use the fourth, fifth, sixth, and seventh floors to get books."

"Which floor were you on today?"

"I was on all floors today."

"Why did you leave work early after the president was shot?"

"I left because of all the confusion. I figured there would be no work performed that afternoon so I decided to go home."

"What did you do when you arrived home?"

"I changed my clothes and I went to a movie," Lee replied.

"Why did you have a pistol on you?"

"I felt like carrying a pistol with me to movie theater, for no other reason," he answered.

"What happened at the movie theater?"

"I fought the Dallas Police who arrested me in the movie theater where I received a cut and a bump," answered Lee.

"Did you shoot President John F. Kennedy and Officer J. D. Tippit?"

"I didn't shoot President Kennedy or Officer Tippit," he said.

"Why did you have bullets in your pocket?"

"I just had them in there."

"That's all the questions I have for you at the moment. Get him ready for the lineup," Captain Fritz said to an officer.

After the first interview ended at 4:45 PM on November 22nd, Lee was taken to a police lineup. Bookhout went to the lineup room and observed for the purpose of keeping up the liaison. He saw four men in the lineup. The lineup was for witness, Helen Markham. She had witnessed the murder of Officer J. D. Tippit. During the lineup, Lee once again complained to the police.

"It isn't right to put me in line with these teenagers. You know what you are doing. I think you are trying to railroad me. I want to speak to my lawyer. You are doing me an injustice by putting me out there dressed different than these other men. I am out there, the only one with a bruise on his head. I don't believe this lineup is fair. Why don't I have on a jacket similar to those worn by some of the other men in this lineup?" he turned and looked at the men standing in the lineup with him. "All of you have a shirt on, and I have a t-shirt on. This T-shirt is unfair."

After the lineup, Agent Bookhout returned to homicide and robbery bureau. Lee was taken to Captain Fritz's officer for a second interrogation. T.J. Nully, David B. Grant (Secret Service), Robert I. Nash (U.S. Marshal), Detectives Billy L. Senkel, Fay M. Turner, FBI Agent James Hosty, and Captain Fritz were present for the 2nd interrogation. Once again, Captain Fritz conducted the interrogation. This interrogation lasted until 6:30PM.

"What did you do when you arrived home after leaving work?" questioned Captain Fritz.

"When I left work, I went to my room, where I changed my trousers, got a pistol, and went to a picture show."

"If you didn't shoot anyone, why did you have a pistol on you?" asked Fritz.

"You know how boys do when they have a gun, they carry it."

"On November 9, 1963, did you write the Russian Embassy?" asked the Dallas police captain.

"Yes, I did write the Russian Embassy." Lee looked and spoke to Agent Hosty, "Mr. Hosty, you have been accosting my wife. You mistreated her on two different occasions when you talked to her. I know you."

"Agent Hosty isn't being questioned, you are. You don't speak to them unless they ask you a question."

"Well he threatened her. He practically told her she would have to go back to Russia," said Lee. "I want to talk lawyer in New York, Mr. Abt."

"Do you know Mr. Abt? Is he your attorney?"

"I don't know him personally, but I know about a case that he handled some years ago, where he represented the people who had violated the Smith Act. He is the attorney I want," replied Lee.

"Can we get you a local attorney?" asked Captain Fritz.

"I don't want an attorney from Dallas."

"What if we can't get in contact with Abt?" asked the captain.

"If I can't get Attorney Abt, then I will get an attorney from the Civil Liberties Union."

"Where did you go to school?"

"I went to school in New Orleans and in Fort Worth, Texas."

"Did you graduate from high school?" asked Captain Will Fritz.

"No. After joining the Marines, I finished my high school education."

"Are you pro-Castro?" asked Fritz.

"I support the Cuban revolution."

"Why do you go by the name O. H. Lee?" asked the captain.

"My landlady didn't understand my name correctly, so it was her idea to call me O. H. Lee."

"Did you bring a package with you to work today?" asked Captain Fritz.

"The only package I brought to work was my lunch."

"Is it true you are a member of the Communist Party?"

"No. I am a Marxist, not a Marxist-Leninist."

"Where did you purchase the pistol in your possession at the time of your arrest?"

"I bought a pistol in Fort Worth several months ago," replied Lee.

"Where did you buy the pistol?"

"I refuse to tell you where the pistol was purchased," said Lee.

"Is it true you mail ordered the pistol and rifle?"

"I never ordered my guns. How can I afford a rifle on the Book Depository salary of $1.25?" asked Lee.

"What irritated you about the president?"

"Nothing irritated me about the President. I think John Kennedy had a nice family," suggested Lee.

"Do you believe in a deity?" asked the captain.

"I don't care to discuss that. Everybody will know who I am. Can I get an attorney? I have not been given the opportunity to have counsel."

At 6:30 Lee was escorted from Captain Fritz's office to another police lineup. This time it was for witnesses Cecil McWatters, Sam Guinyard, and Ted Callaway. On the way to the lineup, Lee was escorted past a group of reporters. As soon as they saw him, the reporters started yelling questions at him. He spoke to them briefly.

"I didn't shoot anyone," Lee yelled to the reporters in the hall. "I want to get in touch with a lawyer, Mr. Abt, in New York City. I never killed anyone."

At 7:10PM Lee was taken to his arraignment: State of Texas v. Lee Harvey Oswald for Murder with Malice of Officer J. D. Tippit of the Dallas Police Department. Lee made a brief statement.

"I insist upon my constitutional rights. The way you are you treating me, I might as well be in Russia. I was not granted my request to put on a jacket similar to those worn by other individuals in some previous lineups," stated Lee.

At 7:55PM Lee was interrogated for a third time by Captain Fritz. It was shorter than the other two interrogations. Before the captain spoke, Lee made a statement.

"I think I have talked long enough. I don't have anything else to say. What started out to be a short interrogation turned out to be rather lengthy. I don't care to talk anymore. I am waiting for someone to come forward to give me assistance."

An hour later, Lee was given paraffin test and his fingerprints were taken in Captain Fritz's office. He questioned the purpose of the paraffin test.

"I will not sign the fingerprint card until I talk to my attorney. What are you trying to prove with this paraffin test; that I fired a gun? You are wasting time, I don't know anything about what you are accusing me," said Lee.

At about 11:20PM, Lee was taking to a room filled with reporters. It was a press conference. Dallas nightclub owner, Jack Ruby, was present for this press conference.

"What happened to your eye?" asked a reporter.

"A cop hit me."

"Were you taken to an arraignment?"

"Well, I was questioned by Judge Johnston. However, I protested at that time that I was not allowed legal representation during that very short and sweet hearing. I really don't know what the situation is about. Nobody has told me anything except that I am accused of murdering a policeman. I know nothing more than that, and I do request someone to come forward to give me legal assistance," replied Lee.

"Did you kill President Kennedy?"

"No, I have not been charged with that. In fact, nobody has said that to me yet. The first time I heard about it was when the newspaper reporters in the hall asked me that question. I did not do it. I did not do it. I did not shoot anyone," answered Lee.

At 1:35AM, Lee was taken to his second arraignment: State of Texas v. Lee Harvey Oswald for the Murder with Malice of John F. Kennedy. Once again he made a statement before the judge.

"Well, sir, I guess this is the trial. I want to contact my lawyer, Mr. Abt, in New York City. I would like to have this gentleman. He is with the American Civil Liberties Union," said Lee.

At 10:35Am, Lee was interrogated in Captain Fritz's office for the third time.

"Do you need an attorney?"

"I said I wanted to contact Attorney Abt in New York. He defended the Smith Act cases in 1949, 1950, but I don't know his address, except that it is in New York."

"Do you own a rifle?"

"I never owned a rifle. Look, the FBI has thoroughly interrogated me at various other times. They have used their hard and soft approach to me, and they used the buddy system. I am familiar with all types of questioning and have no intention of making any statements. In the past three weeks the FBI has talked to my wife. They were abusive and impolite. They frightened my wife, and I consider their activities obnoxious," replied Lee.

"Have you ever been arrested before?"

"I was arrested in New Orleans for disturbing the peace and paid a $10 fine for demonstrating for the Fair Play for Cuba Committee. I had a fight with some anti-Castro refugees and they were released while I was fined," said Lee.

"Do you want to take a polygraph?" asked Captain Fritz.

"I refuse to take a polygraph. It has always been my practice not to agree to take a polygraph."

"Did you shoot President Kennedy and Governor Connally?" asked Captain Fritz.

"I didn't shoot John Kennedy. I didn't even know Governor John Connally had been shot."

"Why does your wife live with Ruth Paine instead of with you?" asked the captain.

"Mrs. Paine was learning Russian. They needed help with the young baby, so it made a nice arrangement for both of them. I don't know Mrs. Paine very well, but Mr. Paine and his wife were separated a great deal of the time."

"You don't live with Ruth Paine, but we found some of your belongings in her garage. Why is that?" question Captain Fritz.

"The garage at the Paine's house has some sea bags that have a lot of my personal belongings. I left them there after coming back from New Orleans in September."

"Where did the name Alek Hidell come from?"

"The name Alek Hidell was picked up while working in New Orleans in the Fair Play for Cuba organization," he said.

"Do you speak Russian?"

"Yes, I speak Russian, correspond with people in Russia, and receive newspaper from Russia," he said.

"Do you own or have you ever own a rifle?"

"I don't own a rifle at all. I did have a small rifle some years in the past. You can't buy a rifle in Russia, you can only buy shotguns. I had a shotgun in Russia and hunted some while there," answered Lee.

"Did you bring the rifle you shot President Kennedy with from New Orleans?"

"I didn't bring the rifle from New Orleans."

"Are you a member of the Communist Party?"

"No, I am not a member of the Communist Party. I belong to the Civil Liberties Union," replied. Lee.

"Do you carry a package to work today?"

"I did bring a package to the Texas School Book Depository. I carried my lunch, a sandwich and fruit, which I made at Ruth's house."

"Why would you shoot President Kennedy? What did you have personally against the president?"

"I had nothing personal against John Kennedy," he replied.

At 1:10PM, Lee Oswald was visited by his mother, Marguerite, and his wife, Marina.

"Is there anything I can do for you?" asked Marguerite.

"No, there is nothing you can do. Everything is fine. I know my rights, and I will have an attorney. I already requested to get in touch with Attorney Abt, I think is his name. Don't worry about a thing."

"What happened to your eye? Have they been beating you?" Marina asked him in Russian.

"Oh, no, they have not been beating me. They are treating me fine."

"Where are you going to get the money to help you?" Marina asked.

"You're not to worry about that. Did you bring June and Rachel?"

"Are you able to talk about what's happening to you?" asked Marina.

"Of course we can speak about absolutely anything at all."

"Did you shoot those two men like they are saying you did?" questioned Marina.

"It's a mistake. I'm not guilty. There are people who will help me. There is a lawyer in New York on whom I am counting for help," Lee spoke in Russian as Marina started to cry.

"Don't cry. There is nothing to cry about. Try not to think about it," he said.

"What do I do if they start asking me questions about you?" asked Marina.

"Everything is going to be all right. If they ask you anything, you have a right not to answer. You have a right to refuse. Do you understand?"

"Yes, Lee, I do. What will happen to me and the girls now?" questioned Marina.

"You are not to worry. You have friends. They'll help you. If it comes to that, you can ask the Red Cross for help. You mustn't worry about me. Kiss Junie and Rachel for me. I love you. Be sure to buy shoes for June."

At 2:15PM, Lee was taken to another police lineup. This one was for witnesses William Scoggins and William Whaley. And once again Lee protested his treatment during the lineup.

"I refuse to answer question. I have my T-shirt on, the other men are dressed differently. Everybody's got a shirt and everything, and I've got a T-shirt on. This is unfair," said Lee.

About an hour after the police lineup, Lee's brother, Robert, visited with him. They were separated by glass and they spoke on telephones.

"I cannot or would not say anything, because the line is apparently tapped," Lee suggested to his brother.

"What happened to your eye?"

"I got these bruises from when they arrested me in the movie theater," said Lee.

"Have they been beating on you?"

"They haven't bothered me since. They are treating me all right," he said.

"That's good, I guess."

"What do you think of the baby? I wanted a boy, but you know how that goes," said Lee.

"Lee, they are saying you murdered a police officer and the President of the United States. What the hell is going on?"

"I don't know what is going on. I just don't know what they are talking about," Lee said.

"Lee, what do you mean you don't know what's going on? They are claiming they have evidence you killed those two men."

"Don't believe all the so-called evidence," Lee said as Robert looked intently in his eyes. "Brother, you won't find anything there."

"What are you going to do about Marina and the girls? Who is going to take care of them until you get out of this mess?"

"My friends will take care of Marina and the two girls," suggested Lee.

"Lee, I know you don't want to hear this, but I don't believe the Paine's are friends to you and Marina."

"Yes, they are," Lee snapped.

"Is there anything I can do for Marina and the girls?"

"Junie needs a pair of shoes," answered Lee.

Lee met with H. Louis Nichols, the President of the Dallas Bar Association, between 5:30PM and 5:35PM.

"Have the police explained to you what's going on?" asked Louis.

"Well, I really don't know what this is all about, that I have been keep incarcerated."

"You are going to need an attorney. Have you been appointed an attorney?" asked Louis.

"Do you know a lawyer in New York named John Abt? I believe he's in New York. I would like to have him represent me. That is the man I would like."

"I think I have heard of John Abt. I don't know him personally," said Louis.

"Do you know any lawyers who are members of the American Civil Liberties Union? I am a member of that organization, and I would like to have somebody who is a member of that organization represent me."

"I do not know any attorney who is a member of that organization. Do you want me help find a lawyer for you?"

"No, not now, you might come back next week, and if I don't get some of these other people to assist me, I might ask you to get somebody to represent me," answered Lee.

After his conversation with the President of the Dallas Bar Association was over he was led back to his jail cell. He was only in his cell for about thirty minutes when he was taken to Captain Fritz's office for some more questions.

"These pictures were found in the Paine's garage. Is that you in those pictures?" Captain Fritz handed two pictures of Lee posing with a rifle.

"In time I will be able to show you that this is not my picture, but I don't want to answer more questions."

"I will not discuss this photograph without the advice of an attorney."

"I think you need to discuss this picture now. This is very damaging to your claim. That rifle you're holding, is that the rifle you shot the president with? And the pistol holstered around your waist, is that the pistol you used to shoot Officer Tippit?"

"That picture is not mine," claimed Lee.

"Well, it looks like you."

"The face is mine. The picture has been made by superimposing my face. The other part of the picture is not me at all, and I have never seen this picture before. I understand photography real well, and that, in time, I will be able to show you that is not my picture and that it has been made by someone else," said Lee.

"Who do you think made this picture of you?"

"The small picture was reduced from the larger one, made by some persons unknown to me. Since I have been photographed at City Hall, with people taking my picture while being transferred from the office to the jail door, someone has been able to get a picture of my face, and with that, they have made this picture," answered Lee.

"Did you keep the rifle in Ruth Paine's garage?"

"I never kept a rifle at Mrs. Paine's garage," said Lee.

"Do you have the receipts for the guns you ordered through the mail?"

"I have no receipts for purchase of any gun, and I have never ordered any guns. I do not own a rifle, I have never possessed a rifle," he replied.

"Who wrote the name of A. J. Hidell on your Selective Service card?"

"I will not say who wrote that name on my Selective Service card," said Lee.

"Why are you carrying this card?"

"I will not tell you the purpose of carrying the card or the use I made of it," he said.

"Why do you have Russian names in your address book?"

"The address book in my possession has the names of Russian immigrants in Dallas, whom I have visited," said Lee.

At 9:30AM on Sunday November 24, 1963, Lee Oswald was interrogation once again by Captain Will Fritz in his office.

"What did you do after everyone started reacting to the shooting of President Kennedy on November 22nd?"

"After the assassination, a policeman or some man came rushing into the School Book Depository Building and said, 'Where is your telephone?' He showed me some kind of credential and identified himself, so he might not have been a police officer. 'Right there,' I answered, pointing to the phone. A co-worker asked if I could eat lunch with them. I told them I could, but I can't at that time. I told them to go and take the elevator, but to be sure to send the elevator back up to me. After all this commotion started, I just went downstairs and started to see what it was all about. A police officer and my superintendent of the place stepped up and told one of the officers that I am one of employees in the building," answered Lee.

"Why did you shoot Officer J. D. Tippit?"

"If you ask about the shooting of Tippit, I don't know what you're talking about," he replied.

"I don't think you have grasped why you are here."

"The only thing I am here for is because I popped a policeman in the nose in the theater on Jefferson Avenue, which I readily admit I did, because I was protecting myself."

"We know you went to Mexico City, so don't lie about that. I want to know, why did you go to Mexico City?"

"I went to the Mexican Embassy to try to get permission to go to Russia by way of Cuba. I went to the Mexican Consulate in Mexico City. I went to the Russian Embassy to go to Russia by way of Cuba. They told me to come back in thirty days," said Lee.

"How big was the package you carried to work on Friday?"

"I don't recall the shape, it may have been a small sack, or large sack; you don't always find one that just fits your sandwiches," Lee recalled.

"Tell me about the Fair Play for Cuba Committee."

"The Fair Play for Cuba Committee was a loosely organized thing and we had no officers. Probably you could call me the secretary of it because I did collect money. In New York City they have a well-organized, or a better organization," he replied.

"Did you intend to organize a Fair Play for Cuba Committee here in Dallas?"

"No, I didn't intend to organize a group here. I was too busy trying to get a job," said Lee.

"Did you place an order for the rifle under the name Hidell?"

"I never ordered a rifle under the name of Hidell, Oswald, or any other name," said Lee.

"If that's truly the case, then is it possible this Hidell used your post office box to receive the rifle?"

"I never permitted anyone else to order a rifle to be received in my post office box," he said.

"Did you order the rifle through your post office box by using a money order?"

"I have never order a rifle by mail order or bought any money order for the purpose of paying for a rifle. I don't know how many times I need to say this: I didn't own any rifle."

"Why do you have a post office box instead of a physical address as your mailing address?"

"We moved around so much that it was more practical to simply rent a post office box and have mail forwarded from one box to the next rather than going through the process of furnishing changes of addresses to everyone," said Lee.

"Why did you have a map with X's marked on it?"

"I presume you are talking about a map I had in my room with some X's on it. I have no automobile. I have to walk from where I am going most of the time. I had my applications with the Texas Employment Commission. They furnished me names and addresses of places that had openings like I might fill, and neighborhood people had furnished me information on jobs I might get. I was seeking a job, and I would put these markings on this map so I could plan my itinerary around with less walking. Each of the X's represented a place where I went and interviewed for a job. You can check each one of them out if you want to."

"Why was there an X on the intersection of Elm and Houston?"

"The X on the intersection of Elm and Houston is the location of the Texas School Book Depository Building. I did go there and interviewed for a job. In fact, I got the job there. This is all the map amounts to."

"What religion are you?"

"What religion am I? I have no faith, I suppose, you mean, in the Bible. I have read the Bible. It is fair reading, but not very interesting. As a matter of fact, I am a student of philosophy and I don't consider the Bible as even a reasonable or intelligent philosophy. I don't think of it, really," replied Lee.

"You said you didn't shoot a rifle on November 22nd. When was the last time you shot a rifle?"

"I haven't shot a rifle since the Marines. It might not be proper to answer further questions, because what I say might be construed in a different light than what I actually meant it to be. I did not kill the President or Officer Tippit. If you want me to cop out to hitting or pleading guilty to hitting a cop in the mouth when I was arrested, yeah, I plead guilty to that. But I do deny shooting both the President and Officer Tippit," stated Lee.

Dallas Police Department had been receiving many death threats directed towards Lee Oswald and homicide detective Jim Leavelle tried to convince police Captain Will Fritz to break his promise to reporters that they could photograph the suspected assassin as he was transferred to a nearby jail and instead sneak him out of the crowded building at an earlier time. Fritz refused, although extensive precautions (including the decision to use an armored truck as decoy) were taken to secure the area where Lee would be briefly exposed to reporters and cameras. Detective Leavelle was handcuffed to him and he was the last person to talk to Lee before he was shot.

"Lee, if anybody shoots at you, I hope they're as good as shot as you are," said Detective Leavelle.

"Ah. You're being melodramatic. Nobody's going to shoot me."

"Well, if they do start, you know what to do, don't you?" asked the detective.

"Well, Captain Fritz told me to follow you and I'll do whatever you do."

At 11:21 am, Oswald was shot and fatally wounded before live TV cameras in the basement of Dallas Police Department by Jack Ruby. Millions watched the shooting of Lee Harvey Oswald; the first time a homicide was captured and shown publicly on live television. Jack Ruby entered the basement from the inside police headquarters. The use of a route through the jail building suggested to some Ruby received help from the authorities inside the building, but many journalists entered the building without having their credentials checked. Jack can be seen on film inside the building on the previous Friday night, apparently posing as a reporter.

Oswald's grave is in Rose Hill Memorial Burial Park in Fort Worth. The November 25th burial and funeral were paid for by Robert Oswald. There was no religious service and reporters acted as pallbearers. Originally his headstone read *Lee Harvey Oswald*, but this marker was stolen and replaced with one which only reads *Oswald*.

CHAPTER 51

———————□———————

"To state the facts frankly is not to despair the future nor
indict the past. The prudent heir takes careful inventory
of his legacies and gives a faithful accounting to those
whom he owes an obligation of trust."

John F. Kennedy

THE NEXT FEW CHAPTERS CONTAINS
A FEW INTERESTING INFORMATION ABOUT THE
ASSASSINATION OF PRESIDENT JOHN F. KENNEDY. TO ME
THEY POINT TO THE PROOF OF THE INVOLVEMENT AND
COVER UP BY THE UNITED STATES GOVERNMENT

The alarming implications of the CIA's Mexico City case against Lee
Harvey Oswald had to be faced on the morning after President Kennedy's
assassination by the new President of the United States: Lyndon Baines
Johnson. At 9:20 AM on November 23rd, President Johnson was briefed
by CIA Director John McCone about *"information on foreign connections
to the alleged assassin, Lee Harvey Oswald, which suggested to LBJ that
Kennedy may have been murdered by an international conspiracy."* At 10:01
AM President Johnson received a phone briefing on Oswald from FBI
Director J. Edgar Hoover. It included the following exchange:

"Have you established any more about the visit to the Soviet embassy
in Mexico in September?" asked Lyndon.

"No, that's one angle that's very confusing, for this reason—we have up
here the tape and photographs of the man who was at the Soviet embassy,
using Oswald's name. That picture and tape do not correspond to this

man's voice, nor to his appearance. In other words, it appears that there is a second person who was at the Soviet embassy down there. We do have a copy of a letter which was written by Oswald to the Soviet embassy here in Washington (A November 9, 1963, letter that Oswald began by referring to 'my meeting with comrade Kostin in the Embassy of the Soviet Union, Mexico City, Mexico,' which was interpreted to mean Kostikov) . . . Now if we can identify this man who was at the Soviet Embassy in Mexico City."

Having just been brief on Oswald by CIA Director McCone, President Johnson was anxious to get to the bottom of "*the visit to the Soviet embassy in Mexico in September.*" Hoover's briefing added to Johnson' anxiety. President Johnson's CIA and FBI briefings left him with two unpalatable interpretations of Mexico City. According to the CIA, Oswald was part of a Cuban-Soviet assassination plot which was revealed by the audio-visual materials garnered by its surveillance techniques. According to Hoover, Oswald had been impersonated in Mexico City, as shown by a more critical examination of the same CIA materials. Hoover left it to Johnson to draw his own conclusions as to who was responsible for that impersonation.

The Central Intelligence Agency devised and executed a setup which played out a scenario to President Kennedy's death in Dallas which pressured other government authorities to choose among three major options: a war of vengeance against Cuba and the Soviet Union based on the CIA's Mexico City documentation of a Communist assassination plot; a domestic political war based on the same documents seen truly, but a war the CIA would fight with every covert weapon at its command; or a complete cover-up of any conspiracy evidence and silent coup d'état that would reverse President Kennedy's efforts to end the Cold War. Lyndon Johnson, for his part, took little time to choose the only option he felt would leave him with a country to govern. He chose to cover up everything and surrender to Cold War prerogatives.

Once the CIA realized its Mexico City scenario was being questioned and could be implicate not the Communist but the CIA itself in the assassination, the Mexico City Station back-pedaled to cover up the false evidence. It began to say the audiotapes of the "Oswald" phone calls to the Soviet Embassy had been routinely destroyed, and therefore no voice comparisons, and reporting their provocative conclusions to President Johnson.

On November 23ʳᵈ, Mexico City CIA employee Ann Goodpasture, an assistant to David Phillips, sent a cable to CIA headquarters in which she reported the Saturday September 28ᵗʰ, call, then stated: "*Station unable to compare voice as first tape erased prior receipt of second call.*"

On the next day, Mexico City cabled headquarters claiming it was now unable to locate any tapes at all for comparisons with Oswald's voice: "*Regret complete recheck shows tapes for this period already erased.*" Although FBI Director J. Edgar Hoover was angry not having been let in initially by the CIA on "*the false story re Oswald's trip to Mexico,*" from this point on the FBI cooperated in revising its story, too, to cover the CIA's tracks. Unknown to ordinary citizens watching President Kennedy's funeral on their television sets, the agencies of a national security state had quickly formed a united front behind the official mourning scenes to cover up every aspect of JFK's assassination.

The consequence of the early 1960s, when John Kennedy became president, was that the CIA had placed a secret team of its own employees throughout the entire United States government. It was accountable to no one except the CIA, headed by Allen Dulles. After Dulles was fired by President Kennedy, the CIA's Deputy Director of Plans Richard Helms became the invisible government's immediate commander. No one except a tight inner circle of the CIA even knew the existence of the top-secret intelligence network, much less the identity of its deep-cover bureaucrats. These CIA "focal points," as Dulles called them, constituted a powerful, unseen government within the government. Its Dulles-appointed members would act quickly, with total obedience, when called on by the CIA to assist its covert operations.

In early September 1963, the Central Intelligence Agency set in motion yet another assassination plot against Castro. This plot was different from the other CIA assassination plots in the past. This plot was meant to serve as a way to blame Robert Kennedy for the killing of his own brother. The CIA's Castro/RFK scheme utilized its key undercover agent in Cuba, Rolando Cubela, who was known by the code name AM/LASH. Rolando Cubela was no ordinary agent but a Cuban political figure whom Fidel Castro trusted. Cubela had fought beside Castro in the Cuban Revolution. He had held various posts in the revolutionary government but became disillusioned by Castro's alliance with the Soviet

Union. In 1961 he was recruited by the CIA, which nurtured carefully its secret relationship with a Castro associate who also had experience as an assassin. In 1959 Cubela had shot to death Batista's head of military intelligence.

On October 29, 1963, Rolando Cubela met a Central Intelligence Agency safe house in Paris with Desmond Fitzgerald, chief of the CIA's Special Affairs staff. In one of the CIA's most blatant attempts to destroy both Kennedy brothers, Fitzgerald, using a false name, posed as a United States senator representing Attorney General Robert Kennedy. The Deputy Director of Plans, Richard Helms, had *"agreed that Fitzgerald should hold himself as a personal representative of Attorney General Robert Kennedy."* Helms had also decided *"it was not necessary to seek approval from Robert Kennedy for Fitzgerald to speak in his name."* The CIA's impersonation worked, convincing Cubela that he had been authorized by the Attorney General's representative to assassinate Fidel Castro. Fitzgerald then put in a special order for Cubela of a poison pen device from the CIA's Operations Division of the Office of Medical Services: *"a ball-point rigged with a hypodermic needle . . . designed to be so fine that the victim would not notice its insertion."*

When Lee Harvey Oswald was arrested in Dallas and was fingered by the United States media as the president's assassin, top-level Soviet officials realized the Oswald letter which had arrived at their Embassy on November 18th had been probably designed to set them up. On Tuesday, November 26, 1963, the day after President Kennedy's funeral, Soviet ambassador Anatoly Dobrynin sent a "Top Secret/Highest Priority" telegram from Washington to Moscow. Its subject was the suspicious Oswald letter received by the Soviet Embassy four days before the assassination. Dobrynin cabled Moscow:

> *"Please note Oswald's letter of November 9, the text of which was transmitted to Moscow over the line of nearby neighbors [for security reasons]. This letter was clearly a provocation: it gives the impression we had close ties with Oswald and were using him for some purposes of our own. It was totally unlike any other letters the embassy had previously received from Oswald. Nor had he ever visited our embassy himself. The suspicion that the letter is a forgery*

is heightened by the fact that it was typed, whereas the other letters the embassy had received from Oswald before were handwritten. One gets the definite impression that the letter was concocted by those who, judging from everything, are involved in the President's assassination. It is possible that Oswald himself wrote the letter as it was dictated to him, in return for some promises, and then, as we know, he was simply bumped off after his usefulness had ended. The competent U.S. authorities are undoubtedly aware of this letter, since the embassy's correspondence is under constant surveillance. However, they are not making use of it for the time being. Nor are they asking the embassy for any information about Oswald himself; perhaps they are waiting for another moment."

Soviet Ambassador Dobrynin recommended in his November 26th telegram to Moscow the Soviet government pass on to United States authorities Oswald's letter, *"because if we don't pass it on, the organizers of this entire provocation could use this fact to try casting suspicion on us."*

Anastas I. Mikoyan, first deputy chairman of the Soviet council of ministers, wired back his agreement with Dobrynin:

"You may send [Secretary of State Dean] Rusk photocopies of the correspondence between the embassy and Oswald, including his letter of November 9, but without waiting for a request by the U.S. authorities. When sending the photocopies, say that the letter of November 9 was not received by the embassy until November 18; obviously it had been held up somewhere. The embassy had suspicions about this letter the moment it arrived; either it was a forgery or was sent as a deliberate provocation. The embassy left Oswald's letter unanswered."

By turning over the Oswald letter to the United States, the Soviets overturned its potential propaganda damage. The Soviet leaders served notice they would not be intimated. The letter was an obvious counterfeit which pointed a finger in the opposite direction from the letter's recipients. Langley had more to fear from its public disclosure than did Moscow.

The Oswald letter was intercepted, opened and copied by the Federal Bureau Investigations before its eventual delivery to the embassy. FBI

Director J. Edgar Hoover described the secret process to the new president Lyndon Johnson, in a phone call at 10:01 AM on Saturday November 23, 1963. Hoover presented President Johnson with evidence from Mexico City of either a Soviet-Cuban plot with Oswald to kill Kennedy or (more likely) the CIA's impersonation of Oswald in its own plot. In the midst of his trying to deal with those unpalatable alternatives, President Johnson also heard Hoover say:

> *"We do have a copy of a letter which was written by Oswald here in Washington inquiring as well as complaining about the harassment of his wife and questioning of his wife by the FBI. Now, of course, that letter information, we process all mail that goes to the Soviet embassy—it's a very secret operation. No mail is delivered to the Embassy without being examined and opened by us, so that we know what they receive."*

CHAPTER 52

—◻—

"Tolerance implies no lack of commitment to one's own beliefs. Rather it condemns the oppression or persecution of others."

John F. Kennedy

On November 25, 1963, Deputy Attorney General Nicholas deB Katzenbach sent a memorandum to Bill Moyers, President Johnson's press secretary, urging a premature identification of Oswald as the lone assassin lest speculation of either a Communist or a right-wing conspiracy get out of hand:

1. *The public must be satisfied that Oswald was the assassin; that he did not have confederates who are still at large; and that the evidence was such that he would have been convicted at trial.*

2. *Speculation about Oswald's motivation ought to be cut off, and we should have some basis for rebutting thought that this was a Communist conspiracy or (as the Iron Curtain press is saying) a right-wing conspiracy to blame it on the Communists. Unfortunately the facts on Oswald seem about to pat—too obvious. (Marxists, Cuba, Russian wife, etc.)"*

To rebut any thought of either kind of conspiracy, Katzenbach's memorandum recommended *"the appointment of a President Commission of unimpeachable personnel to review and examine the evidence and announce its conclusion."*

Before President Johnson jettisoned the CIA's Mexico City case against Cuba and the Soviet Union, he used it (without Hoover's reference to an imposter) as a lever to help put together just such a presidential commission of respected Cold War leaders. He ensured the commission's public acceptance by convincing Supreme Court Chief Justice Earl Warren to chair it. Warren at first refused to become President Johnson's pawn. However, in a taped phone conversation on Friday, November 29th, President Johnson described to Senator Richard Russell how he had co-opted Warren's conscience, by an argument that accepted at face value the CIA's Mexico City evidence. Johnson then manipulated Senator Russell onto the commission, using the same Mexico City argument with which he had coerced Warren: *"Warren told me he wouldn't do it under any circumstances. Didn't think a Supreme Court Justice ought to go . . . He came down here and told me no—twice. And I just pulled out what Hoover told me about a little incident in Mexico City and I said, 'Now I don't want Mr. Khrushchev to be told tomorrow—and be testifying before a camera that he killed this fellow and that Castro killed him and all I want you to do is look at the facts and bring in any other facts."*

After Hoover's disturbing phone call, President Johnson met at 12:30PM with CIA Director John McCone specifically to be filled in further on *"the information received from Mexico City."* Mexico City became Johnson's jumping off point for the Warren Commission.

The Warren Commission would ensure a lone-assassin cover-up of the conspiracy evidence the new president was facing. That would free President Johnson from his dilemma arising from the Mexico City evidence of having to confront either the Soviet Union as the assassination's biggest scapegoat or the CIA as its actual perpetrator. On one hand, President Johnson refused to let the Soviets take the blame for President Kennedy's murder. But on the other hand, he decided not to confront the CIA over what it had done in Mexico City. The presidency was returned to the control of Cold War interests, priorities and profits. Not only was President Kennedy dead, so was his breakthrough with Soviet Premier Khrushchev. In allowing the assassination to go uninvestigated Johnson consented to the total cover-up of both President Kennedy's death and his turn toward peace with the Communists. Once President Johnson and his administration had decided to reject the Mexico City evidence as too explosive, the Warren Commission was given a contradictory mandate.

When President Johnson told Senator Richard Russell he wanted the Special Commission to do was to "*look at the facts and bring in any other facts you want in here and determine who killed the president.*" However, as he emphasized to Russell, President Johnson wanted even more to take the questions of President Kennedy's assassination "*out of the Mexico City arena*," where the evidence apparently implicated the Soviet Union in the foreground the Central Intelligence Agency in the background.

On November 29, 1963, President Lyndon Johnson established **The President's Commission on the Assassination of President Kennedy** to investigate the assassination of President John F. Kennedy. The seven man commission was headed by Chief Justice Earl Warren and included Gerald Ford, Allen W. Dulles, John J. McCloy, Richard B. Russell, John S. Cooper, and Thomas H. Boggs. President Johnson also commissioned a report on the assassination from J. Edgar Hoover. Two weeks later the FBI produced a 500 page report claiming that Lee Harvey Oswald was the sole assassin and that there was no evidence of a conspiracy. The report was then passed to the Warren Commission. Rather than conduct its own independent investigation, the commission relied almost entirely on the FBI report.

At the first meeting of the Warren Commission, Allen Dulles handed out copies of a book to help define the ideological parameters he proposed for the Commission's forthcoming work. He stated that American assassinations were different than European assassinations. European assassinations were the work of conspiracies, but American assassins acted alone. John McCloy claimed that it was important to show the world that the American government couldn't be changed by conspiracy. The Warren Commission was published in 1964. It reached the following conclusions:

1). The shots which killed President Kennedy and wounded Governor Connally were fired from the 6th floor window at the southeast corner of the Texas School Book Depository.
2). The weight of the evidence indicates that there were three shots fired.
3). Although it is not necessary to any essential findings of the Commission to determine just which shot hit Governor Connally, there is very persuasive evidence from the experts which

indicate that the same bullet which pierced the President's throat also caused Governor Connally's wounds. However, Governor Connally's testimony and certain other factors have given rise to some difference of opinion as to this probability but there is no question in the mind of any member of the Commission that all the shots which caused the President's and Governor Connally's wounds were fired from the 6th floor window of the Texas School Book Depository.

4). The shots which killed President Kennedy and wounded Governor Connally were fired by Lee Harvey Oswald.

5). Oswald killed Dallas Police Patrolman J.D. Tippit approximately 45 minutes after the assassination.

6). Within 80 minutes of the assassination and 35 minutes of the Tippit killing Oswald resisted arrest at the theater by attempting to shoot another Dallas police officer.

7). The Commission has found no evidence that either Lee Harvey Oswald or Jack Ruby was part of any conspiracy, domestic or foreign, to assassinate President Kennedy.

8). In its entire investigation the Commission has found no evidence of conspiracy, subversion, or disloyalty to the US Government by any Federal, State, or local official.

9). On the basis of the evidence before the Commission it concludes that, Oswald acted alone.

In November 1964, two months after the publication of its 888 page report, the Commission published 26 volumes of supporting documents, including the testimony or depositions of 552 witnesses and more than 3,100 exhibits. All of the Commission's records were then transferred on November 23rd to the National Archives. The unpublished portion of those records was initially sealed for 75 years (to 2039) under a general National Archives policy that applied to all federal investigations by the executive branch of the government, a period *'intended to serve as protection for innocent persons who could otherwise be damaged because of their relationship with participants in the case.'* The 75-year rule no longer exists, supplanted by the Freedom of Information Act of 1966 and the JFK Records Act of 1992. By 1992, 98% of the Warren Commission records had been released to the public. Six years later, at the conclusion of the Assassinations Records Review Board's work, all Warren Commission records, except those records that contained tax return information, were available to the public with redactions. The remaining Kennedy assassination related documents are scheduled to be released to the public by 2017, 25 years after the passage of the JFK Records Act.

According the *Warren Report*, Lee Harvey Oswald told the United States Embassy in Moscow on October 31, 1959, his new allegiance was the Soviet Union. He said he had promised Soviet official he "*would make known to them all information concerning the Marine Corps and his specialty therein, radar operation, as he possessed.*" However, the *Warren Report* did not mention while Lee was in the Marine Corps he had been a radar operator specifically for the CIA's top secret U-2 spy plane. By not admitting Oswald's U-2 or CIA connections, the Warren Commission avoided the implications of his offering to give "*something of special interest*" to the Soviets.

The Warren Commission's impossible task, "*for the sake of national security*" was to make a convincing, heavily documented case for a lone assassin conclusion. To do so, the commission would have to cover up especially the critical Mexico City evidence. The CIA planted "Oswald letter" dated November 9th, which the Soviet Embassy received on November 18th, and recognized as a fraud, had backfired. The Soviet ambassador's formal diplomatic return of the letter to the United States government made the document a part of the official record. If the Soviet leaders chose to do so, they could make that diplomatic process, and the letter public. The United States government was in a bind. The phony letter had to be covered up or explained.

The Warren Commission's star witness against Lee Harvey Oswald, besides his widow Marina, was Ruth Paine. It was Ruth and Michael Paine who became the Oswald's handlers after George de Morenschildt left Dallas. It was Ruth Paine who arranged for his job at the Texas School Depository Building in October 1963. And it was Ruth Paine whose Warren Commission testimony also put different spin on the Oswald letter which was threatening to uncover the CIA planned plot in the president's murder. In March 1964, Ruth Paine testified on Saturday November 9, 1963, she had seen Oswald type the letter in her home on her typewriter. Besides giving an eyewitness account of Oswald actually writing the letter, her testimony placed on record a different version of the letter from the one the Soviets had received. The new, U.S.-government-preferred version of the letter came, in Ruth's testimony, in the form of a rough draft that she said Oswald left accidentally on her desk. Ruth testified she secretly read Oswald's folded, handwritten draft of the letter left on her desk, while he was out of the room on the morning after he typed the final version. She copied the rough draft by hand while he was taking a shower. Ruth said she took his draft of the letter and hid it in her desk, so she could give it to the FBI the next time they came to see her.

The draft of Oswald's letter which Ruth claimed she hid from him was put on record by the Warren Commission as the more definitive version of the letter than was received by the Soviet Embassy four days before President Kennedy was assassinated. The words that the writer crossed out in the draft have been used to reinterpret the typed letter, in terms of Oswald's intention. Yet the draft stands in significant contrast to the provocative letter which was sent to the Soviets. Moreover, the draft shows internal evidence of having been written by someone other than Oswald, possibly even months after the typed version of the letter. The *Warren Report* tried to explain away the all too revealing Oswald letter the Soviet Embassy received on November 18th:

> "*Some light on [the letter's] possible meaning can be shed by comparing it with the early draft. When the differences between the draft and the final document are studied, and especially crossed-out words are taken into account, it becomes apparent that Oswald was intentionally beclouding the true state of affairs in order to make his trip to Mexico as mysterious and important as possible. . . . In the opinion of the Commission, based upon the knowledge of Oswald, the letter constitutes no more than a clumsy effort to ingratiate himself with the Soviet Embassy.*"

The members of the Warren Commission decided to give the original document, supposedly written by Oswald, back to Ruth, at her request.

CHAPTER 53

—— ❑ ——

"Unconditional war can no longer lead to unconditional
victory. It can no longer serve to settle disputes . . . can
no longer be of concern to great powers alone."

John F. Kennedy

On September 4, 1965, Rose Cheramie's body was found at 3:00 AM on
Highway 155, 1.7 miles east of Big Sandy, Texas. She had reportedly been
run over by a car. Jerry Don Moore, the driver of the car in question, said
he'd been driving from Big Sandy to his home in Tyler. He suddenly saw
three or four suitcases lined up in the center of the road. Moore swerved to
his right so he would miss hitting the suitcases. In front of the car he was
driving was the prone body of a woman lying at a 90-degree angle to the
highway with her head toward the road. He slammed on his brakes as hard
as he could. The investigating officer, J. A. Andrews, stated that Moore
said, "*although he had attempted to avoid running over her, he ran over the
top part of her skull, causing fatal injuries.*" Moore, on the contrary, swore
he never hit Cheramie. He came close to her, stopped, and then drove
her to the nearest doctor in Big Sandy. An ambulance took her from the
doctor's to Gladewater Hospital, where she was declared dead on arrival.
Although Officer Andrews uncertainty as to what happened to Cheramie,
"*due to the fact that the relatives of the victim did not pursue the investigation,
he closed it as a accidental death.*" But was it really an accident?

In 1967 the Louisiana State Police assigned Lieutenant Francis
Fruge to work with New Orleans District Attorney Jim Garrison in his
investigation of President Kennedy's assassination. Fruge interviewed the
owner of the Silver Slipper Lounge. Mac Manuel was the owner of lounge,

which was a known house of prostitution. Mac remembered well the night at the Silver Slipper Lounge when the two men and Rose Cheramie got into a fight. He said they had several drinks when they arrived. She *"appeared to be intoxicated when she got there. She started raising a ruckus. One of the men kind of slapped her around and threw her outside."* Mac told the police lieutenant he recognized the two men with Cheramie as soon as they walked into the Silver Slipper Lounge. He should have because he had worked with them. They were, he said, *"pimps who had been to my place before, hauling prostitutes from Florida and hauling them back."* Lieutenant Fruge had brought with him a stack of photographs from the New Orleans District Attorney's office. From the photographs, Mac picked out his two business associates in prostitution. They were more than that. The two men he identified as having accompanied Cheramie to the Silver Slipper Lounge were Sergio Arcacha Smith and Emilio Santana, two anti-Castro Cubans exiles with Central Intelligence Agency credentials.

Emilio Santana admitted in an interview with Jim Garrison's that the CIA hired him on August 27, 1962, the evening of the day he arrived in Miami as an exile from his native Cuba. Santana was immediately employed by the Agency as a crewmember on a boat sailing back to Cuba, carrying weapons and electronic equipment for CIA-sponsored guerilla actions. He was a CIA employee, he said, during 1962 and 1963. As a Cuban fisherman, he had intimate knowledge of the Cuban coastline, which made him a valuable asset in piloting boats that carried CIA operatives in and out of Cuba. He acknowledges piloting a boat with a CIA team that was off the coast of Cuba for twenty days during the Cuban Missile Crisis. Santana's boat would have been carrying one of the unauthorized commando teams which CIA Special Operations organizer William Harvey dispatched to Cuba at the height of the Cuban Missile Crisis, igniting the fury of Robert Kennedy for the CIA's covert provocation of nuclear war. President Kennedy's refusal then, as at Bay of Pigs, to attack Cuba, and his crisis-resolving pledge to Khrushchev never to do so, provoked a counter-anger in the CIA extending down into the exile community which included Emilio Santana. The man Mac Manuel identified as Rose Cheramie's other companion, Sergio Arcacha Smith, had a more commanding role in the CIA's anti-Castro network. Sergio had been a prominent Cuban diplomat for the Batista regime before it was overthrown by Cuban revolution led by Fidel Castro. He was Cuba's diplomatic consul in Madrid, Rome, Mexico City and Bombay. After he left the diplomatic services, Sergio had prospered enough as a business executive in Latin America to have his own factory in Caracas, Venezuela. He became active there in an anti-Castro group, which may have initiated his involvement with the CIA. On June 29, 1960, he was arrested by the government of Venezuela and charged with plotting to assassinate Venezuelan President Ernesto Betancourt. He was released on July 14, 1960. The American Embassy came to his immediate assistance, issuing nonimmigrant visitor visas to him and his family so they could depart from Venezuela.

After arriving in the United States, Sergio became the New Orleans delegate of the FRD (Frente Revolucionario Democratico), which a CIA document on Sergio states "*was organized and supported by the Agency.*" The FRD "*was used*", the CIA noted, "*as a front for recruitment of Brigade 2506 for the* [Bay of Pigs] *invasion.*" Sergio admitted in a 1967 polygraph test that he and David Ferrie, while working for the CIA, "*helped trained the Bay of Pigs invasion forces with M-1 rifles.*" When the FRD was phased out, Sergio established a New Orleans chapter of the Cuban Revolutionary Council, the Cuban "*government in exile*" organized by the CIA. Guy Banister, the detective/intelligence agent who guided Lee Harvey Oswald in the summer of 1963 in New Orleans, also worked closely with Sergio in 1961-62. Banister helped set up an organization to raise funds for Sergio's branch of the Cuban Revolutionary Council. Banister and Sergio both had their offices in the Balter Building in New Orleans. They moved together in 1962 to the Newman Building at 544 Camp Street, the same address which Oswald used for one of his Fair Play for Cuba leaflets when he was arrested in New Orleans on August 9, 1963, for disturbing the peace. David Lewis, a former employee of Guy Banister, claimed to have seen Sergio and Lee Harvey Oswald. Lewis stated to the New Orleans District Attorney's office he witnessed a meeting in the late summer of 1963 at Mancuso's Restaurant in New Orleans between Sergio, Oswald, and a man named Carlos whose last name Lewis didn't know. It's possible it was a mutual friend of Sergio's and Oswald's' Carlos Quiroga. Lewis claimed Sergio, Oswald and Carlos "*were involved in some business which dealt with Cuban,*" and that Sergio "*appeared to be the boss.*"

Former Marine Corps Lieutenant James Donovan was Lee's radar officer in the Santa Ana radar unit. He claimed Lee "*had the access to the location of all bases in the west coast area, all radio frequencies for all squadrons,*" *all tactical signs, and the relative strength of all squadrons, number and type of aircraft in a squadron, who was the commanding officer, the authentication code of entering and exiting the ADIZ (Air Defense Identification Zone). He knew the range of our radar. He knew the range of our radio. And he knew the range of the surrounding units' radio and radar."*

Former CIA Agent Victor Marchetti wrote in his book, *The CIA and the Cult of Intelligence,* "*at the time, in 1959, the United State was having real difficulty in acquiring information out of the Soviet Union; the technical systems had, of course, not developed to the point that they are at today, and we were resorting to all sorts of activities. One of these activities was an ONI (Office Naval Intelligence) program which involved three dozen, forty, young men who were made to appear disenchanted, poor American youths who had become turned off and wanted to see what communism was all about. Some of these people lasted only a few weeks. They were sent into the Soviet Union, or into eastern Europe, with the specific intention the Soviets would pick them up and 'double' them if they suspected them being U.S. agents, or recruit them as KGB agents. They were trained at various naval installations both here and abroad, but the operation was being run out of Nag's Head, North Carolina.*"

There is no hard proof Lee gave the Soviets real codes to the U-2 spy plane. But the fact Francis Gary Powers' U-2 spy plane went down not long after his defection to Russia can't be just an accident. Francis Gary Powers was an American pilot whose CIA U-2 spy plane was shot down while flying a reconnaissance mission over Soviet Union airspace. At the time Powers' U-2 spy plane was shot down, President Eisenhower and Soviet Premier Khrushchev was in the middle of a peace talk. When the spy plane was shot, the Soviet Premier blamed the American president for the spy plane flights. As a result the peace talk was cancelled. This was the reason for the CIA placing Lee in Russia. Francis was interrogated extensively by the KGB for months before he made a confession and a public apology for his part in espionage. The incident set back peace talks between Premier Khrushchev and President Eisenhower. I think this was the whole point of Lee's defection to the Soviet Union. I believe he was sent over there with the codes for the U-2 spy plane. He was instructed to turn over the classified information in exchange for letting him stay. The peace talk could not be successful and the shooting down of Francis' plane made sure that. On August 17, 1960, Francis was convicted of espionage against the Soviet Union and was sentenced to a total of 10 years, three years in imprisonment followed by seven years hard labor. He was held in "Vladimir Central Prison", some 100 miles east of Moscow. On February 10, 1962, Francis was exchanged along with American student Frederic Pryor in a well-publicized spy swap for Soviet KGB Colonel Vilyam Fisher (aka Rudolf Abel), a Soviet colonel. Shortly after the shooting down of the U-2 spy plane, the CIA shut down the spy plane operation.

By the early 1970's George de Mohrenschildt's behavior leaned towards the erratic. On September 5, 1976, George sent a message to George H. W. Bush, who was the CIA director at the time. I know what you are thinking. Do I mean the same George H.W. Bush who was once the Vice-President to Ronald Reagan and was himself the President of the United States? Yes, I am talking about the one and the same.

George wrote in his letter

> *"Maybe you will be able to bring a solution to the hopeless situation I find myself in. My wife and I find ourselves surrounded by some vigilantes; our phone bugged; and we are being followed everywhere. Either FBI is involved in this or they do not want to accept my complaints. We are driven to insanity by the situation. I have been behaving like a damn fool ever since my daughter, Nadya died from (cystic fibrosis) over three years ago. I tried to write, stupidly and unsuccessfully, about Lee H. Oswald and must have angered a lot of people I do not know. But to punish an elderly man like myself and my highly nervous and sick wife is really too much. Could you do something to remove this net around us? This will be my last request for help and I will not annoy you anymore."*

This was CIA Director George H.W. Bush's reply:

> *"Let me say first that I know it must have been difficult for you to seek my help in the situation you outlined in your letter. I believe I can appreciate your state of mind in view of your daughter's tragic death a few years ago, and the current poor state of your wife's health. I was extremely sorry to hear of these circumstances.*

In your situation I can well imagine how the attentions you described in your letter affect both you and your wife. However, my staff has been unable to find any indication of interest in your activities on the part of Federal authorities in recent years. The flurry of interest that attended your testimony before the Warren Commission has long subsided. I can only speculate that you may have become 'newsworthy' again in the view of the renewed interest in the Kennedy assassination, and thus may be attracting the attention of people in the media. I hope this letter had been of some comfort to you, George, although I realize I am unable to answer your question completely. George Bush, Director of the Central Intelligence Agency."

George had worked with the CIA on a number of occasions, unofficially of course, throughout the years. He knew how the Agency worked. He had the "feeling" he was being watched and followed. He wasn't sure who was tailing him; he just knew it was US Government. He asked for help from the CIA, but the Director turned him away. His life went downhill from there. Two months after he received his reply from Bush, George was committed to a mental institution. He was taken to Parkland Hospital and underwent electroshock therapy. In February 1977, Willem Oltmans met George at the library of Bishop College in Dallas, where he taught French. George confessed to Willem to being involved in the assassination of President Kennedy. He begged Willem to get him out of the country because he felt the government was after him. On February 13, 1977, Oltmans took him to his home in Amsterdam where they worked on his memoirs. Over the next few weeks George claimed he knew Jack Ruby. Willem arranged for George to meet a Dutch publisher and the head of Dutch national television. The two men then travelled to Brussels. When they arrived, Oltmans mentioned an old friend of his, a Soviet diplomat, would be joining them a bit later for lunch. George said he wanted to take a short walk before lunch. Instead, George fled to a friend's house and after a few days he flew back to the United States.

The House Select Committee on Assassinations were informed of George's return to the United States and sent its investigator, Gaeton Fonzi, to find him. Fonzi discovered he was living with his daughter in Palm Beach. On March 27, 1977, George arrived at the Breakers Hotel in Palm Beach and spent the day being interviewed by Edward Jay Epstein. They spent the day talking about his life and career until the late 1950s. George said he had "*on occasion done favors*" since the early 1950s for government officials connected with the CIA. It was a mutually beneficial relationship. In return for his "favors" the CIA contacts helped him arrange profitable business connections overseas. Edward and George broke for lunch and decided to meet again at 3 p.m. George returned to his room where he found a card from Gaeton Fonzi. His body was found later that afternoon. He had apparently committed suicide by shooting himself in the mouth.

Ruth Paine had been studying Russian since 1957 so she was the perfect "sitter" for the Oswalds. In 1963 she signed up to teach a summer class in Russian at St. Mark's School in Dallas but only one student signed up for the class. She met the Oswalds through her interest in Russian. A friend from a singing group, Everett Glover, invited her to a party on February 22, 1963 because he thought she would be interested in meeting people who spoke Russian. She noticed Lee talking to a group of people around him. He talked about the censoring of his mail. He realized after he got home his brother had sent some letters which never reached him. He said all mail from foreign countries addressed anywhere in the USSR must first go to a Moscow office for reading. When the Oswalds came under the protective wings of the Paines, Michael was working as research engineer with a defense contractor, Bell Helicopter, in Fort Worth, Texas. Michael Paine was no ordinary Bell Helicopter engineer. His stepfather, Arthur Young, with whom he worked previously, was the inventor of the Bell Helicopter. By heritage Michael was well connected in the military-industrial complex. Michael Paine's mother, Ruth Forbes Paine Young, was connected to Allen Dulles. Descended from the blueblood Forbes family of Boston, Ruth was a lifelong friend of Mary Bancroft, who worked side by side with Allen Dulles as World War II spy in Switzerland and became his mistress.

Ruth said Lee refused to speak English to Marina. She claimed Lee said he did so to be certain to keep up his Russian. She felt he did this to keep her dependent on him. I think Ruth was "instructed" to get close to Marina and to convince her to live with her so Lee could go on with his mission without restraint. Even though Ruth was introduced to the Oswalds on February 22nd, she didn't attempt to contact Marina until March 8th, when she sent her a note. She visited Marina on March 20th. It is not known what they discussed during this visit. On April 2nd Ruth invited the Oswalds to dinner. On April 7th, Ruth wrote a note, asking Marina to come and live with her. She never sent this note, but she kept it. She visited Marina again on April 11th. During this visit she was trying to convince Marina to live with her. The Oswalds and Ruth had a picnic on April 20th. By the end of the month, Marina was staying with Ruth temporarily, while, Lee went to New Orleans to seek employment and try to find an apartment.

At first I didn't understand why a big deal was made about Marina and Lee living apart from each other. But the more I researched it, the more I realized there was a reason for Marina staying with Ruth. I think it ensured the continued separation of Marina and Lee, allowing Lee to live unencumbered, and with no witnesses to his activities or associates during the principal time leading up to the assassination. They, also, provided a storage space for evidence which would be used against Lee. Almost everything which would convict him in the public mind, including the alleged murder weapon, came out of the Paine's garage. Also found in the garage, among other things, was the Walker photograph, the backyard photograph, the Klein's Sporting Goods tear-out order for the rifle and some radical magazines.

As Lee Harvey Oswald was being set up as an individual scapegoat, so too, was the Soviet Union, together with its less powerful ally, Cuba, being portrayed as the evil empire behind President Kennedy's murder. The Soviet Union, whose leader had become President Kennedy's secret partner in peacemaking, was intended to be the biggest scapegoat of all. On November 18, 1963, the Soviet Embassy in Washington received a crudely typed, poorly spelled letter dated nine days earlier and signed by "Lee H. Oswald" of Dallas. The timing of the letter's arrival was no accident. Its contents made it Cold War propaganda bomb whose trigger would be President Kennedy's assassination. Read in the context of Dallas four days later, the text of the letter seemed to implicate the Soviet Union in conspiring with Oswald to assassinate the United States president. Three paragraphs in particular laid the blame for the assassinations at the door of the Russians. The letter began with, "*This is to inform of events sincem [sic] my meeting with comrade Kostin in the Embassy of the Soviet Union, Mexico City, Mexico.*" It is believed Kostin was actually Valery Vladimirovich Kostikov. Kostikov was a KGB officer was "*the officer in charge for Western Hemisphere terrorist activities—including assassinations.*" He was described as "*the most dangerous KGB.*" This was the same undercover specialist in assassinations who had already set up as Oswald's Russian handler in the phone calls and transcripts in Mexico City. Now the same Oswald-damning connection was being asserted in a letter to the most important Soviet embassy in the world. This propaganda bomb was being sent into the embassy for days before President Kennedy's presidential parade would pass under the workplace of Lee Harvey Oswald. The fuse of the propaganda bomb in the Soviet Embassy in Washington stretched to Dallas. When President Kennedy was murdered, the incriminating letter with its "Kostin"/Kostikov-Oswald connection could then be revealed to the American people. Lee Harvey Oswald, and his apparent sponsors, the Soviet Union and Cuba, could be scapegoated simultaneously in the assassination of the president. It was a scenario whose intended climax was not only the enemies with whom he was talking peace.

The letter's third paragraph read: "*I had not planned to contract the Soviet embassy in Mexico so they were unprepared, had I been able to reach the Soviet embassy in Havana as planned, the embassy there would have had time to complete our business.*" Oswald's original intention had been "*to complete our business*" at the Soviet Embassy in Cuba, which he says was more prepared to deal with him. But, because of his failure to obtain a Cuban visa, Oswald is saying he was forced to take up "*our business*" directly with Soviet assassination manager Kostikov in Mexico City. The letter's fourth paragraph read: "*Of corse [sic] the Soviet embassy was not at fault, they were, as I say unprepared, the Cuban consulate was guilty of a gross breach of regulations, I am glad he has since been replced [sic].*" The problem with this paragraph is this: How did Oswald know the Cuban consulate had been replaced? Eusebio Azcue was replaced as the Cuban consul in Mexico City on November 18th. He was replaced on the same day this letter arrived at the Soviet Embassy in Washington. So, I ask again, how could Oswald possibly know Eusebio Azcue had been replaced before it actually happened? Was this possibly another sign Lee Harvey Oswald was set up?

On November 22nd, at the very moment President Kennedy was shot, a CIA officer was meeting with a Cuban agent in Paris and giving him an assassination device to use against Castro—acting falsely once again in the name of Attorney General Robert Kennedy. Cubela's CIA handler told him that Desmond Fitzgerald had helped write the president's speech which had been delivered in Miami on November 18th. Cubela was informed "*that the passage about the 'small band of conspirators' was meant as a green light for an anti-Castro coup.*" The CIA, by reversing the meaning of President Kennedy's speech to motivate its own hired assassins, created a dogma of disinformation that it would disseminate for decades—that the Miami speech meant an encouragement for murder, not dialogue. The CIA's further device of hiring Cubela in the name of Robert Kennedy to assassinate Castro laid the foundation for the repeated claim that Castro, to preempt the threat on his own life, ordered President Kennedy's murder—and that Robert Kennedy had therefore triggered his own brother's assassination.

On November 25, 1963, Richard Helms sent a memorandum to J. Edgar Hoover that marshaled the CIA's phone-tapped evidence suggesting that Oswald had received not only Soviet but also Cuban government support in assassinating President Kennedy. Attached with the Helms memorandum were transcripts for the audiotapes of seven calls to the Soviet Mexico City embassy attributed to Oswald. Two of them stood out. One was the October 1st call in which Oswald identified Kostikov as the Soviet consul he had met on September 28th. In the other outstanding call, reportedly made on September 28th, the same man, speaking from the Cuban Consulate, made reference to his having just been at the Soviet Embassy.

The head of the CIA Counterintelligence Branch from 1954 to 1974 was James Angleton. He was the supervisor of a CIA assassination unit in the 1950s. The "small assassination team" was headed by Army colonel Boris Pash. At the end of World War II, Army Intelligence colonel Pash had rounded up Nazi scientists who could contribute their research skills to development of United States nuclear and chemical weapons. The CIA's E. Howard Hunt, while imprisoned for the Watergate break-in, told the *New York Times* that Pash's CIA assassination unit designed especially for the killing of suspected double agents. That placed Pash's terminators under the authority of counterintelligence chief Angleton. In the 1960s, Angleton retained his authority over assassinations. In November 1961, the CIA's Deputy Director of Plans, Richard Bissell, directed his longtime associate William Harvey to develop an assassination program known as "ZR/RIFLE" and to apply it to Cuba. When discussing the plans for "ZR/

RIFLE" Harvey scribbled a note to himself. It said: "*planning should include provisions for blaming Sovs or Czechs in case of blow. Should have phony 201 (a CIA file on any person 'of active operational interest') in RG (Central Registry) to backstop this, all documents therein forged and backdated.*" In order to blame an assassination on the Communists, the patsy should be given Soviet or Czechoslovakian associations. In the case of Lee Oswald, his would be Cuban and Soviet. An appropriately fraudulent 201 personnel file should be created for any future assassination scapegoat, with "*all documents therein forged and updated.*" Harvey also reminded himself that the phony 201 "*should look like CE (counterintelligence) file.*"

In the Oswald project under Angleton's supervisor, the CIA's Counterintelligence head blended the powers of assassination and disinformation. In the war against Communism, Angleton thrived on deceiving enemies and friends alike in a milieu he liked to call "*the wilderness of mirror.*" Angleton's Special Investigations Group (SIG) in CIA Counterintelligence held a 201 file on Oswald in the three years prior to the Kennedy Assassination. Considering what William Harvey wrote about creating phony 201 files for ZR/RIFLE scapegoats, the first question which needs to be asked "*How genuine is Oswald's file?*" Oswalds' 201 file in CI/SIG "*implies strongly that either Oswald was indeed a member of the CIA or was being used in an operation involving members of the CIA.*"

Former CIA Finance officer, Jim Wilcott said Oswald served the CIA specifically as a double agent in the Soviet Union who afterwards came under suspicion by the Agency. Wilcott's straightforward testimony on Oswald was made possible by his and his wife's decision to separate themselves from the CIA and speak the truth. After nine years of working for the CIA as a husband-and-wife team, Jim and Elise Wilcott resigned from the Agency in 1966. In 1968 as participants in the anti-Vietnam War and civil rights movements, Jim and Elise Wilcott became the first former CIA couple to go public with what they knew, in spite of the risks to themselves. Jim Wilcott worked in the finance branch of the Tokyo CIA Station from 1960 to 1964. During the same years, Elise was a secretary at the Tokyo station. When President Kennedy was assassinated, the station went on alert. Jim was assigned to twenty-four-hour security duty. He passed the time with agents whose tongues had been loosened by alcohol. They told him the CIA was involved in the assassination. Jim wrote an article about what he had learned at the Tokyo Station. He wrote: "*Oswald* *had been trained (by the CIA) at Atsugi Naval Air Station, a plush super-secret cover base for Tokyo Station special operations . . . Oswald was recruited from the military for the express purpose of becoming a double agent assignment to the USSR . . . One of the reason given for the necessity to do away with Oswald was the difficulty they had with him from the start, and this made him very angry.* Oswald's anger, while he was trying to arrange his return to the United States in late 1960, would have been reason enough for James Angleton to order his Special Investigations Group to keep a security watch on the CIA's double agent.

On the morning of November 22, 1963, a key witness to the assassination possibly saw one of the assassins getting into place. Julia Ann Mercer witnessed a man in a green truck dropping off a man carrying what appeared to be a rifle up the slope of the grassy knoll. That evening and the next morning she was questioned by the Dallas police and the FBI. Four years later, she saw the statements attributed to her. She was unable to recognize them as her own statements.

It was in January of 1968, during Jim Garrison's investigation of President Kennedy's assassination, that Julia's husband called Garrison. He said he and his wife were in New Orleans and wanted to talk to him. When Garrison met them in their hotel suite, he was confronted by *"a most impressive couple. A middle aged man of obvious substance, he had been a Republican member of Congress from Illinois. Equally impressive, she was intelligent and well-dressed, the kind of witness a lawyer would love to have testifying on his side in front of a jury."* Garrison showed Julia her statements as printed in the Warren Commission Exhibits. Reading them carefully, she shook her head.

"These have all been altered," she told Garrison. *"They have me saying just the opposite of what I really told them."*

Julia said on Saturday, November 23, 1963, the day after President Kennedy's assassination, FBI agents showed her an assortment of pictures. She selected four of the pictures as looking like the driver of the green pickup truck. When they turned one over, she read the name "Jack Ruby" on the back.

She told Garrison, *"I had no doubts about what the driver's face looked like. I do not know whether the other three pictures shown me were other men who looked like Ruby, or whether they were three other pictures of Jack Ruby.*

But they definitely showed me Jack Ruby, and I definitely picked him out as looking like the driver."

Julia's identification of Jack Ruby as the driver had occurred on *the day before* Ruby shot Oswald. If her testimony on Ruby delivering a man with a gun case to the grassy knoll had become public, it would have created a major problem for the government's argument there was no conspiracy. Perhaps not surprisingly, the FBI version of her statement claimed, *"Mercer could not identify any of the photographs"* as the driver. After seeing Jack Ruby shoot Oswald on national TV, Julia notified the FBI that she had again recognized the driver of the truck as Ruby. That is not in the FBI report. According to the FBI report, she never identified Ruby at all, much less a second time. The FBI report acknowledges only that she had been shown a picture of Ruby. But the report never disclosed she was shown the picture the day before Oswald was murdered. The FBI again claims, *"she could not identify him as the person"* driving the green pickup truck. The FBI and the Dallas Sheriff's Department versions of her statement not only denied her identification of Ruby as the driver. They also claimed she said the truck had a sign on the side in black, oval letters which read, *"Air Conditioning."* The FBI's and Sheriff's Department's false description of the truck as having an *"Air Conditioning"* sign on its side resulted in a charade. FBI agents then conducted a thorough but unnecessary search throughout Dallas for the driver of such truck. Julia Ann Mercer has been a key witness in the assassination of President Kennedy from the beginning. The government is aware of this and so does she. For that reason, she has been almost impossible to locate for the almost five decades.

At 10:30 am on November 22, 1963, Sheriff Bill Decker held a meeting in the preparation for the President's visit to Dallas that day. He called together all of his available deputies, which was about 100 men. They included the plainclothes men and detectives who were especially important to the president's safety as he passed through the streets of Dallas. The Sheriff told his men, they *"were to take no part whatsoever in the security of that* [presidential] *motorcade."* He instructed his men they were simply *"to stand out in front of the building, 505 Main Street, and represent the Sheriff's Office."* Dallas Police Chief Jesse Curry gave a similar order which would keep his officers away from Dealey Plaza that day. He told his officers, *"to end supervision of Friday's crowd at Houston and Main."* This was just two blocks of the crossfire ambush which awaited the unsuspecting President Kennedy. He gave this order because he claimed the *"traffic would begin to thin out there."* Police Chief Curry would claim years later he was just following the orders of the Secret Service. He claimed, *"The Dallas Police Department carefully carried out the security plans which were laid out by Mr. Lawson, the Secret Service representative from Washington, D.C."*

Chief Curry and Sheriff Decker gave their orders to withdraw security from the presidential motorcade because they themselves were following orders given to them from the Secret Service. They were carrying out orders from Washington. Sounds a little odd, doesn't it? Well, it gets stranger and deeper than that. The Secret Service also made a critical change in the protection the president would normally receive from his motorcycle escorts. The Dallas Police had made plans at a preliminary meeting to assign motorcycle escorts. The Secret Service did not attend that meeting. These escorts were assigned to ride along the side of the presidential limousine. As a result, the motorcycle escort would shield the limousine from any potential gunfire. At a Dallas Police Department/ Secret Service coordinating meeting held on November 22nd, the Secret Service changed the plans. The motorcycle escorts were pulled back from their position alongside the presidential limousine to positions in the rear. This action moved the escorts out of the way of sniper gunfire. It was claimed that the reason for this action was because President Kennedy didn't want the escorts blocking the crowd's view of his limousine. Why would President Kennedy not want escort along the side his limousine in Dallas, when they were clearly along the side the limousine in Houston? The day before in Houston, the Secret Service deployed motorcycles alongside the presidential limousine. What was the difference between the two cities? There wasn't a sniper crossfire awaiting President Kennedy in Houston, where there was one in Dallas. The motorcycle escorts weren't the only change in security on the motorcade in Dallas. The Secret Service withdrew the protection of its agents normally stationed on the back of the presidential limousine. If the agents had been at their usual posts on the limousine, holding the hand rails on the car, they could have obstructed gunfire or thrown themselves on President Kennedy when the shooting began. But they, too, had been removed in Dallas. They were reassigned to the car following President Kennedy's limousine. In this position the agents were useless in preventing an assassination.

CHAPTER 54

—————□—————

"Victory has a thousand fathers,
but defeat is an orphan."

John F. Kennedy

Key Events in Vietnam During The Kennedy Administration

On January 28, 1961, shortly after his inauguration, John F. Kennedy told a National Security Council meeting that he wanted covert operations launched against North Vietnam, in retaliation for their equivalent actions in the South. This is not argue that this was an inappropriate decision, but the existence of covert operations against the North, has to be understood in analyzing later events, especially the Gulf of Tonkin Incident.

Even earlier, he issued National Security Action Memorandum (NSAM) 2, directing the military to prepare counterinsurgency forces, although not yet targeting the North. President Kennedy discovered little had progressed by mid-March, and issued National Security Action Memorandum (NSAM) 28, ordering the CIA to respond to his desire to launch guerilla operations against the North. Herb Weisshart, deputy chief of the Saigon CIA station, observed the actual CIA action plan was "very modest". Given the Presidential priority, Weisshart said it was modest because William Colby, then Saigon station chief, said it would consume too many resources needed in the South. He further directed, in April, a presidential task force to draft a "Program of Action for Vietnam".

In April 1961, the Bay of Pigs invasion of Cuba, under the CIA, had failed, and President Kennedy lost confidence in the CIA's paramilitary operations. President Kennedy himself had taken some responsibility for largely cutting the Joint Chiefs of Staff out of operational planning. The JCS believed the operation was ill-advised, but, if it was to be done, American air support was absolutely essential. Kennedy, however, had made a number of changes to create plausible deniability, only allowing limited air strikes by CIA-sponsored pilots acting as Cuban dissidents. After it was learned the main strike had left behind a few jet aircraft, he refused a follow-up strike; those aircraft savaged the poorly organized amphibious ships and their propeller-driven air support.

The US Air Force, however, responded to NSAM 2 by creating, on April 14, 1961, the 4400th Combat Crew Training Squadron (CCTS), code named "Jungle Jim." The unit, of about 350 men, had 16 C-47 transports, eight B-26 bombers, and eight T-28 trainers (equipped for ground attack), with an official of training indigenous air forces in counterinsurgency and conduct air operations. A volunteer unit, they would deploy in October, to begin FARM GATE missions.

The task force reported back in May, with a glum assessment of the situation in the South, and a wide-ranging but general plan of action, which became NSAM 52.

In June, President Kennedy issued a set of NSAMs transferring paramilitary operations to the Department of Defense. These transfers of responsibility should be considered not only in respect to the specific operations against the North, but in the level of covert military operation in the South in the upcoming months. This transfer also cut the experienced Edward Lansdale out of the process, even though he was an US Air Force officer, the military saw him as belonging to CIA.

Also in May, the first U.S. signals intelligence unit, from the Army Security Agency under National Security Agency control, the unit, operating under the cover name of the 3rd Radio Research Unit. Organizationally, it provided support to MAAG-V, and trained ARVN personnel, the latter within security constraints. The general policy, throughout the war, was that ARVN intelligence personnel were not given access above the collateral SECRET (i.e., with no access to material with the additional special restrictions of "code word" communications intelligence.)

Their principal initial responsibility was direction finding of Viet Cong radio transmitters, which they started doing from vehicles equipped with sensors. On December 22, 1961, an Army Security Agency soldier,

SP4 James T. Davis, was killed in an ambush, the first American soldier to die in Vietnam.

More U.S. personnel, officially designated as advisors, arrived in the South and took an increasingly active, although covert, role. In October, a US Air Force special operations squadron, part of the 4400th CCTS deployed to SVN, officially in a role of advising and training. The aircraft were painted in South Vietnamese colors, and the aircrew wore uniforms without insignia and without U.S. ID. Sending military forces to South Vietnam was a violation of the Geneva Accords of 1954, and the U.S. wanted plausible deniability.

The deployment package consisted of 155 airmen, eight T-28s, and four modified and redesigned SC-47s and subsequently received B-26s. U.S. personnel flew combat as long as a VNAF person was aboard. FARMGATE stayed covert until after the Gulf of Tonkin incident.

Under the operational control of the Central Intelligence Agency, initial U.S. Army Special Forces involvement came in October, with the Rhade. The Civilian Irregular Defense Groups (CIDG), were under Central Intelligence Agency operational control until July 1, 1963, when MACV took control. Army documents refer to control by "CAS Saigon", a cover name for the CIA station. According to Kelly, the SF and CIA rationale for establishing the CIDG program with the Montagnards was that minority participation would broaden the GVN counterinsurgency program, but, more critically, the Montagnards and other minority groups were prime targets for Communist propaganda, partly because of their dissatisfaction with the Vietnamese government, and it was important to prevent the Viet Cong from recruiting them and taking complete control of their large and strategic land holdings.

It was in mid-November when Kennedy decided to take on operational as well as advisory roles. Under U.S. a Military Assistance Advisory Group (MAAG), such as the senior U.S. military organization in Vietnam, is a support and advisory organization. A Military Assistance Command (MAC) is designed to carry out MAAG duties, but also to command combat troops. There was considerable discussion about the reporting structure of the organization: a separate theater reporting to the National Command Authority or part of United States Pacific Command. After meetings in Vietnam by General Taylor, the Secretaries of State and Defense issued a set of recommendations, on November 11. President Kennedy accepted all except the use of large U.S. combat forces.

Robert McNamara held the first Honolulu Conference, at United States Pacific Command headquarters, with the Vietnam commanders present. He addressed short-term possibilities, urging concentration on stabilizing one province: "I'll guarantee it (the money and equipment) provided you have a plan based on one province. Take one place, sweep it and hold it in a plan." Or, put another way, let us demonstrate that in some place, in some way, we can achieve demonstrable gains.

On December 11, 1961, the United States aircraft carrier *USNS Card* docked in downtown Saigon with 82 U. S. Army H-21 helicopters and 400 men. They organized into two Transportation Companies (Light Helicopter); Army aviation had not yet become a separate branch.

Twelve days later these helicopters were committed into the first airmobile combat action in Vietnam, Operation CHOPPER. It was the first time U.S. forces directly and overtly supported ARVN units in combat, although the American forces did not directly attack the guerillas. Approximately 1,000 Vietnamese paratroopers were airlifted into a suspected Viet Cong headquarters complex about ten miles west of the Vietnamese capital, achieving tactical surprise and capturing a radio station.

From the U.S. perspective, the Strategic Hamlet Program was the consensus approach to pacifying the countryside. There was a sense, however, that this was simply not a high priority for Diem, who considered his power base to be in the cities. The Communists, willing to fill a vacuum, became more and more active in rural areas where the GVN was invisible, irrelevant, or actively a hindrance.

In 1962, the U.S. Military Command-Vietnam (MACV) established Army Special Forces camps near villages. The Americans wanted a military presence there to block the infiltration of enemy forces from Laos, to provide a base for launching patrols into Laos to monitor the Ho Chi Minh Trail, and to serve as a western anchor for defense along the DMZ. These defended villages were not part of the Strategic Hamlet Program, but did provide examples that were relevant.

U.S. command structures continued to emerge. On February 8, Paul D. Harkins, then Deputy Commanding General, U.S. Army Pacific, under Pacific Command, was promoted to general and assigned to command the new Military Assistance Command, Vietnam (MAC-V).

Military Assistance Command-Thailand was created on May 15, 1962, but reported to Harkins at MAC-V. In a departure from usual practice, the MAAG was retained as an organization subordinate to MAC-V, rather than being absorbed into it. The MAAG continued to command U.S. advisors and direct support to the ARVN. At first, MAC-V delegated control of U.S. combat units to the MAAG. While it was not an immediate concern, MAC-V never controlled all the Air Force and Navy units that would operate in Vietnam, but from outside its borders. These remained under the control of Pacific Command, or, in some cases, the Strategic Air Command.

No regular ARVN units were under the command of U.S. military commanders, although there were exceptions for irregular units under Special Forces. Indeed, there could be situations where, in a joint operation, U.S. combat troops were under a U.S. commander, while the ARVN units were under an ARVN officer with a U.S. advisor. Relationships in particular operations often were more a matter of personalities and politics rather than ideal command. U.S troops also did not report to ARVN officers; while many RVN officers had their post through political connections, others would have been outstanding commanders in any army. At the same time, the U.S. was beginning to explore withdrawing forces.

The USMC 1st Composite Radio Company deployed, on January 2, 1962, to Pleiku, South Vietnam as Detachment One. After Davis' death in December, it became obvious to the Army Security Agency that thick jungle made tactical ground collection exceptionally dangerous, and direction-finding moved principally to aircraft platforms.

In addition to the U.S. advisers, in August 1962, 30 Australian Army advisers were sent to Vietnam to operate within the United States military advisory system. As with most American advisors, their initial orders were to train, but not go on operations.

1963 was critical not only because the Diem government fell, but that the North, at the end of the year, chose a more aggressive military strategy. Stability in the South, however, would not improve with increasing dissent, coup attempts, and a major coup. It remains unclear as to what extent the South Vietnamese were exploring solutions based a neutralist Vietnam, but this apparently existed at some level, without U.S. knowledge.

Organizations and commands would change with time. In January, for example, Major General Don became Commander-in-Chief of the

RVN armed forces, General William Westmoreland was named deputy to General Paul Harkins to replace him later. In a structural reorganization, the ARVN made the Saigon Special Region the III Corps tactical zone; the former III Corps for the Mekong Delta became IV Corps tactical zone

South Vietnamese forces, with U.S. advisors, took severe defeats at the Battle of Ap Bac in January. This has been considered the trigger for an increasingly skeptical, although small, American press corps in Vietnam. and the Battle of Go Cong in September. Ap Bac was of particular political sensitivity, as John Paul Vann, a highly visible American officer, was the advisor, and the U.S. press took note of what he considered to be ARVN shortcomings.

While the Buddhist crisis and military coup which ended with the killing of Diem was an obvious major event, it was by no means the only event of the year. In keeping with the President's expressed desires, covert operations against the North were escalated. Of course, the assassination of Kennedy himself brought Lyndon Baines Johnson, with a different philosophy toward the war. Kennedy was an activist, but had a sense of unconventional warfare and geopolitics, and, as is seen in the documentary record, discussed policy development with a wide range of advisors, specifically including military leaders although he distrusted the Joint Chiefs of Staff. He was attracted to officers who he saw as activist and unconventional, such as Edward Lansdale.

In 1960 the new administration of President John F. Kennedy remained essentially committed to the bi-partisan, anti-communist foreign policies inherited from the administrations of Presidents Truman and Eisenhower. During 1961, his first year in office, Kennedy found himself faced with a three-part crisis: The failure of the Bay of Pigs invasion in Cuba; the construction of the Berlin Wall by the Soviets; and a negotiated settlement between the pro-Western government of Laos and the Pathet Lao communist movement. Fearing that another failure on the part of the U.S. to stop communist expansion would fatally damage U.S. credibility with its allies, Kennedy realized, "Now we have a problem in making our power credible . . . and Vietnam looks like the place." The commitment to defend South Vietnam was reaffirmed by Kennedy on May 11 in National Security Action Memorandum 52, which became known as "The Presidential Program for Vietnam". Its opening statement reads:

U.S. objectives and concept of operations [are] to prevent communist domination of South Vietnam; to create in that country a viable and increasingly democratic society, and to initiate, on an accelerated basis, a series of mutually supporting actions of a military, political, economic, psychological, and covert character designed to achieve this objective.

President Kennedy was intrigued by the idea of utilizing United States Army Special Forces for counterinsurgency conflicts in Third World countries threatened by the new "wars of national liberation". Originally intended for use behind front lines after a conventional invasion of Europe, Kennedy believed the guerrilla tactics employed by Special Forces would be effective in the "brush fire" war in South Vietnam. He saw British success in using such forces during the Malayan Emergency as a strategic template. Thus in May 1961 Kennedy sent detachments of Green Berets to South Vietnam to train South Vietnamese soldiers in guerrilla warfare.

The Diệm regime had been initially able to cope with the insurgency of the National Front for the Liberation of South Vietnam (NLF, or derogatively, Viet Cong) in South Vietnam with the aid of U.S. material and advisers, and, by 1962, seemed to be gaining the upper hand. Senior U.S. military leaders received positive reports from the U.S. commander, General Paul D. Harkins of the Military Assistance Command, Vietnam, or MACV. By the following year, however, cracks began to appear in the façade of success. In January a possible victory that was turned into a stunning defeat for government forces at the Battle of Ap Bac caused consternation among both the military advisers in the field and among politicians in Washington, D.C. JFK also indicated to Walter Cronkite that the war may be unwinnable, and that it was ultimately a Vietnamese war, not an American war.

Diệm was already growing unpopular with many of his countrymen because of his administration's nepotism, corruption, and its apparent bias in favor of the Catholic minority—of which Diem was a part—at the expense of the Buddhist majority. This contributed to the impression of Diem's rule as an extension of the French Colonial regime. Promised land reforms were not instituted, and Diem's strategic hamlet program for village self-defense (and government control) was a disaster. The Kennedy administration grew increasingly frustrated with Diệm. In 1963, a crackdown by Diệm's forces was launched against Buddhist monks protesting discriminatory practices and demanding a political voice. Diem's repression of the protests sparked the so-called Buddhist

Revolt, during which several monks committed self-immolation, which was covered in the world press. The communists took full advantage of the situation and fueled anti-Diem sentiment to create further instability.

Milestones of the escalation under President Kennedy.

- November 1960—Coup attempt by paratroopers is foiled after Diem falsely promises reform, allowing loyalists to crush the rebels.
- December 20, 1960—The National Liberation Front of South Vietnam (NLF) is founded.
- January 1961—Soviet Premier Nikita Khrushchev pledges support for "wars of national liberation" throughout the world. The idea of creating a neutral Laos is suggested to Kennedy.
- May 1961—Kennedy sends 400 United States Army Special Forces personnel to South Vietnam to train South Vietnamese soldiers following a visit to the country by Vice-President Johnson.
- June 1961—Kennedy meets with Khrushchev in Vienna. He protests North Vietnam's attacks on Laos and points out that the U.S. was supporting the neutrality of Laos. The two leaders agree to pursue a policy of creating a neutral Laos.
- June 1961—Kennedy said, "Now we have a problem making our power credible and Vietnam looks like the place" to James Reston of *The New York Times* (immediately after meeting Khrushchev in Vienna).
- October 1961—Following successful NLF attacks, Defense Secretary Robert S. McNamara recommends sending six divisions (200,000 men) to Vietnam.
- February 8, 1962—The Military Assistance Command Vietnam (MACV) is created by President Kennedy
- February 1962—Attempted assassination of Diem by two air force officers who bombed his palace, fails.
- July 23, 1962—International Agreement on the Neutrality of Laos is signed at Geneva, promising Laotian neutrality.
- August 1, 1962—Kennedy signs the Foreign Assistance Act of 1962, which provides ". . . military assistance to countries

which are on the rim of the Communist world and under direct attack."

- January 3, 1963—NLF victory in the Battle of Ap Bac.
- May 8, 1963—Buddhists demonstrate in Hue, South Vietnam after the display of religious flags were prohibited, during the celebration of Vesak, Gautama Buddha's birthday; but, Catholic flags celebrating the consecration of Archbishop Ngo Dinh Thuc, brother of Ngo Dinh Diem were not prohibited. The police of Ngô Dinh Can, Diem's younger brother, open fire, killing nine.
- May 1963—Republican Barry Goldwater declares that the U.S. should fight to win or withdraw from Vietnam. Later on, during his presidential campaign against Lyndon B. Johnson, his Democratic opponents accuse him of wanting to use nuclear weapons in the conflict.
- June 11, 1963—Photographs of protesting Buddhist monk, Thích Quảng Đức, burning himself to death in protest, in Saigon, appear in U.S. newspapers.
- Summer 1963—Madame Ngo Dinh Nhu, defacto First Lady to the bachelor Diem makes a series of vitriolic attacks on Buddhists, calling the immolations "barbecues". Diem ignores US calls to silence her.
- August 21, 1963—ARVN special forces loyal to Ngo Dinh Nhu, younger brother of Diem, stage raids across the country, attacking Buddhist temples and firing on monks. The cremated remains of Thích Quảng Đức are confiscated from Xa Loi Pagoda in Saigon. New US ambassador Henry Cabot Lodge rebukes Diem by visiting Xa Loi and giving refuge to Buddhist leader Thich Tri Quang. The US calls for Nhu to be dropped by Diem, and threatens to cut aid to Colonel Le Quang Tung's Special Forces if they are not sent into battle, rather than used to repress dissidents.
- September 2, 1963—Kennedy criticises the Diem regime in an interview with Walter Cronkite, citing the Buddhist repression and claiming that Diem is out of touch.
- Late October 1963—Nhu, unaware that Saigon region commander General Ton That Dinh is double-crossing him, draws up plans for a phony coup and counter coup to reaffirm the Diem regime. Dinh sends Nhu's loyal special forces out of Saigon on the pretext

of fighting communists and in readiness for the counter coup, and rings Saigon with rebel troops.

- November 1, 1963—Military officers launch a coup d'état against Diem, with the tacit approval of the Kennedy administration. Diem and Nhu escape the presidential residence via a secret exit after loyalist forces were locked out of Saigon, unable to rescue them.
- November 2, 1963—Diem and Nhu are discovered in nearby Cholon. Although they had been promised exile by the junta, they are executed by Nguyen Van Nhung, bodyguard of General Duong Van Minh. Minh leads the military junta.
- November 1963—By this time, Kennedy had increased the number of military personnel from the 900 that were there when he became President to 16,000 just before his death.
- November 22, 1963—Kennedy is assassinated

CHAPTER 55

———————◻———————

"War will exist until that distant day when the
conscientious objector enjoys the same reputation and
prestige that the warrior does today."

John F. Kennedy

Author's Final Thoughts

This is the part of my book I have found the hardest to write. This is
where I put down my feelings on the Assassination of President John
F. Kennedy. When I first started reading books by other authors on the
Kennedy Assassination I was convinced the Mafia was the sole plotters
behind his murder. But the more I read about the assassination, the sicker
I became. It really disgusts me to think the Central Intelligence Agency
might have been behind Kennedy's Assassination. But it's just so clear to
me now what really led up his death in Dallas, Texas. It's hard to believe I
could have thought anyone else was responsible for his death.

John Fitzgerald Kennedy was destined for greatness. He was destined
to change the world. At least that's the way his part in history should have
been told. It's a shame he never was allowed to accomplish everything he
had set out to do during his presidency. His life was cut down too soon.
He didn't accomplish what he wanted the most; world peace. He wanted
to end the Cold War during his lifetime. But there were stronger forces
who didn't want him to accomplish this goal. They blocked his path every
chance they got. And when they realized he couldn't be deterred, they
removed him from office. They removed him not through impeachment,
but through murder. It's sad to think that the normal everyday citizen

of the United States believe with all of their hearts that the President is the one who runs the country. November 22, 1963 was proof that this isn't the case. The President of the United States is just a puppet who is controlled by the not-so-hidden forces of the Central Intelligence Agency. In my opinion, John F. Kennedy was the last real President to reside in the White House. He was a man who was truly for the everyday man and woman. He was willing to reach out to our enemies with a hand of peace not war.

Regardless what the historians want you to believe, President Kennedy's murder has never been solved. Who and why has never been revealed. The United States government wants the public to believe Lee Harvey Oswald was just a lone nut who assassinated President Kennedy on his own accord. I think the public believed it for so long because they didn't want to know the truth; because sometimes the truth is harder to swallow than the lie. Central Intelligence Agency's ability to flood the media with disinformation worked to perfection. But time has eroded away the cover. In 1991 the JFK Act forced the government to release numerous classified files which dealt with the investigation of President Kennedy's Assassination. But thousands of document are still classified TOP SECRET and hidden from the public. We cannot continue to allow this to be the case. We need to stand up as a united country. We need to demand our Congressmen and Senators to push and make the government release the remaining classified documents. This OUR country and the Kennedy Assassination is part of OUR history. We deserved the right to know the truth. We should not rest until the truth, THE REAL TRUTH, behind the Kennedy Assassination is finally available to the public. And the REAL TRUTH is He Died For Peace.

July 25,2011-March 11, 2012